DIRTY EOIN

THE OUTLAW CHESS SERIES

HARLEY DIAMOND

Published by House of Books Press

www.harleydiamond.com

Edited by Karen Sanders Editing

https://www.karensandersediting.com/

PA Services by Arcane and Reverie

contact@arcaneandreverie.com

Cover Design by Vicious Desires Design

https://www.instagram.com/viciousdesires/

Cover Model is Jerome Adamoli via Daniel Jaems

https://www.instagram.com/jeromeadamoli/

https://www.instagram.com/danieljaems/

Created with Vellum

Blurb

AN UNHAPPILY EVER AFTER?

My life is no fairytale.

I'm no Prince Charming. She's no Disney Princess.

She's the femme fatale in the story.

Fuck. Marry. Kill.

I chose the former. She chose the latter.

My family chose the option neither of us wanted.

For thirty-eight years, I waited to marry the right woman, and then I was forced to marry the wrong one.

I now realize that my temporary paper wife is my equal in every way.

My Ma Duster. My fucking queen.

Fate may not have chosen me for her, but that doesn't mean he never chose her for me.

This future Irish King always gets what he wants, and I want her.

Permanently.

Playlist

Chasing Cars by Snow Patrol

Trigger Warning

This book contains mature content, violence, swearing, and other potentially triggering situations that some readers may find offensive.

Please do not read this story if you are uncomfortable with any of the above.

Thank you.

Author's Note

EOIN'S story starts from where DYLAN's ends (EXCLUDING the epilogue).

DIRTY EOIN is NOT standalone.
DIRTY EOIN is BOOK 5 of a SERIES, which contains an ONGOING STORYLINE that CONCLUDES in BOOK 6, DIRTY PADRAIG.

These books contain MULTIPLE POVs from characters across the entire series.

Due to the nature of the CONTINUING STORYLINE, these books MUST be
READ IN ORDER.

ACE
DIRTY CILLIAN
RAZR
DIRTY DYLAN
DIRTY EOIN
DIRTY PADRAIG

CHAPTER ONE

EOIN

Private Dining Room, Palace Hotel, Manhattan

IF LOOKS COULD KILL.

They can't, unfortunately for Jaine Jones.

Who knew the sight of this golden-haired vixen looking ready to launch herself at me, claws extended, would be quite so appealing to my dick? Given the way he's twitching, he's certainly tempted by what's on offer.

An angel on the outside. A hellion on the inside.

And a succubus in my fucking dreams.

The gauntlet has already been thrown. And by her. So, it's only a matter of time before we step into the ring and go head-to-head. I would far rather it be the bedroom. I can think of several far more enjoyable ways to stop her mouthing off in there, my cock rammed down her throat and making her gag just one. I'd take great pleasure in having her beg to wrap those pouty lips of hers around it before she sucked on it like a popsicle.

Because she would.

I push thoughts of fucking her in the nearest empty room from my mind. Not that she'd let me. She'd put up a struggle. Turn feral.

Hiss. Scratch. Bite.

I'd take anything this woman has to give.

Methinks the lady doth protest way too much. She was lying to herself. She wanted me, the same as I wanted her. She was just playing hard to get.

And it's that pretend indifference of hers that's held me captive for so long. That and the fact that she hates my guts and isn't afraid to say so. Her blatant admittance that she wouldn't piss on me if I were on fire.

Her fearlessness of what I am.

Of who I am.

Of what I'm capable of.

That's why I've always found her so intriguing. That's why this biker female with spitting green eyes and a mouth as blue as a sailor's constantly rides my thoughts.

It was never love. It's simply infatuation. A case of wanting something I can't ever have. It's just made me crave it all the more.

There is no storybook ending. My life is no fairytale. I'm no Prince Charming, and Jaine Jones is certainly no Disney Princess, regardless of what our Paddy thinks.

She's the femme fatale in the piece. The woman to be avoided at all costs.

True love is a fallacy. And even if it does exist, it's for fools. It's much wiser to choose your life partner based on her credentials.

She may have killed, but Jaine's a lawyer. A very successful one, I'll grant her that, but a mere legal professional all the same. In hindsight, I realized she hasn't got what it takes to be a cold-blooded murderer, and the latter's what this future Irish king needs by his side. Recent events have proved just that.

That's the reason I'm about to propose marriage to Molly. After I've visited with her da and asked his permission, that is. The girl saved my life. It's the least I can do.

If not for her, then I wouldn't be marrying anyone.

What would Jaine Jones have done had she known I had a gun pointed at my head?

Nothing.

She'd have cheered the gunman on from the sidelines while sitting on her executive chair as she filed her professional nails and decided which color to paint them.

"Jaine."

"Eoin."

As usual, there are no pleasantries between us. I'm sure she deliberately shuns manners and etiquette just to get a rise out of me. It works every time.

Uncouth. Unimportant. Insignificant.

She wants me to think her all three. At one point, I was naïve where she was concerned. It's why I misjudged her. Why I underestimated her. A fact she likes to remind me of only too frequently.

Fool me once, Miss Jones? I assure you I never make the same mistake twice.

She must be wondering why I'm not surprised to see her.

I am.

She thinks me smug, selfish, and pompous, so that's the mask I wear for her benefit. The one I'm wearing right now. Two can play her game.

She doesn't know me at all if she believes those to be my worst attributes. I'm not sure she'd be quite so blasé about poking continually with her stick of blame if she knew the true monster she could rouse from beneath this polished exterior.

My eyes drift over her. She looks exquisite in the long cream-colored dress she's wearing that gently skims her too-slim curves.

A vision, in fact.

Despite her biker blood and her reluctance to admit it, she fits in. She looks right at home surrounded by the trappings of wealth and the gold flock-papered walls of this ostentatious establishment.

She's a fucking queen.

She could have been my queen once upon a time.

I frown inwardly. The reunion we're all about to witness shouldn't have been on the cards. At least not here. Not now.

Not yet.

But it's unavoidable. Inevitable. And the timing couldn't have been worse with the wedding yet to take place. We don't need my brother getting cold feet. What the fuck is she doing in Manhattan ahead of time?

Her eyes dart from Sophia to Molly. One stands on either side of me. She knows exactly who they are. No formal introductions necessary.

"Eoin, our Dylan's been trying to contact you. He says it's urg…"

Paddy appears.

You could hear a pin drop.

A happenstance moment causes both their worlds to collide like the big fucking bang. Time stands still. Then just one word is spoken.

"Irish."

Her name for him is a whisper on her lips and spoken like a subtle caress. She captures two years of pent-up love, longing, want, and need and crams them into that one single word. My eyes never leave her face as I witness the fleeting myriad of emotions that run through her as she takes him in.

First shock. Then disbelief. Then total and complete adoration.

For the love of her life. For her soul mate.

For my baby brother.

The man I threatened her over. The man I told her to stay away from when he became one half of an arranged marriage with the Sicilian mafia don's baby sister. A union entered into to strengthen our Duster brand and to force him to settle down.

I shouldn't be envious, but I am.

Even though my future lies with another, jealousy is all I feel coursing through my veins. I want her to look at me the way she's looking at him. Like I'm the best thing in the world. Like I'm the only thing that matters.

Like I'm the sun, the moon, and the fucking stars.

He's my brother. My flesh and blood. I love him. But I want to crush his throat with my bare hands because he's getting her undivided attention. And I want it. All of it.

On. Fucking. Me.

He's got what I want. It might only be a look, but it's a look that lays her undying love for him at his feet, along with her sacrificial fucking heart. It's a look that can't be misinterpreted. At least not by someone as observant as me.

I can't see his reaction. Is it mirrored? I hope to fuck not. Then again, Jaine's moment of revelation was gone in the blink of an eye, so did he even pick up on it? Chances are if he did, he'll think it all wishful thinking on his part given she told him she doesn't love him.

Because I told her to.

Right now, I'm invisible. Or am I?

Is Jaine Jones pretending not to see me just to wind me up because she hates my guts? Because she wants to get under my skin? Because she gets off on my adverse reaction as it feeds this toxic, fucked-up relationship we share?

Did the women standing at either side of me witness Jaine

Jones's off-guard moment that lasted for a mere nanosecond before she recovered and switched back to that impressive poker face of hers?

It's unlikely Molly did. But Sophia, our Paddy's fiancée, is sharp. If she witnessed the look Jaine fleetingly bestowed on Paddy, it could spell disaster. More so if it was in any way reciprocated. Things are already terse between the betrothed couple due to his reluctance to welcome her into his bed. We're all aware his unwillingness has nothing to do with practicing abstinence. He's not being a good Irish Catholic boy. He simply refuses to fuck anyone but Jaine.

My phone rings. Walking to the end of the foyer, I take the call.

"Eoin." My other brother sounds panicked. There's no need. The shit has already hit the fan.

"I know, Dylan. We've just collided with her," I grouse.

Serendipitous or not, this unforeseen moment should never have been allowed to happen. Lessons must be learned.

And they will be.

"It's not that, Eoin. We're at the Whisperers' clubhouse in Nevada. Ace and Lucifer have been shot. It's not looking good for either of them. I'm on my way to Rising with Ace."

I don't need to ask why. There's only one reason Ace has asked to return home.

I keep the phone to my ear, but I've switched off from what Dylan's saying. I've heard all I need to. Across from me, Sophia is holding a whispered conversation in rapid-fire Italian. Is it to do with Ace? Is it to do with this Paddy and Jaine collision? Or is it to do with who's just appeared behind the latter?

I make eye contact with Leoluca Di Matteo, my face as impassive as his. I'm well aware he's a long-standing business associate of Jaine's. But he's also a high ranker in the Sicilian Mafia.

What the fuck is he doing here? What the fuck is going on?

Something clearly is, and it's something monumental if he's asked Jaine to come all the way to Manhattan ahead of time.

Having no owing with her, I have no leverage with which to ask probing questions about the many influential people she rubs shoulders with.

And to run this city, I need to know.

Leoluca places a gentle hand on her shoulder. The tactile visual has me wanting to slice the fucker's fingers off one by one for daring to place them on any part of her.

Get a fucking grip, Eoin.

Jaine Jones is not mine. She will never be mine. I don't fucking want her.

I'm marrying Molly McGrath.

Leoluca whispers in her ear then motions his head towards her bag. In the silent chaos that surrounds her, she hasn't heard her phone ringing. Given I've got Dylan on the line, I suspect the caller will be his new wife, Jessie. To warn Jaine of the risk of running into us? Or to tell her about what's just gone down in Nevada?

She takes the call. Her face pales. She's just been told what I have, and then.

She's gone.

CHAPTER TWO

PADRAIG

Private Dining Room, Palace Hotel, Manhattan

SERENDIPITY.

There's no other word to describe it. Fate has brought us together. Right here. Right now. For reasons known only to himself.

Jaine Jones. My cliché blonde. My Disney Princess. My Holy Grail of women and the one I have been in love with since I was nineteen years old.

Too beautiful. Too breathtaking. Too perfect in every way.

Standing in front of me. She's not a dream. She's not a mirage.

That heart-shaped face of hers, those bright green eyes, her upturned nose and pouty lips. Jesus Christ, God really did make perfection when he crafted her.

For me. Or so I once hoped.

They say a picture speaks a thousand words. I'm waiting for the look that speaks a thousand emotions. A sign that confirms that I got it all wrong. That it *is* reciprocated. That she does love me.

Always has. Always will.

My heart pounds in my chest. I'm drowning in a sea of raging emotions I'm struggling to contain below the calm surface of the mask of indifference I have no choice but to wear. I don't speak. Even if I could, words would fail me. What is there to say to the woman who was the constant in my life?

To my soul mate.

To my fated other.

To my one and only.

So I wait and wait for just one sign. For the connection we shared to make itself known. To let me know it was all just a misunderstanding.

Just this one fragile moment in time, I pray that she admits she lied. I pray that she gives away the truth. I pray that she lets me see inside her very soul.

And I pray that it's filled with love for me.

"Irish." She whispers her name for me on an outward breath. I've waited so long to hear it fall from her lips.

A lifetime.

It's the most beautiful thing I've ever heard.

I love her. God, how I fucking love her.

Jaine Jones. My end game that never will.

I want to sink to my knees and roar my frustrations at the heavens. I want The Almighty to tell me what I've done that I'm deserving of this never-ending pain.

But I don't. I can't.

Instead, I allow the tears of regret and self-pity to prick my eyes, but I keep my expression impassive because I have no choice.

There's a flicker of something that crosses her face. Is it love? It's so fleeting, and then it's gone.

I guess I was mistaken.

There's nothing. No outward indication. No sign. No grand reveal that the foolish hope I've been clinging to these past two years hasn't been in vain. It's true. She doesn't love me after all.

Never has. Never will.

I guess it's for the best because it's all too late. Even if the odds weren't stacked against us by my own flesh and blood. Even if she wasn't happily married to her childhood sweetheart. Even if by some small miracle she loved me back.

It's all over. The fat lady has sung.

Last night, I crossed the line. And now I have no choice but to take the vows with Sophia.

I swallow down the sinking feeling rising from my gut. The silent sound of each rusty nail being hammered into the coffin they will bury me alive in echoes through my head.

I stare. She stares.

Right now, for me, nothing else matters. No one else matters. If this is all I will ever have, then I will drink in my very last fill of Jaine Jones.

I want this moment to last forever.

I know this is closure. More so for me. Even if she did care, I'd have to pretend not to. I'd have to let her go.

Once and for all.

Sophia is on the phone. Eoin is on the phone.

Leoluca Di Matteo appears alongside Jaine. He whispers in her ear then places a gentle hand on her shoulder, motioning his head towards her bag. Her phone's been ringing, but she's been so caught up in the moment she hasn't heard it.

When she breaks eye contact, that's when it sinks in. The realization that this is it. That this is the point of no return. There's no coming back from this. Time is running out and there's nothing I can do to stop it. Is this what dying feels like?

For two years, I've waited in the same spot. Tossed aside. Discarded. Abandoned. Where I've wished. Where I've hoped. Where I've dreamed.

In the end, it was all for nothing.

Wishful thinking. Foolish hopes. Pipe dreams.

As here I will remain.

Alone. Unneeded. Unloved.

I want to speak. I want to tell her I need her. That I love her. That she's my reason for being. My reason for breathing in and my reason for breathing out, even if I'm not hers.

Instead, I say nothing.

Resignation. Hopelessness. Acceptance.

She takes the call. Her face pales. And then my life is over.

She's gone.

CHAPTER THREE

ACE

The Ghost Whisperers' Clubhouse, Colton, Nevada

Sitting outside the clubhouse, I stretch my legs in front of me and stare across the Nevada desert. There's nothing to see for miles. Raising my face to the sun, I close my eyes and inhale air that is way too warm and smells of nothing in particular. Not like the sweet smell of my hometown. I'll be heading off at sunrise. Back home.

Now the Whisperers are part of the alliance, there's no need for me to stick around or to even come back. Well, at least not so often. My work here is done for now.

For me, that means things can get back to normal. I can go back to living my life in Rising. With PJ and my boys.

Well, whatever normal is for the prez of an MC.

I'm wearing a smile of contentment, but I figure I've earned that shit. These days, my life is as close to perfect as it's ever going to be, but that hasn't always been the case.

Familiar feelings of regret wash over me at what could have been. What should have been. Regret over all those wasted years.

Ten years.

PJ and I have been handed two good years back in return. The best two years of my life spent with my girl and our two boys. But it's not enough. Nowhere near. I want more. Way more. But I know that's not always guaranteed.

Watching Dylan and Jessie take the vows today, I wish more than anything that my wife was here with me, but I guess I'll see her tomorrow.

The meeting in New York was important to her. Her career is important to her, regardless of her reluctance to admit it. Our lives will change from here on in, and I accept that. I have to. PJ's happiness is all that matters to me. I'm so fucking proud of everything she's achieved in her life.

And I'm so fucking glad that she chose me.

It hasn't been long since the newlyweds showed up. I'm not sure why they'd choose to spend their wedding night here, but Dylan looked troubled. Cillian and Sarah were already here, so I'm guessing whatever's going down is Duster-related and causing them a headache back in New York.

"You expecting visitors, Ghost?" Lucifer yells from across the table, interrupting my thoughts.

Opening my eyes, I glance at him, then cast my gaze to where he's looking in the distance.

There's a hog approaching, kicking up a trail of dust into the hot desert air in its wake.

Ghost walks out of the partially finished clubhouse with Tadgh at his side. Shielding his eyes, he takes in the lone bike as it approaches.

"Nope."

A one-word answer. And a worrying one in our life.

When things seem too good to be true, that's usually because they are. Sometimes you can just tell when something life-changing is about to go down. Like right now.

I know.

We stand as the hog approaches. There are two riders, both wearing full helmets. The moment they pull their ride wide, that's when we know we were right all along about what we silently suspected. This isn't a social call. They're not planning on stopping by to say hello. They're going to pass in front of us for one reason only.

Time stands still as the sun glints off the barrel of the now-exposed gun.

"Get the fuck down," Ghost roars.

Lucifer pushes in front of me, and the first bullet takes him down. I feel the moment the second one fired hits home. I've been shot before, but this time it's different.

The pain in my gut doesn't register straight away. It has me thinking that maybe I haven't been hit after all. I'm not sure how long passes. But when it does register, it's a pain so intense I sink to my knees and almost black out. It's a pain that's letting me know this is it. That the bullet I've taken has devastated my insides so badly there's no coming back. I fall onto my back and sweat prickles my skin, even though I suddenly feel ice cold.

I'm aware of screaming and shouting, but it's like I'm on the outside looking in. Like I'm present but not. The blackness tries to envelop me once more, but I fight it.

For now.

I hate that it's going to end this way.

I'd give anything to see PJ just one last time. More than anything, I want to say goodbye to my plain Jaine Jones, but I know that's not on the cards as the darkness beckons once more and Death himself tries to embrace me in his cold, unloving arms.

"Dylan." My voice is a choppy whisper.

"I'm here, Ace." He sounds broken as he kneels beside me.

I know I only have a matter of seconds at most to say what needs saying. Shit. How can I cram in everything I want to say to PJ in such a short time?

But time is no longer a luxury I have.

I look up at the Irishman. Padraig's brother. Finian's uncle. I can see my eldest boy's eyes reflected in his gaze. His expression is full of kindness and concern.

I grip his arm.

"You tell PJ that I love her. That I have always loved her and that no matter where I am, I will always fucking love her." I grimace and curse as the pain rips through me.

"You can tell her that yourself."

"Dylan," I hiss as I tighten my grip on his arm. There's no time for pretending or denying the inevitable. Not when the darkness is edging my vision once more, offering me a painless abyss as a way out. A darkness there will be no coming back from.

"I will, Ace." He nods and swallows thickly.

I cough and taste the copper tang of blood in my mouth. "You tell her to look after our boys and that she must do right by Fin. Promise me you'll tell her that. It's important." I cough again. More blood.

"I promise, Ace. Is there anything else?" There's an urgency in his tone now. Time is running out. We both know it. And he wants me to have no regrets.

But I have so fucking many. I have ten years' worth of regrets.

Our eyes connect. His show understanding. Mine show acceptance. We both know this is the end of the road for me.

"Get me home. Take me to Rising."

He frowns and slowly shakes his head. "Ace, I'm not sure that's such a good idea. The hospital is an hour away. Rising is four, maybe five."

I know what he's thinking. I won't survive the journey. But I will. I'm not going to make it either way, so if it's the last thing I do in this life… I'll make it home.

"I'll hang on." I swallow the blood in my mouth once more before I let myself be consumed by the darkness.

And then I see her.

A little girl who looks exactly like PJ did all those years ago. And then I realize it *is* her. She's skipping up front, kicking up dust from the familiar well-worn track as she looks over her shoulder at me. She's giggling, but she's not hiding that smile of hers. It's wide and confident. Everything's vibrant. She's vibrant. She's so full of life. I grin back at her as I take in hair like spun gold and green eyes the color of a meadow. Eyes that are filled with so much love for me that, for a second, the intensity of the feeling takes my breath away.

I welcome it as it wraps protectively around me. It's the only thing I've ever needed. She's the only thing I've ever needed.

"Hurry up, slowpoke," she yells.

I laugh out loud as I play catch up. She's wearing the same little blue summer dress she did way back then, and she's still the prettiest thing I've ever seen.

"Where are we going, Jaine?" I shout after her, and she stops in her tracks.

"You know where we're going, Jason Steele." She chuckles as she faces me, then rolls her eyes exaggeratedly. "We're going to the river so you can show me how to skim stones." She holds out her little hand.

I look at hers and then at mine. Hers is clean and mine is dirty.

With a smile, I close my eyes as I raise my face to the Californian sun, inhaling the smell of petrichor and wildflowers deep into my lungs one last time.

I made it home.

Then I take little Plain Jaine Jones's hand in mine and start running with her.

"I love you, Jason Steele," she yells on a breathless giggle.

"I love you too, Jaine Jones. Always have. Always will."

CHAPTER FOUR

JAINE

Dr. Bruce's Medical Centre, Rising, California

Have I told you lately that I love you? Have I told you there's no one else above you?

I'm standing in the same single-story nondescript grey building that baby JJ was born in just three months ago. In the same room where his daddy entered the world.

And the same room he left it in.

The gunshot wound was fatal. Ace knew it. And all he wanted was to come home to Rising. He needed to inhale the sweet air of his hometown and let it fill his lungs and that huge heart of his one last time. Where it will forever remain.

I'm a small-town boy, PJ. I always will be. You know that.

It was all he wanted before he lost consciousness he never regained. My beautiful boy who never asked anything of anyone but who always gave everything he had. Who never wanted to be any trouble and always took the time to appreciate and thank everyone who stopped by his life.

This time, he asked for something.

And that was to go home.

He also wanted Dylan to let me know that he loved me. And that I was to look after our two boys and do right by Fin.

Then Dylan, with the help of Tyler, did exactly what was asked of him and brought him home. And within a few moments of arriving here, in this room where he was born—the room where our son was born—he grew his wings.

And now I stare down at my beautiful boy. My very own Angel of Hellfire as he lays there motionless. Still. Silent.

Gone.

I'm Jason, and I'm eight. I'm Jaine, and I'm seven.

I push back hair that's as black as the midnight sky away from his face. A face that still looks perfect in every way on a boy that was born just to be stared at.

A face that makes him look like he's just sleeping.

Forever sleeping.

You think if our pops are best friends, and our moms are, that we could be best friends too? You want to go to the river? I can show you how to skim stones.

I want him to open his eyes and look at me. I want to look into eyes that are a blue as the bluest thing ever one last time.

Please, God. Let me just do that.

Why am I so plain, Jason?

You're not plain. You're just growing into yourself. From now on, I'm going to call you Plain!

You hid the Aces! You're a big fat cheat, Jason Steele! From now on, I'm going to call you Ace!

Memories cascade through my brain. So many wonderful memories, but there are nowhere near enough. There will never be enough. And who will I have to share them with now? Who will I be able to reminisce over them with? Who will I be able to laugh and cry over them with? It was only ever me and him. Him and me. My best friend.

"Ace."

I say it aloud, and it echoes in the stillness of the clinical white room, bouncing off each wall over and over until it deafens me. It makes no difference how often it's repeated. He can't hear me. He can't answer. He'll never be able to answer me again.

I can't breathe. I want to die with him. Please, God, let me die with him.

And then I cry. I cry loud, painfully. I cry ugly.

For Ace. For myself. And for our baby son who will never know his daddy. Who will never experience firsthand the deep, kind, sensitive soul of Jason Steele. A boy I was so lucky to love and to have been loved so completely by in return. A man who put me and our boys at the center of his world and lived every day showing us just how much we meant to him. A boy who took nothing for granted, living each day like it was his last.

And today, it was.

If I hadn't traveled to New York for my meeting, would he have gone to Nevada? If I hadn't gotten involved in that shitshow in the first place when Razr went in all guns blazing, would he have gone then?

No.

I put him in that position. I put him in danger. I put him in the firing line. I might as well have pulled the goddamn trigger myself.

It's all my fault.

Ten years. We lost ten years.

What I'd give to replay things. To sit my selfish ass down and listen to the words he so desperately wanted me to hear. To read his messages.

You'll always be my creep and my weirdo, same as you'll always be my plain Jaine Jones.

"I'm sorry, Ace. I'm so fucking sorry."

I thought we had forever.

I'll be waiting right here, sweetheart.

And he always will be. He'll never see New York. He'll never leave Rising.

I gently trace the scrolled letter J behind his ear, then lean down and press my nose against his neck. The warmth from his skin has gone. I inhale the smell of his familiar aromatic cologne and all things Ace deep into my lungs before pressing my lips to his.

Warm against cold.

"I love you, Ace. Always have. Always will." I utter the words I never said enough. Words I should have said at least a million more times each day.

Waves of pain wash over me, filling the hollow ache in my chest and drowning me in my harsh, stinking reality.

That Ace will never get to see his boys grow up.

That Ace and I will never grow old together.

That Ace is gone.

And the worst thing?

I never even got to say goodbye.

CHAPTER FIVE

EOIN

The Hudson Dusters' HQ, Manhattan, New York

"He was shot in the gut you say?"

It's just me, Da, and our Paddy. Cillian and Dylan are still in Nevada with their wives, dealing with the aftermath of the shooting. The unfortunate reality is the only reason Ace was in the vicinity was because he was attending Dylan and Jessie's wedding. Then again, if he was specifically targeted, which is what's now strongly suspected, would it have mattered where he was?

"Yes, Da. It was similar to the hit young Rafael Flores took. I spoke to Dylan on the way here. There's reason to believe it was a targeted attack. That it was Ace they were after. No shots were fired at anyone else. Lucifer was injured in the crosshairs. By all accounts, he deliberately stepped in front of a bullet with Ace's name on. It was the second shot fired that hit the intended target. They clearly knew what they were doing, who they were looking for, and they knew exactly where to find him. They obviously did their research in advance, so most likely a pair of professional sharpshooters."

"But why not do it from afar like everyone else? Why be so bloody brazen about it?" Da frowns at me, the pad he never writes in open in front of him.

I shrug. "Maybe whoever was behind the whole thing wanted to make a point. Perhaps they instructed the marksmen to record it to prove the deed was done. Who knows? It's not likely it was personal from the shooters' point of view. It would simply have been a clause in the job description of their hit for hire."

"And we're sure it couldn't have been The Exterminator? We're absolutely certain that's the case?"

"The Exterminator is an ally of the bikers, Da. He would never shoot one of his own without good reason or proper justification. He would also never do anything theatrical. He just gets in, gets the job done, and gets out. And always covertly," Paddy replies.

"Not even if he needed to dramatize the whole thing in order to fulfill the brief and get paid?" Da turns his full attention to him.

"The Exterminator doesn't need the money. It's more a means to an end for him. He's a vigilante first and foremost. At least half of what he earns gets donated to charitable causes representing victims of the wrongdoings he's crusading against to secure them a better future. His sole intention for doing what he does is to rid the world of scum. Ace wasn't scum."

It's all quietly spoken. And likely Paddy's first and only verbal contribution to today's conversation. He's been withdrawn since the news broke. Over Ace? Or over colliding headfirst with the love of his life?

Both probably.

The room is subdued. Morose even.

"And what about this other fella?" Da's frown deepens.

I can tell he's been affected by this. At almost seventy, his hair can't get any whiter, but I'm sure there are a few more lines added to his face since this all kicked off. Regardless of how he and Ma feel about Jaine, as a key member of our alliance, Ace was an extension of our Duster family. At this stage, it's not known if this was a retaliation attack, if proximity to the Nevada situation and him acting as mediator earned him a bullet with his name on, or if it was something else entirely.

The latter would open up a whole new can of worms. Depending on the reason behind his murder, this could well see the start of a targeted killing spree, and the initial concern is who will be next and where will it end.

I exhale slowly. "Lucifer is still in the ICU. Tyler Grayson is adamant he willingly took a bullet for Ace."

"A noble act. But why would he do such a thing?"

"No one knows at this stage."

"And his odds?"

"He's expected to make a complete recovery. A shot to the shoulder. It went clean through."

"Lucky fella."

"Extremely so."

The silence thereafter is deafening, each of us lost in our own thoughts. My eyes drift around the ostentatious room that screams money. How vulgar it is. How pretentious.

And in the grand scheme of things, on days like today, how meaningless.

Paddy, Da, and I are sitting here in the finest tailored suits money can buy like we're royalty. I guess in this fucked-up world of ours, we are.

But moments like this? They make you reflect. They put things into perspective.

We're all just human, regardless of our wealth, status, and power. Just flesh and blood.

One moment here, the next moment gone. How many virtual guns are pointed at our heads right now? How many times a day do our ears burn as our enemies plot our demise?

And when will it be a real weapon that we're staring down the loaded barrel of like Ace did when it was his time? When will my own life flash in front of my eyes as I take my last breath?

Life is short. Ours even more so.

I glance at Paddy. My eyes then stop, and I really take him in. The youngest of us all and arguably the best-looking with his cheeky grin, coal-black hair, and smiling blue eyes. But appearances can be deceptive. It's definitely true in his case because if you scratch the shiny surface and look beneath, you'll see my brother's tired of living. That he's almost given up. That he's mentally and emotionally exhausted at trying to pretend to be something he's not and never will be again.

Happy.

The life and soul have been sucked out of him, reducing him to a shell of the once happy-go-lucky boy he used to be. His outward exterior these days is all an act. And he's an actor. His life is his own personal shitshow. A starring role he has no choice but to play on repeat.

He has to grin and bear it, and we're responsible for that.

An arranged marriage was the best course of action for him when we considered all the facts known to us at the time. When no one was aware of Jaine's existence.

What she doesn't realize is that Paddy was becoming a liability. With his charm and good looks, women simply fell at his feet as he continued to play the field, and in turn, he took full advantage of what was on offer, not caring if they were married or not.

The Dusters had to put an end to the problem or someone else may have.

Permanently.

That aside, it's true that the final decision was reached based on what would be the most advantageous move for the Dusters to increase our power, ranking, wealth, and status.

Paddy was a pawn, and he's now paying the price, as is Jaine.

Right now, she's on the opposite coast having to go through all this alone at a time when she needs him more than ever. Her Irish. Her confidant.

It will be tearing her apart as it is him.

Thousands of miles may separate them, but still they maintain their connection. I felt it when they collided recently. Subconsciously or otherwise, their souls still cherish each other. Their intangible link may be thinner, more brittle, stretched to full capacity, but it's there all the same. Both have stubbornly refused to let the other go. Both have insisted on clinging on. Both have offered a life raft to the other in this tempestuous sea of outlaw life, even if for the past two years it's meant swimming through ever-increasing waves of lies and deceit.

But in a little over three weeks, he'll be wed, and it'll be game over.

And that's when our Paddy will drown. When this connection they both cherish will be ripped apart whether they want it to be or not. When all they've shared will sink once and for all.

What's going through his head now that the woman of his dreams is now a widow? Now, that she's no longer married? If they wanted to, they could wed tomorrow. No one could stop them. No one *would* stop them.

There's just one Sicilian fly in that ointment.

Sophia.

Then again, I've been selfish with Jaine. I've ignored my brother's needs and focused on feeding my infatuation with her. I'm not proud of that fact, and I'm sure one day soon I shall have my comeuppance served to me by my youngest brother. Deservedly so.

I regret the past, but I can't change it. I can only try to make amends and influence my future.

I turn my attention to my da. He's in the winter of his life now, and still he has to come to work most days. He shouldn't have to at his age. He should be spending every precious moment he has left with Ma and little Caoimhe.

"After our Paddy's wed." My firm words are stark against the blinding silence. I pause as they both turn to stare at me. "I will wed Molly McGrath as soon as possible."

And I mean it.

It's time for me to step up and do my Duster duty. Prepare for my future role as the next Irish king.

And for that, I need a wife.

CHAPTER SIX

JAINE

Rising Cemetery, Rising, California

As a child, I used to love the peace and tranquility this place offered and spent hours rubbing the moss off the older headstones to reveal the precious story the passage of time had hidden underneath. The inscribed final words silently spoken between the living and the dead, telling them how loved they were and how missed they'd be.

It's been over two years since I buried my pop on this hallowed ground. Too young to die at fifty-eight, or so I thought.

But Ace. My beautiful boy will only ever be thirty-one years old.

I blink back tears as I sit cross-legged at his final resting place, my hands sifting the still unsettled soil through my fingertips. I never thought I'd be burying anyone else in our family plot. Not for a long time.

I guess God figured I only deserved to borrow Ace for a short while. That he wanted him back. That he needed that beautiful soul of his by his side more than I did.

More than his infant son did.

It doesn't feel real. I keep thinking I'll wake and find that it's all a bad dream. Then I realize it's not. That this is now my everyday waking nightmare.

I'm throwing myself a pity party because I'll never get to see him again. I'm alive. Ace is dead. At least I'll get to see our son grow up.

Tears flow freely. There's no need to hide them here. There's no one to witness one of my many moments of weakness and fragility.

It's just me, Pop, and Ace.

Lifting my hand, I trace the scrolled letter A behind my left ear. I don't need to see it to know its exact outline.

It's forever inked on my skin, but also on my heart.

They say life goes on. It's not really living, though, is it? It's existing. Those of us left behind are the walking dead.

How can it go on without him? Without my best friend. Without my everything rolled into one. Without the other half of my childhood memories.

I wasn't with him at the end.

Treat every day like it's a gift because it is indeed the present. Why didn't I? I took it for granted, that's why, and foolishly thought we had a whole plethora of tomorrows.

I appreciate that death comes to us all, and that for some, the grim reaper comes calling sooner than for others, but the chance to say goodbye was stolen from me, and that's what's unforgivable. It's also what's eating me alive. I can't even put into words how devastating that is.

I know his last thoughts were of me, and I wasn't there for him. With him.

All I can do is whisper in the breeze all the things I never got the chance to say in the hope that, wherever he is, it carries my words to him. I repeat them.

Second after second. Minute after minute. Hour after hour. Day after day.

But what if it doesn't?

What if he never knows how much I miss him? How much I love him. Or how much I wish it had been me and not him.

I try to swallow the lump that forms in my throat every time. In truth, it never really disappears. It stays there, a permanent reminder of everything that will forever remain unsaid between us.

I breathe out, and the sound is shaky with emotion. Then I inhale the petrichor and wildflower air of Rising deep into my lungs. Like Ace did that one final time.

He loved this town. He didn't need anything else.

Just Rising. Me. Our boys.

Our baby son is fatherless, his daddy gone. How is that fair on Ace or JJ? A little boy who'll never know his daddy. All he'll ever have is some snapshots captured over the years, and for everything else, he'll have to rely on the memories of others.

I wish I'd taken more pictures with Ace. Made more memories. Laughed with him more. Talked with him more. Spent more time with him.

Skimmed more stones with him.

I loved every single layer of Jason Steele's beautiful soul.

"You mind if I sit here, Jainie?"

I glance up at my father-in-law and shoot him a watery smile as I shake my head. I can't speak. He knows it's too difficult for me to find the words at times, and even when I do, I struggle to say them aloud.

To speak, you have to be able to breathe. And I can't always do that. Not when a sea of relentless, all-encompassing grief tries to hold me under its unforgiving surface and drown me most days.

Duke sits cross-legged beside me, looking like an older version of Ace. The only difference is he's clean-shaven and keeps his hair short, the black long since peppered with grey.

"He had a good turnout."

I nod as I take in the uninterrupted views over Rising. Ace's send-off was bikers only. Despite protestations, none of the other factions were invited or allowed to attend. There were still hundreds who stopped by to pay their last respects to the prez of the Angels of Hellfire, many having ridden their hogs for days to say farewell to the man who touched their lives in some way.

There's a pause as Duke thinks about how best to phrase whatever he needs to get off his chest.

"It's time for you to return to Manhattan, Jainie."

"And why is that?"

Is he going to admit something that I've suspected for a while now?

"Because that's what Ace would have wanted."

"I know what Ace wanted."

"The club will pass to Clay now."

"I know how the process works, Duke."

There's another pause, this time on my side.

"Ace told you, didn't he?"

He knows exactly what I'm asking.

"He did. But he only confirmed what I'd already figured out for myself."

"And how did you do that?" My voice is calm. I'm not angry, just curious. Pretty soon it will be common knowledge that my eldest son is an O'Connell. If anyone deserves to know in advance of that breaking news, it's Duke.

"I've spent time with Cillian over the years and since the

alliance was formed. I'm aware his and Fin's birthmarks are identical."

I turn to look at him, frowning and shaking my head. "He's not…"

He smiles and interjects "I know he's not Cillian's boy. He's Padraig's."

I exhale.

He turns away and stares into the distance, lost in his thoughts. I do the same. It's several minutes before either of us speaks again.

"I'd like to come with you if that's all right. To New York. There's nothing keeping me in Rising now my boy's gone, and I'd like to see my grandchildren grow up."

Guilt spears me that I'm sitting here selfishly wallowing in my own grief and self-pity without sparing a thought to what Duke's lost.

His only child. His son.

"And what about Darla?"

"She's staying here. Rising is home for her. She has her two boys and their families. My home is where my family is. And that's you, Fin, and little Jason Junior."

I glance at him briefly. "And you're okay with leaving her behind?"

He shrugs. "We were only ever companions, Jainie. She knows if she wants to pay us a visit in the future, then she's more than welcome to."

I stare at the views over Rising this plot affords before turning to look at him once more. "But you were born here, Duke. In this town."

He shrugs again. "And maybe, like my boy, I'll die here someday too. Then again, maybe I won't. I'd still like to come with you all the same. It's not like I can't ever come back. We'll both need to from time to time. To visit Jeremiah. To visit Ace. But you're also going to need all the help you can get."

He's right, of course. I've been trying to figure out how I'll manage juggling a business with two babies. More so when there are so few people I'd trust them with.

I pause before I answer. Not because I need time to think about it. I don't. It's more that I'm feeling overwhelmed that Duke would give up everything he's ever known just for me.

"I'd like that, Duke. For you to come with me. I'd like that a lot." We can both hear the break in my voice as the wave of emotion threatens to drown me once more. He reaches over and squeezes my hand.

"I was thinking, though, that maybe I'll delay my return. Just for a little while."

"The boy needs to know his father, Jainie. You can't put it off any longer." Duke's reply is both instant and firm.

"You're forgetting that Ace was murdered in cold blood."

"I'm well aware of that."

"And there's nothing to say that the O'Connells weren't behind that."

He exhales. "I doubt that very much."

I decide not to tell him about the recorded call. The one containing the blatant threat made against me by the Dusters via Molly McGrath.

"Well, we'll just have to agree to disagree on that. That aside, all I ask is that you give me a little more time because if they were in any way involved, I don't want to give them the satisfaction of seeing me suffering as a result of their actions."

He nods. "How long are we talking?"

"Not long. Trust me, the people who took Ace are going to pay. And not with an engraved goddamn bullet either. Shooting's too good for the likes of them."

And if Eoin O'Connell is behind it, I'm going to take great pleasure in killing that fucker with my bare hands.

CHAPTER SEVEN

EOIN

The Hudson Dusters' HQ, Manhattan, New York

I glance around my office. I'm aware my brothers think it old-fashioned. Maybe it is. But I appreciate the luxury of the dark wood furniture that contrasts magnificently against the same white background the rest of the rooms are finished in. A large antique walnut desk takes pride of place. There's also a wooden case filled with tomes on finance and economics. Subject matters, while not appealing to many, are to me.

My office screams class and wealth. It's only fitting. I am the future Da Duster, after all.

I turn my attention to the matching pair of tan-colored executive chairs that face me. Due to the nature of recent conversations, my brothers and I had taken to meeting in here more often than not to ensure we were out of earshot of our intendeds.

There won't be any need for discussions of that nature moving forward. At least not when it comes to Jaine Jones and me.

That's over and done with. For one, it would be disrespectful to Molly, and she deserves nothing but my utmost respect. For two, the feelings I had for Jaine weren't real. They were merely infatuation.

Both chairs are currently empty. Paddy has all but barricaded himself into his own office as he counts down the days, hours, minutes, and seconds to the end of his life.

His nuptials.

Meanwhile, Cillian and Dylan are both still on the west coast.

Black and white images of our ancestors line the walls. Past Dusters. Some of the most feared men ever to have reigned supreme in New York City all displayed side by side like some sort of Irish mobster line-up. Each one deserves their rightful wall hanging space where they can be dutifully admired and respected. It's the least we can do given their combined significant accomplishments on our family's behalf. I'm proud their blood runs through my veins. At some point, my da's portrait will hang beside theirs as will my own, my brothers', and our future heirs.

Now I've agreed to wed Molly, it will be the next expected step for me. Fatherhood.

Before now, I would have given it a wide berth. I'm selfish. I fully accept I am. Until now, I've always been too precious to sacrifice myself for anyone or anything else. But at thirty-eight, it's time for me to embrace the next stage in my life.

A wife and children. A family of my own.

Again, I push unwanted thoughts of Jaine Jones from my mind. She will be neither my wife nor the mother of my children. She will be nothing to me. She means nothing to me. Not anymore.

While Molly may not have been who I would have chosen, she saved my life. I owe her. It's that simple. And if the pound of flesh she wants in return is to be my wife, the next Ma Duster, and the mother of my heirs, then that is what she shall have.

At least once we're official she can stop tampering with the rubbers. She thinks I don't know about her little game, but I do. I always use a condom from my own supply, never one that's been provided by any female. If they offer, I simply accept then merely discard. I also sheath my own cock. I always have. They're never allowed to roll it onto my dick.

Pin pricks? Sharp fingernails? Tricks as old as time.

If I'd fallen for any of those, I'd have been a da when I was thirteen. If it's a child Molly wants, then she shall have one. Several if her heart desires. Once we're betrothed, that is.

Unlike my brothers, I don't intend to practice abstinence between getting engaged and getting wed. Neither do I intend on wearing a rubber.

Leaning back on my chair I place my feet on my desk and continue to partake in this currently one-sided conversation.

"What do you mean you and Cillian weren't allowed to attend the funeral, Dylan?" Finally. A word in.

"It was bikers only."

I frown. "But you and Jaine have been friends for a long time. You were there with Ace when…"

"The reason Sasha gave was that if Jaine made allowances for one, she'd have to do the same for others. Even Rod wasn't allowed to attend," he interjects.

I get the feeling my little brother doesn't like talking about the biker's passing. He changes the subject. It affected him, listening to his final words and having to be the messenger between him and Jaine. Having to relay what was no doubt a very personal message between the living and the dead.

I understand. Situations like that can also highlight our mortality. That our lives can change on a dime.

"It's my guess it's because Ace was murdered. Right now, everyone is a suspect."

"That's what I'm deducing from it." He exhales frustratedly in response.

"Including the Dusters."

"And can you blame her, Eoin? Our ma blatantly threatened her via your future wife. A conversation that's recorded, most likely duplicated several times over and with copies ready to be distributed to pig aristocracy at the press of a button. Jaine's well aware our parents are gunning for her. In her mind, who's to say that verbal threat didn't encompass her loved ones? I mean, if she really wanted to, she could have our ma arrested on suspicion of murder. And no matter which legal guru we employed, I wouldn't fancy our chances against a vengeful Jaine Jones. She'd wipe the floor with us."

"Jesus Christ, we would never…"

"Jaine doesn't know that, Eoin, and that's the point. After the messaging fiasco, the little trust that did exist has gone," he interjects again. Something he would never have done prior to getting involved with that extremely loud and annoying wife of his. "And then there's your infatuation with her. Who's to say she's not thinking you wanted Ace out of the picture so you could claim her for..."

"I'm marrying Molly." It's my turn to interrupt.

"You've accepted your fate now, but before the Nevada incident, everyone aside from Paddy was aware of your blatant admiration for Jaine. Even Ma. Even Molly. Even Jaine herself."

He's right. On the surface, I could easily appear to be the guilty party in her eyes. But if I'd wanted Ace dead, I'd have handled the matter personally. I wouldn't have resorted to putting a price on the biker's head and letting someone else pull the trigger.

"When are you returning?"

"We're heading back tomorrow. From what I can gather, Duke's going to be moving to New York with Jaine. There's nothing keeping him in Rising now Ace is gone. The club will pass to the current VP. And speaking of Clay, now that he and Sasha have split up for good, I'm led to believe she's also heading back to Manhattan."

"At least Jaine will have a support network around her."

"Yes. But she'll cope regardless. She'll throw herself back into JAL and move on. She has no choice. She has two wee ones to consider. I think having Duke around will help her a lot. JJ's only a few months old, so her life will be pretty full on juggling her professional career, a newborn, and a one-year-old."

We're both now steeped in our own reflective silence. Two little boys will grow up not knowing their father. The type of outcome that could happen to any of us in this life. It makes me realize how much we take our da for granted. I can't imagine a life without him.

"Will you speak to her, Dylan? Pass on our condolences?"

He exhales loudly. "I'll try, Eoin, but I don't think she'll take the call. It's too soon. And I'm a Duster. Until she's sure in her mind we had nothing to do with Ace's death, I'm not sure she'll be prepared to speak to any of us."

There's another pause.

"And how is our Paddy? After… you know."

It's my turn to exhale. "It's difficult to say, Dyl. He's barely spoken since it all happened. I'm not sure if his withdrawal is in relation to Jaine or Ace."

"As much as he had a lot of respect for Ace, it will be Jaine, I reckon. He'll think The Almighty is rubbing it in by letting him see what he wants and can't have just before he has to sign his name on the dotted line with someone he doesn't want and is being forced to have. And I know it's not an appropriate thing to say given Ace has only just been laid to rest, but it must make it ten times worse for him knowing Jaine's single again."

"The same thing crossed my mind too."

"And how did she react when she saw him?"

I snort as I recall the moment, which I'm sure won't go unnoticed by Dylan. I'm fully aware my jealousy is flaring once more. I bite it back before speaking further. "She looked at him like he put the stars in the sky. Thankfully, it was fleeting. I'm not sure anyone else would have picked up on it."

"Not even Paddy? So, he doesn't suspect that she's still in love with him?"

"I doubt it."

"And his reaction?"

"I didn't look."

"Are we any closer to finding out why Jaine was meeting with Leoluca?"

"No."

"Something to do with Sophia and Luc, maybe?"

"It was something of great importance if she flew in just for that meeting. It was a fleeting visit as she had a flight chartered to take her back to LAX straight after."

"If you hadn't fallen out with her, you might have been able to find out."

"I realize that!" I snap, but he ignores my spike in temper.

"Listen, I'll see what I can find out, but I wouldn't hold your breath that she'll speak to me, let alone furnish me with any intel."

"I'm not."

"Maybe you should contact her."

"To exacerbate an already toxic relationship?" I mutter. "Anyway, on a more positive note, our Aidan will be arriving in the next couple of days. Once he's settled, he'll be learning the ropes from

Cillian then helping to ease the burden on the frontline day-to-day issues."

"That's good to know."

"I'll see you tomorrow, Dylan."

"Later, brother."

CHAPTER EIGHT

JAINE

Jaine's Home, Rising, California

"I don't care, Delaney!"

I'm sitting at home on the old cream sofa, trying to absorb the memories of Ace that it holds. It's not working. I'm worried I'm already starting to forget the small things and it hasn't even been two weeks. What if I forget everything and have no memories left to pass on to little JJ?

Guilt swallows me up, then tears of self-pity prick my eyes at the unfairness of my situation. Both are quickly swept away by the now all-too-familiar wave of rage.

We still have no clue who carried out the deliberate attack on Ace, despite Delaney asking discretely via the usual sharpshooting channels. There's not even a whisper, which has us both suspecting that the snipers were employed rather than contracted. Either that or they weren't fully-fledged marksmen, hence why they aren't available for hire. Maybe that was why they had to get up close and personal.

To make sure they didn't fucking miss.

I'll find them. Both monkeys plus their organ grinder. If it's the last thing I do in this life, I will find them, and I will end them.

"You do care, Jaine. You're not thinking straight. It's understandable."

"Well, Ace is dead, so my apologies for not having two flying fucks to give."

He's right. My mood changes like the flick of a switch these days.

Guilt. Sadness. Disbelief. The overriding one being anger. I doubt I'll ever reach the heady heights of acceptance.

I will never accept Ace's death.

"You're grieving, Jaine." His tone is sympathetic. He gets it. Having gone through what he has in the past, he understands better than most, but I don't want his fucking pity. I want my revenge. And right now, he's wrong. Right now, I actually don't give a fuck.

Why should I care about the news that he did manage to unearth on the sniper grapevine? That rumor has it someone is threatening to end an O'Connell life? It'll be well-deserved given the target must be the current king or the future one.

Hopefully, it's the latter. If that's the case, it'll save me the goddamn bother.

Asshole.

"And what do you expect me to do about it, Delaney? You do realize they could be behind Ace's death?"

"That's highly unlikely, Jaine, and you know it." He sighs with frustration at my continual insistence on this matter.

Like Duke, I haven't told him about the blatant threat made by Roisin. That little nugget might just color his thinking when and if I ever decide to spill it. Right now, he's waiting for me to say something constructive rather than sounding like I'm welcoming the news of the imminent demise of an O'Connell with open arms.

Which I am. The eldest brother.

I roll my eyes. I may as well ask, as I know he's going to insist on expanding further.

"So, which one is being targeted? Fergal or Eoin?"

I'm only pissed off I didn't get offered the contract personally. I'll even do it for free.

"Rumor has it that it's Padraig. And on his wedding day." The words are quietly spoken, most likely to lessen their impact.

My brain immediately rewinds to the worst day of my life.

The day Ace died. The day I collided with Irish at the Palace. When he looked at me with such cool indifference as he stood with his big brother and their perfect color-matching fiancées.

Happy families indeed.

I felt like a fool for ever thinking he cared.

All the hopes I'd clung to for two years crashed and burned with just that one detached look. It was clear he didn't miss me at all. He never had. The only reason he'd been messaging me was out of habit or because he was bored and needed something to pass the time. It was obvious he'd moved on as he stood side by side with Sophia.

And it's time I did too. Once and for all.

Tears of self-pity press against the back of my eyes. Not only did I lose Ace, I also lost Irish. And both on the same goddamn day. I'm currently having to deal with the grief of losing two of the most important people in my life.

I will not spill those useless little fuckers, though. I'm all cried out. Now, I'm going to focus my energy on something way more satisfying.

Revenge. Delivering karma personally.

"And why would anyone want to kill Padraig O'Connell?" I try to sound disinterested, but I know Delaney won't buy it. After four years together. I know him inside out, but he also knows me.

"Who knows, Jaine? Maybe the attack's aimed at the Sicilians rather than the Dusters. The Ruoccos have a lot of enemies."

Delaney's right. That's the reason most of their family members are dead. When you're as untrustworthy as the Ruoccos, you tend to upset a lot of people. I lean my head back against the sofa and stare at the ceiling. I wanted to delay my return, not accelerate it, but what choice do I have? I'm already aware something's about to go down with the Sicilians after my meeting with Leo. Precisely what and when, I don't know, but what I do know is that whatever it is, it's imminent.

And I can't let anything happen to Irish.

"Find out if the threat is real and tangible."

"It's real. It's tangible."

"Find out for sure!" I hiss.

"And if it is?"

"Then I'll be left with no option. I'll have to return to New York earlier than planned to take care of business."

I'M NOT SURE HOW LONG HAS PASSED.

I'm still sitting in the same spot, staring at my other phone as it vibrates unwelcomingly on the sofa beside me. I haven't spoken to Jessie since that fateful night at the Palace, despite her calling numerous times since. She wasn't at Ace's funeral. She was at her father's bedside, which is perfectly understandable. Then again, would she have wanted to attend given her new husband was banned from doing so?

Probably not. She's a Duster now, after all.

Truth is, I've barely spoken to anyone apart from Duke, Sasha, and Cherry. Everyone else is involved with the O'Connells in some way. Until I have proof they weren't involved in Ace's death, I can't trust them or anyone around them.

I've got no choice but to speak with Delaney on Exterminator-related business, even though his sister, Sarah, is one of them. But deep down, I know no matter what, he'd never stab me in the back.

It's not about blood with him. He'd kill his own kin if push came to shove. With him, it boils down to honesty, trust, and loyalty. I'd never betray him, and he'd never betray me.

To answer or not to answer. As much as she's one of them, she's still my business partner.

I connect the call.

"Jessie."

There's a pause.

"Jaine." She's surprised I answered. "How are you keeping, partner?" She sounds hesitant.

"I've been better." My tone is clipped. I can't help it. How the fuck does she think I've been keeping?

"I… we… Dyl and I... We're here…"

"I know."

"The family wants to pass on their condolences."

"And which family might that be?"

"Both."

"I'll accept them from the O'Briens."

"Jaine, Dyl was the last person to speak to Ace before… you know. You can't just shut him out."

"While I'll forever be indebted to him for relaying Ace's dying words and wishes, I can fucking shut him out," I bite.

"You're not thinking straight."

"You're the second person to say that to me today."

"Maybe that's because it's the truth."

"I may be grieving, Jessie, but I'm still in control of my faculties. I'm thinking quite clearly, thank you. They threatened me. You heard the recording with your own goddamn ears. Ace was murdered. Now, who do you think might have been responsible for pulling that trigger?"

"The O'Connells would never do something like that, Jaine. Not to Ace."

"And you know that for sure how?"

She pauses. It speaks volumes.

"I don't know for sure."

"Exactly. You don't."

"So, what happens next?"

"I'm moving back to Manhattan."

"When?"

"I can't tell you that."

"So you're keeping secrets from me because my surname's O'Connell now, is that it?"

She has no right to sound hurt.

"And you've never kept a secret from me before, Jessie?"

There's a pause. She knows damn well she has. She told the Dusters about the Nevada unrest when I specifically asked her not to. The trip that resulted in three dead Colombians. An outcome that could easily be behind why Ace was head-hunted personally by the grim reaper. In part, his mediating resulted in the Whisperers being brought in on the alliance. A result that will no doubt have fucked off the still faceless faction behind this trafficking business.

"Anyway, it's not because of that," I continue. There's no point dwelling on it. It won't bring Ace back. "There's an urgent matter I need to attend to and it's not something I can discuss with anybody."

"Not with anyone at all?"

"Apart from Delaney."

"So, it's not because I'm one of them."

"No."

I'm not totally lying. I can't discuss Exterminator-related business with her. I usually could with Dyl, but for obvious reasons, I can't. For one, he's a Duster. There's also the small matter that the person in the firing line of this other sniper's rifle is none other than his baby brother.

"Good, because nothing's changed, Jaine. I'm still your friend. I'm still your business partner."

"How's your pop?" I change the subject.

"He's resting up." She sounds miffed, no doubt at my refusing to discuss the other matter further.

"Why did he take a bullet for Ace?"

"He won't tell anyone. He wants to meet with you. To explain to you why face to face." She sounds hopeful.

"I won't have time to do that before I return to Manhattan, Jessie. I'm sorry."

And I am sorry. Sincerely. Lucifer could have gotten himself killed doing what he did. In the end, his unselfish act was futile. It almost cost him his life and it still didn't save Ace.

There's a pause. I immediately know where this is going.

"Jaine, Dyl wants to speak to you. Can I put him on? Please just talk to him."

"I'll be speaking to the O'Connells soon enough. I said I'd be paying them a visit when I return to New York. That hasn't changed. I have no intention of conversing with any of them before then. That includes Dylan." My tone is firm.

"Shall I at least let them know when to expect you?"

I smile for the first time in weeks. "I'd prefer to keep the element of surprise."

CHAPTER NINE

EOIN

Saint Patrick's Cathedral, Manhattan, New York

"Are you ready, Padraig?"

We're standing in a room just off the altar, its dark wood walls and polished wood floor giving it an almost coffin-like appearance. As if to morbidly complement our surroundings, the flowers of choice for today are lilies.

Funeral flowers. Their strong almost repugnant odor fills the air.

Four brothers tied by blood. Four brothers who must and who do put family first. When push comes to shove, family is all we have.

Nothing else matters. The rest is fake and immaterial.

As Irishmen, our blood binds us. I would kill for my brothers. I would die for my brothers. I seldom display affection or openly discuss my feelings, but they each know that I love them.

Two are wed to the great loves of their lives. That's not going to be the case for our youngest brother. Today, he must be a martyr for the cause and take the vows with a girl he does not and never will love.

He is our human Duster sacrifice.

It's a union that will see us unite with the Sicilian mafia. It will strengthen our position. It will make us more powerful. It will make us more envied. It will make us more feared.

And I'm consumed by guilt.

Not that I will show it outwardly. There's little point. It won't change anything. The oath behind today's proceedings was signed in blood two years ago by both my da and Luciano Ruocco. The only way to be released from its iron-clad grip would have been through the demise of one or other of the two parties locked in.

Sophia or Padraig.

My brother doesn't deserve this fate. When we signed his life away, we thought we were doing him a favor. No female, married, single, or otherwise was safe from his charms. And he showed no sign of ever stopping sowing his wild oats.

What none of us realized was that his actions were a result of him having already found the great love of his life, but she didn't want him.

He cheated on her. Who could blame her?

But it transpired that our Paddy hadn't been playing the field after all. It turns out he had effectively been on a nine-year rebound. And that at the exact moment we were signing his life away, his unrequited love was finally reciprocated.

A love so pure. A love so simple.

If you believe in fated pairs, that's what Paddy and Jaine are.

Were.

By then, it was too late for them.

He looks at me and smiles, but it doesn't reach his eyes. The sparkle they once held has gone. When Jaine walked away from him that day at the Palace, little did she know she took the final speck with her.

By the end of today's performance, he'll be deserving of an Oscar for the part he will have played as he dazzles and entertains New York's finest while pretending that this is the happiest day of his life.

In fact, it's quite the opposite.

Right now, he appears confused. He's like a death row inmate who's finally going to have the drugs injected into his vein to end his life. It's a day he thought would never come, and yet here it is.

There will be no stay of execution. Everyone present here today will witness as our Paddy gets strapped to the gurney he'll have to lie on for the rest of his days.

With Sophia.

"No. I'm not ready, Eoin. I will never be ready. But I accept that I have no choice."

He's resigned to his fate like a lamb being led to the slaughter. There's no point in struggling when the ending is inevitable.

We form a huddle. All four of us together. It's not something we do often, but it's needed today. Our youngest brother needs our combined strength to get through this and come out intact on the other side. How long he stays that way remains to be seen. The fallout from today will have to be managed one day at a time.

We all hear the single painful sob that escapes him.

Heart-breaking. Gut-wrenching. Soul-destroying. Life-ending. It's a sound I know will live with me for the rest of my days.

We all ignore it. To acknowledge it will simply see him fall apart.

I squeeze his shoulder and then we all step back. Motioning my head towards the door, I let Cillian know it's time to go.

We leave Paddy in the coffin-like room with Dylan, who's acting as his best man, and make our way outside. The building is architecturally magnificent both inside and out. It's a venue fitting for a Duster wedding. The congregation is already starting to filter in to take to their seats. The cream of the political crop. New York's business royalty and the high rankers of our world. Manhattan's crème de la crème.

I'm sure if asked, each attendee would have paid handsomely for their invitation given the business cards on offer here today. It's a once-in-a-lifetime opportunity for many on both sides of the law.

Light streams in through each stained-glass window as we make our way to the heavy, bronzed entrance doors, smiling politely but dismissively at anyone who tries to stop us. The time for mingling, fake niceties, and talking business comes later.

The priority is putting an end to the misery our Paddy's been under these past two years.

"Eoin. Brother." I clench my jaw fleetingly before turning to take in Luciano Ruocco, Sophia's elder brother.

Thirty years old, tall, olive-skinned with black hair that he wears tied back at the nape of his neck, and with well-groomed facial hair. From what I can gather, he's a favorite with the elite ladies of New York and so has likely bedded most of the females present today. Married or otherwise and with or without their husband's consent I'm led to believe, hence why he's currently on the receiving end of an array of disgruntled looks from several of the male guests. He's either too arrogant or too stupid to care.

He will never be my *brother* regardless of what he may think.

I offer my hand, but instead, the Sicilian pulls me in, kissing me exaggeratedly on both cheeks before slapping me hard on the back.

"We are family now, eh? Today will see the joining of the Ruoccos and the O'Connells. It's a good day for business, no?"

He smiles. It's as fake as his teeth and his over-the-top greeting. I offer a small one back in return. I don't like him. I have never liked him. But as the don of the Sicilian mafia, I must tolerate him.

"Yes indeed, Luc. Let today mark the day that the Dusters and the Cosa Nostra become firm allies."

His gaze shifts slightly, and his smile seems more fixed. I'm sure most wouldn't have picked up on it, but I did.

What the fuck is going on? Something clearly is.

"Yes, our organizations will of course be allies, Eoin." His fake smile widens further.

"If you'll please excuse me, Luc."

Making my way past the heavy entrance doors, I see who I've been waiting for getting out of his car. I walk down the stairs to intercept him before he can vanish inside the building.

"Leoluca. I'm glad you could make it."

Ever since I saw him at the Palace with *her*, I've needed to know why. Given the awkward interaction I've just experienced with Luc, it's my guess the two are related, and I want fucking answers.

"Eoin." He frowns slightly. Is it over the last time we met and the events that subsequently unfolded, or is it over what's about to take place here today?

"A word, please."

"Of course."

I stand back as he talks in hushed whispers with his driver, who glances in my direction before shifting his attention back to his boss and nodding.

"Come. Let us talk in the car."

We both follow his man to the waiting vehicle. I get straight to the point as soon as the car door is closed.

"Is there something going on that the Dusters need to be made aware of, Leoluca?"

He frowns. "I'm sorry, Eoin. You'll have to explain."

"I've just had an informal chat with Luc during which he was extremely vague and non-committal when I brought up the alliance between the Dusters and the Cosa Nostra. Are there changes afoot that could jeopardize that relationship? As you will appreciate, we've been waiting two years for today's union to take place."

"Luc is vague and non-committal about many things, as you know, Eoin."

He smiles, but I can immediately sense that something is off.

"While I appreciate that's one of several rather unfortunate character traits of his, what I'm asking is is there anything the Dusters should be concerned about? The content of your recent meeting with Jaine Jones, perhaps."

He pauses before responding. "Jaine is my personal lawyer, but then I'm sure you already know that."

He'll be aware I know all there is to know about him within reason, but the same will be true vice versa.

"Let's not play games with each other, Leoluca. You were clearly discussing another matter. And for Jaine to have flown to New York especially, it must have been one of significant importance. Is it in any way related to the somewhat awkward exchange I've just experienced with Luc?"

"I'm sorry, Eoin, but I'm not at liberty to discuss the content of my meeting with Jaine." He smiles once more before continuing. "What I will say is that you are correct. What was discussed was indeed an issue of great importance. Unfortunately, however, our top tier has yet to be informed of the matter. Until that has taken place, as you will appreciate, I can't discuss the content with a third party."

"Be upfront with me, Leoluca. Is my family making a mistake by allowing my youngest brother to marry Sophia Ruocco?"

My tone is sharp, and with good reason.

This is my family. My flesh and blood. And no one fucks with an Irishman's family. Especially not Eoin O'Connell's fucking family. Something I'm sure Leoluca Di Matteo will be only too aware of.

Heads will roll. Sicilian ones.

There's a pause as we assess each other. Leoluca is a similar age to me. These days, he's taken to wearing his hair in a similar style to Luc's. Like Luc, I hear he's also something of a ladies' man. But that's where their similarities end. He has a reputable reputation, unlike the untrustworthy Luciano.

He nods slowly. "Regrettably, I would say yes. But it is much too late to back out of this contractual agreement. Not without life-threatening consequences. It would be seen as a grave insult to the Ruocco family."

"And the alliance that was meant to come from this long-awaited union?"

He must know the importance of his next response. That it may result in outright war if it's not what I want to fucking hear.

"That is not really a matter for discussion today, Eoin. But know this. Our organization is aware of the blood oath the Dusters entered into with Luciano, but it was undertaken with him personally. That aside, the Cosa Nostra does not wish to make an enemy of the Irish mob. Neither do we wish to start a civil war in New York. We may be many things, but we are not fools. The opportunity exists to build a powerful alliance between our organizations without the need for any arranged matrimony. Once the dust has settled on the planned changes within our organization, then you and I will discuss the many business opportunities that are available to us. You have my word on that."

We stare at each other once more before we each give a slight nod of acceptance and acknowledgment.

He's right, of course. If we go to war, there will be no winners. Only losers and bloodshed.

"I look forward to having that conversation." I hold out my hand

and he shakes it with his. "It's been an informative chat, Leoluca. I do hope you enjoy the wedding."

His driver opens the car door and I step out into the sunshine.

"Please. Call me Leo."

An olive branch.

Only a handful of people call him Leo. I nod at him once more before turning to walk back inside the church.

He's clearly a master of his craft having told me everything I needed to know without actually saying the words.

'You and I' confirmed exactly what I thought. That the future don of the Sicilian mafia wants to have a tete-a-tete with the future Irish king, and the wedding taking place today offers no political advantage to the Dusters whatsoever. That aside, as a point of honor and to avoid unnecessary conflict or bloodshed, the alliance with the mafia is ours for the taking.

My pressing concern now is Luciano. What the fuck has he done to have himself ejected from his own organization when, typically, the only way a founding family member can leave is in a wooden box?

What he decides to involve himself in moving forward could be extremely damaging for the Dusters. This revelation doesn't make him less dangerous. It makes him more so. More importantly, what the fuck have we done? But I already know the answer to the latter.

We've destroyed my brother's life for nothing.

CHAPTER TEN

JAINE

Saint Patrick's Cathedral, Manhattan, New York

Delaney: *Have you set off?*
Jaine: *I'm already here.*
Delaney: *Your plan?*
Jaine: *To walk in, shoot Eoin O'Connell in the head, then throw a party / wake to celebrate.*
Delaney: *Your actual plan, Jaine.*
Jaine: *I'm dressed like a guest and I'm carrying a huge flower arrangement.*
Delaney: *That's your plan? I'm sure the flowers will be gratefully received, but you can't kill someone with a rose.*
Jaine: *Lilies. The flowers of the day are lilies. I checked in advance.*
Delaney: *Is it a wedding or a funeral?*

Jaine: *It's a wedding, but someone's going to die today, so I guess it's both.*
Delaney: *So, a dual-purpose flower arrangement.*
Jaine: *Yup.*
Delaney: *Fingerprints?*
Jaine: *I'm wearing gloves.*
Delaney: *Weapon?*
Jaine: *Already hidden inside. I attended service yesterday so I could confess my sins to The Almighty in advance. I found a safe place to hide it at the same time.*
Delaney: *You got an invitation?*
Jaine: *Like they'd invite me. I'm going to pretend I'm with the florist, hence the flowers. Failing that, I'll play my dumb blonde act. Works every time.*
Delaney: *Are you sure they'll let you in?*
Jaine: *Trust me. It's the O'Connells we're talking about. It's all about keeping up appearances. The event will be over-the-top and vulgar. There will be so many people in attendance if they were sheep, you'd fall asleep trying to count them. I'll never be noticed. Plus, I'm wearing jaw-droppingly expensive clothes, a huge hat, and sunglasses that cover most of my face. I'll fit right in. More importantly, no one should recognize me.*
Delaney: *Use the location finder if anything goes wrong. I'll come straight away. I'll stay local.*
Jaine: *I will. And good to know. Why aren't you attending the big day again?*
Delaney: *Bailey's in Nevada visiting her daddy. I've used the excuse I have a prior appointment with my shrink.*
Jaine: *Mental health comes first.*
Delaney: *Always. Please be careful, Jaine.*
Jaine: *Quit worrying, dad.*

I SMIRK AT MY BURNER BEFORE PLACING IT BACK INSIDE THE LINING of my jacket. Aside from asking if the person is deserving of my engraved bullet, I never discuss a hit. Yet here I am having a full-blown message conversation beforehand. I know Delaney's worried about me. I'm sure that completely out-of-character exchange will have made him even more so. He'll be thinking I'm choosing not to focus on the matter at hand because I've got a death wish or something.

I haven't. I don't want to die. I have two little boys to live for.

But I feel numb. Detached. Like I'm not residing in my own head space. Like I'm experiencing some sort of weird surrealistic episode.

I know it's grief. That it's all too much too soon. I'm still healing. I'm still trying to process Ace's death, and yet here I am trying to save the life of a man whose family may be responsible.

A man who's also the father of my eldest son.

"I can't let anything happen to Irish, Ace," I whisper. I hope he can hear me. I pray to God he can each time I talk to him.

All day. Every day. Like he's still alive and not dead.

There's no acceptance. Can't. Won't. Never will.

The familiar lump forms in my throat. They're getting easier to swallow these days. Let's face it, given their number, I've had plenty of practice.

I know Ace would understand my predicament. I also know he wouldn't want anything to happen to Fin's biological daddy. At least not before he gets the chance to meet his beautiful son.

I close my eyes and raise my face to the sky then exhale slowly. It's a warm, sunny day with a gentle breeze. The perfect weather for a wedding.

Irish's wedding.

Another lump forms.

Blinking back tears, I gaze up at Saint Patrick's. The large spires of the medieval-looking cathedral almost reach the heavens themselves and the bells are already ringing loud and clear to ward off any evil spirits, suggesting that they rethink any plans they may have had about dropping by here today.

Guess I'm just Plan B. That if The Almighty's bell tolling fails to ward off the sniper bad guy who's no doubt being handsomely rewarded for ending the life of Padraig O'Connell, then it'll be down to The Exterminator to save the day.

Flower arrangement in hand, I join with a large party of wedding guests before slowly making my way inside the church. As I suspected, invitations aren't being checked. Why would they bother? Who in their right mind would turn up to a mobster wedding uninvited?

Me. That's who.

Inside, sunlight streams through the stained-glass windows, creating a kaleidoscopic visual effect, but I have no time to stop to admire it.

The smell that greets me causes me to wrinkle my nose. The whole building stinks of lilies. It's not subtle. It's intense and overpowering. An odor that I'm sure will forever remind me of today. An unpleasant stench for an even more unpleasant memory.

Extracting myself from the group of guests and holding the flowers in front of me, I make my way upstairs, nodding and smiling at anyone who looks in my direction. Despite being inside, I keep my hat and sunglasses firmly in place. While I may be attracting one or two curious stares, I still remain mostly inconspicuous. If I'm recognized, it will be game over.

For me as well as for Irish.

The room I've *borrowed* is one of two located just above the entrance, and the rifle I'm using is currently hidden behind a statue of the Virgin Mary. I'm sure the mother of Christ will be only too delighted that I've singled her out to bear witness and keep schtum on the atrocities I'm about to commit.

It's the most compact and straightforward weapon I own. It's lightweight enough that I can pull the trigger from a standing position, which is a priority for today. There's also no disassembly required. Another priority. Given I'll need to get out of dodge pronto, I can leave it under the watchful eye of Mary here and pick it up at a later date.

In the unlikely event it's found, it will be clear of prints. Each part is also individually handmade by several different gunsmiths, so they're completely untraceable.

Locking the door, I put the flowers, my hat, and my sunglasses to one side then replace my white gloves with a thinner pair. I only ever wear fingerless, but needs must today, and I have to be able to feel the trigger.

Picking up my rifle, I balance it on the small ledge that has been perfectly positioned to allow an unwitnessed bird's eye view over the proceedings from the room. Then I stare through the scope of my weapon, and I wait.

I see Leo. Then Luc. So many familiar faces. People I'll need to reacquaint myself with in the not-too-distant future now I'm back living in Manhattan.

If I make it out of here in one piece, that is.

It's then I see the O'Connells. Sarah. Jessie. For the first time, I see Roisin and Fergal in the flesh.

My little boy's grandparents.

Ma Duster is petite. A small woman with a big bite. I know that only too well having been on the receiving end when it comes to my relationship with her precious boys. If only she knew my secret. She will soon enough. It's not a reveal I can put off much longer.

Fergal is exactly how his eldest son will look in thirty years. White-haired and too handsome for his own good.

My trigger finger itches the moment I see *him*.

Eoin O'Connell. Looking as pompous as ever with his arm snaked around Molly McGrath's waist. Meanwhile, she looks like the cat who got the cream.

Pair of narcissists. They really are deserving of one another.

Maybe one day I'll spill her secret. That she never saved his arrogant ass in Nevada. That The Exterminator did. Then again, maybe I won't. At least not until after they're wed because, by then, even with the truth laid bare, he'll be stuck with a liar forever.

Good luck with that in this life.

That would be at least one checkmark in the karma box, and I have a whole host of those fuckers lined up just for him.

My gaze then shifts to the movement at the front of the church. Tears prick my eyes when Padraig appears, followed by Dylan. Another lump forms in my throat and I swallow it down.

With his hair slicked back and wearing a tux, my Irish looks as handsome as ever. He's smiling. He looks happy. He raises his hand and waves to his adoring fans for the day.

The congregation.

"Irish." It's a whisper on my lips. Does he know I'm here? Can he feel my presence?

He doesn't care. He looked at me like I meant nothing to him at the Palace.

Unimportant. Forgotten. Discarded.

His past.

How can I feel the connection when he can't? This invisible thread that links us. I know my heart is beating in time with his right now.

"Our souls have always been intertwined. You feel that too, darlin'?"

"I feel it, Irish," I whisper-sob.

I watch as he immediately raises his head and glances around.

Who or what is he searching for? And then? He's staring straight at me. But then again, he's not. He can't see me. No one can.

Does he sense I'm here after all?

"Don't be so goddamn stupid, Jaine," I whisper-hiss.

I shake my head in denial while trying to hold back the tidal wave of emotions that's been threatening to drown me all day. I can't let those fuckers get the better of me.

Not yet. Not here.

I've been gullible enough. I needed him in my life as much as I needed air to breathe, and when he was gone, I substituted him with the next closest thing.

Dylan. Or so I thought.

Fool.

The web of lies was spun larger and larger until it became two years' worth of deceit. And all because it suited Eoin O'Connell's self-serving purpose. I was used to stop Irish drinking himself to death so he could fulfill his Duster duties here today. Not that any of that matters now. In the end, I see it for what it was.

That it helped me. That it helped Irish.

And now here we are.

Once friends.

Once confidants.

Once everything

Now strangers.

Now parents.

Now nothing.

Get a grip, Jaine. You're here to work, not mope over what could have been. After today, what can never fucking be.

I drag my gaze away from him and switch my focus to the guests. It's my guess if anyone's going to attempt anything, it will be after the ceremony. Why wait until today otherwise? There's a reason. I just don't know what it is.

Yet.

But I will. I'll make it my mission to find out. Same as I'll make it my mission to find out who killed Ace.

Maybe both are related.

A stray tear runs down my cheek as self-pity pays me his daily visit to deliver me a cake of despondency for one. Something to snack on as I witness this whole fucking debacle.

I quickly wipe it away.

Have I got what it takes to carry this through? I'm already feeling overwhelmed. What if I miss the shot and Irish gets killed right in front of me? What if I'm successful but I get caught afterward? I haven't thought this through properly. Maybe Delaney's right. Maybe subconsciously I do have a death wish because, right now, I'm acting the way Razr would.

Still. It's too late now. I have one shot at this. No pun intended. So, what will be will have to be.

"Focus, Jaine," I whisper-hiss at myself once more.

I look through my scope for any unusual signs. Let's face it, it's not like I can search for someone who looks like a serial killer. Most of the congregation gathered here today could wear that cap.

When the Wedding March is played, I ignore it.

When Sophia walks down the aisle on Luc's arm looking beautiful and radiant, I ignore her.

When they say their vows in front of The Almighty, I ignore them.

I ignore it all because I have to. I put thoughts of Irish out of my head because I have to. They'll only distract me and get one or both of us killed.

My finger rests on the trigger as we near the crux of the proceedings. I breathe slowly.

In on four. Out on four.

Repeat.

I don't want to fucking hear it.

I now pronounce you husband and wife.

But I just did.

My heart shatters as those life-altering words are spoken, the emotional pain instantly turning to physical as my empty chest cavity constricts in on itself.

Irish lost. Ace lost.

So much heartache in such a short space of time. But I'll survive. I have to.

In on four. Out on four.

Repeat.

Breathe, Jaine.

I just need to focus my energies on hand-delivering karma now.

It's then I spot who I suspect could be the marksman. He's sitting immediately behind the O'Connells and fidgeting in his seat. Is it him? I watch as his hand reaches inside his jacket. I frown. If it is, then there's no way he can get a clear shot at Irish from his position. At least not without standing.

Show me the gun.

I can't react until I know for sure he's the shooter. I wait and I wait until the kaleidoscopic sunlight glints off the barrel of the now-raised weapon.

Jesus Christ. Is this guy a suicide sniper? Is he going to do what I think he is? Is he going to attempt to take out the O'Connell family? From where he's seated, that's what it appears he's primed to do.

One? Two? As many as he can before turning the gun on himself?

I watch as he points the weapon at the back of Eoin's head. I hesitate; I'm tempted to let him get on with it.

Let justice be served.

You have no proof, Jaine.

My conscience is right. I don't. Plus, if that asshole is guilty, he'll die by my hand, no one else's. I pull the trigger and the goon falls forward the moment my bullet connects with the back of his skull.

Then?

All hell breaks loose. Shouting. Screaming. People running for their lives.

Just as I'm moving to hide my weapon behind the statue, that's when I notice the second marksman. This sniper is on a ledge to the right of me and he's armed with a rifle. Again, his weapon is pointed at the family and not at Irish.

This isn't good.

I should be out of the goddamn building by now. Every second I remain increases my chances of being caught. I know that. But what can I do? I have no choice. I delay my escape by raising my weapon once more.

Line up. Check scope. Pull trigger.

Click. Boom.

I watch as he topples from the balcony and lands in the middle of the congregation.

What follows next is pandemonium. There's no other word to describe it.

Taking a deep breath, I hide my rifle, put on my hat and sunglasses, leave the room, and make my way downstairs.

When I reach the bottom, Eoin and Cillian O'Connell are already ushering the panicking guests outside.

Please don't recognize me.

I spin around to walk the other way and my gaze connects with Sophia's. Irish's wife.

His future.

She's talking to Fergal. She knows it's me under this disguise. She points in my direction and Fergal looks across.

I turn and walk. I don't panic. I don't run. But I know he's now following the girl who dared turn up here today without an invitation.

I speed up and try to lose him in the mayhem before making my way behind the building. He's more likely to think I'll make a run for it rather than hang around, right?

Wrong.

A hand grabs the top of my arm. The grip is vice-like. It's the grip of a murderer. It's the grip of a madman. It's the grip of death himself.

I turn and stare briefly into the eyes of Da Duster just as something connects with the side of my head, and I lose consciousness.

CHAPTER ELEVEN

DYLAN

Saint Patrick's Cathedral, Manhattan, New York

CARNAGE. THAT'S WHAT IT'S TURNED INTO.

The day from hell has turned into a bloodbath. A fitting end to a mobster bash some might say. The shootings have provided us with an impromptu finale as they've put a stop to any of today's other pre-planned festivities taking place.

I'm sure our peers will be talking about the events of today for generations to come, so we've definitely made an impression and gone out with a bang.

Pun intended.

Aside from me, Paddy, and Sophia, the rest of the family is now wearing liquified brains down the back of their clothing as a result of The Exterminator dispatching what appears to have been a fellow sniper who was sitting directly behind them.

We know it was The Exterminator as we've already recovered one of the two engraved bullets fired.

The vigilante then totally saved the day by shooting down another bad guy who was perched in the rafters. That one fell and landed right in the middle of the congregation. It was like a scene from an action movie.

Only, this was no stunt. This was real life.

This is our life.

The second bullet? Eoin's upstairs hunting it down before the pigs get here.

I've explained to him that even though The Exterminator had our backs today, he can't be seen to be playing favorites. It won't do the sniper any favors. It certainly won't do us any either.

Thankfully, he saw sense and agreed.

No bullet equals no proof. The pigs might query their absence, but in the resultant chaos that ensued, anyone could have taken them. That's our excuse and we're sticking to it. They can't argue with that. And they won't if they know what's good for them.

I'm sure a lot of people present would have been only too happy to take away a bullet engraved with an X as a memento from today's aborted proceedings. It's not quite the wedding favors the unhappy couple was looking to hand out, but still.

The newlyweds have left the building now that today has effectively been canceled. Sophia has insisted on traveling to Sicily for their honeymoon, so that's where they're now headed.

It's my thinking their visit may be extended to incorporate *the foreseeable future* with a certain female biker scheduled to return to Manhattan imminently. An individual the O'Connell family should be grateful was covertly with us here today.

Our Paddy shot me a look before he left. It was an *I told you so* look. He was adamant he could sense Jaine. I told him he was imagining things. That it was all wishful thinking on his part. That she was still doing her grieving in Rising.

But he was right.

It was similar to what we witnessed before at St. Peter's. The connection between them so strong they can sense when the other's near.

It made his day. Not that she had to bear witness to him taking the vows with Sophia. I'm pretty sure that's the last thing Jaine would have wanted a front-row seat at. But it will have meant the world to him that after everything that's happened, she still cared enough to come here today to save an O'Connell life.

Maybe even his own.

He's resigned to his fate now having taken that precious purity of Sophia's. Apparently, in the absence of having a Jaine Jones in his life, he gave in to the sweet siren song coming from the whiskey decanter, then gave in to Sophia's juvenile advances.

Or so she says.

He can't remember a thing, but the virginal blood on the sheets the next day was all the proof he needed.

I know he felt like he'd cheated on Jaine all over again. The same as he did when he was nineteen. And that the shitty karma he was being served a heaped plateful of was deserved for all the lies and deceit he subjected her to over and above his initial betrayal.

He'll be eating it cold for the rest of his days now.

I turn my attention to my own wife, who's currently splattered in brains. I can't help but snicker at the grimace on her face as she looks down at the back of her pretty lemon frock.

She elbows me in the ribs for my efforts, and I grunt. She'll pay for that later.

"Was it him, Dyl?"

I smirk. I know she's referring to The Exterminator. "It was, Jessie."

"So, Mr. X-marks-the-spot was here? In this actual building?"

"I reckon so."

"Who were the bad guys trying to kill?"

I shrug. "I have no idea."

"But Mr. X does?"

"I reckon he does."

She sticks out her bottom lip huffily. "I wish I could call Jaine to tell her, but she knows what day it is today. It wouldn't be fair. Plus, she'll still be getting settled in."

"Settled in?" I frown at her.

"Back in her apartment."

I look at her in confusion. "You never mentioned she was back in Manhattan."

She shrugs. "I knew she was heading back sooner than she wanted to, but she couldn't or wouldn't say why. Apparently, it was something she could only discuss with Paul Delaney."

I nod knowingly. "So Razr mentioned her return to Bee…"

"And Bee told me, yup."

"So, you weren't meant to know."

"I guess not. No one was." She at least has the decency to look and sound sheepish.

I turn as our Eoin approaches, the sound of wailing pig sirens now filling the air.

"Got it." He holds up the other engraved bullet.

Molly rushes to his side and wraps her arms around his waist like he's somehow saved the day by finding it.

I smirk at her, and it's met with a scowl. There's no love lost between us. Everyone is aware that I don't like her. I make no attempt to disguise it either, and the feeling's mutual.

I've gone a complete one-eighty. From never saying boo to a goose to having an opinion on everything and everyone.

That lot should have been more careful what they wished for.

I glance at my eldest brother, who's wearing a frown as he surveys the wrecked church. I reckon at least one gun was pointed at Eoin's head today. And if that's the case then this is the second time Jaine Jones will have saved his life.

I excuse myself, leaving Jessie talking to Cillian, Sarah, and Ma, and make my way outside. I need to make an important call.

Standing on the church steps, I dial his number. He answers within three rings.

"Razr. The Exterminator paid us a visit today." I get straight to the point.

"Is that right." It's not a question.

"Have they been in contact with you?"

"Not yet, no."

I pause as my blood runs cold in my veins. I'm sure my delayed response causes his to do the same. It's been almost an hour since the fateful shots were fired. Jaine should have touched base with him by now. If she hasn't then there's a reason for that.

"Where the fuck is she?"

This is the first time either of us will have acknowledged the fact that we each know who The Exterminator is.

"She has her burner."

"What if she can't use it?"

"Who would have taken her? She was dressed as a wedding guest."

"I have no idea… Actually, wait."

My cold blood now turns to fucking ice. "I have no idea where my da is either." I whisper my thoughts aloud.

"Dylan…" he growls. I hear the threat behind it. A threat that's letting me know that if my da so much as harms one hair on Jaine Jones's head there will be outlaw war. That the bloodbath witnessed today will be nothing in comparison.

"Leave it with me, Razr. I'll keep you posted." I hang up before he can threaten to cut out my throat.

Spinning around, I jog back inside. "Eoin." The others look at me as I beckon him over, likely wondering why I'm being secretive.

"What is it, Dyl?" He frowns at me.

"Jaine was here today," I murmur.

His look turns to one of confusion. "What the fuck do you mean?" he hisses.

"She came to watch, I think."

There's no way I'm spilling her secret. As a result, I'm well aware I'm making her sound like some sort of crazed stalker.

"Why would she want to bear witness to something that would have been painful for her?"

"Who knows? It's a question we'll need to ask her." I shrug in an attempt to appear clueless.

"So, she came all the way to Manhattan to watch Paddy get married. And where is she now? On her way back to California?"

"Rumor has it she's moved back to Manhattan. That she's back living at her old apartment. And right now, no one knows where she is. Trouble is, I don't think anyone knows where Da is either."

"Shite."

CHAPTER TWELVE

JAINE

Play Gentlemen's Club, Manhattan, New York

IT'S THE SOUND OF DRIPPING WATER THAT WAKES ME IN THE END. There's only a second or two's respite before the pain in the side of my head makes itself known. I feel like I've been hit by a goddamn baseball bat. Maybe I have.

Memories come flooding back. Manhattan. Irish's wedding. The two snipers. Being caught.

Being. Caught.

I open my eyes and he's staring straight at me.

Fergal O'Connell. Da Duster himself. My abductor.

I blink to clear my blurry vision and the movement causes the pain in my head to ratchet up a couple of notches to borderline intolerable levels. It's a pain that makes me feel sick. Faint. But I show no outward sign of either.

I will not give this fucker the satisfaction of seeing me react to anything he's going to throw at me today.

By doing what he's done, he's already decided I'm guilty without trial. He's moving straight on to my execution with no clear evidence of any wrongdoing on my part aside from being in the wrong place at the wrong time.

I save his life and, in turn, he ends mine.

I try to move, but I'm tied to a plastic chair. Looking down, I take in the dirt and blood that's now covering my cream pantsuit. Most likely my blood from the wound on my head. I glance around. I know where we are. It's where the Dusters extinguish the lives of those who would dare disrespect them, save for the ones who are deemed important enough to be worthy of one of my very expensive engraved bullets.

It's a disused area of the subway. They own several. It feels a bit like a concrete tomb. The cold bites into your bones, and it's so quiet the silence echoes in your head. It's only broken by the constant dripping sound. If you had to spend any length of time in here, you'd no doubt go as insane as the man standing in front of me.

The smell? Death.

Lysol. Piss. Shit. Copper. All sprinkled with a generous pinch of good old-fashioned fear.

The floor's recently been hosed down, so someone's already met their maker today. The O'Connells must have squeezed one in just before the ceremony.

It was probably Irish. One for the road.

Maybe the deceased's wedding gift wasn't up to scratch. One less guest to wine, dine, and impress, I guess.

I've never been in one of the Dusters' torture chambers before, although I have seen inside when Sarah live-streamed her cutting out the throat of the Colombian trafficker.

I finish looking around, then return my gaze to Da Duster.

He's wearing black dress pants and a white shirt with the sleeves rolled up, likely because my blood, when he spills it, will be a fucker to get out. The rest of his wedding attire has been discarded.

"You're awake, girlie." It's an observation. He can quite clearly see that I fucking am. His voice is deep, quiet, and soothing in its tone. No doubt he's perfected it over the years. He's got the balance just right. It lures people in by pretending to be someone who gives an actual fuck in an attempt to hide what he truly is.

A demon who doesn't.

He stares at me with eyes that are identical to Padraig's and Fin's. I ignore his words and hold his gaze.

"What were you doing at my son's wedding?"

I ignore him. He doesn't deserve my response. He doesn't deserve anything from me when he's already made up his goddamn mind. He breaks eye contact, but only so he can pace the floor as he runs his hand repeatedly through his white hair.

It's clear the hand movement is to stop him from doing something else. What exactly? Slitting my throat? Throttling me?

What can I say anyway? That I'm a vigilante sniper and I decided to stop by and save their unworthy Irish necks? Right now, I wish I hadn't bothered.

"Answer me." It's a threat. I stare at him. I'm looking at evil itself right now, all wrapped up to look like a kind old granddaddy.

My son's grandaddy.

"Fuck you." The words in my brain slip out of my mouth. Jesus Christ. Delaney's right. I do have a death wish.

Fergal reaches me in two strides and backhands me across the face with such a force my teeth rattle against the inside of my mouth. Blood is now all I can taste. My head throbs so violently I feel like I'm going to pass out.

Don't give him the satisfaction, Jaine.

"The bride told me she'd seen you skulking around. Were you involved with the shooters? Were you trying to harm my family?" His voice sounds pained. Like the thought of anything happening to his family keeps him awake at night and tortures him relentlessly twenty-four-seven.

Ditto.

So, even though Sophia recognized me, she decided not to tell Da Duster who I am. Figures. It was most likely in the hope he'd react first and ask questions later. She was right. That's exactly what he has done.

She'll get hers. In this life or the next.

He's in my face now. Eyes of sparkling blue contrast against a face that's lined with age and from living in this life. My gaze connects with his. I hide nothing. He hides nothing. Neither of us looks away.

Thousands of tortured souls clawing to get out. That's what I see when I look into his eyes. Does he expect me to show fear as I witness the depth of death, destruction, and depravity that resides within his fucked-up head space?

I fear no one.

I wonder what he sees when he looks into my eyes. Does he see the same? The countless souls of the vermin whose lives I've ended. I truly fucking hope so.

"Speak, girl. Don't make me have to drag it out of you."

It's then I hear the blade. I'd know the almost silent sound of a switchblade being flicked open anywhere having spent four years of my life with a madman who used one as his weapon of choice.

I exaggeratedly spit out the blood that's been pooling in the side of my mouth before replying.

"I said. Fuck. You."

His eyes bore into mine. He's trying to make me back down and cower like a frightened dog.

I cower from no one.

He can do his worst. He'll never break me.

A look crosses his face. Only fleetingly. Pride? Respect? It's gone as quickly as it arrived.

He nods. To himself? To me? I'm not sure why. I'm not sure of the reason.

I can see the shiny silver blade out of the corner of my eye as he lifts it. He won't cut my throat. At least not yet. This is a torture chamber first and foremost. Far below the city streets where no one can hear you scream or beg for mercy.

I won't scream. I won't beg either.

Hell will freeze over first.

I feel the moment the blade connects with my cheek. The initial sting as the sharp piece of metal kisses my skin almost apologetically.

Still, I stare into his eyes. I make no sound. I give nothing away. Not even when I feel the blood trickle down my face. He's not fucking worth it. The O'Connells are not fucking worth it.

This is a battle of wills, and I will not be beaten.

Neither of us hears the elevator behind us, we're so engrossed in our mind games.

"Da!" It's Dylan.

I'm not sure what feeling it is that floods me. Relief that I'm to live to see another day. Regret that I didn't get to finish what twisted shit I started with Da Duster.

A combination of both maybe.

I can see the reluctance in his gaze as he's forced to break eye contact with me. It's clear he wanted to keep playing our mind games too. He steps back.

"What the fuck is it, Dyl? Can't you see I'm busy?" He moves to the side, and that's when I take in Dylan and Eoin O'Connell.

I make eye contact with the eldest son. He frowns in silent response. No doubt at the state I'm in. I don't want his sympathetic looks. I don't want his pity. I don't want his regret. I don't want his excuses. I want out of this chair, and I want to fucking kill someone.

Preferably him.

"What the fuck, Da? Jaine!" I switch my gaze to Dylan. He's visibly upset. Running his hands through his hair the same as his da was just doing like he doesn't know what to say or do. Like he's wondering how to fix this shit show he's been confronted by.

He knows what I've done for his family today. The risks I've taken. The rewards I'm now being personally delivered in thanks. He'll know that I've been pre-judged simply for turning up uninvited.

He'll also know I'll now want my revenge for this over and above everything else I've been subjected to by the O'Connells these past two years. More importantly, he'll know that my sniper secret is to be kept just that.

A secret.

And one that's mine alone to spill.

"Jaine?" Fergal frowns as he looks between me and his sons.

Eoin nods as he breathes in slowly then exhales. "Yes, Da. This is Jaine Jones."

CHAPTER THIRTEEN

EOIN

Play Gentlemen's Club, Manhattan, New York

SHE SITS TIED TO A CHAIR IN A CREAM TROUSER SUIT THAT'S covered in blood and dirt. One side of her blonde hair is caked in blood, her face is bruised down the same side, and her other cheek is bleeding from where my da's cut her with a blade.

She's a mess.

A hot fucking mess.

"Unbind me." She barks the order at Dylan. She won't want to interact with me. My brother's suspicions will be correct, I'm sure. That she believes me guilty of playing a part in Ace's murder. And now here's my da almost ending her life.

Who can blame her for thinking the Dusters have it in for her?

Dylan represents the safest ground. Despite everything, there's still a modicum of trust there. He's the best of a bad bunch in her eyes.

Well, aside from our Paddy.

But given what she's gone out of her way to witness today, she must know that he's now lost to her forever.

What was she thinking?

I look at my da, but his eyes are trained on her.

Watching her. Observing her. Taking her in.

Can he now see what I see?

Not that it matters. Whatever toxic relationship Jaine and I fleetingly shared is over. I'm scheduled to fly to Dublin next week to meet with Molly's da.

Da wanted to meet Jaine. Had asked to do so.

Well, now he has.

But Jesus Christ, it should have been under different circumstances.

Dylan remains silent as he unties her. He won't know what to say. That the patriarch of our family has acted in such an appalling manner. He'll be angry. Maybe even ashamed. That her first interaction with our da has seen her strapped to a chair and manhandled.

But then, we are mobsters, and she did turn up to a family event uninvited. In his defense, my da has never seen her before. He had no idea who she was when he abducted her. Yes, he acted without thinking. But his family was threatened today, and quite understandably, he reacted.

Never trifle with an Irishman's flesh and blood. And definitely not one as unhinged as my da.

I'm sure he'll be annoyed with himself. Not that he'll ever admit as much to anyone outside of the immediate family. More so to Jaine Jones.

All actions have consequences.

I'm sure she'll let us know what those are in due course. Because there will be payback for today.

"Should I ask Jessie to come, Jaine?" Dylan volunteers quietly.

"You will do no such goddamn thing. What happened goes no further than this room." she hisses at him, but the laced-with-venom warning is loud for a reason. It's directed at all of us.

He stops what he's doing and stares at her.

"There will be repercussions if it does, Dylan O'Connell. You have my word on that." She blatantly threatens him.

He nods his agreement before continuing to unbind her, silent once more.

Will she go to the pigs? She's a lawyer. She could quite easily have my da sent down for the rest of his life for what he's done to her. But she'd never betray her own kind. So, what exactly does she mean?

Repercussions? I want to fucking know.

"Shall I call for a doctor to attend?" It's only right that I offer. She is bleeding, after all.

She laughs dryly. "What? Like the useless Dr. Kelly?"

"We have others," I add, choosing to ignore her scathing response.

"I'll pass. What's another scar or two when my body's already littered with the goddamn things?"

I curse my dick for twitching and my brain for instantly imagining each and every one of those scars. Scars that will no doubt caress her skin like works of dark fucking art. I push the unwelcome thoughts from my mind of tracing every single one of them.

With my tongue.

Now is not the time. In fact, there will never be a fucking time for such thoughts. Not of her.

Not. Ever. Again.

We silently assess each other. Time passes. I'm not sure how long. The moment only ends when her phone starts to vibrate. I watch as she reaches inside her jacket and pulls out her burner. She knows exactly who's calling her. Dylan must have given him the heads-up.

"I'm fine, Delaney," she mumbles.

There's a pause at her end. He's shouting. We can all hear the depth of his anger even if we can't make out the precise words. He'll be even more unhappy when he sees the state she's in. As much as our Cillian's married to his sister, it won't make Razr any less likely to want to slit our throats over what the Dusters have done to Jaine today.

"I'll see you in five minutes." She disconnects the call, then looks at us one by one. "Leave Delaney to me."

It's a statement. She doesn't want or expect an acknowledgment.

There's a pause.

"So, now you know I'm back in Manhattan."

Another pause.

She suddenly looks resigned. Like what she's about to say she doesn't want to but has no choice in the matter.

She exhales slowly. "I have back-to-back meetings tomorrow. The last one finishes at three p.m. I'll be at your offices by three-thirty. There's something I need to discuss with all of you. Sophia and Molly are not to be present."

She won't want Sophia or Molly in attendance because she trusts neither. With the latter, who can blame her given she blatantly threatened her? A conversation which will no doubt form the basis for her thinking we're connected with Ace's death in some way.

"Sophia and Paddy have gone on honeymoon to Sicily. Ma's flying out to the Ruocco family home tonight at Luc's insistence."

She stares at me once more. Her face gives nothing away, even though I'm sure my reminding her that my youngest brother is now a married man will sting.

Guilt flows through me. The harsh reality that his arranged marriage achieved nothing. I still have to reveal my findings to the rest of the family. Explain the content of my recent conversation with Leo.

Jaine will already be aware given their close relationship. I'm sure it will have been touched on during their recent meeting. I'm also sure she'll take great pleasure in saying *I told you so*.

"When is he due back?"

"We're not certain. He's able to work remotely, so there's no real rush. It's not been discussed, but we believe Sophia wishes for them to remain in Sicily long term."

I'm sure she can read between the lines. That Sophia's deliberately keeping Paddy away from Manhattan as she doesn't want him anywhere near her.

She nods. "Well, it can't wait indefinitely. It's already waited too long."

She stands, then walks to the elevator and presses the call button.

"Tomorrow. Three-thirty p.m."

The doors open. She steps inside. They close.

And then she's gone.

"I'M SORRY, BOYS."

Dylan is now sitting on the chair Jaine was bound to, his head in his hands.

"What the fuck happened, Da?" He runs his hand through his too-long black hair as he looks up at him.

"We saw her trying to leave the church. Or at least Sophia did. She mentioned she'd seen the girl skulking around and looking suspicious. After what had just happened, I immediately saw red."

"Sophia. I should have fucking known," I grouse.

"She wanted this reaction." He frowns at me.

"She did, Da. She must have recognized Jaine and then decided to use the fact that you'd never met her to her advantage. She'd have been quite happy for you to take her life so she could never tempt our Paddy again. So, you clattered her over the head and dragged her here kicking and screaming."

"The first part is correct, Eoin. I'm ashamed to say I did clatter her. But there was no kicking or screaming on her part. The girl gave nothing away. There were no reactions from her whatsoever. She remained deadpan throughout. Even when I cut into her flesh, she didn't flinch."

Something akin to pride races through me. That even facing certain death, Jaine Jones still maintained that defiance of hers.

"Did you not ask her who she was?"

"Aye, but she wouldn't say. She likely thought it was too little too late for all of that. And she was probably right. The only words she uttered were *fuck you,* and she used them twice."

There's a silent pause before Dylan starts to snicker, the sound lightening the dark mood.

"That's Jaine Jones for you, Da. She backs down from nothing and can always be relied on to turn the air blue."

He looks at me as he speaks, and I start snickering too, while Da just continues to stare at us.

CHAPTER FOURTEEN

JAINE

The Hudson Dusters' HQ, Manhattan, New York

Closing my eyes, I exhale the last of Rising from my lungs before inhaling the familiar trash and exhaust-fume-filled air of the concrete jungle that represents my second home.

I've missed New York.

With a small smile, I listen to the symphony of the yellow cab drivers as they honk their horns and cuss at each other, the sound of their camaraderie only drowned out by the ever-present wail of sirens.

I haven't told anyone where I'm going or what I'm doing. That way, no one can either encourage me or tell me I'm making a mistake. It doesn't matter what they think. It doesn't matter what I think either. All that matters is that it's time. I can't delay the inevitable forever.

It's also what Ace wanted. His living wish and also his dying one. My beautiful boy, selfless until the end.

I stand on the sidewalk and gaze up at the imposing skyscraper, the sun reflecting off its glass-covered exterior.

Duster HQ.

Irish surrounds me the moment I step through the revolving entrance doors. I'm sure I can smell his cologne, Old Spice. Or is it just wishful thinking?

It's most likely ingrained in the foundations of this over-the-top pretentious environment with its marble flooring, white walls, and putrid pieces of art.

Not that it really matters. Our connection is one-sided these days. Which is perhaps just as well given he's now happily married.

Tears threaten, but I blink them back. I'm done crying. I've cried me a goddamn river. Tears don't help. They only hinder. They only drown.

Married or not. Connection or not. I still wish he were here.

This is his breaking news. He deserves to be the first to hear it. But it's not a reveal that can take place over the phone. And I can't wait for his return with the date unknown. A date that could be tomorrow. A date that could be never.

I can't put it off any longer. If not now, then I may decide never to spill my closely guarded secret. And that wouldn't be fair on anyone. More so Fin. Whether I like it or not, these people are his blood family.

Four females sit side by side behind the mile-long reception desk, the white marble monstrosity rising like a vulgar wave from the ostentatious floor.

The girls are all as to be expected. Decorative. Black-haired. Blue-eyed. Most likely Irish. Their uniformed exteriors are matched right down to the color of their regimented nail varnish and lipstick.

All Duster-approved, I'm sure. And probably inspected and signed off by the resident asshole himself.

The one closest looks up at me. Her smile is as fake as the veneered teeth behind it. It's clear I'm expected as no introduction is necessary.

"Right this way, Miss Jones."

Polished. Professional. Proficient. I expected nothing less.

We walk to the bank of elevators. I'm shown into the first one, and she presses the button for the top floor.

While traveling up, I take in my reflection in the all-mirrored wall surface. My navy pin-striped suit was hand-made by the best tailor in Manhattan. My overall appearance screams top-tier business professional.

Apart from my face.

I've hidden the damage Fergal inflicted as best I can, but the bruising on one cheek from the back-handed slap he gave me is still clearly visible, as is the switchblade cut on the other. A wound that is currently being held together by surgical tape. I'm wearing my hair down in a futile attempt to disguise the golf ball-sized lump on the side of my head which, even now, throbs as a constant reminder of yesterday's unfortunate events.

Thankfully, my meetings today were all internal. My team is used to me wearing cuts and bruises. No questions are ever asked. Given I'm a biker and who we represent in the main, it's to be expected that not every day will be challenge-free. They accept that it comes with the territory and that the risks faced are reflected in the exorbitant prices both JAL and JAA charge.

The elevator pings to announce my arrival. The doors open and I step out.

"Candice."

She looks up, and I take in the tall, willowy female who's positioned just outside the meeting room door. She's as beautiful as the last time I saw her with her creamy skin, dark hair, and large hazel eyes. I find myself wondering who she's fucking now since Molly will have put a stop to her daily desk sex shenanigans with Eoin. Then again, maybe she's still pining over the future Irish king.

She smiles at me. For once, it seems almost genuine.

Almost.

I smile back. For once, I almost feel sorry for her.

Almost.

I haven't seen her since Leo's function. She was with Cara then. The deceitful blonde who has now departed God's green earth courtesy of Sarah O'Connell's blade.

"They're waiting for you, Jaine."

I nod. Trepidation butterflies flutter through my stomach. Not because, having heard about them for so long, I'm about to attend my first reservoir dogs-style meeting. I'm not in the least bit nervous about confronting or holding my own with the majority of the O'Connell clan in one sitting. Not at all. I can handle myself in any business arena. It's because when I say what I have to, it can't be taken back. Pandora's box will have been opened and its contents revealed. I have no idea what the reaction or fallout will be. All I know is that from this day forward, everything will change.

For better or worse? A union forged in heaven or hell.

Well, that remains to be seen.

CHAPTER FIFTEEN

EOIN

The Hudson Dusters' HQ, Manhattan, New York

"SO, WE DON'T KNOW WHY JAINE'S CALLED THIS MEETING."

"No, Jessie. We don't." I reply even though I'm tempted not to bother.

"Didn't you think to ask her?"

"When she suggested we meet, it was neither the appropriate time nor place to pose such a question."

"And she wants all of us to hear what she has to say."

"That's what she insinuated, yes. But as we've all already agreed, Jaine will be dealing with me today."

"Can I at least say hello to my business partner?"

"Yes, of course you can. We're all fully aware of how much you'll struggle to keep that mouth of yours closed," I bite, then I'm immediately annoyed with myself for reacting to her persistent fucking needling because that's precisely what she wants.

She ignores my adverse reaction. Instead, she just smirks in that annoying way only she can having achieved her desired result.

"And why isn't Molly allowed to attend again?"

"Jaine didn't give a reason."

"She didn't have to. It's obvious." She rolls her eyes exaggeratedly.

"Is it really?" I'm not sure why she bothered asking the question when she clearly already knows the answer.

I don't know why I bother replying. She'll just continue conversing with herself regardless. She has no zip. And no filter. She's much like Jaine in that regard, but without the cussing.

"Yes, it is. It's because Molly threatened her and then suggested her success was down to the fact that she has a mattress attached to her back. There's a word for that. Two, in fact. Professional envy."

"I'd be very careful what you say about the future Ma Duster."

The most fitting word to describe Jessie O'Brien is intolerable. Each day she sets her stall out to wind me up, and every day she succeeds. Just as I'm fully aware that Dylan has no time for Molly, I have no time for Jessie.

"Why? What's she going to do? Shoot me in the head?"

She and Sarah snigger at each other. Those two are as bad as each other at causing trouble and egging each other on. We've enough trouble heading our way in the shape of Miss Jones.

"Eoin's right, Jessie. Jaine isn't coming here today to take afternoon tea with us all. She's got an announcement to make, and she wants the Dusters' full attention when she does so. We don't need her manipulating the situation any more than she has already."

Jessie smiles sweetly at Da. "Manipulation is what Jaine does best, Fergal. She's a lawyer, don't you know."

"We realize that, hence why we need to keep the conversation confined to the matter at hand, whatever that may be. While we appreciate you're her business partner and that you and Sarah are her close friends, please don't forget that you're also both O'Connells."

"Don't ask me to pick sides, because I won't."

Backchat now from Sarah, no doubt inspired by Jessie's outspokenness.

"No one is asking you to pick a side, Sarah. All we're asking is that you pipe down and let Eoin handle the woman. Once Miss Jones has left the building, we can then discuss her revelation between us as a family. Which is how it should be. But please can we all just find out what it is first."

Da's borderline hissing now, so no one will dare speak further. Not if they know what's good for them.

He's annoyed. It's understandable. Jaine's calling the shots. She told us she's coming. Demanded we all be present. And here we are, doing as we're told like good little mobsters.

There's a reason for that. For Jaine to insist on delivering whatever the fuck this news is on our turf means it's something monumental. Something life-changing. And potentially something that means we can't touch her after it's been publicly announced.

And I'll bet she can't fucking wait.

I look around the table. We're all here apart from Sophia, Molly, Paddy, and Ma.

I glance once more at Jessie.

She's one of Jaine's two loyal supporters present today. Our Dylan's new wife is seated to his right. They say opposites attract and it's true in their case. Dylan is an introvert, or at least he was. Jessie, on the other hand, is an extrovert who loves to be the center of attention. Looking ever the business professional, the tall model-esque blonde accountant now has her poker face firmly in place.

She'll hold her tongue for now. She won't want to upset Da and the same will be true vice versa. For whatever reason, they share a soft spot for each other.

I then turn my attention to Sarah, our Cillian's wife, seated to his right. Both are redheads with matching fiery temperaments. Sarah lives in the moment. Most of the time, she does so without a single thought or care as to the outcome of her fly-by-the-seat-of-her-pants approach to life. Sarah is Paul Delaney's baby sister. She's also one of Jaine's closest allies and her other great supporter.

She's currently biting her lip nervously. It's that skittish reaction that gives her away. She knows. Whatever it is, Sarah Delaney already fucking knows.

For how long I wonder?

Da looks deep in thought, a frown marring his forehead. He has done ever since his tete-a-tete with Jaine yesterday. Today, we'll see first-hand the results of his handiwork now that all the blood and filth will have been washed away. No one will know the reason Jaine will look like she's been through the wars.

We've been sworn to secrecy or else there will be *repercussions.*

A blatant threat, not a veiled one, and one our Dylan took extremely seriously.

I look at the only other person in the room. Blonde-haired and green-eyed like his ma and hailing all the way from Dublin, I take in our cousin, Aidan O'Connell.

He catches my eye and grins. This is all new to him. The professional business side of the organization. He's used to getting his hands dirty dealing with the supply and shipping of weapons from the Irish end. As he'll be working closely with Cillian, we thought it only right that he witness today's showdown.

He has no real idea what's going on or who Jaine is, but he's soaking it in all the same. He'll no doubt be enjoying every entertaining moment of witnessing the big bad Dusters being made to jump through silly little hoops by a female fucking lawyer.

Still, he's part of our inner circle. It's his birthright the same as it is ours. He's blood. Family. It's the most important thing to us O'Connells.

And no matter the earth-shattering news Jaine Jones announces today, she will never bring our family to its knees. She will never bring me to my knees. She may try like many have done before her. But she will fail just as they did.

Silence.

So quiet we can all hear the elevator door as it opens and closes, then the mumble of conversation as Jaine speaks with Candice.

The latter knocks on the door.

"Come in." My tone is firm. Today, Jaine Jones will meet her match when she enters the den of the lion himself.

Candice's smile is polite but forced. Now I've agreed to wed Molly, what we shared has ended once and for all. A reality she's not pleased about. She'll get over it, I'm sure. It's not like I ever promised her anything.

"Your visitor has arrived."

"Show her in, please."

The door closes.

Seconds later, it reopens and Jaine walks into the room.

I take in the woman I allowed to haunt my thoughts for far too long. She looks immaculate in a navy suit with matching heels. Her golden hair hangs down to mid-back. It's a far cry from her typical tank girl look.

If she'd been dressed like this when we first met, then maybe I wouldn't have made the mistake of underestimating her. I know now it was likely deliberate on her part. She's manipulative. Extremely so.

She makes eye contact with me first. Her cheek is badly bruised, and the cut inflicted on her by my da's blade is being held together by surgical tape. She shifts her focus to him. Not many can hold my da's stare, but she does, and with ease. Then again, she'll have looked into the depths of the madman's condemned soul yesterday when her life was hanging by a thread.

She showed no fear then. She's displaying none now.

I thought he may appear sheepish at having to survey the results of his overreaction in the harsh light of day, but he gives nothing away either.

"Partner, have you been in a fight?" Jessie breaks the elongated silence, which is typical of her need to always be heard.

Jaine smirks at her. "You know what curiosity did to the cat, don't you, Jessie? I suggest since you've not been blessed with the nine lives of a feline that you mind your own goddamn business."

Jessie laugh-snorts in response. Very ladylike. Almost as ladylike as Jaine's cussing little mouth.

The things I want to do to that fucking mouth.

Unwelcome thoughts.

"Jaine." Sarah speaks next.

Jaine looks at her and simply nods, confirming what I thought. That she does indeed know what the rest of us don't.

Three biker females. Three close friends. Family in their world. Blood or not. Two form part of our inner circle and one is currently an enemy on the outside.

"Dylan. Cillian." Jaine acknowledges both and they nod. She then turns her attention to our Aidan.

"And you are?"

He grins at her. "I'm Aidan."

She continues to stare at him, no doubt waiting for him to divulge further. She raises an eyebrow when he doesn't.

"Well, it's good to know your folks decided to keep you and so thought you deserving of a first name, Aidan. But do you know anything else about yourself beyond that, or is that all the intel they thought you'd be able to handle?"

Jessie snickers, and Aidan's grin widens. He leans back on his chair, stretches his arms upwards, then places his hands behind his head. Jaine's gaze lingers on him, which I'm sure was exactly what he was aiming for.

Is she admiring him?

My hand tightens around my Mont Blanc pen, imagining it to be his neck. I don't want her looking at him. I want her eyes to be on me at all fucking times.

"Smart mouth," he replies.

"Smart everything," she quips in response.

"I like you already."

Try as she might, she can't stop the small smile from forming as her mouth curves upwards. She likes him too. That much is obvious. And I know why. Aidan is the blonde-haired version of our Paddy when it comes to confidence, looks, and winning fucking personality.

"That's good to know, but I'm still waiting."

I respond on his behalf. I don't want him interacting with her.

"Aidan is our cousin. He flew in from Dublin last night and will be working alongside Cillian."

Aidan raises an eyebrow at me. He knows exactly why I intervened. He'll know now that she's off-limits to anyone but me.

Meanwhile, she's now glaring at me.

Good. It's best she doesn't forget who the future Irish king is.

"Given you've answered on your cousin's behalf, am I to assume that I'm only permitted to converse with you today, Mr. O'Connell?"

"That is correct, Miss Jones."

"So be it." She glances at the circular table. There are two spare chairs. One to my right, which is where Molly typically sits, and one to Aidan's right, which would see Jaine facing me. She walks to the empty chair beside my cousin. Two reasons, I suspect. She doesn't wish to be anywhere near me. She also wants a front-row seat to witness my reaction to the announcement she's about to make.

Aidan smiles at her, and she smiles back. Right now, I want to rip off his fucking head and piss down his neck.

I don't. But only because I'm not sure how the rest of my family would react if I did.

Jaine places her briefcase on the tabletop. Just as she's about to take her seat, her phone vibrates. Removing it from her inside pocket, she glances at the handset. It's different from yesterday's, so it's not her burner. It's the phone I've been permitted to have the number of. She's deliberately not given me the other number, even though she's fully aware that I have it.

To wind me up. To dare me to use it uninvited. Both, probably.

"Excuse me. I have to take this."

"Leo." She walks to the window, speaking in rapid-fire Italian. It's his native tongue, but it won't be for that reason. It's so the rest of us won't know what's being said. She won't be discussing anything confidential. She's not naïve. She'll be aware that all conversations that take place in this room are recorded. It doesn't go unnoticed by the rest of us, however, that Luc's name gets mentioned on more than one occasion.

"Ciao. Ciao, Leo."

I want to know what they were talking about, but that will have to wait. That's not what today is for. It's my guess today is about something far more important.

Jaine remains standing, deep in thought, her gaze fixed out the window.

She finally turns, making eye contact with Sarah once more. Cillian side glances at his wife. I'm not sure how happy he is now he realizes she's in on the act and that she's kept a secret from him. From the entire family.

A big one.

Jaine takes her seat beside Aidan, her gaze now fixed on me. She'll get straight to the point like she always does.

"As you all know, Padraig and I dated briefly when we were nineteen. We kept in touch but then reconnected in person a little over two years ago when we were taken by the Russians, along with Ace."

She pauses briefly. Her face is void of emotion, but everyone sitting here is aware its grief related. She tilts her chin in preparation for what she's about to reveal before continuing.

"That reconnection resulted in my eldest son. Finian Fergal Jeremiah O'Connell Steele."

Cue the mic drop.

Jaine nods at her partner in crime, and in response, all of our phones vibrate simultaneously. I unlock mine immediately. It's a message from Sarah. A picture. I open it and find myself looking at a little boy with hair as black as coal contrasted by the pale skin of the Irish and with sparkling blue eyes and a cheeky smile identical to his da's. He's holding a soft toy in his hand, his exposed chubby arm displaying the O'Connell horseshoe birthmark.

Padraig has a son.

My ma and da's first-born grandchild and a male Duster heir.

I can't speak at first. I'm not sure what I expected, but it wasn't this.

Envy suddenly courses through my veins. That she's carried my brother's offspring when it should have been mine.

I shouldn't be thinking that way when I'm about to wed someone else, but I can't fucking stop myself.

"You kept him from us!" I hiss at her.

She frowns momentarily, my adverse reaction clearly not what she expected. She doesn't need to know it's fueled by my spiraling jealousy.

She stares at me. "You as good as ran me out of town, or have you forgotten? You threatened to have me exterminated if I didn't do as you asked. Stay away from my brother, you said. For two years, you said. I was simply doing as I was told."

She speaks matter-of-factly, but I can tell my outburst has infuriated her. I'm sure she already feels victimized. As a result, she's now struggling to control her own rage.

"That's no excuse. You should have informed us the moment Finian was born." I stand and push my chair back.

So this is the secret she's been hiding all this time. From my family. From my brother.

From me.

She also stands, resting her hands flat on the table with one eyebrow raised. "Nothing would have been gained by my doing so. On the contrary, Padraig would have signed his own death warrant by insisting that we marry, and you know it."

"You could have told me!"

She snorts, her anger finally surfacing. "Why the fuck would I tell *you* anything, Eoin? In fact, why the fuck would I tell your family anything? Separating Irish and me was a combined Duster decision, after all. *It was nothing personal, Jaine*." She mimics me.

"THE CHILD IS AN O'CONNELL," I roar.

She stares at me. Time passes before she speaks, and when she does, she's managed to rein herself in.

"I did what you asked. I played by your rules. You wanted me out of sight and mind until Padraig was safely wed. I did exactly that. If you're angry, then you have no one to blame but yourselves. His family is the reason he's missed out on Fin's life. That all of you have. Not me. And for what? It turns out it was all for nothing."

"I told you so." My voice is low.

She doesn't reply.

"Say the words, Miss Jones. I know you're dying to."

She still doesn't respond. Instead, she walks around the table before stopping right in front of me, her defiant green gaze boring into mine.

If this room were empty, I'd pin her down on that table and fuck that defiance right out of her.

She nods slowly. "It proves you don't know me at all if you think I'd take any pleasure from saying those words." She pauses. "You may have your precious alliance, but at what cost to Padraig? You and I both know the coalition is in no thanks to him marrying Sophia as we both also know Luc is to be overthrown as the reigning don in the not-too-distant future. That rumor has it he's setting up his own mafia organization. That, in fact, he may have already done so. So, Irish has a son he's never met, and for what?" She glares at me, her eyes filled with undiluted hatred. "Leo mentioned your discussion, so let's not pretend this is breaking news to you, Eoin."

I glare back but say nothing. I can't deny it and she knows it.

If she's spoken with Leo, then she'll also be aware that I was only party to this revelation yesterday, and given everything that's subsequently happened, the likelihood is I won't have had time to share this sorry state of affairs with my family yet. She's deliberately gone out of her way to cause mayhem here today.

No doubt all part of her big payback plan.

"And why would he discuss the content of our private conversation with you?" I ask the question even though I already know the answer.

"It was business-related. Leo has no business secrets from me."

"And why is that, Miss Jones?"

She laughs dryly. "Has the reason I returned to Manhattan ahead of time been eating away at you, Mr. O'Connell? I'm sure you know the answer, but if you want to play games by having me spell it out, then fine. Leo has asked that my companies represent the Sicilian Mafia once he takes over as the new don."

"And have you agreed?"

"Not that it's any of your business, but yes, I have."

There's a pause. She'll know what I'm thinking, I'm sure. That if she and Paddy had married, we would have had the alliance we wanted anyway, and potentially many more.

"So, yes. I can say I told you so if that's what you wish to hear. I can also say I warned you to steer clear of the Ruoccos on the very day you as good as told me to pack my bags and leave Manhattan. But it would give me no satisfaction. Because not only has Irish suffered as a result of your poor decision, but his son has too. Fin is sixteen months old, and he's never met his biological father. I hold you personally responsible for that."

We glare at each other as we stand inches apart.

"Can we meet him? Young Finian?"

Da interrupts whatever the fuck this is between me and her. I frown and squeeze my eyes shut briefly. Given he almost killed Jaine yesterday, I'm now just waiting for her to tell him to fuck off.

That's what he deserves. What we deserve, and we all know it.

"Tomorrow. I'll make the necessary arrangements through Dylan."

Her gaze never leaves mine. Even though my face remains impassive, she'll know I'm both surprised and grateful for her unexpected favorable response. She eventually breaks eye contact. I want to take some sort of satisfaction that she looked away first, but I know she did so because with both of us being stubborn as fuck with each other, we would have stood here all day.

Having thrown her grenade, I watch as she retrieves her briefcase before leaving the room without uttering another word.

Manipulative, evil woman.

CHAPTER SIXTEEN

JAINE

Jaine's Apartment, Upper East Side, New York

"Jaine. I wasn't sure who was meant to call who. Sorry if it's not a convenient time. I can always …"

"It's fine, Dyl," I interject.

He'll no doubt have been put under pressure by the rest of the O'Connells to touch base and find out where my head's at. Have I changed my mind about letting them see Fin today or haven't I? Was my agreement a spur-of-the-moment decision and on reflection, I've had a change of heart?

There's a pause.

For the first time ever, we share an awkward silence. It's what I half expected. He won't know what to say.

Ditto.

I share a child with his closest sibling. A little boy I've kept hidden.

From him. From his family. From Irish.

He'll feel like he doesn't know me anymore. Like he never really did. Maybe now he'll understand how I felt when the dirty secret he kept from me came to light. How let down I was when I found out that for two years I'd been messaging Irish, believing it to be Dylan. I felt like I didn't really know him then either. On top, I felt betrayed at the extreme lengths of covert manipulation they had all gone to to stop me from finding out, my own thoughts and feelings on the matter obviously unimportant in the grand scheme of things.

At least I didn't pretend to be something or someone I'm not. And I kept quiet for the right reasons. My news wasn't withheld for selfish gain or political purpose.

It was done for Irish.

But then, the deceitful part Dylan played was in his brother's best interests too. I get that. Even though what he did was wrong, his heart was in the right place. Unlike Eoin. That asshole doesn't have a heart. He kept up with the pretense as it fit right in with that all-important goddamn masterplan of his.

"Jaine."

"Dyl."

We speak at the same time, both of us no doubt feeling the need to fill this shared alien silence. We've never not known what to say to each other, but so much has happened in such a short time I guess neither of us knows where or even how to start.

"You go first, Dyl."

"It's what Ace was talking about, wasn't it? What he meant when he said you needed to do right by Fin?"

I pause, blinking back tears as Dylan recaps Ace's final words.

"I'm sorry, Jaine."

"It's fine, Dyl." Another pause as I try my best to keep my head raised above the tidal wave of grief that still threatens to drown me most days. "Yes, it was. I wanted to tell you, but I'm glad I didn't because with what I now know, it might not have been you I revealed it to. It could have been Irish."

"I'm so sorry about all of that."

"I know you are." And I know he is. Unlike his older brother.

"And I understand the reasons you did what you did. Why you never mentioned anything about Fin."

I sigh while running my hand down my face. I feel emotionally wrung out. "Do you? Eoin clearly doesn't."

"I do, Jaine. And you're right. Our Paddy would have dragged you straight down the aisle at St. Peter's whether you wanted to wed him or not."

"And earned himself a bullet in the head from the Ruoccos whether I said yes or not."

"I agree. So, my opinion, for what it's worth, is that you did the right thing. And the rest of the family will realize that in due course. Everyone's just a bit shell-shocked, that's all. We expected your announcement to be something noteworthy. We didn't expect it to be a living, breathing little person."

"Does your ma know about Fin?"

"She does. She and Da have been speaking on and off ever since he broke the news to her."

"About?"

"No clue. It's all been hush-hush. I don't even think our Eoin knows. I guess we'll all find out today."

"And Irish?"

There's a pause.

"He's not been told. We have no way of knowing how he'll react. It's too risky telling him while he's away."

Tears prick my eyes once more. "It just seems wrong that he's going to be the last to find out when he should have been the first."

"I understand. But knowing Paddy, he'll make the journey straight back to Manhattan and all hell will break loose."

"Because the shit will then hit the fan and it will all have been for nothing."

"Exactly."

There's another pause.

"The wedding. Jaine… what you did."

It's his turn to sound emotional. He likely now suspects I saved more than one O'Connell ass that day.

"How did you know? I mean…" Dyl began.

"We were trying to find out who was responsible for Ace… you know… his…." My voice breaks once more, and I exhale slowly as I try to compose myself. "Delaney heard a rumor on the sniper grapevine that someone was planning on killing Irish on his wedding day. I couldn't let anything happen to him. I had no choice but to return to Manhattan earlier than planned."

"So, you witnessed him marrying Sophia."

"I did."

There's a pause. He'll know how hard that would have been for me.

"Anyway, it soon became clear that it wasn't Padraig they were targeting. It was the rest of the family. I almost missed the second sniper. I spotted him just as I was readying to leave. It was the delay in dispatching him that resulted in me being seen by Sophia."

I pause before I continue. Tell the truth or not?

"Dylan…. the first gun. It was aimed at the back of Eoin's head. I'm sorry to say but I almost let the marksman pull the trigger."

There's a pause as he no doubt digests what I've just said. That I was prepared to witness his eldest brother being killed in cold blood.

"But you didn't. That's the important thing."

"Only because I have no physical proof."

"Proof of what?" For the first time ever, Dylan O'Connell raises his voice at me. "That the Dusters were behind Ace's death? You really believe us capable of such a thing, Jaine? You will never find proof because we had nothing to do with it! Jesus Christ, Ace was killed on my wedding day. I was the last person he spoke to before he... before he..."

His voice breaks and tears fill my eyes for the nth time as my brain slowly and painfully slide-shows through the memories of the worst hours of my life.

"Ace was a good man, Jaine. In fact, he was a great man. I'm only sorry that I never had the opportunity to get to know him better. I regret that I didn't embrace this Duster side of me earlier so I could have done just that."

A sob escapes me. Then another. And another.

"Jaine." His tone is sympathetic as I throw my daily fucking pity party, only this time, I have a guest.

"I miss him, Dyl."

"I know you do."

"And all of this. It's just too much too soon." I'm aware I sound broken and pathetic. And I am.

But it's only temporary; the time for grieving has passed. Ace is gone. He's never coming back. I need to pick myself up, dust myself down, and get over it. And that's what I will do. That's what Ace would want me to do.

Dyl and I both know when I put the phone down that I'll piece myself back together. I have no choice. This is a fleeting moment of weakness and fragility. Nothing more. The life I lead allows for neither. Both will only get me killed, and I have two little boys to live for.

"I don't know what to expect from today, Dyl," I whisper.

"Then don't expect anything. Just go with the flow. I'm sure things will work themselves out and fall into place naturally. Do you want me to come and pick you up?"

My response is immediate. "I think it would be best if I make my own way there."

"So you can leave when you want to?"

"Exactly."

He snickers. "I'll message you the directions."

The O'Connell Home, Darling, New York

It's a gated entrance, so I have to wait to be let in. For once, I don't complain or criticize. For once, I understand. Fergal and Roisin want to protect their family at all costs.

Even from me.

Having a family of my own, I get it now. The security will be state of the art and Fort Knox equivalent. They have a lot of enemies. From this day forward, so will Fin.

Having parked up, I step out of my recently purchased SUV. Like the Duster vehicles, it's effectively a bullet-proof, bomb-proof tank disguised to look like an innocent black four-wheel drive. I bought three. One for me and one each for Duke and Sasha to use. A must for any time they're transporting Fin, JJ, or both.

I take in the O'Connell family home. It's vulgar. No surprises there. It's a mansion-like property finished off with over-the-top water fountains and manicured gardens, the lawns so perfect they look like they've been cut with a pair of nail scissors. They probably have. It's not like they can't afford it. Security cameras immediately fix on me. They'll no doubt follow my every move. Big brother is watching, but I can't see him.

Figures.

I raise my face to the sky and close my eyes. It's a beautiful day weather-wise, and the sun caresses my face with its warmth, the air laden with the perfume of freshly mown grass. It's pleasant. But I miss the smell of petrichor and wildflowers.

I miss Rising.

I miss Ace.

I swallow the familiar lump that appears in my throat. I will have my revenge. But that's for another day. Not today.

Fin's fast asleep but wakes when I unstrap him from his car seat. Familiar blue eyes gaze up at me.

Like his daddy's.

Like his grandaddy's.

"Hey, little big guy." He's teething again, so I'm answered with a drooling smile. He then immediately starts to chatter and tell me his stories. Some of the words are recognizable now, but most are made up. He loves the sounds of his own voice.

Just like his daddy. I so wish Irish were here to meet his son.

Balancing Fin on my hip, I grab his bag, then I stand and stare at the front door of the O'Connell house.

Run. Run. Run.

But I know I can't. I know I have to do this.

For Fin. For Irish.

It was also Ace's dying wish, and I can't let my beautiful boy down.

I start to walk forward. I'm dragging my heels reluctantly. Who will open the door, I wonder? Aside from Cillian and Sarah, who will be first to set eyes on Padraig O'Connell's son?

CHAPTER SEVENTEEN

EOIN

The O'Connell Home, Darling, New York

"FERGAL, YOU'LL WEAR A HOLE IN THE CARPET IF YOU'RE NOT careful, and let me tell you, Roisin won't be best pleased if you do." Jessie tries to lighten the mood, and for once, I'm grateful. Despite her best efforts, it still doesn't have the desired effect. Da continues to pace the floor regardless.

He's agitated, and I know why.

He's had several covert conversations with Ma since Jaine dropped the Finian bombshell, and that's only the ones we're aware of.

Their content? No one knows. Not even me.

Yet.

My brothers, their wives, and our cousin Aidan are all here. Everyone is dressed casually. Today is about family, not business.

There's no Paddy or Sophia. There's no Ma or Molly either. Not that the latter is best pleased about her lack of an invitation.

We're in the family room. It's a comfy space, all neutral colors with a massive TV hanging from the wall and two large black leather sectionals to lounge on.

Today, there's no joking or bickering.

Today, the TV is off.

Today, no card games are being played.

The only sounds are the happy gurgles coming from the strawberry blonde-haired Caoimhe. The smiling eleven-month-old girl is sitting on the floor among a huge pile of toys and under the ever-watchful eyes of her proud parents, Sarah and Cillian.

We're all silent, each of us lost in our thoughts.

Waiting. Wondering.

I glance at Da. I appreciate he's had a surprise grandson sprung on him, and one he's about to meet face-to-face for the first time. I also appreciate much of his nervous energy is to do with the fact that the child's mother is currently residing in the Duster's *public enemy number one* spot. But there's clearly something else afoot. Something no one else is aware of.

Only Da and Ma.

"Tell me again, please, why Molly wasn't allowed to be here?" I disturb the silence.

I'm still not sure it's entirely appropriate that my future wife has been excluded from this extraordinary family meeting. At some point, the past will have to remain in the past. None of it can be undone. She and Jaine will have to tolerate being in the same room together. At some point, they will need to interact and be civil to one another. Fin is family. Blood. And as his mother, that makes Jaine family too now. But so is Molly.

"Molly blatantly threatened the girl, Eoin. That's likely the reason she suspects we had a hand in her husband's death. Do you really want to start World War III today when there are wee ones present?"

"I appreciate that, but having to placate an angry Molly who feels pushed to the side simply because Jaine has born a Duster heir makes my life extremely difficult. This situation won't be able to continue. Molly is the future Ma Duster. As part of this family, Jaine will have to answer to her as the head female whether she likes it or not."

Da's saved from answering by the doorbell. We all glance at each other. We know who it is. It's more in surprise than anything. It never rings. The only people who visit this house are family, and there's no need for them to ever use the bell.

Why do I get the feeling that Jaine will never see herself as family? That she will always wait to be invited in? That she will always see herself as an outsider?

That she will always *choose* to be an outsider?

I leave the room to answer the door. As I make my way through the house, I take in the interior of the property. I'm well aware Jaine will scrutinize it. I'm also aware she'll find it both ostentatious and vulgar. But there's one thing she can't accuse my parents of and that's not being family orientated. There are photos everywhere. The most recent one being the image of Fin that we all simultaneously received.

I open the door and my gaze immediately sinks into hers. I inwardly curse my traitorous eyes for being unwittingly drawn to her time and time again. I can't seem to stop them from drinking her in. She's dressed down in camo combats and a white tank top. It's the outfit she was wearing the first time I met her. Is it deliberate? A reminder of the fact that in this guise I underestimated her? I suppose the professional image doesn't work in Ma mode. Business suits and baby sick don't mix.

Maybe I'm overthinking things. Maybe it's just a coincidence.

I'm not sure how I feel seeing her standing with a small child balanced on her hip.

I scan her face. Her bruises are healing and the lump on the side of her head has reduced. Did she think wearing her hair down yesterday hid it?

It didn't.

Her hair is tied back today, and my gaze is instantly drawn to the tattoo behind her right ear. The scrolled letter I now has a small F beside it. For Irish and Finian, no doubt. I'm guessing the A behind her left ear has a small J alongside it these days.

My observation doesn't go unnoticed, but nothing is said.

My attention then switches to the little boy in her arms. A little lad with a mop of unruly black hair that looks the spit of our Paddy but in miniature form.

Guilt.

It's all I feel when I think of my brother. Our Paddy could have had it all. The wife. The child. A ready-made family.

And now he has nothing.

As soon as I make eye contact with Finian, he smiles and holds his chubby arms out, his little horseshoe birthmark on display.

Jaine chuckles as she looks at him. "He'll go to anyone he thinks will listen to him talk before you think to flatter yourself, Eoin."

I laugh out loud in response. "Charming as ever, Jaine."

"Nice to know I haven't lost my touch."

"Can I?" I motion my head toward the little one.

There's a pause. She's thinking about it. She's probably worried I'll grab him and slam the door in her face. That she'll never see him again.

Who can blame her? In her eyes, we've taken everything from her.

She gently leans him forward, and I scoop him up in my arms.

He's heavier than I thought, and he smells of baby powder. He smiles up at me, all bright blue eyes, tiny white teeth, and with saliva hanging from his bottom lip.

"He's teething." Jaine laughs as she wipes the drool away with the back of her hand before wiping it down her combats. It's nice to see her smiling so openly, but I'm not foolish enough to think it's for my benefit. It's because she loves this little lad more than life itself and doesn't want him to ever see her with any expressions aside from positive ones.

Like those of love and happiness.

"So, are you going to invite us in, or are we going to stand here all day?"

She breaks my trance. I'm conscious I've been staring at her. We both are.

"Of course." I motion my head for her to step inside. She closes the door behind her, and I watch as she takes in her surroundings.

She stares at the shrine of photos, her gaze drifting to the one of Fin that has been placed beside one of our Paddy at the same age. It could be the same child. A flicker of emotion crosses her face as she takes it in.

Regret. Hurt. Anger. Blame.

I know she blames us. Blames me. That she always will. And I accept that. Or at least the part I played.

But life moves on. It has to.

Her husband is dead. Paddy is married. I'm about to get wed. Then again, in this life, by tomorrow, everything could have changed.

She follows me into the family room. Everyone stares. Not at me. Not at Jaine.

But at Finian O'Connell.

He immediately spies the stack of toys and wriggles in my arms, wanting down. I look at Jaine and she nods. Standing him on short chubby legs, I can't help but smile as I watch him toddle across to where Caoimhe is playing.

Cousins.

I glance at my da and he's entranced. Fin grabs a unicorn plush and then lets out a noisy yell before trying to stuff the whole thing in his mouth all at once. His actions earn him a chuckle from everyone in the room, which causes him to stop what he's doing. He looks around wearing a beaming smile when he realizes he has a captive audience.

Like father, like son.

Knowing all eyes are on him, he stands back up, waddles across, and passes the now saliva-soaked toy to my da.

"Thank you, young Finian."

Tears prick his eyes that his grandson has brought him a gift, but I know it's also over the fact that Jaine, despite hating us, still saw fit to name the little boy after my own granda. I know that unselfish act meant the world to my da.

He lifts him, sits him on his lap, and immediately switches to granda mode, talking in a silly voice and making the plush dance around. Fin giggles as he tries but fails to catch the toy, Da pulling it out of his reach at the last minute every time.

It's a beautiful, childlike sound.

Innocent. Pure.

I look at Jaine, and she's smiling at the visual and at da. I look again at him and he's smiling back at her in return. He's grateful. His expression speaks volumes.

And she understands. Family is all that matters to him. And to her.

I'm well aware this lightheartedness and bonding is over Fin only. The Dusters are still her enemy right now. More so me.

"Can I hold him, partner?" Jessie interrupts the moment as is her way.

"Provided you don't drop him on his head, Jessie." Jaine laughs out loud. It's another beautiful sound.

Unfiltered. Natural.

Jaine stares at Fin with such love as Jessie lifts him from my da's reluctant arms.

I want that for me. I want to experience that unconditional love. I never realized until now how much I really want children.

With her.

More unwelcome thoughts.

Da turns his attention to Jaine, his expression now serious. "Jaine. Can I have a word with you in private, please?"

She looks at da, her expression now poker-faced. Will she or won't she leave Fin unattended?

"He'll be fine with us, Jaine. I promise." Our Dylan speaks, and she stares at him, searching his face forensically for any signs that he's lying to her. What she sees must reassure her as she nods slowly.

I have a feeling we're all about to find out what's been causing my da to wear out the carpet.

CHAPTER EIGHTEEN

JAINE

The O'Connell Home, Darling, New York

I follow Fergal through to his office. Could this be a trap? They lull me into a false sense of security then steal my son away. I wouldn't put anything past the O'Connells. Or at least not past Da Duster and his heir. The only saving grace is that Roisin's not here to add fuel to their family fire and fan their fucked-up flames. I'd never have left Fin unattended had she been around. She's still in Sicily with Irish and his new wife.

Hopefully, she'll stay there.

Fergal's office is made up of dark wood shelving in the main, with an arsenal of guns and other weapons carefully laid out across each surface. It's my guess each gun is loaded and ready to use. Just point and pull the trigger.

I look at the sniper rifle on display. It has me wondering if he knows how to use it or if it's just for show. It's not a natural talent everyone possesses.

I run my finger down the smooth cool length of the straight metal barrel, the familiar feel instantly soothing my sniper soul. It reminds me that I need to collect my own weapon from St. Patrick's. It's probably best to wait. Let all the fuss die down beforehand. As expected, the headline news is that the fatal shots were thought to have been fired by The Exterminator.

It's speculation. Nothing more. There's no proof it was the surreptitious sniper as no bullets were ever recovered.

"You like guns, Jaine?"

My wandering thoughts are interrupted.

"I do."

He's not worthy of a lengthier response. I might have to smile and play happy families in front of Fin, but I'm not interested in unnecessary small talk with him. It wasn't so long ago he was carving into my flesh with a switchblade. I'm having to wear surgical tape as a memento.

Does he think I'll forget? He's a fool if he does. I'll neither forgive nor forget.

I turn around. Fergal is now seated at his desk, which is clad in the same finish as the shelves.

"We have a shooting range on the property. Would you rather we talk there?"

"Here will do just fine."

Common sense tells me to decline in case my head becomes the unofficial target.

He watches closely as I take a seat on the matching brown tub chair that faces his.

"Next time, then."

My silence speaks volumes. It's telling him all he needs to know.

That I'm hoping there won't be a next fucking time. There's no point saying it aloud, though. We both know there will be. We're tied for life now. Only death can release us from this unwanted entrapment.

"I won't apologize for what I did."

Just like that, he's confronting the elephant in the room. Or at least one of them. I know he's talking about what happened at the wedding. At least he's honest. I've got to respect him for that if nothing else. This isn't the reason he's brought me in here, though. It's a smokescreen.

"I'm neither expecting nor asking you to." I shrug.

"If history repeated, I'd do the same thing."

"Good to know."

"I won't ask why you were there."

"Closure." I stare at him, my expression impassive.

A blunt, one-word answer. Also a blatant lie. It's not like I can tell him the truth. I immediately turn the tables.

"Did you have Ace killed?" I toss it out there like a grenade. It's fitting given there's half a dozen stacked in the corner of the room. Fuck him if he doesn't appreciate my line of questioning.

Time passes.

Tick. Fucking. Tock.

Every silent second convinces me further of their guilt.

"Direct, aren't you?" he eventually replies.

"I'm a lawyer. It's in the job description."

"And are you at work now?" He leans forward, placing his elbows on the desk. Is he trying to intimidate me? Because it won't work.

"Well, I'm certainly not playing happy families regardless of what you may think."

"But you are family."

"Fin is your family. I will never be your family. You made sure of that."

"Paddy's situation…."

"Is your fault."

"We didn't know."

I laugh dryly. "Same old bullshit."

"Mind your manners, girl," he hisses.

"Like the Dusters minded theirs when they walked into my apartment and threatened me two years ago?" I reply matter-of-factly while raising one eyebrow.

"We can't change the past."

"Nope, you're right. We can't."

"I have a question I want to put to you."

"Answer mine first. Did the Dusters have any involvement in Ace's death?"

"No."

An immediate response.

I stare at him. He stares at me. I'm not sure for how long. Until it's clear he's telling the truth. That's how long. I don't say out loud that I believe him when I finally realize that I do.

"What did you want to ask me?"

"You're a widow." He states the obvious.

"Go to the top of the goddamn class."

"Are you always this rude, girl?" he hisses again.

It's my turn to lean forward to place my elbows on the desk. "Only with *family*."

We stare at each other. More time passes.

"If I have my way, that's what you'll be. I want you to marry into the family. In fact, I must insist that you do."

"You must insist?" I raise a mocking eyebrow.

"Yes."

"You tell me to do something, and I'll do the opposite. Same as I did with Roisin." I smirk.

"Childish."

"Perhaps, but still goddamn satisfying if it fucks up your plans."

I watch as he runs his hand through his hair. Same as he did that day in the subway. It's to stop him from doing something else.

Shooting me. Throttling me. Cutting me. Probably all of the above if I don't do his bidding.

"The child is not safe out of wedlock, and you know it. As soon as news of his existence gets out, he'll become our Achilles heel. You all will. You and both your boys."

He has a valid point. I'm neither naïve nor stupid. I know the moment it's announced that Fin is an O'Connell, he'll have a target on his back, as will I and JJ.

Not to kill per se, although that can't be ruled out. It's more likely any enemy would capture to use as blackmail. And a very powerful bargaining tool that would be against the Irish mob given they're all about family and flesh and blood.

"The only O'Connell I would ever consider marrying is already married."

"For the love of God!"

It's a day for hissing it would seem.

I smile politely. "God had nothing to do with it. The Dusters made that poor decision all on their own."

There's a pause. I'm grating on his last nerve. Maybe Jessie and I have more in common than we realized.

"Even for your boys' sake, you would consider no other?" he asks.

"No."

"Then that would leave us in a difficult position."

"Don't threaten me."

"What will happen if we do?"

We stare at each other once more. His gaze is penetrating, but I've already looked into the bowels of hell and fucking survived.

I'll be permanently wearing the scar to prove it.

"You really don't want to know that answer," I tell him. "But don't underestimate who you're dealing with. Eoin's been paying the price for doing just that for the past two years."

"Then work with us. We can't leave the child exposed. You must have heard about what happened at St. Patrick's."

"The fact that The Exterminator saved the day, and several O'Connell lives in the bargain?"

"You know the sniper personally?"

I nod. "Although, apparently, Molly does too. She told me she spoke to him at length. That he was considering working exclusively for the Dusters. The sniper can't remember their little heart-to-heart. Likely because it never fucking happened."

Good luck with having a bare-faced liar in your top tier. I don't say the words aloud, but he knows that's precisely what I'm thinking.

Another pause. He's digesting what I've just said. But then he already knows what Molly is. Another Sophia. Another poor choice. Another mistake.

I almost feel sorry for him.

Almost.

"Anyway, who would you have me marry in this grand master-plan of yours, not that I'm agreeing to anything."

I already know who he's going to say. It's obviously the reason we've been recently introduced.

Aidan.

"Eoin."

I'm momentarily speechless that Fergal O'Connell is suggesting I marry his eldest son. The asshole I hate with a goddamn passion.

My nemesis and the bane of my fucking life.

"Now I know you really are certifiably insane. My answer is no. My answer will always be no."

"Then who would you consider, pray tell, girl?"

"I thought you were going to suggest Aidan."

"You would consider him?" He raises an eyebrow at me.

I snort. "I'd give consideration to digging up Lebedev and marrying his corpse before I'd ever consider Eoin."

There's another elongated silence. He's trying to read me. He never will. No one ever will. Unless I want them to, that is. He picks up his phone.

"Come through. Bring our Aidan with you."

I WATCH AS MR. GQ MODEL HIMSELF STRIDES IN LIKE HE OWNS THE place. Let's face it, one day, he will. He's dressed down today in dark blue denim jeans and a pale blue denim shirt. Even double denim suits him.

Asshole.

He's wearing stubble and his black hair is curling over the top of his shirt collar. Some might say it's too long, but he suits it. Maybe someone should tell him it adds a human element to the tin man with no heart. The man who always has to appear immaculate and pristine.

Maybe someone should also tell him that it's okay to be imperfect every once in a while. That it's okay to remove the poker from your ass every once in a while too. That life's too short to continually strive just to keep up appearances.

When, in the end, none of it fucking matters.

Eoin looks like Irish. His nose may be longer, his arrogant jaw more squared, and unlike Irish who has a full pout going on, Eoin's bottom lip is way fuller than the top. But there's no mistaking they're siblings.

It's then I realize I'm staring at the damn thing. His bottom lip.

His mouth. My focus shifts to his eyes. Aquamarine. Neither green nor blue. He must hate the fact that his sublime self dared be indecisive about something. They're laughing at me. No doubt because he interprets my staring as me blatantly admiring him.

He wishes.

Right now, I just want to kill the fucker. This situation is all his fault.

I glare at him, then switch my attention to Aidan. He's not as tall as Eoin, maybe six-three to Eoin's six-five, but he's just as lean. It's obvious he works out a lot. The white t-shirt he's wearing looks to be a size too small.

There's a reason for that.

It's so it can hug his torso like a second skin to best display his hard-earned efforts. Unlike the rest of the O'Connells, Aidan's hair is blonde, the top styled messily. That's also done deliberately. It's to make you itch to reach up and tidy it with your fingers. He wants you in his personal space. Then he can make his move by drawing you in with all the charm in the world.

Aidan's handsome. Too handsome. All the O'Connell men are. The Almighty gave these boys an unfair helping of good looks when he was serving them up.

His eyes meet mine. Green on green. He reminds me of Irish with his cocky stance and smart mouth.

A player.

"Take a seat, boys."

Fergal interrupts our silent appraisal of each other. He misses nothing. Good. Hopefully, he saw the sheer loathing in my eyes when I looked at Eoin.

They each collect a spare tub chair from the corners of the room. Aidan places his between mine and Eoin's.

"Da, what the fuck is going on?"

"Allow me." I turn to look at each of them in turn. "Fergal here wants me to marry either you." I nod my head in Aidan's direction. "Or you." I look at Eoin.

CHAPTER NINETEEN

EOIN

The O'Connell Home, Darling, New York

I FROWN AT HER, AND SHE RETURNS IT WITH A LOOK OF DISTASTE. Good. I'm pleased the suggestion of our getting wed is as unattractive to her as it is to me.

I've confronted my unwanted reality.

I want to fuck her. It's nothing more. That doesn't mean I wish to marry her.

Maybe once I would have rejoiced at the thought of us taking the vows together. But not now. Not when I'm planning on marrying Molly and have all but given her my word.

Aidan laughs heartily before leaning back and putting his hands behind his head as he did in the meeting. Jaine runs her gaze over him. Jealousy courses through my veins as it did before.

Jesus Christ, I need to rein this in.

"Well, Uncle Fergal. At thirty years of age, I'm not saying

marriage isn't on the cards for me sooner rather than later, but I was hoping my future bride would at least court me before she had me take the vows with her. What do you say, Jaine? Are you planning on wining and dining me before taking me to your bed and having your wicked way with me?"

His accent is broad Dublin, like Molly's.

Jaine smirks at him. "Have you heard yourself? Wine and dine you? You flatter yourself way too much, Aidan O'Connell, that you think yourself worthy of my precious time."

Aidan clutches his chest dramatically as though to appear mortally wounded. To me, he looks the fool, but Jaine's smirk broadens, and she rolls her eyes exaggeratedly.

She fucking likes him.

"Fair enough, sweetheart. For you, I'll make an exception. No dating required. Provided you make an honest man of me beforehand, I'm all yours. Just tell me where and when."

"Not so fast, Aidan," Da interrupts.

We all look at him. It's not like anything's been decided or agreed, but he already wants to throw a spanner in the works.

"There's one small problem." He frowns.

"Go on." I want to know what it is. Surely Jaine marrying Aidan is the answer to all our prayers.

"Finian."

"What about him?" Jaine frowns.

"Sophia can't know about him."

"Why not?" she hisses. Who can blame her? She's had to keep the boy hidden his whole short life as it is.

"Because with all that's going on with the Sicilian mafia and with Sophia and her brother earmarked for the off, we can't chance antagonizing the girl. At the moment, we have no idea what alternative organization they're setting up. How ethical or deadly it may be."

"I was pregnant with Fin before the arranged marriage was entered into. There was nothing going on between Irish and me after it was announced."

"She won't see it that way, unfortunately. All she'll see is you having a hold over our Paddy."

"Can't we just say that he's Ace's son? Jaine's been passing him off as such until now, and with his coloring, surely it's believable enough."

"The birthmark, Eoin," Da replies.

"What about it?"

"Anyone who sees it will know he's an O'Connell, including Sophia. The girl's sharp. The moment she spots it her brain will start whirring. She'll immediately suspect that Fin is Paddy's son given his age and the timings. We need to be proactive. We need to eliminate that thought process by someone else claiming parentage of the child beforehand. If we attempt to do anything reactively, she'll see it for the ruse that it is. And we need to act now. While there's every reason to believe her and Paddy will remain in Sicily long term, it can't be guaranteed."

"Are you suggesting I keep Fin a secret from Irish forever?" Jaine asks.

Da shakes his head and frowns. "No, of course not. But until we know what the Ruoccos are up to, we have no choice." He pauses. "The boy must be protected at all costs. Right now, we don't know who was behind the church attack. Or Ace's attack, for that matter. Were they related or weren't they? The Dusters have a lot of enemies. The Ruoccos even more so. Fin would be tied to both through Paddy, so until we know for sure exactly who and what we're dealing with, we need to keep his true parentage under wraps. We can't rely on The Exterminator turning up to save the day every time."

So, Da's finally managed to convince her that we had nothing to do with Ace's death. That I had nothing to do with it. Maybe now she'll drop this ridiculous personal vendetta.

"Why did he?" Aidan disturbs my thoughts.

"Why did he what?" I turn to look at him.

"Save the day. I mean, it wasn't a hit for hire. He wasn't being paid by anyone as far as we know. So he was there for one reason and one reason only. To safeguard at least one O'Connell."

I shrug. "He has a solid relationship with our Dylan. Maybe he was looking out for him."

"Jaine knows him personally," Da adds, nodding at her.

We all turn to look at her. As a lawyer, why would she need to have dealings with the sniper? Then again, she was in a relationship with Paul Delaney for four years and the marksman always operates through the Scorpions. Maybe their connection grew organically as a result.

"Have you any idea why we were targeted, Jaine?"

She shakes her head. "I don't. But what I do know is The Exterminator went in believing it to be Padraig who was at risk. It transpired to be the opposite. It was the rest of the O'Connells who were."

"So, the sniper potentially saved us all." Da looks stunned at this revelation.

Jaine shrugs. "Well, as many as the two hired marksmen could have taken down before they were dispatched."

We sit in silence digesting this, but while important, it's not a matter for discussion today. It's not the reason we've been summoned into Da's office.

"Anyway, we've digressed," I mutter.

"Yes, we have, Eoin. Sorry."

"So why not Aidan? He has the same birthmark." I frown.

"Aidan wasn't in New York two years ago."

"So he couldn't be the father," I mutter.

The realization dawns on me what I'm going to be expected to do.

"Not just that, but there's also Fin's coloring. Jaine and Aidan are both blonde, and Fin is black-haired. I'm not saying it's not possible, but it could still raise unnecessary questions over his parentage."

"I won't do it," Jaine challenges as it finally dawns on her too.

"What choice do we have, Jaine? It would be easy to pass Fin off as Eoin's son. You met him around then, did you not?"

"Irish would think I tossed him aside and then cheated on him with his brother!"

"He's married, so it's irrelevant now."

"It's relevant to me. He'll hate me," she snaps back.

"You won't know he hates you if you're dead. And imagine how he'd feel if, God forbid, something happened to little Fin as a result of us not keeping his parentage hidden."

"I won't do that to Molly." It's my turn to decline. She may not have been hand-picked by me, but I won't go back on my already given word.

"What choice do we have, Eoin? Fin is family. Blood family. He needs our protection. His needs must come first."

"What does Ma have to say on the matter."

Ma detests Jaine. I'm hoping mentioning her will make him see sense.

"I have your ma's blessing to do whatever is necessary to protect young Finian. That aside, I am head of this household, not your ma. The final decision rests with me."

He turns his attention to Jaine. She hates my guts. There's no way she'll agree to marry me regardless of my parents' wishes.

"Jaine?"

She turns to me, then smiles saccharinely sweetly. "I'll marry Eoin, but I have three conditions."

"Go on."

She turns her attention back to Da. "I decide if and when the marriage is ever consummated."

He stares at her for a time before nodding. "Agreed. And the next."

"I decide when it gets publicly announced."

He exhales in frustration, obviously not pleased with the second condition. "Agreed. And the last?"

"I can be granted an annulment to the marriage provided my request is made within the first six months of the event taking place."

Is Jaine trying to make a mockery of me or of the act itself? She's fully aware that an annulment goes against all of our beliefs. Marriage is a sacred union. It's for life in our religion, hence why it's not something that's ever entered into lightly.

We all stare at Da. He knows I'll carry out his wishes, as is my duty. Will he or won't he accept a condition that goes against his own faith? By accepting all three, he's effectively agreeing to me having a temporary, paper wife.

"Agreed." It's said with reluctance.

CHAPTER TWENTY

JAINE

Jaine's Apartment, Upper East Side, New York

"Do you know what you're doing, Jainie?"

"I have a tentative plan that I'm not going to share with anyone." I answer Duke honestly, albeit distractedly while slowly pacing the floor.

Yesterday, I agreed to marry Eoin O'Connell. Right call. Wrong call. Guess it's way too late for second thoughts.

"Not even me?" He raises an eyebrow.

"Not even you." I shoot him an apologetic look.

"You do realize you're effectively signing yourself up to becoming the next Ma Duster."

"I know what I'm doing, Duke."

"Do you? From where I'm sitting, it sure as hell seems like it was a spur-of-the-moment decision."

I frown. "It was, sort of, and then it all fell into place in my head."

I can't tell him that I've decided to do something useful with my grief. That I'm going to channel all that negative energy into something way more positive and way more satisfying.

Revenge. Delivering karma personally.

Eoin and I are on a promise, after all.

He stands up from the sofa, walks across, then pulls me against him in a vice-like hug, no doubt to put an end to my constant pacing. Closing my eyes, I press my nose to his cream cotton shirt, welcoming the familiar smell of his cologne and cigars. He's taken to not wearing a cut these days now he's living in New York.

I miss the smell of leather.

I miss Ace.

"So long as you're sure, Jainie. I'll support whatever decision you make. You know that."

He retakes his seat while letting out a small sigh. Meanwhile, I resume my pacing. He's trying his best not to show it, but he's worried about me. He likely thinks I'm making a hasty decision.

I'm not.

My reasons for doing what I'm about to are valid.

We're in my apartment. It's all still monochrome in shades of black, white, anthracite, and silver. I've purchased the one directly below, so Duke can have his own space but still be close at hand. He complains it's too big for just him, and that it's also way too expensive. I've argued that it's a good investment, which it is, even though I insisted on paying Delaney full market value. It's a small price to pay to have Duke here with me. He's Ace's dad. Aside from my boys, he's the only real family I've got. Well, aside from the faceless father I've yet to meet. And while I may be about to gain another, Duke will always be my father-in-law.

"So, when is this happy event taking place?"

"This evening," I admit.

"So soon." He frowns, his face now clearly displaying the concern he was trying his best to hide.

I shrug. "Well, there's no point in delaying the inevitable."

"Your witnesses?"

"Jessie and Dylan."

He exhales. "You spoke to Jessie about all this yet?"

He's likely hoping she'll talk some sense into me. That she'll tell me I'm rushing into things. That I'm obviously still not thinking straight.

That she'll make me change my mind.

She won't. My thoughts are crystal clear. My mind is made up.

"Nope. Eoin's going to speak to Dylan when I speak with her. He's just waiting for me to give him the nod. I wanted to discuss it with you first. Explain my reasons. I don't want you to think I'm over Ace or that I'm in any way disrespecting what we shared by marrying again so soon. I will never be over Ace, but after what happened to him and what went down at St. Patrick's, I need to do everything I can to ensure Fin and JJ are protected, and that you and Irish are too."

"Don't marry the Duster on my account, Jainie. At the end of the day, I'm an old man and you're still a young girl. You've got your whole life ahead of you."

"I would die for you, Duke. Same as I would gladly have taken Ace's place. You know that. And you're not old. You're sixty. Plus, Sasha doesn't seem to think you're old."

I smirk at him, and he shoots me a small smile. Sasha and her mom have taken Fin and JJ out for the day. I've noticed the way she is with him. I can't say it's not a little weird seeing my friend flirt with my father-in-law given he's twice her age, but who am I to judge? Age is just a number. Life's too short to get hung up over that or anything else.

"Have you thought about how Padraig will react to the news?"

"I can't let that influence my decision. He's married now, and when we crossed paths recently, he couldn't have looked more indifferent if he'd tried. He's clearly moved on with his life, just as I have to do with mine."

"Are you sure it wasn't an act?"

"He looked happy at St. Patrick's, and he didn't know I was there."

He frowns. He can't argue with that. Neither of us can.

I pause my pacing. "Listen, Duke, all I know is that I have to do everything in my power to protect his son and Ace's son. Nothing else matters. Not my feelings. Not your feelings. Not Irish's feelings. Someone is gunning for the Dusters, and as soon as it becomes common knowledge that Fin is an O'Connell, he'll immediately become their weakness. We both know how these games work."

"But marriage is a big commitment, Jainie. It's for life with the Irish. Once you're in, there's no way back out. And the rest of your life could prove to be a long time if you have to spend it with the wrong person."

"I know that." I don't mention my get out of jail free card, as he'll only ask questions as to why I need it.

"Do you love him?"

"What? No!" I sound appalled, and it causes Duke's frown to deepen further at the realization of the true extent of what I'm signing myself up for.

"So, what's in this for you?"

"That's between God and me, Duke. You'll just have to trust that I know what I'm doing. I just need your blessing before I do it."

"You have it, Jainie. You've always had it."

I know he's worried, but my reasons for going through with this arrangement stack up, and he knows it.

He doesn't need to know that there's any more to it than that.

The rest is personal.

The rest is between me and Eoin O'Connell.

St. Peter's Church, Upper East Side, New York

I park up my hog, which I've had transported to New York. I figured I'd just use Ace's whenever I'm back home in Rising. It's not like he needs it anymore, and it's not like I'll ever allow anyone else to use it. It would be a crying shame for that classic never to be ridden again.

Taking off my helmet, I shake my hair free. Then, running my hand through its mid-back blonde length, I stare at the building I imprinted to memory the last time I was here.

This is all wrong. This is his place.

Regardless of how Irish feels about me now, it still feels like I'm betraying him. Not only by marrying his eldest brother, but by doing so in a building that he holds so close to his heart.

I'm glad he didn't marry Sophia here.

Maybe one day this place could be for me and him.

I curse myself inwardly. It would seem I'm living in cloud cuckoo land with all the pipe dreams and wishful thinking that I've got going on given what I'm about to do.

It will never happen.

I stare up at the church, and a feeling of déjà vu washes over me.

Ancient grey stone walls and a spire that reaches into the night sky as though to part the very heavens themselves form the imposing building. The same bats as before flit playfully around my head as I raise my face and gaze up at a festoon of glittering stars. I inhale the same earthy smell of freshly dug soil. A smell that lets me know that the small graveyard with the uneven headstones has a few more permanent residents to help push up daisies.

The O'Connells should be grateful that, thanks to The Exterminator, it's not their names on the newly-etched grave markers.

With a shaky breath and a heavy heart, I start my journey toward my doom. Do they have cameras trained on me?

Most likely.

They'll no doubt be able to witness the dead woman walking as she drags her reluctant feet. That I'm doing this against my will, despite the speed with which I accepted.

But this isn't about me. It's about Fin. It's about JJ. Among other things. What I want counts for nothing. What I'm about to do I have no choice in.

It's all a means to a fitting end for a well-deserving individual.

I continue towards the most aged of imposing doors. They'll all already be inside, I'm sure.

Watching. Waiting. Wondering if I'll even show up.

Anger suddenly barrels through me at the unfairness of my situation. I didn't ask for any of this. To lose Irish. To lose Ace.

It quickly dissipates, calmed by the realization that my forced desperate measures at least have a silver lining.

I place my hand on the black circular metal handle before turning it and pushing the door forward. It creaks loudly in protest, its weight pressing against me as though to keep me out before finally relenting and letting me in. It's clear The Almighty doesn't want me inside the walls of his place of worship.

This time around, it's him and me both.

The bright lights inside contrast the darkness I leave behind as I once again take in the place that's been a staple to Irish throughout his life.

My chest feels hollow. Empty. Tears prick my eyes. Full. Unlike last time, I can't smell him. Unlike last time, I can't feel him here.

But then, the connection we shared has gone. Ripped apart and tossed aside by him because after two years of deceit, he then decided that he no longer needed it, whereas I need it now more than ever.

He doesn't miss me. He doesn't love me. He loves her now. Sophia.

I told him I didn't love him. That I never had. Would telling the truth back then have made any difference? The Dusters backed me into a corner until my freedom of choice was no longer my own.

History is repeating, but with one marked difference. This time around, I'll make it worth my while.

"Jaine." It isn't Sarah's voice, it's Jessie's. I'm not going to throw myself a pity party this time around. Two years on, I'm able to hide the forever pain that became my permanent bed partner the moment I lost him from my life.

Today, I shall wear my very own mask of indifference.

Pain should never be displayed in this life unless you want others to know that you're weak. I will show no weakness.

I take a second to compose myself.

Deep breaths. In for four. Out for four.

"Are you sure you're doing the right thing, partner?"

Am I sure?

Desperate measures call for extreme lengths.

Jessie is wearing her leathers like I asked her to. I'm a biker. She's a biker. I will never be a mobster's moll. Or at least not Eoin O'Connell's.

"We've been through all this, Jessie."

"But there must be another way." She frowns.

"There is no other way."

She stares into my eyes. She's searching for evidence of doubt. A sign of second thoughts. There are none.

I know what I have to do. The reasons I'm doing it. Jessie only knows the ones I've told her about. Same as Duke. She thinks I'm doing this to protect Fin and JJ.

And I am. In the main.

Jessie nods in understanding.

She knows this isn't about me. This is about doing what's necessary.

My eyes glance over the tall, vaulted ceilings, the ancient wooden pews, and the abundance of stained-glass windows that no doubt look breathtaking with the sunlight streaming through. It's a beautiful place. Serene. I feel its history wash over me a second time.

It's then I hear the footsteps. I know it's him.

My nemesis. My enemy. The antagonist in the story of my life.

"Eoin." I stare at my future husband as his name echoes around Irish's church.

Mr. Smug. Selfish. Pompous.

His face is impassive. He's got the look down to an art form.

We're both playing the game today, both of us experts at our craft.

I take in his expensive suit. It's clear he's taking this union seriously. I'm wearing my leathers. It's clear I'm not.

Maybe I should have made more of an effort. Perhaps I should feel guilty for being so blatantly dismissive of this whole sorry affair. He is Irish Catholic, after all. This is a once-in-a-lifetime event. There's no way out for him unless I grant him one. He's waited thirty-eight years for this life-altering moment to take place. A moment I know he doesn't want to share with me. A moment he wants to share with Molly McGrath.

Does he love her? I fucking hope so. Because when he's married to me, she'll be lost to him forever, and vice versa. Maybe then he'll experience what it feels like to lose someone you love. What it feels like to face the rest of your life without them in it.

He has no option but to fulfill his Duster duty whatever that may be and whatever the cost to him personally.

Just like Irish had to.

They gave me no choice. I'm giving him no choice either.

Is this payback? You bet your goddamn life that's what this is. But taking the vows with me will only see the games begin. That's where they start, not where they end.

I told the asshole two years ago I would make his life as miserable as he made mine.

That promise will be served from today onwards. I will achieve my goal.

I *will* bring Eoin O'Connell to his knees.

CHAPTER TWENTY-ONE

EOIN

St. Peter's Church, Upper East Side, New York

Opposites. That's what she and I are.

Jaine Jones holds my gaze as she stands wrapped head-to-toe in black leather, while I face her wearing a suit that cost five figures. It's not that she can't slot into my life. She'll refuse to.

She has her reasons, I'm sure.

For one, she has no need to as she has a full and very successful life of her own. Then again, even if armed with no reason, she still wouldn't simply because she hates my guts. She'd fight to the death before she'd ever submit to me.

I curse as my dick twitches at the thought of that battle. Of pinning her defiant little self down before making her beg for my cock. Because she would.

Unwanted thoughts. I push them aside.

Her, or should I say our, unfortunate reality is that she birthed an

O'Connell, and with that comes risks and enemies. A plethora of both, and we protect our family first.

Always.

She's dressed the way she is for a reason. Perhaps I should feel flattered as it's entirely for my benefit. It's to remind me that underneath it all, she's a biker. That she's never going to change. Not for anyone.

But especially not for me.

"Jaine."

She breaks eye contact and turns away. "Father O'Reilly."

She answers the short, stout man with his mop of white hair with a warm smile as he shakes her hand. A man I've known all my life.

"How are you, Jaine? Baptized and confirmed if I recall?" He returns her smile with a bright one of his own.

"I'm fine, Father, and yes. Your memory serves you well."

"It's not too late to back out, you know," Dylan whispers in my ear, interrupting my silent appraisal of my soon-to-be wife. I glance at him before turning my attention back to Jaine.

"It's not that simple, Dyl. This is a Duster mess and we've got to clean it up."

"You're about to take the vows with a woman who hates your guts."

"I'm well aware of that."

"Jesus Christ, our Paddy could have had it all. His woman. His son."

"I'm well aware of that too."

"So, what happens after today?"

I side glance at him before returning my eyes to Jaine. "I'm not sure anyone's thought that far ahead. Including Da."

"How did Molly take the news?"

"I haven't told her."

I feel his eyes boring into the side of my head. "Holy shit, Eoin. Why not?"

I shrug. "There was never any guarantee that Jaine would turn up. I didn't see the point in letting the girl down for nothing."

"Do you love her?"

"Which one?"

"Molly?"

"No. But I owe her."

"You don't owe her."

"She saved my life."

"Maybe she did. Maybe she didn't."

"What's that supposed to mean?" I turn and frown at him, but he doesn't make eye contact.

"Nothing. Ignore me. Anyway, do you still fancy yourself in love with Jaine?"

I pause before I answer as I take in the too-slim blonde who's wearing that defiant attitude of hers like a badge of fucking honor. "I thought I did. But it was more of an infatuation. A simple case of wanting something I couldn't and shouldn't have. It just made me crave it more."

"Do you think you'll grow to love her?"

"Do you think she'll grow to love me?"

I answer his question with a question. His silence speaks volumes.

He exhales slowly. "This union will break Paddy's heart."

"I'm sure he'd rather his heart broken than anything happen to his son."

"True. Anyway." He steps in front of me before giving me a hug. "For what it's worth, I wish you well, brother."

He releases me and I nod at him. He then turns and nods at Jaine. She looks between us both then nods slowly back at him in silent response. She and I are doing our duty to our respective families today. Nothing more.

Father O'Reilly motions for Jaine and me to step forward.

What happens next is as much a blur for me as it is for her, I'm sure. For thirty-eight years, I've waited to marry the right woman. Now, I'm marrying the wrong one. Still, we're in the same boat. We're both having to take the vows with someone we'd much rather not.

I'm holding Jaine's hands in mine. They're tiny. For all her big-mouthed defiance, she really is delicate and fragile. I'm sure if I called her either of those things to her face it would be met with a torrent of abuse and foul language. I have to remember that these small hands broke the neck of a man twice her size.

I watch her, and she catches me. Our gazes hold as she slips the ring on my finger.

It feels intimate somehow. In a way, it is. Regardless of the reasons, we're making a commitment to each other. From today onward, she is mine. To protect. To care for.

To love.

I'm about to place the ring on her finger when I notice she's still wearing her wedding band from Ace. Her eyes connect with mine. She looks emotional. She either thinks I'm going to ask her to remove it or that I'm going to slip it off and replace it.

She really does think me that heartless.

I would never ask her to remove it. It's a narrow barely-there band, much like the ones I've had made. I slip the new one on, so it rests just above.

She looks up at me. I see gratitude. It's fleeting, but it's there all the same. It will be short-lived, I'm sure.

"You may kiss the bride."

Neither of us will have given this part any thought. The part most couples look forward to. A kiss that holds the promise of what's to come later.

The wedding night. The consummating of the marriage.

Maybe we should have discussed and agreed on how best to approach this beforehand.

My gaze drifts over her natural beauty with her blonde hair and large green eyes before coming to rest on that pouty mouth of hers.

She steps forward, and my eyes connect with hers once more. It's clear she wants to seal this deal in the traditional way.

With a kiss. No doubt a chaste one.

She licks her lips in silent invitation and my gaze drops to her mouth.

JAINE

I feel emotional at having to repeat the vows. More so as I should only have had to say them once in my life.

This is wrong. What we're doing is wrong.

Me with him is wrong.

I want to bolt for the door. Refuse to go through with it. But I know I can't. My son is an O'Connell. For that reason, in their insane minds, it means I need to be one too. What would they have done if I'd still been married to Ace? Taken Finian away from me?

There's no point dwelling on that. I'll never know.

I'm not married to Ace. Ace is dead.

I'm remarried. But to the wrong brother.

I swallow down the guilt and the feeling of betrayal. I'm doing this for the right reasons. I just need to keep focused on the silver lining.

I know I need to go through with the next part. That I need to kiss him for my plan to work. I feel sick at the thought. Not in disgust. In I don't know what. For two years, he and I have shared whatever the toxic fuck this is.

I guess we're about to find out.

His gaze drops to my mouth.

I'm not sure who moves. Me? Him? I'm conscious he's in my space now. Or am I in his? I don't fucking know anymore.

My heart is pounding so hard it feels like it's going to explode in my chest.

Nerves. Apprehension.

Something else?

I focus on the strong column of his throat. I can see his heartbeat. It's fast. For whatever reason, its speed calms mine and slows it back down.

Mr. Impassive is actually affected.

I raise my hands to his shoulders. He feels solid beneath my fingers. Like a wall of hard steeled muscle wrapped in a ten-thousand-dollar suit.

Does he have tattoos? Scars? Beneath this professional image he portrays, is there an inked, scarred bad boy underneath?

I'm suddenly enveloped in the spicy scent of his cologne. It's overwhelming. He's overwhelming.

This whole situation is overwhelming.

He snakes one strong arm around my waist and pulls me flush against him. I lift my eyes and they're instantly captured and held captive by his. I can't look away.

Aquamarine.

Neither blue nor green. They're on a face that's totally defined and so fucking perfectly masculine.

I bite the bullet and press my lips to his.

Soft. Warm. Unmoving.

He doesn't know what to expect or how to react.

Ditto.

Push. Pull. Push. Pull.

That right there sums up the fucked-up relationship we've both rightly or wrongly gotten off on to date.

And now, he's letting me take the lead. He's waiting for me to let him know exactly what I want. The problem is, I don't know. I've never known exactly what I want from Eoin O'Connell. It's all been as confusing as fuck.

It's my guess the feeling's mutual. That he hasn't known exactly what he wants from me either.

I lick his bottom lip, then bite down until I can taste blood.

Fuck. Him.

That right there is the moment I unleash what lies behind that polished facade of his.

He growls as he fists my hair and yanks my head back. He stares down at me briefly, his nostrils flaring in annoyance as his eyes scan my face before his lips capture mine.

Hard. Demanding. Unforgiving. Ripping the air from my lungs, he sucks out my very soul.

I groan against his lips, the sound silenced by his tongue which thrusts deep into my mouth, filling it with his unique taste of arrogance and sheer male fucking dominance.

A myriad of emotions spirals through me.

Loathing. Lust. The latter the most prominent, causing me to kiss him back equally hard. Equally demanding. Equally unforgiving. My fingers tangle in the too-long hair curling at his collar before yanking on it. He growls before devouring me like a wild fucking animal.

Fight. Run. Escape. I should do all three, but I don't.

Because I want more. Because I've reached some sort of sick, fucked-up high. Because, like a junkie, I'm instantly addicted to the rush of intensity and desire unleashed in me by that punishing mouth of his.

Reluctantly, I pull my lips away.

He leans his forehead against mine and we pant against each other's mouths. I breathe him in. He breathes me in. He stares at my swollen lips. I stare at his. Blood pools on the surface of his. I want to lick it off, but I stop myself.

I raise my gaze and stare into eyes that are now burning green.

Anger. Arousal. Adrenaline.

Which is the trigger, I wonder?

It was my one concern. The only potential fly in the karma fucking ointment. That this toxic game we've been playing would turn out to be something.

It is.

And I prayed for the something to be one-sided.

It's not.

The only thing that could go wrong has. There was nothing fake about the part I played in that kiss. And doesn't this asshole just fucking know it?

I push him backward, then storm past the wide-eyed, open-mouthed stares of Dylan and Jessie on my way out of the church, cursing inwardly as I do.

I dread to think what Father O'Reilly made of that spectacle. If I wasn't already going to hell, then I sure am now.

But that's now the least of my worries.

My thoughts switch to Ace.

Gripping my hog, I gulp the frigid night air into my lungs before leaning over and heaving my guts onto the grass verge.

It's bile. Nothing else. I haven't eaten a thing today. All I did was contemplate what I was going to have to do.

Standing upright, I wipe the tears from my face as I try to swallow down the guilt.

This is all too soon, but I have zero control over the timings of all the things that continue to go wrong in my life. All I can do is roll with the punches and keep reminding myself that I'm doing this for the right reasons.

CHAPTER TWENTY-TWO

EOIN

Eoin's Apartment, Hudson Yards, New York

"Eoin, where are you?"

"I'm at home, Dylan."

Pouring myself a whiskey, I glance around my apartment with its dark brown furniture and accents contrasting against a cream backdrop. It's a warm, calming space which is exactly what I need. I seldom drink, but Jaine is going out of her way to drive me to it.

Infuriating, evil woman.

It's no wonder our Paddy is a borderline alcoholic having had to handle her for over a decade.

"So, you left the rest of us standing at the altar and just fucked off home?"

"The runaway bride had already absconded after the deed was done. I went in search of her, but she had ridden off into the night on that hog of hers."

"The deed was definitely done all right. I mean, what the hell was that all about?"

"What do you mean?" I frown as I swirl my drink around the crystal glass.

"That X-rated display you and Jaine put on. I almost felt the need to place my hands over poor old Father O'Reilly's eyes. He'll be scarred for life after witnessing that. I'm surprised he didn't start crossing himself before chucking a bucket of holy water over you to separate you both."

"I'll send him a note of apology."

"There's no need to apologize. He did tell you to kiss your bride, after all. I guess none of us expected you and Jaine to react with quite so much enthusiasm given how terse your relationship has been until now."

"Her responsiveness took me by surprise also."

I can still taste the unique addictive sweetness of her mouth as it surrendered to mine. I want more. Way more. I want fucking all of her. And I will have her.

It's only a matter of time.

"So, are you now going to hate-fuck each other?"

"That's unlikely." *But, if I have my way...*

"Why not? She obviously doesn't find you as repulsive as she's been making out. What happens now?"

I throw back the whiskey in one, welcoming the sensation as it burns and warms my throat. "I need to explain things to Molly."

"When?"

"Tonight. But only after I've spoken with my new wife."

Because, like it or not, Mrs. O'Connell, that's exactly what you are.

My wife.

I POUR MYSELF A SECOND WHISKEY AS I RESORT TO MESSAGING HER. Having tried several times, she still won't pick up.

Eoin: *Answer the phone.*
Jaine: *I have nothing to say to you.*
Eoin: *We need to discuss what just happened.*
Jaine: *We got married.*
Eoin: *Not that.*
Jaine: *Nothing else happened.*
Eoin: *We kissed.*
Jaine: *Did we? Oh yes, so we did. As kisses go, it was pretty forgettable.*

My fingers tighten around the glass as she blatantly fucking lies to me and herself.

Eoin: *Stop lying.*
Jaine: *Sorry. Am I offending that dick-shaped ego of yours? I'm not lying. You're not the first man I've ever kissed, and you won't be the last.*
Eoin: *I will be the last. I'm your husband.*
Jaine: *For now, and only on paper.*
Eoin: *So, you really want to play that game, do you, Miss Jones?*
Jaine: *I specialize in games.*
Eoin: *Have it your way.*
Jaine: *Goodbye, Eoin.*

I stare at the words on the screen, a small smile playing on my lips. She can be as blasé as she likes with her throwaway remarks, but she knows that I now know. That her pretend indifference to me is, in fact, quite the opposite.

Well, two can play your game, Mrs. O'Connell.

Permanent wife or temporary? *When you're on your knees and begging to suck my cock, it will make no difference to me.*

The Hudson Dusters' HQ, Manhattan, New York

"I had a message from Jaine this morning. She said she wasn't sure if she could make our meeting, which is perfectly understandable as she does have companies of her own to run."

Jessie is clearly getting off on the fact that she knows more than the rest of us put together when it comes to Jaine's movements.

She tosses me the smirk that's reserved solely for me, which I ignore.

She's been quieter than normal today. Something we should all be grateful for. She'll be missing her tag teammate, Sarah. She and Cillian have gone out with Caoimhe, and they've taken Finian along for the ride. Sarah says some cousin bonding time is exactly what the doctor ordered now we're all one big happy family.

Jaine's obviously not broken the news to her yet. That the happy family Sarah wants to embrace is merely temporary as far as she's concerned.

"You have to remember that she's a successful professional in her own right."

I roll my eyes inwardly as Jessie continues to place her business partner on a pedestal, despite the fact we're all already aware of her considerable successes.

As usual, it will be for Molly's benefit. She's still never forgiven her for the mattress on the back comment.

"Jaine's a temporary O'Connell. Nothing more. Her and Eoin's marriage is a sham." Molly pouts as she adds in her two cents worth.

Whether a permanent arrangement or not, I had no option but to explain to her what had taken place between Jaine and me. That with all the unrest, we had no choice but to wed to safeguard Finian, but that the marriage is on paper only.

The only truth she's not been made aware of is that Fin is Paddy's son. For now, she thinks I had a dalliance with Jaine and that he's mine.

Understandably, she's not best pleased that this means I can't marry her, but given the annulment clause Jaine slipped in, I suspect it's only going to be a temporary delay.

I never mentioned the kiss Jaine and I shared, even when Molly questioned my bruised lip. Some things are better left unsaid.

Da frowns at Molly's comment. Did he really think Jaine and I would live happily ever after?

She's manipulative. She'll never toe the Duster line. Not if she can help it.

It's clear she's only tolerating this marriage until the faceless enemy is dealt with and the immediate danger to her sons has passed. Then she'll request the annulment.

It's also clear that she's chosen to take the vows with me rather than Aidan simply because it prevents me from marrying Molly. No doubt another part of her big payback plan.

I'm impressed. She's coordinated it all perfectly. There's just one tiny little thing she didn't fully consider.

That this toxic relationship we share has an underlying mutual attraction. The fact that we're both now fully aware that my temporary wife is mine for the taking. Physically, at least.

"When does Ma return?" I pose the question. Aside from Da, no one knows her take on everything that's gone down.

"Today," Da answers distractedly.

His response is met with silence. We're all now considering the confrontation that will inevitably take place between Ma and Jaine. The woman she was dead set against joining our family to the extent she had Molly verbally warn her off. The woman who's Finian's ma. As my wife, Jaine is also set to fill her shoes as the next Ma Duster.

"So, if your marriage is fake, does that mean there's a chance for me?"

His question interrupts the silence. We all turn to look at Aidan.

He smirks. "I would be happy to take Jaine as my wife."

I clench my jaw to stop myself from saying something inappropriate. Is he deliberately trying to wind me the fuck up? Because it's working.

Then again, why should I care? Jaine's made her position quite clear, and I wanted to fuck her, not marry her. This way I can get her out of my system while we're still wed, then when she plays the annulment card, which she inevitably will, she can become Aidan's headache. At that point, I can fulfill my obligation and marry Molly.

Problem solved.

"Why would anyone want to marry that biker woman?" Molly answers, wrinkling her nose in disgust.

Aidan puts his hands behind his head in what I now know to be his signature pose.

"Let me think." His smirk widens as his mind drifts to Jaine. "She's beautiful. Intelligent. Successful. And I'll bet she looks sexy as fuck in all that leather gear."

My thoughts drift back to when I took the vows with her. He's right. She does look sexy as fuck wrapped head to toe in her biker attire.

Jessie laugh-snorts in response just as there's a knock on the door.

"Come in."

Candice enters the room. "Jaine's here." She smiles at me as she makes the unexpected announcement. I glance at Da, and he nods.

"Send her in," I reply.

All eyes are on Jaine the moment she walks through the door. She's wearing a pale grey pantsuit today, the fit displaying her slim shape so perfectly Aidan's tongue is almost hanging out of his mouth.

"It's good to see you, Jaine." Da cuts the silence with a pleasantry.

"Is it?" She smiles.

It's clear she thinks herself so clever at having manipulated this situation to her own advantage. Is this the best she could retaliate with? If it is, then I'm sorely disappointed. I expected so much more after she threw down the gauntlet so vehemently before threatening to destroy my life. I thought I'd be deserving of at least something noteworthy, not simple delaying tactics. That's all this is.

She takes the same seat as before, placing her briefcase on the table. Aidan smiles charmingly at her, and she returns it with one of her own. She then turns her attention to Molly, who's sitting in her usual place to my right. The atmosphere instantly turns frigid. It's understandable. I'm not naïve enough to think, in Jaine's case at least, that it has anything to do with any high regard for me.

Her gaze switches to my bruised lip, and my traitorous dick twitches as my own gaze drops to her lips. The things I want to do to that cussing, disobedient little fucking mouth.

She looks between Molly and me. I can tell she's not best pleased that we're acting like a couple and like nothing's changed.

I'm not sure why. Nothing has.

Maybe she thought the moment she became my paper wife that I'd behave like an obedient dog and come to heel. If she wants that sort of loyalty, then she'll have to fulfill all of her wifely duties, both in and out of the bedroom.

When Molly places her hand possessively on my thigh, I don't immediately remove it like I normally would. Everyone is well aware of its placement. Even Jaine.

Jaine looks between us both. Do I detect a hint of jealousy?

"How did the meeting with Rod go, partner?" Jessie pipes up, interrupting the prolonged silence. So, she knew exactly where she was all along.

"As planned." She opens her briefcase as she responds. "I'm between meetings. I was passing so I thought I'd drop the latest order in."

"Rod's in New York? He never mentioned anything." I raise an eyebrow at her.

She looks at me. Her gaze then flits to Molly once more before returning.

"He flew in this morning. I've already explained he asked that I personally handle all business affairs between the Dusters and La eMe moving forward. With that in mind, he perhaps thought there was no need to let you know the minute he landed in town."

She throws the paperwork on the tabletop.

"The weaponry order is twenty-five percent larger than previous. Rod asked for a reduction because of the sizeable increase. I perused the contract there and then, reviewed the figures with Jessie over the phone, then provisionally agreed to his offer on the Dusters' behalf. It made complete business sense to accept. I just need a signature on the paperwork. I can of course revert back with a counter-offer if you prefer, but I think you'll find that they've been more than fair."

"Surely, I should be the one reviewing that information. I am, after all, the Dusters' external legal representation, not you," Molly retorts.

Jaine ignores her barb. "Rod asked for a provisional yes or no during the meeting. I reviewed the detail, discussed it with Jessie, and based on our findings, I called it."

"It probably benefits La eMe." Molly snorts.

There's a pause before Jaine responds. "Are you suggesting that I would agree to a deal that would be in any way detrimental to the Dusters?" Her tone is cool.

"That's exactly what I'm suggesting," Molly tosses back.

Jaine pauses again. "Rather than make unsubstantiated accusations, why don't you take a look at the contract yourself? Then again, maybe you should source some unbiased legal representation beforehand to assist you with that given you're not qualified to do so."

Perfectly professionally delivered.

Molly ignores the dig. But Jaine does have a valid point. Now that Paddy's no longer here to oversee her, we are exposing ourselves by allowing Molly to operate quite so unrestricted. After the accountancy fiasco, lessons must be learned.

"I'm sure it will be exactly as I predicted. I mean, why would you want to help the Dusters?" Molly laughs exaggeratedly. She smiles at me before turning her attention back to Jaine.

"You say that like I've never undertaken legal work on their behalf before now."

"Only because you *owed* them."

Jaine glances at me. "That's both arguable and debatable."

"So, if you don't owe them, why help them?"

"Because my son is a Duster."

The words are spoken quietly and to remind us of that all-important fact.

She's right, he is. And for that reason, Jaine would never harm this organization or the O'Connells as we're Finian's blood family.

She looks at me once more. "As said, I was simply between meetings. Please peruse the order from La eMe and sign the contract if you're happy with the content. I can arrange to have it collected tomorrow. Rod's also asked me to mention that he's hosting a small function while in town. As business associates, the Dusters will, of course, be invited. I'll forward the details to Jessie, and she can distribute them accordingly."

She breaks eye contact with me. Then, in complete silence, she closes her briefcase, stands, and then leaves.

CHAPTER TWENTY-THREE

JAINE

Jaine's Apartment, Upper East Side, New York

I'VE JUST STEPPED INTO THE ELEVATOR TO GO FROM MY APARTMENT to the office when my phone rings in my hand. I look at the caller ID.

Jessie.

I exhale as I let it ring out. Any non-work-related conversations we've had of late have been strained as, despite what she claims, she's still reeling from the big reveal. Like Dylan, she says she fully understands the reasons I didn't tell anyone about Finian, aside from Ace and Sarah, that is, but I know she's disappointed that I didn't include her on the list of people in the know given how close we've gotten over recent months.

I get it. But I just couldn't. There was too much at stake.

I haven't verbally spoken to her since church-gate, but I can't put it off any longer. I've been deliberately avoiding the confrontation as I knew it would mean spilling even more lies.

I can't tell her what I'm planning.

I've only held that conversation with Ace. Dead people can't talk or answer back, which is maybe just as well as I'm not too sure he'd condone the completely out-of-character thing I'm doing.

In fact, I know he wouldn't.

I answer the phone second time around.

"What game are you playing, partner?"

She gets straight to the point. That's the trouble with accountants. They're as forensic as lawyers. It's not easy pulling the wool over their eyes. Unfortunately, yet again, I have no choice but to do just that.

"I'm not playing any game, Jessie."

Liar, liar pants on fire.

"No? Well, you may not like big bad Eoin all that much and you may also think he's an asshole, but you can't tell me you don't want to fuck him after that display in the church."

"I don't."

"Okay. Let me rephrase that. Your brain might not want to fuck him, but your body sure as hell does."

"Even if I was interested, it would be wrong on every goddamn level."

"Ace wouldn't want you to be on your own, Jaine."

"It's not just about Ace."

"Paddy's married."

"He's already going to think I cheated on him."

"He cheated on you."

"He was nineteen," I argue.

I shouldn't be making excuses for Irish. He was young, but he was still old enough to have known better. I guess everything happens for a reason, though. If he hadn't cheated, would we have stayed together? Would I then have missed out on these last two years with Ace?

I wouldn't trade that time with him for anything.

"He was at an age where he knew that sticking his dick in another female when he was in a committed relationship with you was the wrong thing to do. Anyway, it's not my decision to make, but as you're now married to Eoin, whether that be temporary or otherwise, you do have permission to fuck him and not be judged by me or anyone else. It's allowed between married couples. Even God himself condones it."

"Really? Well, that's good to know. Thanks so much for pointing that out."

She ignores my half-assed attempt at sarcasm.

"I also wanted to let you know that Roisin's back from Sicily." She's speaking quietly now, no doubt in an effort to break the news gently. I don't let on that Sarah's already told me in her typical *just say it how it is and fuck the consequences* way.

"That's not so good to know."

"I gave her your number."

"Did you now?"

"Well, she is your mother-in-law and the grandma of your little boy."

"Well, lucky me for hitting the family jackpot twice over."

"She's actually not that bad."

"Says you." I snort. "She didn't indirectly threaten your life. Anyway, she's Team Molly."

"She's Team Finian."

"She hasn't met him yet."

"She wants to."

"It's in hand. Sarah's picking him up in the morning, and then taking him to see her and Fergal."

"Aren't you going to insist on tagging along in case she tries to abduct him?"

"I trust Sarah, and for some reason, I trust Fergal. I don't trust Roisin, but what choice do I have?"

"Speaking of daddies. When are you going to pay mine a visit? He's been asking. I think he just wants to get everything that happened with Ace off his chest now."

Guilt sweeps through me. I've been so focused on my plan I haven't given Lucifer a single thought. The man willingly stepped in front of a bullet with Ace's name on and I still haven't thanked him.

"Next time I'm back in Rising, I'll take a trip to Nevada at the same time."

"He'll appreciate that. Thank you. Also, this shindig of Rod's."

"What about it?"

"Dyl and I have abstained, as have Cill and Sarah. Eoin is taking Molly as far as I'm aware, or that's what she says. It's all a bit…"

"That's fine with me," I interject.

"Are you taking a plus one?"

"Maybe."

"Dropping any names?"

"Nope."

"Spoilsport." She huffs.

"That's me. Now, have you finished your interrogation? Because last I heard, it's me that's the lawyer and not you."

She snickers. "There's just one final thing. Eoin has the signed paperwork for Rod with him today. He's asked if you can drop by and collect it personally."

"From HQ?"

"Nope. I have no clue where from. He's asked if he can send a driver. I'm guessing what with you currently earmarked as the next

Ma Duster that he'd like for you to be chauffeur-driven around these days. Shall I approve the car?"

I stare at my reflection in the elevator mirror. To the naked eye, I look quite the business professional. Like a mobster's moll rather than a biker's old lady.

"Yes."

I press the button for the ground floor. Did he think I'd turn him down?

The Docks, Hudson Yards

"What's your name?"

"Liam."

"Thank you for picking me up, Liam."

I make eye contact with the bald driver in the rear-view mirror of the now stationary black SUV. The Dusters probably have a fleet of identical vehicles. With the blacked-out windows, no one can tell who the passenger is or indeed if there are any.

It's my thinking Liam has worked for the Dusters for a long time. He spoke only once, and that was in acknowledgment of who I am. He also kept his eyes trained on me the entire journey.

Well, as much as it was safe for him to do so.

The only words that left his mouth were 'Mrs. O'Connell'.

I didn't correct him, but I won't be changing my name.

I wasn't a Steele. I won't be an O'Connell either.

I will always be Jaine Jones.

His two spoken words were accompanied by a single head nod. Since news of Eoin and my nuptials has yet to be publicly announced and Liam's been furnished with that currently classified piece of intel, I reckon he's a toy soldier of the highest-ranking variety. With his advanced years it's also my guess he reports directly to either Fergal or Roisin.

He waits for the plethora of locks to unravel before alighting the vehicle. Maybe I should be more concerned given that we've pulled up at the docks. That perhaps there's a custom-made pair of concrete shoes with my name on waiting for me to slip my feet into.

There's no point in trying to second guess. The way I see it, if the O'Connells want me dead, then there's not much I can do about that.

He opens the car door for me, and I step out.

There's a chill in the air, and it's depressingly overcast. There's no real view from where we've parked. We're hidden behind sky-high walls of stacked containers. Some old. Some new. Many with their paint or advertisements peeling off thanks to the saltwater content in the brackish water of the Hudson River.

There's a reason we're hidden. Why anyone who pulls up here is kept out of sight. They're either a Duster, one of their high-rankers, or an unfortunate individual who's destined never to leave.

High ranker. Checkmark.

I guess I'm just about to meet the other two.

"This way, please, Mrs. O'Connell."

I nod at Liam, then follow his tall, lean frame through a maze of containers until we reach our final destination.

Hopefully not mine.

The rusty door's already ajar. It's almost welcoming.

Almost.

Liam motions his head for me to follow him inside. When I do, my eyes are instantly drawn to the man bound to the canteen-style chair that's been placed in the center of the old container. A chair that's been set in a slab of concrete so it can't topple over. It's my guess the slab, the chair, and the unlucky person currently residing on it will be tossed in the Hudson when what's done is done here today.

Unfortunate individual. Checkmark.

The balding, rotund man looks to be mid-forties. He's wearing pants and nothing else aside from a thin layer of what I take to be his own lifeblood.

His eyes are currently bulging on his face as though trying to silently communicate with me.

To plead. To beg. To lie. He needn't waste his time. I've heard every excuse before.

He's barefoot, so I'm guessing it's his socks that are filling his mouth and being used as the makeshift gag to prevent him from talking. His chest is heaving. Either he can't breathe or it's in fear. I think it's the latter considering the other person with us in this freezer-like metal box.

"Leave us." The other person finally speaks, addressing Liam.

Duster. Checkmark.

My eyes shift from the soon-to-be-deceased to Eoin O'Connell.

He's dressed professionally like me, but he's removed his tie, his suit jacket, and rolled up his sleeves.

Like father, like son.

I guess it's a sign that they mean business. Something to bear in mind for the future, perhaps.

He needn't have bothered with the sleeves. His shirt is already drenched in Mr. Unfortunate's blood.

My gaze connects with his. Green on green.

Anger. Arousal. Adrenaline.

Which one this time, I wonder?

I wait for Liam to leave before I speak.

"What's he done?" I motion my head toward the man strapped to the chair. The instant I show Mr. Unfortunate some attention, he tries to plead his case past his gagged mouth. Maybe he thinks that as a woman I'll find the art of cold-blooded murder offensive. As a woman, perhaps I should. As a biker and a serial killer, I don't.

What Mr. Unfortunate here doesn't realize is that depending on what he's guilty of, I'd gladly do the honors myself.

"He's part of the male choir at St. Peter's. Has been for years. We found out today he's been grooming a young Irish boy. That he's been fucking him for months. His parents only discovered the atrocity when the ten-year-old lad tried to hang himself before finally confessing everything."

I clench my jaw in disgust. With two little boys of my own, I know this is every parent's worst nightmare. The dirty pedo fucker deserves everything that's coming to him.

"What are you going to do to him?"

I know he's not expecting me to take part. That the future Da Duster wants to command the stage and have me his captive audience so I can witness all three hundred and sixty degrees of his fucked-up darkness.

Maybe all the wives have to go through this initiation ceremony as a welcome to the O'Connell family.

Or perhaps not.

Sarah's never mentioned it. Neither has Jessie.

Maybe I'm receiving this preferential treatment as, having already birthed a Duster heir, I'm as good as blood in their eyes. That it doesn't matter what I witness as I'm guaranteed to forever keep quiet.

He walks towards me until we're inches apart, and my eyes scan his face. He's obviously run his hands through his hair several times as it's streaked with blood, and he's also wearing flecks of it on his skin.

My eyes drop to his full bottom lip, and he licks it in silent response. Arousal flows through me. I want that mouth on me, and he knows it.

I lift my eyes and our gazes connect. Lust is blazing in his green depths, and it's no doubt reflected in my own. He wants me. The feeling's mutual, no matter how much we try to deny it.

I curse my body's betrayal as much as I curse him.

"You tell me, Jaine." It's whisper-like. His gaze never leaves mine.

Today's a Ma Duster test. I realize that now. Have I got what it takes? How will I react? What sentence will I hand out? Will it fit the crime in his eyes?

The latter is what's most important.

The Dusters run a tight ship, but at the heart of their organization beats a strong sense of kinship from the top tier all the way down. Same as bikers.

Mr. Unfortunate hasn't stolen or killed. He's done something far, far worse. He's hurt their family.

"I want you to rip out his heart and make him eat the fucking thing." I announce the pedo's death sentence loud and clear.

His nostrils flare then he nods slowly.

"As you wish... wife."

A reminder of exactly what I am.

For now.

He's staring at me with his head cocked, making him look slightly deranged. He's trying to gauge my reaction to his use of that one single word.

My reaction? Wet. Because right now, he looks hot, dark, and dangerous.

A heady combination. And my favorite.

I swallow thickly, which I'm sure won't go unnoticed by him. I'm playing a dangerous game. I may have bitten off way more than I can chew, but there's no turning back now.

He finally breaks eye contact before walking toward the only other piece of furniture in this frigid space. A wheeled trolley filled with various surgical instruments and torture devices similar to the one in the dripping concrete tomb under Play.

I watch as he picks up a scalpel before holding it up to inspect its gleaming surface.

"At my wife's request, your last supper will now be served, you filthy piece of scum."

For whatever reason, his voice sounds more Irish when he's in killer mode. It's then I realize that he's not so dissimilar from Delaney. That there are two sides to this Irishman. Unlike Delaney, Eoin is in complete control of his inner demon, just like he is with everything else in his life.

I watch as the scalpel cuts deep into the pedo's torso, blood pushing past the splitting flesh to spill and pool on the floor. The smell of shit fills the air, and the puddle is instantly made bigger by the added contents of his bladder.

He can't scream, but he makes harrowing sounds as Eoin uses his bare hands to rip apart his flesh to expose his ribs. He then uses surgical shears to hack open his rib cage.

I taste vomit.

Mr. Unfortunate passes out. Eoin throws water over him. He wants him fully conscious for the grand finale. The piece de resistance. He wakes with a start. He's struggling to breathe, likely due to blood loss.

Eyes bulge. Tears stain. Snot streams. All topped off by a river of bright red blood.

He's no longer trying to speak. If he could, he'd beg for a quick demise and for this dance with the devil to be over.

But he knows what's coming next. He'll be dished up what I ordered from the menu on his behalf.

I watch as Eoin uses both hands to prize out Mr. Unfortunate's still-beating organ. I want to put my hands over my ears at the inhuman sounds he makes, but I don't. Instead, I watch his eyes widen in pain and shock as Eoin shows him the last thing he will ever see before shoving the thing in his mouth.

His own heart.

I'm sure I can feel the texture against my own tongue. That I can taste the copper tang of his blood mixing with the taste of my vomit.

It's over.

Or is it?

Because I will never forget what I witnessed here today. Eoin O'Connell has made sure of that.

The sounds. The sights. The smells. The tastes. They're all now branded to memory. And for the first time in my life, I felt it. Only fleetingly. But I did all the same.

Good old-fashioned fear.

I'm also sure I felt the ice-cold fingers of death himself as they whispered across my skin, causing it to prickle in awareness.

I always insisted that Eoin O'Connell had The Almighty stuffed in his back pocket. It's quite the opposite. He has Satan.

And I take back what I said. He's nothing like Delaney. Delaney might be an insane killer. But Eoin O'Connell?

He's a monster, but given I chose the sentence and he merely delivered it, what does that make me?

Today, the future Irish king extended me an invitation to witness him in all his mobster glory.

He offered. I accepted.

Contract in place, he then allowed his dark soul to wrap itself seductively around mine in some sort of fucked-up invisible claiming.

I think in his twisted mind that now makes me his.

CHAPTER TWENTY-FOUR

JAINE

The Meeting Rooms, New York

It's been over two years since Sarah and I were abducted from this place. So much has happened since.

Finian born. Jason Junior born. Irish married.

Ace gone.

While the tears have subsided, the relentless sadness still holds me in its unforgiving grip.

What if. What if. What if.

It's how I start each day and how I end it.

The waves of grief still feel tidal wave-sized most days, and the frequency with which they crash against me is relentless. All I can do is fight to hold my head above water and breathe. What other choice do I have?

This isn't about me. It never has been.

And life has to go on for everyone else, even if not for my beautiful Ace.

I look around. All that's changed in the time I've been away is that more bling has been added.

More crystal. More gilded gold. More over-the-top furnishings and accents. More identical waiting staff dressed like little penguins, strutting around in their matching black and white uniforms while expertly balancing flutes of the finest champagne on silver serving trays. More vulgar. More ostentatious.

And it's filled with everything fake.

Fake smiles.

Fake laughter.

Fake kisses.

Fake people.

Fake relationships.

To most present here tonight, all that matters is business cards. Events like this are ticket-holder only, and to even be invited you need to be of suitable high ranking. It's the way it is in any business world, not just ours.

"Thanks for agreeing to come with me." I smile at him. He looks good in his tuxedo. His blonde hair is still messy, but I think Aidan O'Connell is perfectly happy being imperfect and unique. He doesn't want to blend in. I'm not sure he could even if he tried.

"Well, I couldn't see you being without a date, Jaine."

"Is that what this is? A date." I chuckle as I roll my eyes at him.

"It's whatever you want it to be." He grins cheekily.

I'm waiting for him to add the word 'darlin' at the end. He doesn't, thankfully. And I'm so glad. He reminds me way too much of Irish as it is.

I push thoughts of Padraig aside. I can't go there. If I do, my plan will never work.

"Being my plus one was only one of the reasons I invited you along, Aidan. Given this is a business affair, I thought it might be beneficial for the Dusters for me to introduce you to Rod. I do believe you and he speak the same language, so I'm hoping you may be able to mend some much-needed bridges."

And save me from having to be the go-between forevermore.

It's then I notice him out of the corner of my eye. Eoin.

I watched him murder Mr. Unfortunate in cold blood. I left immediately thereafter with the taste of vomit still lingering in my mouth. I haven't had any contact with him since, and that was over a week ago. He's tried to call, and he's messaged several times, but I've blown him off completely.

I think I'm about to pay for giving him the brush-off.

He's mid-conversation when his eyes connect with mine, and there's no sign of Molly, more's the goddamn pity. Now's neither the time nor the place for a confrontation with him.

I try to pull my eyes away, but I can't. There are a lot of powerful men here tonight, but none can match his dark presence. It's hypnotic almost. We stare at each other across the room.

"Jaine."

"Rod."

Our silent scrutiny is interrupted. I turn to grin warmly at the newly announced silent leader of La eMe. It's a genuine smile for my old school friend.

At an event where outward appearances are almost as important as net worth, he's also dressed elegantly in a tuxedo. Unlike most of the businessmen here this evening, however, Rod doesn't have a fawning female gushing over him.

Rumor has it he's under pressure to find himself a suitable wife. The Mexicans like to promote a family image among their own. Family is important to their organization and comes before everything else. It won't sit well with the other La eMe high rankers that Rod is still single and unwed.

"Rod. It's good to see you again."

We hug each other in a tactile embrace, our relationship perhaps one of the only non-fake ones in the room.

"You too, Jaine."

"Rod, this is who I was talking to you about. Aidan O'Connell. Aidan has just come over from Dublin and he's something of a weaponry expert. I know you were looking to mix up your order and try out some new firearms. I do think it would be beneficial for you to have a discussion with him."

Aidan smiles widely at the Mexican as he shakes his hand. "Jaine perhaps sings my praises a little too highly, but I'm more than happy to assist in any way I can."

I leave them to it before doing the rounds. Most of the other people present are already clients of JAL. Our kind like to deal with their own, after all, so it's more a case of smiling politely and touching base.

Eventually, I make my way into the restroom. The door opens and closes moments later. I already know who it is.

My skin prickles.

Fear. Anticipation. Arousal.

A combination of all three.

"What do you want, Eoin?" I stare at him in the over-sink mirror and watch as he moves to stand behind me, looking tall, dark, and devilishly handsome dressed head to toe in black.

I inhale the scent of his spicy cologne. He's so near I'm sure I can feel the heat radiate from his body as his dark soul wraps itself seductively around mine once more.

"Are you fucking my cousin?"

I stare at his reflection, searching for signs that this is a joke. But it's no joke. He's being serious. He actually thinks something is going on between me and Aidan. He's as insane as that old man of his.

"I'm not sure that's any of your business."

He grabs my arm with a firmness that will bruise before spinning me around to face him. I'm conscious my heart rate is now rocketing.

He's so close. Too close. Dangerously close.

"You've been avoiding me, Jaine. You won't take my calls. You won't answer my messages." His voice is soothing. Like his da's was when he tried to lull me into a false sense of security before cutting me with a fucking blade.

It's all smoke and mirrors. They're peas in a pod.

"I had nothing to say to you. I still don't," I toss back flimsily.

Wrong answer. I watch as he switches from the cool professional I normally deal with into the monster I witnessed at the docks.

"I asked you a question. Are. You. Fucking. Him!" He steps back, then proceeds to pace the floor while running his hand repeatedly through his hair.

"No. And even if I were, I'm not sure what it's got to do with you."

He stops pacing and glares at me. "You're my wife!"

"On paper. We both know the marriage was entered into for the protection of Finian only. Nothing else. I bet you're still fucking Molly. Am I right, *husband*?"

His silence speaks volumes. I'm not sure how I feel about that admission.

He walks towards me until we're so close our bodies are touching. His eyes burn into my flesh as they track the movement of his finger, which he's slowly trailing up the outside of my arm.

"What are you doing, Eoin?" I roll my eyes exaggeratedly in an attempt to appear immune, but it's betrayed by my shaky whisper of a voice. I curse myself inwardly for letting him know how much he's affecting me.

His lips curve upwards. He's pleased with himself. Pleased with this reaction.

His fingers drift from my arm to my shoulder, unexpectedly hard and calloused. His hand then lingers against my throat before wrapping around it.

Perfect fit.

His fingers feel like they belong there, holding me in place, acting like some sort of possessive collar. He uses his thumb to tilt my chin up, so I have no option but to look at him.

Green on green.

I don't want to know what the trigger is this time. Hopefully not anger. Given his hand placement and after what I witnessed at the docks, I'm fully aware one squeeze could end my life. That if he had reason to, he wouldn't hesitate, wife or not.

"Why did you kiss me, Jaine?" His eyes search mine.

Watching. Waiting. Expecting.

Demanding.

"Father O'Reilly asked us to." It's partially true, but I'm still aware my answer lacks any real conviction, leaving it sounding pathetic and weak.

His eyes drop to my mouth. "Don't. Lie. To. Me."

I swallow thickly. His hand will be able to feel it. It will also be able to tell just how fast my heart's fucking beating.

"Because I wanted to know." I change my response to the truth.

"Know what?"

"If it was something or nothing."

"And which was it? Remember. Don't lie."

"Something." It's barely a whisper.

There's no point in denying it. We both felt it at the church. Then again at the docks.

I should grab his hand. Pull it off. Push him away. Run for my life, but I don't.

Because he knows exactly what I want. He knows exactly why I'm not running. He knows I want more.

Way more.

I lied to Jessie. My brain isn't in control. My body is.

And I hate it.

"Do you want me to kiss you again, Jaine?"

"No," I answer quickly. Too quickly. He growls in frustration; he knows I'm lying. The low, animalistic sound is like a fucking aphrodisiac. Maybe I need to lie some more because it's making me wet. Weak. Wanting.

His fingers tighten around my throat. I'm testing his patience.

I close my eyes and swallow thickly once more.

"Yes." I keep my eyes closed. I can't look at him. I don't want to see his smug expression or what's lurking in the dangerous depths of those green eyes of his.

He walks me backward until my ass is pressed against the edge of the basin so there's no escape. My hands clutch the edge of its surface so hard my knuckles must be white.

When his breath mingles with mine, I let out an audible sigh.

Lust. Desire.

A deep-rooted hunger that's been present for I don't know how long.

I feel light-headed with anticipation. Is he going to kiss me or isn't he? He runs his tongue across my bottom lip before sucking it into his mouth. I know he wants to bite down. He wants payback.

He wants to make me fucking bleed.

But he can't. Not here. Not with all these people present.

He bites down hard enough for it to hurt, and I groan in response.

"You like pain mixed with your pleasure, don't you, Jaine?"

Right now, I don't know what I like. I can't even think straight.

My brain is betraying me too.

"Don't you?" He bites down harder before letting go completely.

I groan louder. I want him to bite me some more.

He's asking a question he already knows the answer to. He just wants to feed that massive ego of his. Asshole.

"Say. It."

"Yes," I hiss.

"And are you wet, Jaine? If I lift this exquisite sequin dress, will I find that sweet little pussy of yours drenched with desire for me?"

The voice he uses as part of his art of seduction is like melted fucking chocolate. I press my thighs together. The thought of him touching me there is too much.

This wasn't meant to happen. My plan was meant to be straightforward.

This *something* was meant to be nothing.

He was meant to be a bland, self-absorbed asshole.

I've misjudged him. I've underestimated him. Same as he did with me. And he's let me. All this time, he's encouraged it.

Mr. Smug. Selfish. Pompous.

It was all a front.

Mr. Dominating. Dangerous. Deadly.

That's who I'm married to. That's my harsh reality.

Eoin O'Connell was never meant to have so many complex, addictive layers. Layers that he deliberately kept hidden behind that narcissistic façade of his.

He must notice my subtle leg movement because he snickers softly.

"Admit it."

I don't confirm. I don't deny it either. He's right. I am wet.

He raises an eyebrow. In response, I simply nod while licking my lips. His breath mingles with mine once more.

Is he going to fucking kiss me or isn't he?

I'm conscious there's a phone ringing. Is it mine or his?

He steps away.

"FUCK!" He runs his hand through his hair once more as he looks at the caller ID. Then he answers.

"Molly."

While he's on the phone, I use the opportunity to escape, even though I know it's only temporary.

This is unfinished business. He has me in his sights now.

Push him away. Wait. Push him away. Wait.

Then when the time is right, reel him in.

It was always the method I was going to adopt because Eoin O'Connell doesn't like being denied. The word *no* doesn't exist in his vocabulary. Not for the man surrounded by yes-people.

Everything is going according to plan. Which is just as well, as I'm not sure there's anywhere I could run where he wouldn't find me now.

I need to get out of here. I need to regroup. I silently curse the unwelcome situation I find myself in.

This was never meant to be a two-way street. It was meant to be a one-way ticket for him straight to karma-ville.

I just pray to God that my plan doesn't backfire leaving me the one burned.

CHAPTER TWENTY-FIVE

EOIN

Eoin's Apartment, Hudson Yards, New York

"YOU LEFT THE FUNCTION BEFORE IT HAD BARELY BEGUN. WHY IS that?"

I pose the question the moment she answers her phone, which she did after one ring, I suspect because she now realizes the inevitability of our situation.

That I always get what I want in the end.

It's exactly the same as what she wants, so I'm not sure what her problem is. Not that she'll ever admit to it.

"You obviously did the same if you're no longer there. Why don't you ask yourself that very same question."

"I didn't ask for a smart-mouthed reply. I asked why you left."

I pour myself a whiskey and throw it back in one. I'm still cursing Molly for calling when she did. Her timing was fucking impeccable as always. My wife's pouty little mouth was mine for the claiming, along with anything else I wanted.

She was putty in my hands.

"I achieved what I needed to. I introduced Aidan to Rod. They hit it off, which is what I hoped would happen. Maybe now Rod will deal with the Dusters direct, and I won't have to play piggy in the middle. Molly can then stop insinuating that I'm entering you into shitty contracts."

I ignore her as she blatantly tries to change the subject. I have no interest in Molly, Rod, or La eMe right now. My only interest is in her.

"Why. Did. You. Leave?"

"I had a headache."

The glass I was holding shatters against the opposite wall on impact. She's lying to me. And to herself. Again. I don't want her fucking lies.

"I want your truths."

"You want my truths? Okay. Here's the truth. An insane Irishman followed me into the restroom and manhandled me, so I left."

"You haven't seen anything if you think that manhandling, Mrs. O'Connell" I smile to myself.

"I've seen more than enough, thank you."

"Stop lying."

"I'm not lying."

I laugh dryly. "Really? You and I both know if I'd wanted to fuck you in that restroom, you'd have let me."

"Narcissus is on the other line. He's asking for his arrogance back."

Yet another smart-mouth reply, which I ignore. "You and I both know it's true, Jaine."

"Speculation. We'll never know for sure."

"And why is that?"

"Because from now on, I'll make sure I'm never alone with you."

"Really? Well, you'll be alone with me imminently as I'm on my way to your apartment."

"Don't you fucking dare, Eoin. I won't let you in," she hisses.

"Then I'll just break the door down."

She disconnects the call and I smile at the phone. If she thinks a door will stop me from getting to her then she's even more insane than I am.

Jaine's Apartment, Upper East Side, New York

"Open the door, Jaine. I meant what I said. I'll break it down."

It swings open almost immediately. The glamorous dress has gone. Once more, she's attempting to hide behind her uniform tank top and combats.

I drag my gaze slowly up her body. By the time I reach her nipples, they're already crying out for my attention, and when I reach her face, I find flushed pink cheeks as a result.

Her body's betraying her. She wants me. She can't fucking deny it anymore. That body of hers is screaming out to be possessed by mine.

And it will be.

Imminently.

"You have five minutes." She stands back and motions for me to step inside. I lean against the door frame.

"You do me an injustice, Mrs. O'Connell, if you think all I can last is five minutes." I smirk as I make my way past.

I glance around. It's all unchanged since I was here last, but then she has been living in California for the best part of two years.

"That's not what I meant, and you know it. And my name's Jones. Jaine Jones."

She sounds flustered. I'm making her nervous and it's because she doesn't trust herself around me.

"You're married to me. That makes you an O'Connell," I answer while continuing to look around.

Whether permanent or temporary, for as long as she's my wife, she will carry the family name. Anything else is simply unacceptable.

Uninvited, I sit on the sofa, stretching my arms across the back. I've changed into a fitted white t-shirt and a pair of dark blue jeans. From the way Jaine's staring, she's highly appreciative of the t-shirt's snug fit. I stretch out my legs in front of me and her eyes drop to my crotch. She stares longer than could ever be considered polite before she realizes and quickly raises her gaze to meet mine.

"Enjoying the view?"

She ignores my question. We both already know the answer.

"What do you want, Eoin?"

"Do you want me to start reciting things off in explicit detail, Jaine?" I half-smile as I raise an eyebrow at her.

She doesn't want to know what I want from her right now because most of it is downright degrading and involves her being on her knees. My dick's already twitching at the thought.

She doesn't reply.

"Aren't you at least going to offer me a drink?"

"If I must."

My eyes drift over her slim shape as she proceeds to open the drinks cabinet in the far corner of the room. She doesn't ask me what I want. She already knows.

She passes me the glass. I deliberately let our fingers touch, and she jerks her hand away.

I'm clearly affecting her. And badly.

"Did you put anything in it?"

"A little water. Trust me, if I wanted you dead, I'd put a bullet in your head."

I laugh. "So, you think yourself quite the marksman."

"I don't think. I know."

"Not joining me?" I hold up the glass then toss the amber liquid back in one.

"I prefer to keep my wits about me."

"Around me?"

Again, she doesn't reply.

"Do you think me a wolf in sheep's clothing, Jaine?"

She laughs. "No. You don't even bother trying to hide what you are anymore."

"And what is that exactly?"

"A monster."

"Is that because you've seen the other side of me now?"

Once more, she doesn't reply.

"Come now, Jaine. I'm the future Da Duster. I have a dark side with an unquenchable thirst for violence. Surely that's to be expected given what I do for a living. But that can't be intimidating to someone like you. You were in a relationship with Razr for four years. You also went toe to toe with my da."

"It was different."

"Why was it?"

"It just was. Look, just cut to the chase, Eoin. What is it that you want?"

I place the empty glass on the floor, then stand and walk slowly toward her. Her heart is pounding. I can see its forceful beat in her throat.

"What do I want? Well, you may think me deserving of nothing from you, Mrs. O'Connell, but as your husband, I demand everything."

CHAPTER TWENTY-SIX

JAINE

Jaine's Apartment, Upper East Side, New York

"WHAT IF I DON'T WANT TO GIVE YOU EVERYTHING?" I WALK backward until I connect with the wall.

"We both know you'll give it to me willingly."

"I was to decide if and when the marriage was ever to be consummated. Not you." My argument is weak.

He smirks. "Then tell me to stop, wife… if you can."

He crosses the room like a panther readying to pounce on its prey, his eyes darkening as they drop to my already pebbled nipples. He's deliberately showed up wearing clothes designed to best display a mouth-watering physique that he clearly works very hard on.

He wants me to admire him.

And I can't seem to stop myself from doing just that.

And he's right. He and I both know that with minimal effort, he'll have me begging him to take everything and anything he wants.

Smug asshole.

I take in that full bottom lip of his on that model-like face. It's no longer bruised. No longer marked. I want to bite it. Claim it all over again. I want to cause him pain.

I want to make him fucking bleed.

Then I want his bloody lips on my skin. Marking it. Staining it. Along with his teeth and tongue.

I hate that I want him.

My eyes rise to meet his as the room becomes suffocating.

He's staring down at me like he wants to eat me alive.

I hate that I like him looking at me like that.

His lips hover over mine, and his breath feels like it's sucking the life out of me. I stare at his mouth, then drown in his gaze. Over and over, my eyes flick from one to the other.

I lick my lips, and his eyes drop.

"If we're doing this, then you're finishing things with Molly. You're not fucking me while you're fucking her."

He stares down at me, his eyes narrowing. "You're in no position to negotiate, Mrs. O'Connell. I think we both know you won't be able to deny me."

"My pussy. My rules. You end things with her or this doesn't happen. Not ever. Do we have a deal or don't we?"

"It's not that simple." He exhales.

"It is that simple. Let me make one thing clear. I play second fiddle to no one. Do. We. Have. A. Deal?"

There's a pause. Is he going to decline? He's already made Molly a verbal promise since she supposedly saved his life.

"Demanding, evil woman," he whispers as his thumb drags roughly across my bottom lip.

I push his hand away. "Is that a yes?"

Have I done enough? If he says no, I'm fucked because he's right. My betraying body won't deny him and it will then all have been for nothing.

There's a lengthy pause. Is my plan about to blow up in my face? I can almost hear the non-existent ticking of a goddamn bomb.

"Yes."

"Your word. Give me your word."

"I give you my word."

Silence.

Offer and acceptance. Contract in place. We both know I've now given him the green light to take anything he wants. To do anything he wants.

And doesn't he just fucking know it? He grips my hip with one hand, deliberately digging his fingers in to bruise my flesh, no doubt in punishment at my having backed him into a corner. From stopping him having his cake and eating it too.

Two words.

Tough. Shit.

His other hand wraps around my throat, gripping it tightly. My breath hitches at the connection, welcoming the feel of this human collar once more.

His thumb tilts my chin up, and he stares down at me, drinking me in as his eyes flit from aquamarine to green. With a growl, his lips capture mine, his tongue immediately taking ownership by thrusting deep into my mouth.

Searching. Tasting. Remembering.

Arrogance has an addictive flavor. I know because I'm tasting it right now. It tastes like Eoin fucking O'Connell.

And then it's payback. He bites down hard.

I taste blood.

He sucks on my bleeding lip before he devours me once more, sharing the metallic taste as his tongue fills my mouth possessively.

I yank his top free from his jeans, and he pulls it over his head to give me the access I crave to his hot, sculpted flesh all covered in scars and black ink. Underneath his clean, shiny surface, Mr. Impeccable really is a very dirty boy.

So perfectly imperfect. So tall, lean, and totally defined. The man is the carnal sin of lust itself disguised as a hot as fuck mobster.

I drag my nails down his chiseled torso, my fingers dipping inside the front of his jeans until I can feel the heat emanating from his hard dick. He growls his annoyance when I move them away.

In retaliation, he releases my throat, knowing I'll immediately miss its possessive hold. He's letting me know who's in charge. I hiss in complaint, which he ignores as he pulls my top over my head.

"You're mine." His breath is hot against my lips. "Say it."

"No."

"Say. It."

"I fucking hate you."

"Such a perfect cussing little mouth that I'm sure I'll find plenty of uses for later. Hate me all you want, Mrs. O'Connell, but admit that you now belong to me."

"You're an asshole."

"Say. The. Words."

"I belong to you."

"Good girl."

"I'm not a good girl. I will never be a good fucking girl. I'm a bad girl. And I lied. I will never belong to you," I hiss.

"I admire your determination, but we both know that you already do."

Conceited fucker.

"No more talking." Pushing my tongue into his mouth, I silence him as I unbutton my pants and let them fall to the floor. My naked flesh shivers. It has nothing to do with temperature.

Anticipation. For something that's been building between us for years.

His mouth drops to feast on my nipples. Sucking them in turn. Biting them. Punishing them with his teeth and mouth. I arch my back as I groan my approval, my hands fisting his hair. I want more. Way more of this pleasure. Pain. Perfection.

He bites and sucks on my flesh as his hand drops to my swollen folds. I'm drenched. No foreplay necessary.

"It's clear this little pussy of yours already knows that it's mine."

He growls his appreciation as he uses my slickness to lubricate his fingers before thrusting them deep inside. He's not gentle. Not that I expected him to be. I whine as he scissors them, stretching me and getting me prepared for his undoubtedly massive dick.

Because let's face it, The Almighty wouldn't dare bequeath Eoin O'Connell with anything less than a cock that's truly fucking magnificent.

I don't hear the sound of him losing the rest of his clothes. I don't hear anything as he finger-fucks me.

Hard. Fast. Wet.

The sound of how aroused I am fills the silence along with my appreciative groans of pleasure as his fingers perfectly destroy me. Just as I'm about to reach the pinnacle, they're gone. Before I can complain, he lifts me so I can anchor my legs around his hips.

His breath is hot against my mouth as he rests his forehead against mine. His green eyes bore into my soul.

"Now watch as I claim what's fucking mine."

We both watch as he drives his dick inside me with one punishing thrust.

"Fuck." I hiss at the intrusion.

"Did it hurt, wife?" His breath is hot against my ear.

"Yes."

He's big. Too big.

"Good. Feel the burn and remember the pain. We made a deal, Jaine. A deal that means from here on in, this is the only cock your tight little pussy will fucking know. From today, you will take everything I have to give. From today, you will give me everything I ask for, and each time I'm done with you, you will thank me afterward."

"You're not wearing a condom."

"You're my wife. No rubber will ever come between us. I will fill you with my cum in any orifice of my choosing and you will thank me for that too."

He pulls out and thrusts straight back in. The orgasm denied me now clawing for release as his dick bottoms out, and doesn't he just know it as he deliberately thrusts deep and then stops.

"Eoin, please," I whine.

"Do you want me to fuck you, Jaine?"

"Yes," I hiss.

"Then ask me."

"Asshole."

"For cussing, you'll now have to add please. Now. Ask. Me."

"Please fuck me, Eoin." I dig my nails deliberately into his shoulders until I can feel blood. "That's for making me fucking beg."

He curses me under his breath before proceeding to pound me into oblivion against the wall.

Ruthless, determined, selfish thrusts.

Everything hurts. Everything burns. But when he angles my hips, I'm lost to my pleasure as his dick connects with my sweet spot and I finally reach my high. My walls clench around him, and my release drenches his cock. My teeth find his neck and sink in, and he growls his annoyance before fucking me harder.

Pain. Pleasure. Alternating perfect thrusts.

Hot skin, damp with sweat. I lick the saltiness off, the raw taste of him combined with the spicy scent of his cologne turning me on even more.

He drops my feet to the floor, then spins me around before pushing my front against the wall with such force he knocks the air out of my lungs.

"Spread your legs."

I do as he asks, then he tilts my hips upward and thrusts into me from behind. I hiss in complaint at how deep he's gone. His response is unforgiving. He grips my hip, fists my hair painfully with the other hand, pulls me flush against his torso, then fucks me harder, faster, and deeper until his movements become erratic.

"Come with me." It's not a question, it's a command, and he'll expect me to do as I'm told.

The animalistic sound of his low growl as he finds his own pleasure causes me to spiral once more, my clenching walls demanding that he spill his seed deep inside me, his twitching cock obliging as he empties himself in long, steady thrusts.

We stay there leaning against the wall.

Hot. Sweaty. Panting.

Finally, he pulls out and steps back. I know exactly what he's doing. He's clearly fucked a thousand women in order to hone his craft to such perfection, but this will be his first ever time without a condom. And the neanderthal wants to witness his cum run down my inner thighs.

I spread my legs farther, and he grunts his appreciation as it immediately starts to escape and coat my skin. Catching it with his hand, he thrusts it back inside. Even though I hurt, I groan my approval as he then fucks me slowly with his cum-covered fingers.

In and out. Over and over until I start to soar once more. His breath is hot against my ear as he brings me right to the edge.

"From this moment on, if any man looks at you the wrong way, I will kill him with my bare fucking hands."

"Possessive much?"

"You're mine."

The heel of his hand presses against my clit, and I welcome my release as I groan my new husband's name.

In response, he growls his approval in my ear.

CHAPTER TWENTY-SEVEN

EOIN

The Hudson Dusters' HQ, Manhattan, New York

"JESUS CHRIST, YOU ACTUALLY FUCKED HER."

We're in my office. I look up at Dylan, wondering how he could know that as I've not said a word.

"Your neck."

I frown at him as he sits on one of the tan-colored executive chairs that face me, still none the wiser.

"Hickies. And since I've never seen you with one before now, I reckon the resident female vampire is none other than Mrs. Jaine O'Connell. Tell me I'm wrong."

I pause to consider whether responding to such a personal question is in any way inappropriate, but considering the clearly damning evidence left by Jaine herself, there's no point in trying to deny that our relationship has moved to the next level.

"No. You're not wrong."

He snickers. "I never thought I'd see the future Da Duster sporting hickies like a high schooler. So, you finally fucked your wife which means sex without a rubber for the first time in thirty-eight years. How was that for you?"

"That, Dylan, is none of your business. And let's be clear. What I do intimately with Jaine is not something I intend on sharing with others. And if you know what's good for you, you will never ask or expect me to."

He nods with a knowing smirk. "I see she's brought out your possessive side."

"Not at all. As my wife, she deserves my respect, that's all."

He snickers again. It's clear he doesn't believe a word of my fucking lies.

"And are you in love with her all over again?"

"I'm not sure how I feel about her." It's the truth.

"But you're sure that you want a repeat of whatever happened between you last night. I'm not asking for any details. I may not be the most handsome of the O'Connell brothers, but I quite like my facial arrangement as it is, as does Jessie."

Before I get the chance to reply, there's a knock on the door.

"Come in."

"Jaine is on her way up."

"Thank you, Candice."

"Should I…." Dylan makes to rise from his chair.

"Stay where you are."

We both stare at her as she walks in. She's wearing another pantsuit. Navy. But this time she has a small matching scarf tied around her neck. An accessory that's no doubt necessary to hide what my *monster* inflicted on the delicate skin of her perfect throat. My fingers are already itching to wrap themselves around it again.

To use it as my own accessory and as a means with which to pin her down as I slide my cock into her tight little pussy.

Tempting, evil woman.

Without being offered, she takes the spare seat beside Dylan. She's clearly playing her uncouth card today.

She seldom if ever wears make-up but she's wearing lipstick. Blood red. How appropriate for a femme fatale such as her. No doubt it's to hide the bruising inflicted on her bottom lip by my teeth.

My payback, which I know she enjoyed far more than she'd ever admit.

I want those scarlet lips wrapped around my cock. I want to watch that pouty mouth stain my dick red as it gags on my length. It twitches at the thought.

Placing her briefcase to the side, she stares straight at me. I can see the desire in her eyes. She's doing nothing to mask it.

I fucked her so many times last night. Each time harder than the last, and each time, she asked for more. She's insatiable. I've never known anything quite like it. I'm surprised she can walk today, let alone sit. I wish Dylan wasn't here so I could fuck her over this desk.

"I know exactly what you're thinking, Mr. O'Connell, and it will never goddamn happen."

"I see your tongue is back to its favorite activity of mouthing off. And what is it that you believe I'm thinking?" I raise an eyebrow at her.

"That you want to fuck me over this desk."

She side-glances at Dylan, who's now squirming in his seat not knowing where to look. He won't speak. He'll be scared he'll say the wrong thing and then I'll want to snap his neck. Or she will.

We both know she's more than capable. We're both aware of what she did to the Colombian who tried to throttle Sarah.

"Are you a mind reader now, Mrs. O'Connell?"

"I don't need to be a mind-reader. Having first-hand experience, I now know exactly what goes on inside that twisted head of yours."

"Is that right?" I can't stop my lips from curving upward.

"Yes, it is." She returns my smile briefly before it disappears. "And I want this desk gone."

"It's going nowhere."

"I'm burning it."

I lean back in my chair as I observe her while she sits there pretending to be all prim and proper. I too have first-hand experience. I now know that neither word could be used to describe the real Jaine O'Connell.

"And why would you want to do such a thing?"

"You've been fucking your PA over it for years."

"Careful, Jaine. Your jealousy's showing."

She smiles politely. "It has nothing to do with jealousy, so please don't think to flatter yourself. My reason for wanting to throw it on a bonfire is because this piece of furniture must breach every sanitary code in the state of New York. It's going, but don't worry, I'll buy you a new one, *husband*."

One single word and my dick is instantly rock hard. She's claiming me as hers by calling me her husband for the first ever time.

And now I want to claim her. Over this fucking desk.

"And do I get any say in this new desk that you're proposing?"

"Nope. But don't worry, I'll make sure it's large enough to accommodate that huge ego of yours."

Dylan sniggers, and I draw him a glare.

"Anything else?" I raise an eyebrow at her once more.

"Have you told her yet?"

I frown and exhale. "I'm handling it. It's not as straightforward as you may think."

She stands and places her hands flat on the desk. Her top is low enough that the position perfectly displays her small cleavage.

"It seemed pretty straightforward last night. Or was that because all your decisions were being made by the wrong head?"

"That. Fucking. Mouth," I hiss-whisper.

She smirks as she retakes her seat. "That fucking mouth that you won't have access to any longer."

"She saved my life, Jaine. I owe her!"

There's a pause. She side-glances at Dylan once more before turning her full attention back to me.

"Well, I'm sorry that you feel indebted to her for that reason, but unfortunately, I'm all out of fucks to give. You gave your word."

"And I will honor it. I just need some time. It's a difficult situation all around."

"It's not difficult. You open your mouth, and you tell her that it's over. I want it done, and I want it done today."

"I can't do it today."

"Today, or don't call me, I'll call you. And I will never fucking call you. You have *my* word on that."

Standing, she picks up her briefcase, then leaves the room.

Dylan instantly smirks at me.

"Don't say a word," I warn him.

"Take a seat, Molly."

She closes my office door and walks into the room. I know she won't take a chair willingly. We're alone. She'll attempt to sit on my lap like she always does. Under normal circumstances, I wouldn't mind, but if Jaine were to walk in and find her there, there would be hell to pay.

To avoid any compromising situations, I stand and move towards the window. The view is magnificent. The best the building has to offer. It affords me the very best sight over my extensive kingdom.

I turn around. Having removed all temptation, Molly's now seated exactly where Jaine was earlier.

I can't help but compare the two.

Molly's also professionally dressed, but aside from that, it's a complete contrast. Jaine's blonde hair and green eyes on a too-slim figure and Molly's black hair and pale blue eyes on a body that's slim but curved in all the right places.

I know which one I want. Then again, haven't I always?

She looks up at me and smiles. She's not right for me. Far from it. She also has several attributes that make her wrong for the role of Ma Duster.

But she saved my life. She was there for me when it mattered. She sank a bullet into the skull of the Colombian scum who was pressing a gun to my head and was about to pull the trigger.

And that changed everything.

Still. Family comes first. It has to. Finian is family. That makes Jaine family. I'm telling myself that's all this is with Jaine. That I'm simply doing the right thing. But I know I'm lying. It's more. Way more. How much more I don't know, but I want to find out. I need to find out.

I will find out.

And if the only way I can do that is by letting Molly go, then that is what I'll do. If I don't and this *thing* with Jaine develops further, then Molly stands to get hurt a whole lot more further down the line. It's best to nip it in the bud now for everyone's sake.

I know she won't take it lying down. She had her sights firmly set on being my wife and the next Ma Duster.

"I can't marry you, Molly."

She stares at me, her eyes unblinking, and then she laughs exaggeratedly. "Very funny, Eoin."

I keep my expression impassive. "I'm being serious. I can't extract myself from the marriage with Jaine. Protection of young Finian has to take priority over everything else."

"I know he's your son. But maybe we could adopt him. Make him our son. Give him brothers and sisters. I know you want a large family. I want that too, I…"

I interject. "He's not my son. He's Padraig's son."

A frown mars her forehead. "What are you saying?"

"What I'm saying is that Jaine and Paddy reconnected before he was entered into the arranged marriage with Sophia. Fin is the result of that reconnection. But with the current unrest within the Sicilian mafia, more specifically between the organization and the Ruoccos, it's not safe to reveal his true parentage at this time."

She frowns. "But why couldn't Jaine just continue to pretend that he was Ace's child?"

"The O'Connell birthmark."

She nods. "And why couldn't someone else have married her? Aidan or one of the other cousins."

"They weren't living in New York at the time. It was around then that I first met her as you already know."

"So you were chosen as the scapegoat."

"Unfortunately, yes."

"Then why can't we just continue as we are? That we're together and your relationship with her is fake."

She stands and walks slowly towards me. It's her walk of seduction. I've been the recipient of it more times than I can count. I watch as she sashays her slim hips invitingly while licking her lips. Sadly, for her, neither has the desired effect on me now.

She snakes her arms around my shoulders as she stares up at me before putting on her well-rehearsed pout. I look at her lips briefly then raise my gaze to meet hers.

"Because I won't cheat on my wife." Again, I just say it how it is because, in every sense of the word, Jaine is now exactly that.

There's a deafening silence.

I watch as Molly's eyes drift to my neck. I'm doing nothing to hide the *hickies*.

Her face pales as she drops her arms to her sides. "You've been sleeping with her," she whispers in disbelief.

I don't reply. There's no point. It's obvious that's the case.

She glares at me. "You've been cheating on me with her."

"Not cheating. Last night was the first time we were ever intimate. She insisted I end things with you beforehand. I had to give her my word that I would before she would consent to anything happening between us."

She laughs bitterly as she steps back. "So, this is you finally getting around to letting the third party in the triangle know that she's been dumped." There's a pause, then she frowns. "If it's just to keep Finian safe, then why do you have to have a physical relationship with her?" She nods slowly, a wry smile crossing her face before she finally answers her own question. "Roisin was right all along, wasn't she? You do have feelings for her."

I don't reply. Not because I don't want to, but because I can't. I don't have that answer. I'm not sure if I have feelings for Jaine or not. What I do know is that I want her.

Crave her. Desire her.

"Do you love her?"

"No."

"Do you love me?"

"No."

I'm as honest as I can be.

Silence. We've spent several intimate months together and now neither of us knows what to say. I verbally promised to make her my wife, and now here I am reneging on that because deep down I know that having now had a taste of Jaine, I will never be able to stay away from her. And that's not fair on Molly.

I turn to look out the window once more. "I'm sorry, Molly, but you deserve better than anything I can offer you."

"Bullshit!" she snaps. "You're saying that to appease your guilt. We both know you're doing this for yourself. Not for me. Not for Jaine. Not for Finian or for Paddy. You're doing this for Eoin. You've fallen for the same woman as your brother. So, tell me, how will you explain all of this to him? That you've effectively stolen his life?"

I frown. The view is no longer of interest. She has a valid point. I know how this all looks. But it wasn't like that. None of this was intentional or pre-planned. Until I was forced into taking the vows with Jaine, I was set on marrying Molly. Not that she would ever believe that now.

I turn to face her once more. "He's living in Sicily, working remotely and with no return date scheduled. He could be due back tomorrow. He may never return. He's also married. Nothing can change the latter."

"How very convenient for you." Her tone is bitter as she stands. "Very well. I'm not going to beg to be in a relationship with you when you don't want to be in one with me. But know this, Eoin. My da won't take kindly to you humiliating me in this way. He won't take kindly to Jaine humiliating me in this way either. With that in mind, I can't be held responsible for whatever action he may or may not decide to take."

She turns and storms out of the room, slamming the door behind her. It's my guess that's the last I'll ever see of Molly McGrath. Whether I hear from her da is another matter.

She's completely right. I have dishonored her, and in turn, I've dishonored her family. And in this life, you reap what you sow. It may amount to nothing. Then again, the Dusters have so many enemies. What's one more?

My curiosity is piqued. I'm surprised she never threw in my face the fact that she saved my life.

CHAPTER TWENTY-EIGHT

JAINE

Jaine's Apartment, Upper East Side, New York

Eoin: *I'll be at your apartment imminently. Be there.*

I STARE AT THE MESSAGE ON THE SCREEN.

It's just as well my office is located in the same building. I know immediately what it relates to.

My ultimatum.

Her or me.

It was one or the other. The decision was his alone to make. Last night, and in the heat of the moment, he chose me.

I make my way to my apartment. There's a knock on the door less than ten minutes later. I open it. He makes no eye contact as he strides in. The spicy scent of his cologne wraps around me.

He removes his suit jacket, leaving him in a white tailored shirt that he wears like a second skin. I now know that every inch underneath is toned and defined. I've explored his perfect imperfections several times over with my hands.

Lips. Tongue. Teeth.

He's agitated. I watch as he paces the floor, running his fingers repeatedly through his hair.

To stop him from doing what exactly? Killing me? Or fucking me? It's either one or the other.

He rolls his shirt sleeves up.

I guess he means business.

Masculine arms covered in veins. He must work out a lot. But then, what would I know? I know the businessperson. I know Mr. Smug. Selfish. Pompous.

The paradox that is Mr. Dominating. Dangerous. Deadly? I'm still trying to figure him out.

All we've ever done is go out of our way to aggravate each other with our constant back-and-forth needling. Our hate banter somehow started a fire that drew us both in and eventually made us want to reach out and touch the naked flame.

And last night we did.

It culminated in one night of intense hate-fucking, both of us taking what we needed, not knowing if the opportunity would ever arise again. Not knowing if we'd ever want it to again.

But my own cold light of day has me facing a raging hot inferno that I'm not sure I can ever put out.

Was it the same for him? I guess I'm about to find out.

"It's done."

He stops pacing and stares at me. He feels guilty. I know he does. And I guess that's an alien feeling for him because Mr. Inconsiderate just walks over everyone and takes what he wants. He never stops to consider others.

But he did in her case because he thinks she saved his life.

She didn't, though. I did. Twice.

But he doesn't know that. Will he ever? Who knows? That's not a decision I have to make right now while he's staring at me like I'm the sun, the moon, and the stars.

I walk across and stand in front of him. His hair is messy, and his forehead creased.

"She…"

I place my finger against his lips. "I don't want to know how she reacted. I would never gloat in the face of another woman's misery. I've been the other woman, remember? I know how it feels being her. I'm sorry I had to make you choose, but I refuse to be anything less than someone's everything. I have too much respect for myself. And, whether deserved or not, I have too much respect for Molly to allow her to be deserving of anything less either."

He stares at me. Aquamarine eyes search mine, neither of us giving anything away. We haven't reached the baring of souls stage. We likely never will. He and I will always be the classic example of enemies to lovers. A lethal cocktail mixed with a dash of twisted and taboo.

The main ingredient? Toxicity.

I lick my bruised bottom lip and his eyes drop to my mouth. His heartbeat instantly increases. I can see it in his throat. I feel mine doing the same.

Reflected.

We may not share our thoughts or feelings, but our bodies are so incredibly attuned they don't need dialogue to communicate their wants, needs, and demands.

I hate mine for it. I hate his for it.

I curse him, because one taste and, like a junkie, I was hooked. Neither of us can hide this physical bond that we share. At least not from each other.

I want him, rightly or wrongly.

Wrongly. Wrongly. Wrongly.

I turn away, suddenly over-whelmed by a fusion of guilt and grief.

Too much. Too soon. Too much. Too soon.

Tears threaten. I bite them back. I have no choice. I can only release them when I'm on my own.

When it's just me and Ace.

Now is not the time for grief or self-pity. I can't afford to drop the ball. Not now I've got him exactly where I want him. I just need to stick to the goddamn plan.

Composing myself, I turn back around. I watch as he removes his tie. Strong hands working deftly. Strong hands that have now explored every inch of my body. That have given me intense pleasure and inflicted intense pain. Strong, possessive hands that have wrapped around my throat so many times I now miss their presence.

I run my fingertip down his crisp white shirt. My heart pounds even faster.

He's all fucking mine. And I can do whatever I like with him. *For now.*

With both hands, I rip his shirt apart. Buttons scatter. The visual is skin. Perfectly inked. Imperfectly scarred.

Placing my nose against his neck, I inhale the scent of his cologne, sighing as I welcome back his darkness as it wraps its addictive arms around me once more. Pressing my lips to the same spot, I allow my hands to glide down the smooth, chiseled flesh of his torso before stopping to rest at the top of his suit pants. Raising them upward, I place them against his chest to let him know I want him to stay exactly where he is. Then, stepping back, I strip.

His eyes follow my every move, drinking me in. I feel light-headed with how much lust and desire I see in his eyes.

Moving forward, I press my hands against his chest once more. His heart is pounding, the same as mine. I then run them slowly back down his body, but this time, my lips and tongue follow their path until I'm on my knees in front of him.

His gaze now burns green.

I unzip him to freedom, letting his pants drop to the floor. He steps out and kicks them aside. My eyes feast on that magnificent cock of his. He's too big. Every time he fucks me, it hurts. But that's intentional on his part.

The pain is for my pleasure.

I run my fingertips along his impressive length with its throbbing veins and leaking tip. His abs clench as it jerks under my touch, and my tongue laps up the bead of pre-cum that appears on the head.

Growling, he fists my hair with one hand. Waiting for his instruction, I inhale his addictive, musky scent.

"Suck."

That one spoken word is like an aphrodisiac. I groan as my core melts.

His eyes darken as he uses his thumb to smear my lipstick. It's my guess he wants my mouth to stain his dick blood red.

My eyes never leave his as I run my tongue over the blunt head to lubricate him before sucking hard on the nerve endings right under the tip. He hisses, his grip on my hair tightening.

"I said suck, wife. Do something useful with that bossy little mouth of yours for once and wrap it around my fucking dick."

"Asshole." I smirk up at him, but I can hear the command in his tone. He has expectations now that he's publicly chosen me. Now that he's claimed me.

Now that he's chosen me over her.

I gave him no other option.

He feels vulnerable but empowered at the same time. I get it.

We're tied. *For now.*

My gaze never leaves his as I open my mouth and take him

deep. I gag at his length, my eyes instantly watering. It's his turn to smirk. I'm right where he wants me to be. On my knees and choking on his cock.

Fisting my hair with both hands, he starts to fuck my mouth.

Hard. Fast. Wet.

He thrusts deep. Too deep. He deliberately cuts off my airway before pulling back, his nostrils flaring as he watches me gasp.

Saliva and precum dribble down my chin. His stamina is impressive, but I already know that. My jaw and scalp hurt. In retaliation, I dig my nails into his thighs to inflict my own pain, but he ignores my pathetic payback attempt and continues to ruthlessly fuck my mouth.

I squeeze his balls hard, and his movements quickly become jerky. His eyes bore into mine as he grips my hair and pulls my head back.

"Don't fucking swallow. I want to see my cum in your mouth." It's a snarl. He's not hiding his true self now that he's openly staked his claim.

I wrap my red lips back around his length and then, with a low growl, he erupts, letting his ropes of salty thickness fill my mouth.

"Show me."

I tilt my head back and he uses his thumb to drag down my chin, his nostrils flaring further as he watches his cum drip from my parted lips.

"Now forever taint your soul with my darkness, wife, by drinking every last fucking drop."

I swallow him down then use my finger to gather the spill from my chin and suck it clean.

"That. Fucking. Mouth." He growls.

"Is all yours." *For now.*

CHAPTER TWENTY-NINE

EOIN

The Hudson Dusters' HQ, Manhattan, New York

I SMILE AT MY PHONE AS I MESSAGE HER.

Eoin: *Nice desk.*

And it is a stunning piece. Large and impressive in hand-made dark walnut and with a leather top. The potent smell of the black finish reminds me of her.

Biker.

Jaine: *It's over the top and vulgar, so I thought it matched your personality perfectly.*

I laugh out loud. She has me doing that a lot these days.

Eoin: *Thank you. I'm extremely grateful.*
Jaine: *You're welcome. I thought the leather was a nice finishing touch. Much easier to wipe clean should you ever wish to dick Candice at lunchtime again.*
Eoin: *Why would I want to fuck her when I can fuck you? Let's be honest, you claim my cock every opportunity you get.*
Jaine: *Have you even heard yourself? Your arrogance should see you banned from speaking. Then again, from what I've heard, most of the conversations you have are with yourself and about yourself. Anyway, I've had the other desk thrown on a bonfire.*
Eoin: *Beautiful, evil woman.*
Jaine: *But you love me anyway.*

It's a statement rather than a question. And it's meant in jest, I know. But it still has me questioning after almost three months. Do I love her? Will I ever love her?

Eoin: *Ma says you're still avoiding her.*
Jaine: *Can you blame me? She pretty much threatened to have me exterminated.*
Eoin: *We have to put the past behind us if we're to have any chance of a future.*
Jaine: *The future is never guaranteed, so why bother?*
Eoin: *Perhaps not, but it's impossible for us to continue to live day by day.*
Jaine: *Us? Does that mean you and me?*
Eoin: *What do you want it to mean?*

There's a pause on her side. For Jaine, that means she's either thinking, she's gotten emotional, or she doesn't wish to discuss the matter any further. At least not at this time.

I know her ways now.

Jaine: *I'll message her.*

Eoin: *Thank you.*

Jaine: *I didn't say when.*

Eoin: *You're being deliberately unaccommodating, Mrs. O'Connell.*

Jaine: *On the contrary. I'm very accommodating. You insinuated just as much last night. And you weren't complaining then, Mr. O'Connell. In fact, I can repeat what you said word for word if you like.*

Eoin: *Don't.*

Jaine: *Why? Am I making you hard, husband?*

Eoin: *Jaine, I have a lot of work to get through.*

Jaine: *Best work* hard *then.*

Eoin: *I'm on my way to your apartment, wife, and you know what will happen when I get there.*

Jaine: *Have you even heard yourself? I'm surprised your neck can support the weight of that big, fat conceited head of yours.*

Eoin: *Flattery won't save you.*

Jaine: *Only someone as pompous as you would consider being called conceited as flattery.*

Jaine's Apartment, Upper East Side, New York

"Thank you, Dec."

Declan O'Malley. One of my high rankers and my former driver, now used exclusively to tail Jaine wherever she goes. His role is the single most important one in the Duster organization.

To me, at least.

I'm sure she hasn't picked up on his presence. She won't think I'm having her followed. It's for her protection and for that of Finian and JJ. All the women in our immediate family are. Most end up embracing it in the end and using their *tail* as a driver, much like Ma uses Liam. It kills two birds with one stone. I'm not sure someone as headstrong as my wife will ever view it as a benefit, however.

"You're welcome, boss."

Dec's brought me here in one of our many custom SUVs. He complements the vehicle. He's dressed head to toe in black. His hair and eyes also match. His skin in direct contrast is pale. Dec's my age. Maybe slightly older. Being trained in several of the martial arts, it's instilled in him to fight to the death. He's also versatile with most weapons. It's for those reasons he's the only person I trust to keep Jaine safe when I'm not around to do so.

I wait for the locks to unravel before stepping out onto the sidewalk. It feels alien coming here during daylight hours. Things will be so much easier once she's moved in with me. I frown as I make my way inside the building. Whenever I bring up the subject, she changes it, but it's one that must be broached.

Two of the conditions Jaine raised have now been ticked off. The marriage has been consummated more times than I can count, and while our union has not been publicly announced, it's no longer a secret.

I'm sure our outlaw peers will be fully aware that Jaine is my wife.

The only other stipulated condition was her ability to seek an annulment should she choose to do so. I suspect this condition was only inserted on the off-chance it transpired that we weren't compatible in any way. Given three months have now passed with no major issues then I'm not expecting this to be put into play.

My only concern right now is over her unwillingness to take things to the next level. I appreciate that Jaine's an independent woman. I also appreciate what she's been through and understand that she may just need more time. But my gut is telling me there's more to it than that. That she's keeping me at arm's length for reasons she's unwilling to share. We've yet to spend a full night together. Not that I ever have with any female. But it's time. I want to.

Even now, she's never spoken with my ma nor met her face to face. She makes every excuse under the sun not to visit our family home. Who can blame her? She went once, was backed into a corner, and was forced into an arranged marriage with me.

It's been almost three months since I chose her. I have no regrets about my decision, and I'm confident she doesn't either, not that it's ever been openly discussed.

Jaine is my intellectual equal.

We spend our evenings talking of a great many things – business, politics, current affairs. There are no topics off-limits when it comes to healthy debating, but she refuses to discuss anything of a personal nature, and if I mention Ace or my youngest brother, she simply changes the subject.

What we do share is a physical connection that I've never experienced before. Our intimate relations are animalistic to the point of being frenzied.

I see her. I want her. I fuck her. And as soon as I'm done with her, I want her all over again. I never seem to be sated, and the feeling's mutual. She's a walking map of bruises and bite marks as I stake my claim on her skin repeatedly and for the world to see.

I'm confident that she's mine. Physically, at least. But is that still enough? There's most definitely no whispered sweet nothings nor tactile pillow talk. Do I want any of that? How do you know if you want something when you've never experienced it before?

I knock on the door, and it's opened by an older man. I know who he is the moment I see him, the resemblance uncanny. Aside from the short greying hair and the lack of a beard on his lined face, he looks just like Ace.

He smiles broadly as he holds out his hand. "You must be Eoin."

I return his smile with a genuine one of my own as I shake his hand. "And you must be Duke."

He motions for me to step inside.

I'm used to seeing Jaine with Fin from time to time. The little lad who's a million miles an hour, never sits still, and is back and forth between anyone who will listen to his constant chatter. He's just like his da.

Guilt barrels through me as it does any time I think of my youngest sibling, but I quickly push it aside. It won't change anything.

Is he happy? We're told that he is by the only family member he actually speaks to these days. Ma.

Texts messages are ignored. Calls go straight to voice mail. Business emails stick to business only. Any attempt to interact with him on family or personal matters just falls on deaf ears.

I take in my wife.

She's dressed professionally but is currently jacketless. This time, she's not holding Fin. She's holding a small baby. He doesn't have a lot of hair, but what he does is inky black curls. He stares at me with open curiosity, his blue eyes looking huge on a small face with a chin that has a little dent in.

Jaine stops what she's doing and watches me as I take in JJ. Finian's baby brother. Ace's son.

"Do you want to hold him? I need to speak to Jessie quickly."

I drag my gaze from the little one and look up at her with a smile. "I'd like that."

JJ doesn't hold his arms out like Fin did when I first met him. I have to scoop him from Jaine's hold while he continues to stare up at me with the bluest eyes I've ever seen.

"He's his father's son, that's for sure." I watch my wife leave the room before I turn to face Duke. "Duke. About Ace." I frown.

His face is lined, I'm sure much is attributable to grief. With a melancholy sigh, he pats me on the shoulder. "I know. We all sure as hell miss having him around." He looks at me, silent for a moment before speaking further. "I'm glad you've come here today. I've been hoping I might run into you for a while now, but with you and Jainie only spending your evenings together, our paths never crossed."

Does Duke know why our relationship feels almost pigeon-holed? Why Jaine seems reluctant to commit to anything further? Then again, if Duke knew anything, would he tell me? I'm thinking probably not as he'd never betray her confidence.

He pauses, a frown creasing his forehead. "Now, I know your family has been spending a lot of time with Finian recently, and rightly so. He's an O'Connell and I'm told he's his father's son too. But I'm glad you've finally had the chance to meet little JJ today." He pauses once more. "You see, with Jason gone, any new man in Jainie's life will immediately become JJ's father figure. I know the same could be said for Fin, but we both know he has a daddy who's alive and well, and while he may not know about him just yet, we also know that will change. At some point, he'll become part of his life. It's different for little JJ with his daddy having passed."

He looks at the little boy and smiles. It's bittersweet. He's lost his son but gained a grandchild. Like Fin looks like Paddy, I'm sure JJ looks just like Ace at the same age.

He turns his attention back to me.

"If you and Jainie ever decide to make a proper go of this marriage, and by that, I mean if you ever decide to live together as a family, then you'll instantly become the man JJ looks up to. You'd have to be prepared to accept him as your son, even though he's not your flesh and blood because, growing up, little JJ won't know any different. Not until he's older and it's all explained to him."

He rubs his hand over his face. Despite several months having passed, it's clear Ace's death is as raw a subject for him as it ever was, as it still is for Jaine. The fact that he was murdered and the party responsible is still at large must make it even more difficult to accept and move on.

He exhales.

"See, I'm getting on in life now, son. I won't be around forever. And I don't want JJ to miss out on having a well-rounded childhood. To experience that, he needs to be surrounded by family." He pauses once more as he glances at JJ, then back at me. "So, if it's all right with you and your folks, I'd like for little JJ to be included in your plans every once in a while and that you take time getting to know him too. Because despite him not being an O'Connell, Fin and JJ are blood brothers. They deserve to grow up together. To be there for each other much the same as you are with your own siblings. I'm guessing between you four boys, you'll produce many grandbabies for your folks in due course. That yours will be a large close-knit family of siblings and cousins. Neither Jainie nor Ace had that growing up. They only really had each other. In a way, it was a good thing. In a way, not so good. They loved each other so much. Maybe too much. They became dependent on each other. When they stopped talking, my boy struggled to move on with his life. It was like something died inside him the day Jainie left Rising. He never got over losing her, and I'm not sure she coped either.

"I know one of Jaine's biggest regrets is that it was only ever her and Ace. Now he's gone, she has no one to reminisce with. I know she's mentally boxed up a whole truckload of her childhood memories because she has no one to share any of them with now. I know she doesn't want that for Fin or JJ. She wants them to grow up part of a large, loving family."

He pauses once more.

"The boys aside, I know Jainie has feelings for you, Eoin. She may not have said anything, and maybe I shouldn't be saying anything either, but I've known her since she was seven years old, so there's not much she can hide from me. I just want what's best for her. For all of them. I guess what I'm trying to say is that you need to decide if the feelings you have for her are enough that you're prepared to take on a ready-made family. They come as a package. You can't pick and choose. Don't sign up and then decide it's not worth it or it's all too much effort. They've been through enough as it is."

I stand, silently taking on board what Duke's said word for word. I understand. My family has unintentionally been separating the siblings because all we've been focused on is getting to know Fin. In making up for lost time.

He's a Duster heir. An O'Connell. It was a natural and understandable reaction. But in doing so, we've stopped him from spending time with his baby brother. A little boy who needs his older sibling around to learn from and to be there for him. Same as my brothers always relied on me and, on occasion, still do. We need to welcome both children into our family. Treat JJ as an O'Connell and include him in our future organizational plans. Duke's right. I'll be the only da he'll ever know.

Is this why Jaine's refusing to commit further? Why she's limited my involvement in her life and in her children's lives? Because she's concerned I won't accept them as a package. That I won't grow to love Ace's son and treat him like my own?

I look down at him. JJ is quiet and reserved, much like his da was. I'm sure he sees everything and misses nothing too, just like his da did.

He lifts his head and stares up and me with an expression so open and honest. Can I be the father he needs now that his own has been taken from him? He's already lost so much in his short life.

I smile down at him, and he smiles a gummy one back, causing me to laugh out loud.

Yes. I think I can.

CHAPTER THIRTY

JAINE

Jaine's Apartment, Upper East Side, New York

I WATCH AS EOIN DISCARDS HIS JACKET THEN YANKS OFF HIS TIE before taking a seat on the sofa and running his hand through his hair.

He's agitated.

No sooner had he turned up here today then he was called away again.

We both have successful companies to run. We may not appreciate their demands at times, but it comes with the territory.

The reason he's so frustrated is because he was hoping to spend some quality time with me and the kids. That we could do something together for once as a real family.

In his haste to get here, he's come straight from the office as he's still wearing his business suit, and now he's frustrated because, despite his best efforts, he's still arrived too late.

It's seven p.m. and both boys are already tucked up in bed.

If he lived with us, he wouldn't have to try to squeeze himself into an allocated timeslot. If he lived here, we could take meals together, watch movies together, play games together, and do normal family stuff together.

But he doesn't. Because I won't let him. He feels pigeon-holed. I know he does.

I pour him a whiskey as I do every evening. He only has one as he likes to keep his wits about him around me and the kids.

He's always alert. Always protective. Unbelievably so.

"Jaine." He's staring at me now, his forehead creased. I know what he's going to say even before he opens his mouth.

Walking across, I pass him his drink. I wait as he throws back the whiskey in one the same as he always does before passing me back the glass.

I remain standing, my hands fidgeting with the now empty crystalware.

"I appreciate our marriage was somewhat enforced, but I believe I've given you adequate time to adjust and accept our situation." He runs his hand down his face.

He thinks I'm going to change the subject like I always do. I won't. For once I'll give him the truth. I let him continue.

"I think it's time we started living together as a family. We're married. We should be under one roof, not residing in two separate apartments. You and I shouldn't be limited to only spending our evenings together after the children have gone to bed."

I know how much he desperately wants this. How long he's always wanted it.

I know how much I need him to want it.

The only positive is that what I'm about to say isn't a lie. It isn't because it's part of my game plan. It's more important than that.

"It's just too much too soon for me, Eoin. It wasn't so long ago that I was Ace's wife. And he was such a big part of our family. An irreplaceable part of my life. Since he left us, everything has happened so fast. I just need time to come to terms with it all."

His eyes never leave mine. I know he's searching for any sign that I'm lying to him, but I'm not. At least not about that.

Every day, I still wake up and reach for Ace until I remember that he's not there, that he never will be again, and that I've been sleeping alone all these months. It's then that I talk to him.

That's our time. And it may be selfish, but I still need that for now.

"I'm sorry, Jaine. I never even thought."

"You have nothing to apologize for. I completely understand where you're coming from. I just want you to understand where I'm coming from."

"What about the children?"

"What about them?"

"Could we do something with them? I appreciate Sarah takes them to visit my ma and da often and I could spend time with them there, but I'd like for you and I to do something with them on our own."

As parents.

"What did you and Duke chat about?" I change the subject while I ponder what he's asked. Fin doesn't need a replacement daddy. He already has one, even if he is absent for now, but JJ does need a father-figure in his life.

He smiles at my question like it's something top secret. Eoin doesn't smile often. Usually, it's that pompous smirk of his that he shoots in my direction.

"He said he wants me to be more hands on with JJ and for him to be included in our Duster plans."

I chuckle. "So, let me get this straight. He wants JJ to become a mobster like his big brother as opposed to a biker like his folks?"

He laughs out loud. "I believe the point he was trying to make was that he doesn't want them spending any length of time apart, which is perfectly understandable. He feels that as brothers they should be allowed to grow up in close proximity."

I know Duke's thinking about me and Ace.

That it was always me and him. And now that he's gone, I don't know what to do with all these memories.

"He's right. It's important that they playfight and build memories together. We only ever get one childhood. Siblings are part of the same jigsaw. Growing up together lets them figure out which piece they are and which part they have to play in order to be there for the others."

There's a pause. I know we're both now thinking of the fourth O'Connell brother. The missing piece. The fact that their family is currently fractured.

As is mine.

"I'd be honored to."

"Honored to what?" I smile-frown at him.

"Help you raise JJ." He pauses. "I understand I can never replace Ace, but I'd like to be there for him all the same."

He's asking if it's okay for him to love my little boy. I instantly feel tears prick my eyes. There's no way he won't be able to see them, but he says nothing.

"And what else did Duke's big mouth have to say for itself?"

There's a pause.

"He said that you have feelings for me." It's quietly spoken. He's unsure of himself because he's not sure if it's true or not. "Do you?"

I nod slowly. I'm not going to lie, but I'm also not going to tell him that they're feelings I wish I never had. Feelings I never in a million years expected to have. Feelings I don't know what the fuck to do with.

Feelings that make me feel all kinds of other feelings, none of which are positive.

Guilt. Betrayal.

I don't want to know if he has feelings for me, so I don't repeat his question.

I just want to live in the present for now, just for a little while longer. It will all be over soon enough.

"If you can get tomorrow off, we can take the boys out for the day." It's time for the final push.

"Consider it done." I watch as he pulls out his phone.

I DON'T THINK IT WOULD HAVE MATTERED WHAT EOIN HAD planned. He cleared his calendar so he could spend the day with me and the kids.

We didn't go anywhere fancy. Just to the local park.

It's amazing what new adventures you can find just by being outdoors and using your imagination. It's all me and Ace ever relied on when we were kids. I want my boys to grow up the same way, even if it's not in Rising.

We pushed the kids on the swings. Then we ate a picnic, and Finian emptied his Jell-O over the top of his baby brother's head. JJ cried, not because of the injustice of it all, but because it went all over his precious soother.

Fin, knowing he was in trouble, ran as fast as his chubby little legs could carry him, which wasn't very fast at all. His childish laughter filled the air as he was chased and then caught by his Uncle Eoin, who proceeded to throw him so high in the air I had to close my eyes as I couldn't bear to watch. When I opened them, he had already been caught in his safe, strong arms.

I smile as Eoin laughs heartily, something I've never seen him do.

Today, he's not a mobster. Today, he's a man enjoying a rare day out with his family. The kids are appreciating every minute with him, just as he is with them.

For a man who has it all, he actually wants very little.

He wants a wife. He wants children. He wants a family. Because this man was born to be a husband. Born to be a father. Born to head a family.

He makes eye contact with me as I sit with JJ on a blanket on the grass.

And I see it. It's clear as day.

Love.

I watch as he then takes Fin's hand and leads him to the little pond. It's not big, it's not deep, but it's enough to show him how to skim stones.

Because that's exactly what he does.

I have to hold in the sob that's bursting to escape.

For the first time since I hatched my plan, guilt courses through me. The end is now in sight, but I'm not sure it's the ending I want anymore.

CHAPTER THIRTY-ONE

JAINE

The Hudson Dusters' HQ, Manhattan, New York

"AND HERE I THOUGHT YOU AND I WERE GOING TO LIVE THE happily ever after, Jaine." Aidan smirks at me, but from across the table this time. Eoin has insisted that I sit by his right-hand side.

He tenses beside me at the thought of his cousin laying so much as one finger on me. I can't see his face, but Aidan's reaction tells me all I need to know.

"Green's not your color, cousin," he quips with a smile.

Aidan needs to quit while he's ahead. Eoin may not end his life because he's family, but it doesn't mean he won't spill his blood.

Jessie laugh-snorts. Standing, she crosses the room barefoot to swing the Newton's Cradle into action.

Aidan's testing Eoin's patience and pushing his boundaries. It's meant in jest, but Eoin's operating on a short fuse. Little JJ has started teething in earnest, and for the past few days, he's been screaming the place down twenty-four-seven. It's resulted in several sleepless nights. And what I've discovered is that Eoin O'Connell doesn't cope well with abstinence.

Self-imposed or otherwise.

He wants to fuck daily. Several times a day. But he's currently feeling the effects of the many sexless evenings. While being totally understanding, he's become grumpy and reactive at having to do without. I pick up my phone just as Cillian starts to discuss the clubs and hotels side of their business.

Jaine: *Can Dec drop me off at my office after this meeting is finished?*
Eoin: *Dec who? And why are you messaging me when I'm sitting right beside you?*
Jaine: *Because this is a private conversation. Dec. The guy you have tail me on a daily basis.*
Eoin: *I didn't think you'd noticed.*
Jaine: *I miss nothing.*
Eoin: *Obviously. Well, I certainly miss something.*
Jaine: *One track mind?*
Eoin: *Not at all. Just a case of blue balls.*
Jaine: *It takes fifteen minutes to get to my office. Twenty if we take the scenic route.*
Eoin: *What are you suggesting?*
Jaine: *Nothing. Why? What did you think I was suggesting?*
Eoin: *That I fuck you in the back of the SUV.*
Jaine: *How dare you think I would ever suggest such a thing.*
Eoin: *Teasing, evil woman.*

"Any update on the snipers?"

We all turn our attention to Fergal. He's not around so much these days, and no doubt he'll be leaving as soon as this meeting is concluded. Sarah, who seems to have become the Duster equivalent of Mary Poppins, has taken Caoimhe, Fin, *and* JJ to visit with Grandma Roisin.

Now he has two male grandchildren to bond with, Fergal won't want to miss out on any opportunity to start grooming them into becoming perfect little mobsters. I'm sure he will have started the process early on with his own sons. No doubt by reciting aloud the atrocities of what their ancestors had gotten up to over the decades while they were still in the goddamn womb.

"I'm hopeful for an update on the Nevada ones imminently," Dylan answers as he side-glances at me. "I spoke to Ty before the meeting. There's a rumor going around that one of the hitmen is a local. They're still looking into it."

"And the vermin behind the attack at the church, Cill?"

Cillian shakes his head. "Both marksmen were clean, Da. It looks like one was a suicide sniper. He went in knowing the only way he was coming out was in a body bag. The other was just as prepared to die. No doubt their families were handsomely rewarded for their combined efforts despite both being unfruitful, thanks to The Exterminator."

Fergal frowns. It will be giving him sleepless nights knowing his family is under threat.

"And your da, Jessie. How has he been keeping?"

She smiles sweetly at him. They have a close bond. Something he and I will never have. All we share is a mutual tolerance.

"He's fully recovered, thank you for asking, Fergal."

I catch her eye and subtly shake my head, letting her know not to mention that I may be heading to Rising soon, then on to Nevada to meet with Lucifer. I know for a fact that Eoin will throw a hissy fit and insist on going with me. And I can't have that.

Anyway, my plan may have fallen into place by then, and what he wants will no longer matter.

I turn my attention to Dylan. "If Ty discovers something concrete, then you let me know straight away."

"And why would Dylan do that?" Eoin frowns at me.

"Because if either of those two snipers get unearthed, I'll be the one to kill them, that's why."

"You're not going anywhere on your own."

I glare at him. "I'm a big girl, Eoin. I've managed to survive thirty years in this life without your guidance or assistance."

"You're my wife now, Jaine. An O'Connell. And last I heard, we all potentially have targets on our backs. I will not have you put yourself at risk. You're not going anywhere on your own and that's the end of it!"

"I'm my own goddamn person!"

"You're my goddamn person!"

"Jesus Christ." I roll my eyes exaggeratedly. "Are you going to piss on me so everyone knows I'm your property."

"I might."

"Fuck you, asshole!"

"Anytime, Mrs. O'Connell."

I leave it there. There's no point poking him. No one needs Eoin's monster coming out to play, and he won't take much encouragement given the foul mood he's already in. Heads will roll, quite literally, family or not.

In a way, I can understand his protective stance. He thinks I'm a lawyer. Nothing more. He doesn't know what I do in my spare time, even if it is infrequently these days since I'm being tailed more often than not.

I glance around the now silent table, conscious all eyes apart from Dylan's are watching our back and forth with what appears to be amusement. I'm not sure why. There's nothing remotely funny about the seriousness of this situation and the fact that it resulted in Ace's death.

I cut the silence. "Dylan, I meant what I said. The Nevada snipers are mine. Big brother here can go fuck himself if he thinks otherwise. It was my husband they killed. For doing so, my face will be the last thing they see before I personally hand their diseased souls over to the goddamn reaper."

I ANSWER THE PHONE WITHIN THREE RINGS. WHEN SOMEONE CALLS at this time of night, it's not to ask after your health. I sit bolt upright in bed.

"Dylan, what's going on? It's two a.m."

"Jaine. They've picked one of them up."

"The snipers." It's not a question, more a confirmation. "Where is he?"

"He's currently being flown to New York."

"When?"

"He'll be here in around six hours."

"Where?"

"Where Da took you."

"So, underneath Play."

"Yes."

A shiver runs through me, my life flashing in front of my eyes as I think back on my own dalliance with da Duster.

"I'll get Duke to stay with the kids."

"I'll see you there."

A small smile crosses my face. I forgot that Dylan likes to slice and dice these days. He's finally reached his true Duster potential thanks to Jessie's influence and is now as bloodthirsty as the rest of the O'Connell family, although perhaps not as bloodthirsty as his eldest brother.

"And, Dyl?"

"Yeah?"

"No one lays a finger on him until I get there. That dead man walking is all fucking mine."

Play Gentlemen's Club, Manhattan, New York.

It's just gone eight a.m.

Daylight has broken. The familiar cacophony of honking yellow cabs and wailing pig sirens somehow warms the frigid morning air of New York City.

Stepping down from the back of my hog, I type in the code to the parking facility underneath Play Gentlemen's Club. You can tell from the exterior alone that it's a Duster establishment. It screams luxury and wealth while silently warning you that you enter at your own risk. That by simply crossing the threshold, you take your life into your own hands as you've sold your soul to the devil.

The exorbitant membership fee you pay will buy you silence. A personal guarantee that what goes on here stays here. Anyone found guilty of spilling secrets will have their blood spilled in return.

The unluckiest of all may find themselves locked inside a dock-side shipping container with the eldest O'Connell.

I swallow thickly as the unwelcome memory of what I witnessed that day causes a shiver to run down my spine, reminding me that Death himself is Eoin O'Connell's right-hand man.

Ever-present. Watching. Waiting. Collecting. And all on my husband's behalf.

Influential men on both sides of the law come to Play to drink, gamble, and fuck women who aren't their wives or girlfriends.

Many of the females will have a unique look. Many will appear younger than they are. Many will have a sought-after skillset.

It's whatever floats your perverse boat.

Money talks. Anything can be bought here and, potentially, anyone.

On the side, you can also purchase a variety of weapons, and everything is, of course, sprinkled with a generous dusting of cocaine. If that's not your drug of choice, there are plenty more options on offer.

The black matte metal gates swing slowly open, and I ride inside. Dismounting, I make sure they're firmly closed behind me before making my way down the ramp.

The moment I see him, my stomach flips.

It was always a given that Dyl was going to let Eoin know I was on my way. He's dressed all in black. Snug jeans and a fitted sweater that clings to his abs and biceps. Rather than being sated, over time, the physical attraction between us grows stronger.

I can't take my eyes off him, his deadly presence almost commanding me to worship him like some sort of dark god.

I pull up my Softail and yank off my full helmet, swinging my blonde hair free. The biker blood that runs through these veins now shows on the outside and I don't give a damn who can see it. I'm leather-clad from head to toe. The same outfit I wore when we married.

He strides over to me then stops. He looks menacing. Deranged almost. I'm sure it's the prospect of killing and spilling blood that makes him appear so. His monster is surfacing at the welcome smell of death.

His hair is longer.

Mr. Perfect suits the imperfect look.

He's staring at me like he wants to eat me alive.

"Eoin…"

His mouth captures mine before I can say another word. His hand fists my hair as he yanks my head back to suck and bite on my throat.

Marking me. Claiming me.

I groan in appreciation. I want more of his mouth on my skin. Licking. Sucking. Biting. I want those sinful lips all over my fucking body. He devours me once more, kissing me harder than he's ever done. I can taste the desire. The emotion.

The love?

His tongue plunders my mouth as his hands drop to my ass. He growls as he runs them slowly across the smooth black leather before yanking my front against his so his erection rubs deliciously against my clit.

I pull my mouth away. I can't breathe.

I want him.

So. Fucking. Much.

I swallow down the bitter taste of guilt.

Ace knows why I'm doing this as I fill him in on where things stand every day during our morning conversation. When I talk to him like he's still alive and not dead.

The familiar feeling of betrayal still lingers, but I'm accepting of it these days because my own reality is that I'll be delivered my own comeuppance at the precise moment Eoin is served his. That I'll be suitably punished for having inappropriate feelings for him that I neither expected nor asked to have.

And it's no more than I deserve.

"Eoin."

His hot breath is against my ear. "I want to fuck you fast. I want to fuck you hard. I want to fuck you every single way that there is to fuck you and then I want to start at the beginning and do it all over again because you drive me fucking insane, Jaine O'Connell."

I stare up at him with his too long hair and his eyes of flashing green.

So dark. So dangerous.

I lean my forehead against his. "Let's take care of business first, husband."

He likes when I call him that. He's possessive. I am his and he is mine. I realize that's now his mentality.

He nods. Then, taking my hand possessively in his, he leads me to the elevator.

He's turned up here today because he made a vow to God to protect me. He also wants me to know that we're in this together. That we're a team. That he will always be there for me whether I need him to be or not. I know he expects the same in return.

When he chose me, I made a pact with this devil.

CHAPTER THIRTY-TWO

EOIN

Play Gentlemen's Club, Manhattan, New York

We own several disused areas of the New York subway system. The section below Play is perhaps the most depressing of all because there's a constant dripping sound.

Water.

I used to hear it constantly like some sort of auditory hallucination. A non-existent reminder, perhaps of the number of lives I've ended within the confines of this grey concrete tomb.

It's the reason I moved to the docks. Bodies are easier to dispose of at the riverside location. You can also breathe in air that's not permanently laced with the stench of death.

Jaine doesn't look around. She witnessed all this place had to offer firsthand when she went toe to toe with my da. That's not the only reason she doesn't take in her surroundings. It's because her gaze is immediately fixed on the man bound to the chair.

Or should I say boy.

Dylan gave me the heads up. It's the reason I asked him to stay away. To let me handle this unwelcome news with her on my own. We both knew she was going to be disappointed and upset by what she found.

"Abel."

She closes her eyes, evidence of disbelief and regret etched clearly across her face. That Ace was betrayed by one of his own.

A biker.

"I'm sorry, Jaine," he whispers.

She stares at him, then slowly walks across to stand in front of him. He can't be any more than nineteen years old. He's wearing a cut that still looks new.

The Undertakers.

His blonde buzzcut is smattered with blood. Going by the lump on the side of his head, it's obvious he's been clattered by something. Aside from the usual stench of death and Lysol that lingers in this place, the smell of urine is also strong. He's already pissed himself.

She stands there with her head in her hands, looking completely broken. What's going through her mind? Is it to do with Ace? Or is it over what's she's going to have to do here today?

Even a trained murderer like me, a person with numerous killings under his belt, wouldn't find it easy ending the life of someone so young. Someone who's simply made a careless, foolish mistake.

But in our world, we do what we have to do.

With a loud sigh, she crouches down in front of him, and he stares back at her, wide-eyed, confused, and disorientated.

"You gave him a ride to the Whisperers' compound, didn't you?"

He nods.

"Do you know who was behind it?"

"The Colombians. I… I don't know any more than that, Jaine. Honest I don't. I just picked him up from behind the diner and then dropped him back there after. He wore a helmet the whole time. He didn't speak, and I didn't see his face."

He starts sobbing, tears and snot running down his young face.

"Why the hell did you do it, Abel?" She runs her hand through her hair in desperate frustration.

She won't want to do what she has to, but she has no choice.

"They pulled me aside. They threatened to kill my folks and traffick my baby sisters if I didn't do their bidding or if I told anyone. I didn't know what else to do, Jaine. I thought he'd just fire some warning shots when we got to Ghost's place. I didn't think he was going to point the trigger at Ace."

She closes her eyes tightly when he mentions his name, regret now replaced by raw pain. She's letting her guard down and showing her emotions because no one's here to see.

It's just me and this dead boy walking.

Eventually, she speaks. "You see any faces?"

He shakes his head. "Nothing. They wore balaclavas the entire time. I only knew it was them because of their accents. Their type used to come calling at the clubhouse regularly when Reaper was prez."

"Is there anything else you can tell me, Abel?"

Before she ends his life.

The words aren't spoken aloud, but we all know they're silently implied.

He sniffs. "Rumor has it they've been threatening some of the other brothers with the same thing. I don't know if they'll react or not. But…. but family's family, Jaine. No one's going to just stand by and watch something happen to their loved ones," he sobs.

She exhales slowly. "I understand that, Abel. I also understand that you did what you did in order to protect your family. But your actions left my youngest without a daddy at only three months old." Her voice breaks.

"I'm so sorry, Jaine."

She stands up straight and stares down at the crying boy with his downturned face, his upset the only sound apart from dripping water.

When she finally speaks, her voice is contained. She knows she has to be strong for both their sakes. "You patched in now?"

He nods without looking up.

"Then you know the rules, Abel. That you have to live and die by the patch that you swore your allegiance to. It's the way it is. The way it's always been. The way it always will be. There are no exceptions. The rules apply to all of us. You and I both know that." She speaks quietly but firmly.

He nods as he starts crying in earnest. "But… my family… Jaine."

She places a comforting hand on the shoulder of the young boy who, in part, was responsible for Ace's death.

She's forgiving him.

"They will be kept safe and provided for. Nothing will happen to them. I give you my word on that, and I stand by my word. Always."

He nods.

"You're a man, Abel. A young one, but still a grown man. You knew what you were doing. I respect that you did what you did for your family, but I can't condone the fact that you betrayed your club and your brothers. That your actions resulted in the death of another biker. If you'd told us, we could have helped. But you made the choice to go it alone. So while I can't grant you absolution, I can grant you a quick redemption."

He looks up and watches as she approaches the wheeled trolley holding the vast array of torture devices that our Paddy liked to put to use on a daily basis. It's my thinking none of those will be needed today.

Just one.

She picks up a flick knife.

Simple. Silver. Steel.

And then she walks over and stands behind him.

He knows this is it. That today, Jaine is his judge, jury, and executioner. He tilts his own head back, his lips quivering in fear. Their eyes connect and she holds his gaze. He nods in acceptance, and she returns it in silent response. I then watch my wife as she cuts the throat of a teenage boy.

Because he was disloyal to his club. Because he betrayed his brothers. Because he hurt her family.

Because, even though he didn't pull the trigger, he killed Ace.

His body tenses briefly as his blood spills, and then he's still. Dripping is the only sound once more.

Water. Blood.

She walks back around and stares down at him as he sits there in a pool of his own lifeblood and bodily fluids.

I pass her a towel. She uses it to wipe her hands and the blade before passing it back. She doesn't look at me. She hasn't made eye contact the entire time we've been down here. I watch as she puts the knife in the front pocket of his cut. A gesture from one biker to another. A weapon for him to use in his next life.

"Send him back to Nevada. He died for his family. And for that, he's at least earned them the right to have a grave to mourn him at."

I stay where I am as she leaves. I hear the elevator door open then close. I don't look at her. I don't follow her.

She needs time to grieve. For Ace still, but also for young Abel.

She needs time to come to terms with what she's had to do here today. She knows if she had been in his position, she may well have done the same thing.

Family is all that matters.

And today, he's lost his life because he put his family ahead of his brothers and his patch.

Abel's life may be over, but for Jaine, his death marks only the beginning. She'll forever have to wear his invisible blood on her hands. She'll also have to carry the heavy burden of associated guilt. Ending his life will have brought her no satisfaction nor a sense of justice. It will just have brought her more pain.

She's done what she had to do. She had no choice, and I now realize that in every way, she's my equal.

My Ma Duster and my fucking queen.

The Hudson Dusters' HQ, Manhattan, New York

It's been a week since Jaine took the life of the young biker. She's kept to herself during that time. She's been coming to terms with it. Dealing with it in her own way.

The mood is morose as we sit around the circular table.

I glance at Jessie. She's been quiet of late, which is unlike her, and the Newton's Cradle has also been deathly silent. Normally, I would rejoice, but it would be a shallow victory. Her eyes are red-rimmed because a young boy from her hometown has had to lose his life for protecting what he loved most.

His family.

Her sister, Bailey, is beside herself. He was her school friend. A lad she'd known her whole life.

But the boy almost cost them their own father. Would they rather he lived and their da died because the grim reaper wanted a soul? It was one or the other.

In my opinion, Jaine did the right thing. In our life, if we don't abide by the rules, then where will it all end? We can't choose when to apply them or who to apply them to. They must be applied consistently, no matter how difficult that may be at times. Had it been a forty-year-old man that had surrendered his life to Jaine's blade, would they have been feeling such guilt? Probably not.

The boy protected his family the way he thought best. It was his choice to make.

Unfortunately for him, a biker died as a result, and another was gravely injured. Abel knew what would happen if the truth ever came out. He was simply living on borrowed time.

Who are we to judge if it was the correct decision that he made? None of us will ever know what the outcome would have been had he chosen the alternative path. There was no guarantee the threats made against his family wouldn't have been carried out had he not done the Colombians' bidding. It's not like they could have been protected twenty-four-seven.

In the end, he sacrificed his life for theirs. It was his to do with as he wished.

The unfortunate reality is now his parents will have to spend the rest of their lives without their son. His brothers and sisters without their sibling.

But that's a daily occurrence in our world. When you join our ranks, while you're handsomely paid, you're signing yourself up to live the remainder of your life day by day. We make a lot of widows and create a lot of orphans in this game. Only the individual can decide if the rewards outweigh the risks.

There's a knock on the door.

Candice walks in. She's dropped the sour look. She's admitted defeat. She knows I belong to Jaine.

"Your wife's here."

I nod.

Seconds later, Jaine enters the room. Another pantsuit. This time dark grey. She looks good. It's not really an appropriate time, but my dick twitches at the sight of her. It's been a while, and I've fucking missed her.

Jessie immediately gets up to hug her. Jaine hugs her back. They're united in their biker grief, both families having been betrayed by the same brother.

"How are you, Jaine?" My da poses the question.

I frown as I look at him. He's aging in front of my eyes. This life is starting to take its toll on him. He needs to step down.

And now I have Jaine by my side, I'm more than equipped to take on the role of Da Duster.

She smiles at him. "I'm doing okay, thank you, Fergal. I just needed a moment to gather my thoughts and clear my head."

She's been appreciative of my ma and da's help with both children this week, when her grief blew up and she needed some space and time out.

I wanted to be there for her. But it was neither appropriate nor what she needed. She can't smile and play happy families with a new husband when she's still mourning the death of the previous one.

She takes her seat beside me and places her briefcase on the table. Her hand then reaches down to squeeze my thigh. It's an acknowledgement. She realizes I wanted to be there for her, but I accepted that this was something she had to do alone. With just one touch, she's letting me know she's grateful I gave her the space and time she needed.

She then looks around the table.

"We have to find them." Her firm tone contrasts the utter silence.

"Find who?" Dylan asks.

Jaine stands and starts to slowly pace the floor. "The faction behind this. According to Abel, the Colombians are blackmailing brothers by threatening their families. His life ended because of poor choices. Choices he made because he didn't know what else to do. How many others are they poisoning the minds of? How many others don't know what else to do? We can't just assume this is confined to the MCs."

"What are you suggesting, Jaine?" I frown at her.

"That we need to explain to our people what to do if they're approached. And if they already have been, then we need to encourage them to step forward so we can deal with this together and head on. If we don't, Abel won't be the only casualty. Who knows, maybe this faction's plan is to divide and conquer. Whatever the fuck mind games they're playing, we need to be one step ahead, and that starts with clear lines of communication."

I nod. She's right. We seldom call meetings, but maybe we need to share this threat with our high rankers and have them filter it down the Duster masses. Perhaps she could stand by my side as I relay the news. It's high time our union was formally announced to the rest of the Duster organization.

"We'll call a meeting with the top tier."

She nods. "Meanwhile, I'll speak with Rod, Delaney, and Clay. Jessie, Dylan." She looks at them in turn. "You speak with Lucifer and Ty. Tell them they need to put on a united front and call church for all three MCs. This affects Colton as a town, not just their own individual clubs. And tell them no bickering or pissing up the wall contests. Now is not the goddamn time."

"On it, partner." Jessie salutes her, adding that annoying smirk of hers.

I don't say anything as she'll only make some smug, smart-mouthed comment, but it's good to see the old Jessie resurface.

It's my turn to speak.

"The key parties behind this faction have remained invisible for quite some time, so it's clear this isn't their first rodeo. If we are able to identify them, it's my guess they won't be easy to take down. With that in mind, when unearthed, can we rely on The Exterminator to take care of business personally if required."

Jaine stares at me, her eyes defiant and her chin tilted. "I'm sure the sniper will be only too happy to oblige."

CHAPTER THIRTY-THREE

JAINE

Eoin's Apartment, Hudson Yards, New York

I'VE TURNED UP UNANNOUNCED. I'VE HAD DEC BRING ME AND asked him not to pre-warn Eoin. Has he told him? I guess I'll never know. It's not like he'll tell me even if he has. I think that Dec's one of Eoin's own trusted high rankers, so he'll follow his boss's orders, not mine.

He's been tasked with tailing me to keep me out of trouble. What Eoin doesn't realize is that I don't need anyone to keep me safe. I've been keeping *me* safe for years. It's other people that need to be protected from my engraved bullets.

It's been ten days since I took Abel's life. I've killed hundreds in my time. His death is the only one that will forever weigh on my conscience because at his age and given the same set of circumstances, I would have done exactly the same thing. I would also have expected the same end result had I been found out. I would never have been naïve enough to think otherwise.

But knowing that doesn't make it any easier to process.

He was so young. Too young. His whole life ahead of him. What happened to Ace was unintentional on Abel's part, but it still happened.

Ace is dead.

And Abel might as well have pulled the trigger himself for the part he played.

He made a foolish decision, and he paid the ultimate price.

What his death has done is given me even more incentive to track these goddamn fuckers down. I'm no longer just doing it for Ace. I'm doing it for Abel too now.

I stare at the grey door. It looks like any other, but it's my guessing it's everything proof to safeguard the future Irish king. I've never been to Eoin O'Connell's apartment. Dec had to put the relevant codes in for the building entrance and also for the elevator.

Any shared evenings have always been spent at my place.

When I messaged earlier, I could tell from his underlying tone that he wanted to see me. Not just for fucking, but to spend time together like we're a regular couple.

But we're not. We're a pair of cold-blooded murderers.

I know he wants us to spend the night together. That he has done for some time. That he wants us to take things to the next level.

Spend the night together.

Move in together.

Play happy families together.

Live the happily ever after together.

If only he knew my plan. He will do soon enough.

He's never asked why I've never invited him to stay over, and he's way too proud to have invited himself. I don't think he's ever spent the night with any female.

Not even Molly.

I think his whole life it really has been a case of 'wham bam thank you, ma'am'. That he's always been way too selfish to ever share any part of himself. That he's always just taken what he wanted then left once he's had his fill before moving on to his next willing victim.

Until now. Until me.

Our relationship has evolved into something way beyond physical. It's what I wanted, and even though we've reached this stage more slowly than I thought we would, it still feels like we've reached it way too soon.

Because the tables have turned. It's now me who wants to have my cake and eat it. That I'm the one being the glutton. I'm trying to cram as much of Eoin O'Connell in as I can.

My plan will come to fruition imminently because he's getting impatient that our relationship isn't moving forward quickly enough, and there's only one reason for that.

The signs are all there.

In this outlaw game of chess that he's insisted on playing, I'm about to say one word.

Checkmate.

And five short months of intense intimacy doesn't feel anywhere near long enough. Not after two years' worth of push and pull foreplay. My plan now comes with a guaranteed blowback, and I guess I deserve nothing less. Two wrongs don't make a right. I never realized how true that was until now, but it's way too late to back out.

I knock on the grey door. He'll have security. He'll know it's me, as will his brother. Dylan has surveillance on all the Duster properties, including their own private homes. Can he see me standing outside Eoin's apartment? Will his big brother appreciate me turning up at his home unannounced? I guess I'm about to find out.

The door opens.

He's shirtless, and he's obviously just showered as his hair is mussed and wet.

This dark lord is truly fucking breathtaking.

My eyes drift over the map of ink he wears on a lean chiseled torso that's on full and welcome display. They then sink lower to take in the pair of grey sweatpants that are hanging dangerously low on his slim hips, deliberately positioned to show off the start of the toned V that instantly captures your attention then drags your gaze downward. The material is doing nothing at all to disguise the sheer size of the appendage that lurks just underneath.

"Jaine."

He raises one eyebrow, a small smile tugging on his lips at my blatant ogling.

Did he expect me?

If the visual I've been greeted with is because he didn't, then I'm fucking glad I turned up unannounced. I've never seen him this dressed down before. Dressed down looks good on him.

Too fucking good.

Let's be honest, nothing would ever not look good on Eoin O'Connell. He really is one hot as fuck mobster.

And he's my mobster.

For now.

I walk past and step inside. I expected his home to be cool and clinical, with everything immaculate and perfectly positioned. It's quite the opposite. The open-plan living space is calm and relaxing in warm shades of creams and browns and with throws and cushions scattered welcomingly around to encourage you to make yourself right at home.

It's an inviting space.

I pause, frowning inwardly.

There's so much about him that I don't know. That I want to know.

But that I never will know.

I'm wearing a tank top and combats. Nothing underneath. I pull the tank over my head and kick off my high tops. The only clothing that remains between us is his sweats and my combats.

"Fuck me."

His nostrils flare and his eyes darken as he immediately picks me up bridal style.

"Not your bedroom."

He frowns down at me as he walks.

"You're not fucking me in the same bed you fucked her in."

I'm jealous that he fucked her and that she had access to something that's mine, even if only temporarily.

He smirks, his conceited self no doubt savoring my possessive tone.

"Do you want me to throw the bed on the bonfire and get a new one?"

"That's exactly what I want. You're mine."

He kicks open a door. A bedroom. Is it a guest one? He throws me on top of the bed then stands back with his hands slung low on his hips.

It's obviously because he wants me to admire him some more. He knows he looks good. I lick my lips. I want to lick his body.

Every. Perfect. Fucking. Inch.

"I'm yours. Is that right, Jaine?" A cocky smile plays on his lips.

I rest on my elbows as I stare up at him with one eyebrow raised. "That's exactly right. I have a marriage license that says just that. So, why don't you quit standing there staring and help yourself to those conjugal rights of yours?"

I've pressed the button. With a low growl, he leans forward and his scent washes over me. Spicy cologne mixed with his personal take on dark and dangerous.

I want to inhale it exaggeratedly.

Bottle it, keep it, and never forget it.

But I will.

Strong hands grip my waist as he drags me down the bed towards him.

"Going by your mouthy demands, I'm guessing you've missed my cock, Mrs. O'Connell. Am I right?"

I nod, now too breathless to speak.

"And I'm also guessing that you've missed my fingers marking that pretty little neck of yours."

I nod again, then groan as his hand circles my throat, squeezing until I can't breathe before slowly releasing. Using his other hand, he unbuttons my pants and yanks them down my legs before quickly discarding his own.

"On all fours."

I do as he asks, the bed dipping when he joins me.

Running the blunt head of his shaft through my slickness, he immediately thrusts inside. No time to prepare. I whine as I'm suddenly filled with his dick. One hand grips my hip and the other pushes my upper torso against the sheets as he begins to fuck me into oblivion.

Hard. Fast. Deep.

Perfect.

"I swear to God that weapon of mass destruction between your legs is rearranging my insides."

"Flattery won't get you anywhere, wife. You asked for my cock. You're getting my cock. We made a deal. You take. You give. I'm sure you wouldn't want me to go easy on you."

He slaps me on the ass as he fucks me so hard, I have to brace myself against the wall.

"Is that all you've got, husband?"

I whine in pain as his dick bottoms out, but it instantly turns to mewls of pleasure as he expertly lifts my hips and gives me what I need by railing my sweet spot over and over. He orchestrates my body so fucking well. Welcome waves of pleasure spiral through me, but he never lets up. He pounds into me like a machine, his sweat dripping down and mixing with my own as he sucks and bites on my flesh anywhere he can so he can mark me for the world to see.

I clench around him, and I'm rewarded with another slap on the ass.

"I decide when I come, not you," he growls against my ear.

I arch my back and push back, making him go even deeper before clenching around him once more."

"Disobedient, evil woman."

His breath is hot as he bites my shoulder for not doing as I'm told.

He then thrusts deeper. Too deep. I shatter once more. My walls tighten, claiming that beautiful cock of his as mine. He curses me under his breath when I break his perfect stride, his strokes becoming erratic before he spills deep inside me.

I ache all over. I'm bruised all over. And he'll be ready to go again in less than ten minutes.

Any sane woman would have had enough after just one round, but it seems I'm just as insane as him.

Because all I want is more.

CHAPTER THIRTY-FOUR

EOIN

Eoin's Apartment, Hudson Yards, New York

It's an alien feeling to be lying in my apartment and in my bed with a female draped over me, her fingers trailing gently across my chest.

Not just any female. My wife.

To me, beds are useful for two things. Fucking and sleeping. The latter I've always done alone. I've never been tactile. Never cuddled. I've never taken part in pillow talk either.

I fuck. Extremely well, the same as I do everything else in life. I make sure my partner comes several times, and I only claim my release when they're beyond physical exhaustion and no longer of any use to me.

What Jaine doesn't realize is that none of that has ever taken place in my home. Always theirs. No woman has ever been invited back here. My apartment is my sanctuary. I share it with no one. I've never wanted to until now. Until her.

"How many women have you slept with?"

I frown inwardly in surprise more than anything else. We never share anything of a personal nature. Why now? Is she finally ready to take our relationship to the next level?

Her head is resting on my shoulder. She doesn't stop her caressing hand movement. She's asked the question like it's an everyday run-of-the-mill thing to query. In her biker world maybe it is. I'm used to Jaine's lack of airs and graces now.

"None."

"Okay, let me rephrase that. How many women have you fucked?"

"Why would you want to know that?" I frown outwardly, even though she can't see me.

She shrugs. "I'm just curious. I heard rumors that you O'Connell brothers had slept with most of the single women in Manhattan and quite a lot of the married ones too."

I exhale. I'm not sure how to answer. Truthfully is probably best.

"Hundreds."

"One hundred? Two?"

"Several."

"So, three figures?"

"Perhaps."

"Right."

Her hand stops briefly. Does that number bother her? I'm not sure what she expected. I'm thirty-eight years old. I've sown my wild oats countless times over the years before finally becoming bored and reducing my harem down to a handful of pre-selected women, all of whom have signed watertight NDAs. Even Candice. Even Molly.

All of them apart from her.

"And what about you?"

"What about me?"

"Your number."

She chuckles loudly. "Oh, it's nothing impressive, Mr. O'Connell, I can assure you of that."

"So, not hundreds."

She chuckles again. I like the sound. It's not forced or fake, but then that's one thing Jaine could never be accused of being.

"I may be a biker, but I'm not a cum slut."

"Sorry. I wasn't insinuating that you…"

"Four."

I frown again. Is she saying what I think she is?

"So Ace, Razr, Padraig, and me."

"You sound disappointed that it's not some big fancy number."

"Not at all. I'm just surprised."

"That I don't have a professional mattress attached to my back after all?"

It's my turn to chuckle. I can't help it. "I'm sorry about that, Jaine. It was wrong that we allowed Molly to insinuate such things."

She shrugs. "I'm a big girl. I'm also thick-skinned. I was more concerned that she might spread malicious rumors and my clients might start approaching me over these other professional services I'd been holding out on."

We both laugh before a comfortable silence resumes once more.

"Tell me about them, Jaine. Your past relationships."

"What do you want to know?"

I shrug. "Whatever you feel comfortable telling me."

There's a pause.

After all this time, is she finally going to let me in?

"Well, Ace was my first. I was eighteen. He was the son of the prez of the Angels, so all the girls my age were after him. We were best friends. We had been since I was seven years old. I was so fucking in love with him."

There's a pause. I'm fully aware that it's grief related.

"I thought he slept with me then immediately slept with someone else. That shit stung so badly I ran from my hometown and never looked back."

"And did he sleep with someone else?"

"No."

"He never tried to explain?"

"He did, but I wasn't prepared to listen. We lost ten years as a result."

I refuse to let her get more melancholy, so I move straight on. "Then you went to Yale and met our Paddy."

"I did. Mr. Gift of the Irish Gab himself." She chuckles, but it quickly evaporates. "We dated for three months, then he cheated on me."

Another potential melancholy moment. I move on again. "And then?"

"And then I finished law school, started JAL, and met Delaney. We were together for four years. My pop was killed by the Bratva. I returned to Rising, reconnected with Ace and Irish. Got pregnant. Then I returned to New York where you proceeded to chase me out of town."

"In a nutshell."

"In a nutshell. You know the rest."

"So, the first time you slept with my brother was when you reconnected."

"Yes."

"And you fell pregnant."

"Yes. Anything else?"

"Your song with Padraig. It was played at the church at Cillian and Sarah's wedding. Remind me. What is it?"

"*Kiss Me* by Ed Sheeran."

"And why did you choose it?"

"I didn't. Irish did. Around the time I got pregnant with Fin."

"And your song with Ace?"

"*Creep* by Radiohead."

"Why that choice?"

"Jesus Christ. Maybe you should become a goddamn lawyer."

I ignore her barb. "Why that choice?" I repeat.

She shrugs. "I was an ugly duckling growing up. I was skinny with zero shape. I wore glasses. I had train track braces. I also liked guns and practiced MMA several times a week at my pop's insistence. I was different from the other girls. Aside from having a bedroom that was pink and fluffy, I was never a girly girl. I was a classic tomboy. I guess in many ways I still am, hence the tank tops and combats. It's what I feel most comfortable in. Back then, the kids my age thought me a creep and a weirdo, hence the song choice. I guess rather than try to hide my freak, I just flew the flag as high as I could and embraced it."

"But he loved you? Ace? Regardless of the way you were and how you looked?"

"I guess he did."

"And Paddy?"

She shrugs again. "Who knows? I was still a creep and a weirdo when I met him. I never was sure what he saw in me because even back then he was turning every female head. Did he love me? You tell me. Do you cheat on someone you love?"

"Razr?"

"Delaney and I fell into a relationship at a time when we both just desperately needed someone. That was our priority, I guess.

Being there for each other. We never felt the need to share a song. You done interrogating me now?"

"I'm just trying to understand you."

"There's nothing much to understand. I grew up around an MC compound. My pop was their lawyer and I followed in his footsteps. That's about it."

I'm sure there's more to her than what she's just summarized, but I leave it for now. It's one step forward. I don't want to risk taking two steps back by pushing her too hard. We've got the rest of our lives together for me to glean the finer details. I want to know everything there is to know about my headstrong wife.

"What's our song?"

There's a pause. I've asked a question she doesn't wish to answer.

"We don't have one." Her voice is quiet, the guilt evident.

Am I disappointed? I'm not sure. She clearly thinks me undeserving of a song. That nothing springs to mind because I don't inspire anything like that in her.

I'm not sure how I feel about that given how much she inspires in me.

"And why is that?"

"I guess because you and I didn't start off in a conventional way. There was no real relationship beforehand. Well, apart from an extremely toxic one."

I pause. "And what do you…"

"Do you want us to have a song?" she interjects. She clearly doesn't wish to discuss our relationship. I want to know if she sees us as conventional now. If she ever will. Or will she forever think of us as toxic?

I pause again as I consider what she's asked. "I think I'd like that."

There's a shared silence. Is she thinking what I am? About what having a song together actually means? It's not something you share with just anyone. A special song is something you hear that makes you instantly think of the other person.

Your person.

I've never shared one with a woman. Aside from the physical act of sex, I've never shared any part of myself with any female before now.

"Do you want me to run my choice past you or are you okay with letting me decide?"

"I trust you to pick the correct song."

"You trust me." Her tone is quiet, almost hesitant.

"Yes, Jaine. I trust you."

She pauses, no doubt to digest what I've just said. What it's silently implying. That I trust her, and I'm not only referring to a simple song choice.

"So, tell me about you."

It's my turn to shrug. "I've been groomed for the Da Duster role since I took my first breath."

"And there's no pattern to your madness, it was simply inherited from your da."

I chuckle. "That's correct."

"Women?"

"My first fuck was when I was thirteen, and my first kill was a week later. And before you ask, it wasn't the girl I fucked that I killed."

She snickers. "Who was this girl?"

"She was an escort. My da thought it best to get my first sexual experience out of the way so I could focus on my duties. He chose someone who knew exactly what to do with a post-pubescent boy."

"How very Dusterly of him."

I chuckle again. I can't help myself. She does the same in response.

"Does it bother you?" I ask.

"What?"

"That I've been with so many women."

"No."

She answers too quickly.

"Does it bother you that I've fucked your brother?"

"No."

That was a lie. I don't wish to be reminded of the fact that she fucked my brother. Or Razr. Or Ace.

There's a pause.

"Did you love any of those women?" she asks.

"No." My response is immediate. It's true. I didn't.

"So, they fell in love with your O'Connell charms, but it was never reciprocated."

"They didn't love me either."

She stops her hand movement. I immediately miss it.

"What do you mean?" She glances up at me.

I shrug. "No woman has ever told me they love me."

She frowns. "Not one?"

"No."

"Not even Molly?"

I shake my head.

There's a pause. Does she feel bad on my behalf once more that for whatever reason I'm not deserving of love?

That I'm clearly unlovable?

Her hand movement resumes, and I'm content once more.

"Most were with me because of who I am. Some perhaps had their sights set on being the next Ma Duster. Others may have wanted access to the luxurious lifestyle I could afford them. Some may just have been curious about what it was like to be fucked by a mobster."

"So you were just using them for sex."

"Correction. We were just using each other for sex."

"That's…."

"Shallow?"

"I was going to say sad."

Maybe she's right. Maybe it was sad. But it was all I'd ever known, so it was all I'd ever come to expect. I never really thought about it before now. That I was simply using others and in return being used myself.

"From my experience, most people take what they want from relationships, whether that be sex, companionship, or anything else."

She exhales slowly as her fingers slowly skim down my abs before wrapping themselves around my semi-hard cock. I guess my first ever pillow talk is at an end. That Jaine's now going to take what she wants from *this* relationship.

In a way, I'm disappointed. She didn't ask more about me because she has no wish to know more.

Does she not want to scratch the surface? Find out what makes me tick as a person? It makes me feel quite unimportant. That she's pretending to be interested in me when, deep down, she's not.

If my own wife's not interested in getting to know me, then who ever will be?

No one?

I swallow down the disappointment. Maybe after five months, this is all I should expect.

Was this all Ace got from her?

I suspect not. It was clear he was always front and center in her life whereas I appear to be more of an afterthought.

I watch as she strokes my dick to life while her mouth licks and bites down my torso, tracking the path of her fingers. I grunt my approval when her little pink tongue flicks out to lap up the bead of pre-cum that's formed on the tip.

Smiling at me, she sucks it into her mouth before releasing it with a loud pop. I yank her head back by the hair.

"If you want my cock, you can have it, Mrs. O'Connell. But in return, I will make you gag on every last inch. Now, open wide."

She does as she's told and parts her pouty lips. Fisting her hair in both hands, I hold her head steady, then thrust into her waiting mouth.

"Suck it. Don't play with it."

Her mouth feels like a tight vacuum around my shaft, its sole aim to suck me dry.

I fuck her hard. Fast. Deep. She chokes and gags, but she takes everything I have to give.

"If you want my cum, you'll have to work harder for it than that, wife."

She smirks in response, then proceeds to run her tongue up my entire length like it's a fucking popsicle before taking the whole thing in her mouth and squeezing my balls. My eyes roll to the back of my head. I've been sucked off more times than I can count, but she's got it down to a fine art.

"That. Fucking. Mouth." I hiss as my balls instantly tighten.

I yank her head back. She's not getting my cum just yet. Her eyes are watering. A mixture of saliva and precum dribbles down her chin, which she wipes off with the back of her hand.

"There's only one thing I enjoy more than having that cussing little mouth of yours wrapped around my dick and that's having your tight little pussy strangling it."

Pulling her forward so she's straddling my hips, I connect our mouths. I need to taste myself on her tongue.

"I want to come down your throat, Jaine. But I also want to fuck you. Decisions, decisions." I smirk against her lips.

My hand circles her throat as the other lines up my cock, then I thrust into her.

"Pussy wins," I whisper in her ear.

I sink deep. She whines her appreciation as I pull her hips down to meet mine. She's small. If my cock were any thicker, it wouldn't fucking fit.

I watch as she grinds on my dick, using my body to chase down her pleasure. She's a vision. The smattering of scars she wears just adds to her perfection, letting me know she's lived a fucked-up life and survived.

That she can live in my world, stand at my side, and survive.

Her walls tighten around my cock, her movements now erratic. She's getting close. I'm not done with her yet.

I will never be fucking done with her.

Yanking her head forward, I connect our mouths once more before flipping her onto her back. Pushing her knees back, I admire her pink folds that are glistening with her arousal and screaming out for more cock.

Fisting my shaft, I coat my length in her slickness before thrusting deep. She grimaces in pain as I bottom out once more, her expression quickly changing to one of pleasure when I angle her slim hips and nail her sweet spot.

Her body is singing. I orchestrate it so fucking well.

Her walls tighten once more, her pussy trapping me like a vice.

"More," she whines.

"Greedy woman," I whisper in her ear.

Then I give her exactly what she's begging for. More. I fuck her so hard she has to brace herself against the wall, and I watch as she comes once, twice, three times in quick succession.

"Eoin." She's ruined. I've fucking destroyed her.

"Yes, Jaine," I hiss as I continue to piston into her.

"Come with me."

Her nails scratch at my thighs as her walls convulse around me once more, strangling my cock just fucking perfectly. My own release claws at the base of my spine as I let her tight pussy swallow my entire length. I growl at the intensity of the sensations as the first strokes of pleasure cause my cum to start spilling deep inside her.

Exactly where it belongs.

Coating her. Claiming her. Making her mine.

She winces when I eventually pull out of her tender flesh before kneeling in front of her.

"Show me."

"No. Neanderthal."

"Show. Me."

I look at her as she lays there spent and used with my covers twisted around her then watch as she spreads her legs farther apart to let me witness my cum leak from her swollen pussy onto the sheets.

It's right then that the reality of the situation hits me.

This is no infatuation. Neither is it a simple case of wanting what I can't have.

Jaine will forever be my kryptonite because I love her.

CHAPTER THIRTY-FIVE

JAINE

Eoin's Apartment, Hudson Yards, New York

DAWN WILL BREAK SOON, AND WHEN IT DOES, I'LL FINALLY HAVE spent the entire night, but there's been no sleeping involved.

Bruised. Sated. Content. I feel all of them.

We lie there with our exhausted limbs tangled together. My head rests on his chest and he places a soft kiss on top.

Things have changed between us, and I know why. It was only ever a matter of time. It's been building for months. Some could argue for years.

In silent response to his affectionate gesture, I place a light kiss on his chest while inhaling the scent of spicy cologne, clean sweat, and raw masculinity. I then trace the outline of one of his tattoos.

He has several. As many as Ace.

But he doesn't have a J behind his left ear or a PJ over his heart because he's not mine. He was never going to be mine. He can't ever be mine.

So, my initials will never brand his skin.

"Jaine."

His voice is gentle, which is unlike him. Eoin O'Connell doesn't really do gentle unless it's with either Fin or JJ. He cares about JJ now. He's spent a lot of time bonding with him recently, and I know my little boy has grown to love him.

But there are some things more important than love.

Some may call it revenge. I call it justice.

"Yes?"

Time passes. He's thinking about what he's going to say. How he's going to phrase it. I already know what it is. I can *feel* it wrapped around me, infused with his darkness.

He may fuck me hard. He may fuck me painfully. But it's all about me now. It's no longer about him.

"I love you."

And there it is.

Three. Little. Words.

Words that mean so much to the person saying them. Words that represent their hopes and dreams for a future together, and of two souls becoming forever intertwined. Words that leave them feeling exposed and vulnerable until they're returned.

Words that can mean absolutely nothing to the person they're being said to. Words that, once spoken aloud, simply represent just another part of the past.

I lie there in silence. I know he's hoping I'll reciprocate.

I won't. Because this is it. The time has come to draw a line under it. I hatched my plan in a split second in Fergal's office that day, and it worked.

Maybe too well. Maybe too quickly.

Definitely too quickly.

For months, I've been holding back from him. For months, I've been keeping him at a safe distance and pushing him away. I could sense his frustrations and I deliberately let them build.

Then tonight, I gave him what I had to to seal the deal once and for all.

False hope. A sign that I was ready to move forward with him.

But I'm not ready. I will never be ready. I can't ever be ready.

Letting him in after all this time was the final piece of the jigsaw. What it took to push his feelings over the line.

And now here we are.

But letting him in was also my own personal blowback, because having done so, with my plan accomplished, I now need to let him go.

Truth. Honesty. Trust. He gave me all three.

He then gave me a fourth. Love.

While all the time I was setting a trap.

Am I glad I did it? Yes. He and I were on a promise.

No. Because I'm not sure I'll ever be able to rid myself of the guilt. That he's never been loved, that he clearly thinks himself unlovable and even perhaps unworthy. That I'm about to hammer both home.

That despite all the women and all the relationships, he's never once had those words said to him. That he's never experienced the overwhelming rush of emotion that comes from hearing them fall from the mouth of the person you love.

Three little words. And what he wants more than anything in the world is to hear them from me.

But he won't. He never will.

Sad. That the man who, on the surface, looks like he has it all really has nothing.

That he's been surrounded by so much and so many, but he's

simply been used, his life on the surface appearing so full but underneath the façade is stark and echoingly empty.

That all he has is worthless and immaterial.

Money. Possessions. Power.

What does any of that matter when you're alone? When you have no one to share any of it with. When, like Ace, you could be dead tomorrow.

Guilt. When I realize how difficult it must have been for him to say those words aloud. Words they refer to as little when they're, in fact, quite the opposite. They're the biggest words you will ever say out loud in front of another person.

The most important. The most exposing. Potentially, the most damaging.

Words that can make you or break you. The thumb up or thumb down resting solely in the hands of that other person. Of the person you love. Your person. A person who may or may not love you in return. Words that Eoin O'Connell won't have said before. Words he may never repeat again for fear of further rejection.

He's sacrificed his heart to me by saying them aloud. He's made himself weak. He's made himself vulnerable. He's also just made his final move in the game he and I have been playing for over two years because he trusts me to do the right thing with his heart.

But I won't. His trust is misplaced and always has been.

I pause before I respond. There's no rush. Neither my sadness or my guilt will see me deviate from my laid-out plan.

"I don't have three words for you, Eoin. I only have one."

He tenses beneath me. "And that is?"

"Karma."

CHAPTER THIRTY-SIX

EOIN

Eoin's Apartment, Hudson Yards, New York

In silence, she stands, gets dressed, and leaves as I lie there watching her.

With her scent all over me and the echoes of her cries of pleasure still ringing in my ears, I let my harsh reality sink in.

I've been fucking played.

You will pay for this. Not the Dusters. You personally. They say revenge is a dish best served cold. It is. Today, you have underestimated who you're dealing with. That's a mistake on your part. A grave one. Mark my words, Eoin. One day I will make your life as miserable as you have made mine.

Bravo, Jaine.

It would seem that I've underestimated you yet again.

Now it all makes sense. Your reluctance to take things to the next level. Why you maintained such a distance between us and kept me at arm's length. I'm not sure why you let me spend time with your children when I was never destined to become part of your family.

For five fucking months you've been game-playing. Who knew you could keep up the act for so long?

It's clear Jaine Jones has set out to ruin my life because, as far as she's concerned, I ruined hers.

She insisted we marry. She gave me an ultimatum. Her or Molly. Decision made, she then let me fall in love with her, all so she could teach me a valuable lesson, I'm sure.

All because I took from her the person she loved. My brother.

All because I took from him the person he loved. Her.

All because she wanted me to experience firsthand the loss of losing the person you love most. Of having someone rip them away from you with no consideration as to how it makes you feel.

Fine.

I now know exactly how my brother feels. Are you happy now, Miss Jones?

How long has it been since she uttered the word *karma*?

Ten minutes? Fifteen?

It feels longer. It already feels like something's physically missing. Like there's a part of me that's no longer functioning properly.

My heart.

For the first time in my life, I feel fucking bereft. But then, he's been bereft for over two years, hasn't he?

Yes, Jaine. I get it. I played a small part in a wrong decision that fucked up my brother's life.

I love my baby brother. Never underestimate how much I fucking love him. I don't need you to serve me up a dish of stone-cold revenge for my involvement in his reality.

You. Have. No. Fucking. Idea.

And why would you? You've never bothered to ask. You've just gone ahead and made your own assumptions. From day one, you chose to have me typecast as the villain in your little pre-scripted story of vengeance. The pre-judged Prince Uncharming to your vigilante Disney princess.

An Oscar winning performance on your part, I have to say, in a tale where there will be no happily ever after for any of the characters involved.

With a frustrated sigh, I lie there and watch as the dawn finally breaks.

Jaine Jones successfully accomplished what no one else ever has. She brought me to my knees. And by using the one thing I've never experienced before now.

Love.

My future, it would seem, is to remain quite the opposite.

Unloved.

The Hudson Dusters' HQ, Manhattan, New York

We've just had our meeting. It was obvious Jaine wasn't going to turn up. Now that she's achieved her goal, she likely won't attend another. I'll explain the situation to my parents in due course, but only once I've had the chance to digest it myself.

Aidan was, of course, full of questions as to her notable absence. I didn't answer any of them. When everything comes to light, he'll likely think he's in with a chance. That if she refuses to remain wed to me, he should be next in line as the only possible alternative.

If he goes anywhere near her, I'll break his arms, legs, and fingers.

In fact, I'll just break him, period. Fuck what the rest of the family thinks.

I'm now back in my office.

"What's going on, Eoin?"

For a moment, I forgot Dylan was even in the room.

Did he see her outside my apartment last night? Now he has a wife to occupy his evenings, it's unlikely he'll be as forensic with the surveillance as he once was. He'll have better things to do with his time, I'm sure. I still thought it best to mention it on the off chance he did notice.

I'm looking out the window distractedly. The view means nothing today. I may as well be staring into fucking space.

Jaine's patience was commendable, I have to say. She waited over two years to exact her revenge, and she did so perfectly. In her defense, she did remind me on several occasions of what she had in store for me. It was extremely short-sighted of me to think she wasn't playing some sort of game all this time. I naively thought she had developed feelings for me. Hoped they mirrored my own. That, as a result, we were wiping the slate clean.

Obviously not.

Thanks to our shared levels of intimacy, Jaine Jones really did fool me twice. Was that also an act? Would she really have gone to such extreme lengths to avenge our Paddy? To lower herself to sleeping with the enemy? Clearly, that's what I still am to her.

In truth, I thought each cussed reminder nothing more than an empty threat. Not once did I think her the vengeful sort.

How wrong I was.

I turn to look at my brother. "Jaine came to my apartment last night."

He raises both eyebrows. Given how surprised he looks, it's clear he didn't see her on the surveillance. I understand his reaction, but there has to be a first time for everything, and she is my wife.

"You mean you finally allowed a female to enter the hallowed ground that is your home?"

I exhale and roll my eyes at him.

"And then what? You hate-fucked each other?"

I glare at him initially before replacing it with a frown. "There's no point in trying to protect her modesty when she's quite happy to go into explicit detail with anyone who cares to listen."

He snickers. "That's biker chicks for you, brother. They grow up in the midst of sex and debauchery. To them, being surrounded by people actively fucking is just a normal part of their everyday…."

"I told her I love her, Dylan," I interject.

There's a pause. "Right. And since you look as miserable as sin, I'm guessing she didn't reciprocate?"

"No, she didn't. She said one word before she left."

"And that was?"

"Karma."

He frowns at me, his expression changing to one of shock when the realization finally dawns on him too.

"Jesus Christ. This is payback for Paddy."

I don't respond. It's not a question.

"So, are you telling me that Jaine's intention all along was to make you fall in love with her all so she could dump you?" His frown deepens when he realizes just how carefully pre-planned this whole episode was.

"Well, it's currently only speculation. I never asked what she was referring to when she uttered the word karma, and she didn't offer up any explanation, but that was my interpretation."

"Jesus, Mary and Joseph. I never thought Jaine could be so vindictive."

"Nor I. In hindsight, I can understand her personal vendetta against me, but why drag Molly into it? She made me choose, Dylan. She left me with no other option. After giving my verbal word to Molly that I would marry her, I had to renege on the deal."

Dylan shrugs. "You would have to have chosen at some point,

brother. You and Jaine were together for months. You couldn't have strung both along all that time."

"I know, but given Jaine's plan was most definitely pre-meditated, the least she could have done was afford me a little time. I could have let Molly down far more gently than I did. Miss Jones backed me into a corner. And for what? It's quite clear she never had any intention of committing to this marriage or honoring her vows."

"Maybe she did you a favor."

His voice is quiet. Too quiet. He's hiding something.

"Molly saved my life. It was she who did me the favor, not Jaine."

He gives it away with his small frown.

"Explain that look."

"What look?"

"The one that crosses your face anytime I mention Molly saving my life!"

And then it dawns on me. What a fucking fool I've been. I run my hand through my hair in frustration.

"It was him, wasn't it?"

"Who?"

"Don't play games with me, Dylan. I've been party to enough playground tactics in the last twenty-four hours to last me a fucking lifetime. It was him. The Exterminator. He was in Nevada because you were there. In case you got into trouble. Tell me I'm wrong!"

"For the record, it was also in case you got into trouble." He mumbles once more.

"And why would he care what happens to me? He doesn't know me from Adam!"

"I wouldn't be too sure about that." More mumbles as he switches his attention to the floor.

"Why do you say that? Is he someone known to the family?" I'm curious now. I want to know who the fuck he is.

He exhales. "I can't reveal his identity, Eoin. You know that."

"Then just confirm that my suspicions are correct. That it was him. Both in Nevada and at St. Patrick's."

He nods.

"And Molly took the credit for Nevada because she was the only one holding a gun." I'm talking out loud more than anything now, but he nods once more before answering.

"Tyler has the physical proof that it couldn't have been her. She did discharge the weapon as we all heard it go off, but it was most likely accidental. Her shot hit the floor to the right of where she was standing. The bullet ricocheted off the newly laid concrete and landed in the corner of the room."

"So that's why Jessie went foraging around in the Colombian's brains. To retrieve the engraved bullet so the rest of us would be none the wiser."

Again, a silent nod.

And that's why Molly never tossed the fact that she saved my life in my face. She didn't.

"Jesus Christ. Why didn't you tell me this before, Dylan?"

I pace the floor, my hand running repeatedly through my hair as anger spirals through me at the sheer level of deceit and game-playing that's been going on around me yet again.

I stop and glare at him. "I could have made the single biggest mistake of my life. What if I'd married the girl and this had then come to light?"

"I'm sorry, Eoin. I honestly thought you'd started to develop feelings for her. That you were taking the vows with her for that reason as well as for the fact that you thought she'd saved your life."

He at least has the decency to look and sound sheepish.

"I never loved Molly."

He exhales loudly again. It's the sound of guilt.

"The sniper didn't want anyone to know, Eoin. It wasn't a hit for hire. There was never any guarantee any shots would be fired. If it became common knowledge that it was him who saved us, it would have looked like he was favoring us over others. It could then have been suggested that we were working in cahoots. His remaining invisible was the only way."

I appreciate he felt a sense of loyalty to the marksman. I also understand his reasoning. But all of this at what potential cost to me?

"You should have told me, Dylan. I could have offloaded Molly months ago had I known. And more importantly, when there was no third party involved. She now thinks I've jilted her for Jaine. And that means we now have another potential enemy in the shape of big Malky McGrath. He'll most likely want blood for what he'll perceive to be me dishonoring his only daughter." I run my hand down my face and exhale in frustration.

What a fucking mess.

"I'm sorry, Eoin. As soon as Fin's existence came to light, everything just spiraled, and you were immediately married off to Jaine."

There's a pause.

"So, what are you going to do now?

I stare at him. "Have you seen Da these days? How old he's looking? I'll have no choice but to move on with my life, with or without Jaine Jones in it."

"But you love her." He frowns.

I snort. "And what difference does that make when she clearly doesn't love me?"

CHAPTER THIRTY-SEVEN

JAINE

Jaine's Apartment, Upper East Side, New York

"You did what?" I'm pissed off and pacing the floor.

The pacing has got nothing to do with what Dylan's just announced. I've been doing that since I got home this morning at just before dawn.

We never did spend the night together.

Do I regret it now?

Do I regret any of it?

The pissed off mood I'm in is, however, over the news he's just spilled.

"I had to tell him, Jaine."

I stop pacing. "I call bullshit."

"Jaine…"

I close my eyes and try to calm myself down. "Did we or did we not agree that it would remain a closely guarded secret unless I decided otherwise. There was no reason for you to ever tell Eoin." I'm hissing through my teeth now.

"He needed to know it wasn't Molly. He felt beholden to her. The fact that you made him choose didn't sit right with him as he thought himself indebted to her."

"Well, I'm sorry he had to decide which of us he wanted to fuck. That the poor big glutton wasn't able to spend the rest of his days pigging out by having his cake and eating it too. All I did was give him an ultimatum. I didn't force him to pick me. He made that decision all on his own."

"You know the point I'm making, Jaine. He thought he owed her. He felt guilty that he wasn't able to let her down more gently."

"Listen, Dyl." I close my eyes once more and rub my hand across my forehead, sighing loudly. "I'm really sorry that Molly got caught up in the crosshairs. and I truly mean that, but if he was only marrying her because he thought she'd saved his life, then I did him a favor. In fact, I did both of them a goddamn favor. And more importantly, I did so without having to reveal my alter-ego's involvement in the Nevada situation!"

"I understand what you're saying, but the rushed way it was handled. The fact that he jilted her pretty much at the altar for you. We're concerned her da's now going to be on the warpath because he'll see Eoin as having humiliated his only daughter."

"The revealing of my secret wouldn't have changed that."

"No, but if Eoin had not been made aware, his conscience and sense of loyalty might have gotten the better of him and he may have decided to take her back. She'd have jumped at the chance. You know that."

"Do you think he would have?"

Jealousy spirals through me, but I push it aside. He was only mine temporarily. He was never going to be mine for the long term.

"I guess we'll never know."

There's a pause. I'm waiting for the interrogation. I'm sure the O'Connells will have been speculating about my marked absence around that circular table of theirs. Then again, maybe not. Jessie hasn't said anything. If she suspected something untoward, I'm sure I'd have heard about it by now.

"Why, Jaine?"

Here we go.

"He deserved it." I hate the fact that I immediately sound defensive.

"We all deserved it in some shape or form, so why single him out?"

"Because he showed no remorse for what he did."

"He's a mobster, Jaine. He's not supposed to show remorse. He's supposed to get the job done."

"Not even when it comes to his own flesh and blood?" I snap.

I know what he's going to say even before he says it.

"Paddy's arranged marriage wasn't Eoin's decision. It was Ma's. A mother knows best. You know that's her viewpoint. She tried the same with the rest of us. Eoin may have agreed in principle with my parents' choice for Paddy, but even if he hadn't, it was already a done deal. The contract had already been signed. You're also forgetting that it was a decision made without any knowledge of your existence. If the family had known about you, I'm sure the outcome would have been different. Unfortunately, most of the responsibility for Paddy's situation lies with Paddy himself. He kept you a secret for nine years, Jaine. A secret that he kept even from me."

He's telling me things I don't want to hear.

"Eoin lied about the messages for a year. In what way was that right? He should have put an end to the charade as soon as he found out."

I close my eyes and rub my hand across my head in frustration. I was meant to feel ecstatic. After two long years of push and pull, I won.

But right now, I don't feel like a winner. In fact, I feel quite the opposite.

I can still feel his eyes on me as I dressed and then left. He never said a word. He didn't have to. I already felt like I'd stabbed him in the back.

"In hindsight, I should never have allowed it to start in the first place. Am I to be punished for my involvement too? It was more my fault than Eoin's."

I want to stick my fingers in my ears because it's yet more truths I don't want to hear or accept. I don't want to listen to excuses for him. I want to blame him. I *need* to blame him. If I don't, then all this time I'll have focused my efforts and energies on toxic mind games for nothing.

I wanted revenge so badly. But why when I'm not the vengeful sort and never have been? Grudge holding is a waste of everyone's time. And time is not something we always get a lot of in this life.

Look at Ace.

If this bitter taste is what serving payback tastes like, then I really wish I hadn't bothered.

"I kept my secret. You kept yours. Both of us did what we did for Irish. Eoin did it for himself."

A last-ditch attempt at convincing myself that I haven't spent all this time waging a war I should never have started in the first place. I've been reduced to clutching at flimsy fucking straws.

"I'm not saying Eoin's blameless, Jaine, far from it, but then none of us are. He did it for Paddy in the main. You weren't to know, but he was pickling his liver on a daily basis. It became clear pretty early on that Paddy needed you to anchor him. That he always had."

"He doesn't need me anymore." I hate that I've gone from sounding defensive to sounding pathetic.

"He's moved on. He had no choice."

"Why message me for two years to then just stop? I just don't get it." Even I can hear the frustration in my voice.

"He made his bed, Jaine." He sounds sympathetic. I don't want his pity. I want to know why Irish messaged me all that time to then just blank me when we met face to face.

"What do you mean?" I ask.

"He took Sophia's purity the night of my engagement party."

Everything falls into place. From turning hot to cold. The look of indifference. Now it all adds up.

"Paddy's the loyal sort. You know that better than anyone, Jaine. Sophia's his wife now. Nothing can change that. He will never disrespect her. And he will never leave her."

Dylan's just telling me what I need to know. That Irish has let me go and that I have to do the same with him.

I disconnect the call and stare at the wall.

"Did I do the right thing, Ace?" I ask the question out loud. I wish he could tell me what to do next. About Eoin. About Irish. About how to keep placing one foot in front of the other now he's gone. "Why did you have to go and fucking leave me?" My frustration releases in a sob.

Because I know if he were here, everything would be okay. But he's not. So the way I see it is nothing will be okay ever again.

Tears don't help, especially ones of self-pity, but I can't stop them from falling. I'm overwhelmed by guilt, sadness, and betrayal.

I spend the rest of the day with the kids. Just me and them. We play games and we watch movies. Disney ones where the cliché blonde princess really does find her happily ever after.

In the evening, with Duke minding the children, I leave for the

MMA club. I'm going to take out my frustrations by punching a fucker legally in the face.

CHAPTER THIRTY-EIGHT

JAINE

Jaine's Apartment, Upper East Side, New York

I've put both babies to bed, and Duke's just preparing to leave. His presence is comforting. Familiar. In so many ways, it's like Ace is here with me. They look so alike and have so many similarities. I hope little JJ shares them too. Then again, Ace will have picked most up from Duke due to proximity. Tears prick my eyes that JJ will never have any relationship with his own beautiful daddy.

I miss Ace so much. Since returning to New York, it feels like I haven't had chance to breathe, let alone grieve.

"Jainie."

My face must give my feelings away as Duke sits beside me on the sofa and pulls me against his chest. He knows I'm fragile right now. He's known me since I was seven years old.

I can't hide from him. Not even if I wanted to.

And then I cry.

For Ace. For Duke. For JJ.

And then I cry tears of self-pity.

Over Ace. Over Padraig. Over Eoin.

"He cares about you a great deal, you know."

"Who?" I mumble between sobs, my face pressed against his cotton shirt. I've asked the question, but I already know who he's referring to.

"Eoin. Can't you find it in your heart to forgive him for what he did? For whatever part he played in the Dusters' bigger picture that day? I mean, you know now the final decision wasn't his."

I sit up and rub the heel of my hand over my swollen eyes. "I deserve justice, Duke. Irish deserves justice. Fin deserves justice."

"But Padraig and Fin aren't asking for it. And even if Padraig knew the truth, he'd still most likely forgive his big brother."

"What are you saying?"

"That it's only you who's seeking revenge, and I never thought you the vindictive type."

"I'm not. Not usually."

"Then why with Eoin?"

My mind drifts to the Irishman. The bane of my life. My arch-nemesis. The villain of my story. My husband.

I chose to make him all of the above. He didn't ask to be any.

"Because he infuriates me. Because he drives me insane. I want to kill him with my bare hands, and I want to kiss him at the same time, and that just makes me hate him more."

He chuckles. "So, what you're saying is that he frustrates the hell out of you. There's a thin line between love and hate, Jainie."

"I don't love him."

"Are you saying that because you feel you have to? You don't need to say it on my account or on account of Ace. Ace knew you loved Padraig as much as you did him. He accepted that you had the ability to love more than one person."

I sigh. "Even if I did love Eoin, which I don't, how can I ever forgive him? He still played a part in all the pain and suffering."

Duke chuckles again. It's a warm sound. It makes me realize how fucking glad I am that he came to New York with me. "Look at the pain Ace caused you over the years. And you forgave him."

"That was different."

"Why? Pain is pain, Jainie. Padraig caused you pain too. If I recall, he cheated on you. That's the reason you and he split up in the first place."

I stare into space as I take in what Duke said.

"All I'm saying is, don't throw away a chance at happiness because you want someone to blame for all the things that have gone wrong in your life."

"And is that what you think I'm doing? With Eoin?

"I think you've focused on that moment as being the time when everything went wrong, and as Eoin delivered the unwelcome news, rightly or wrongly, you've held him responsible. But look at all the good that came from that day. You came home to Rising. You married Ace. There were a lot of positives, little JJ being one of them. The point I'm trying to make is that a lot of people contributed to the unhappy events that have been scattered throughout your journey. I'm sure in some ways even I did. But you didn't bear a grudge with them. Or with me." He kisses me on the forehead before he stands. "If you don't want to be with Eoin, that's your choice. All I'm saying is make that decision for the right reasons and not because of something he dropped the ball on in the past. All of us have dropped the ball at some point, yourself included. Ace is gone and Padraig's following his own path. You need to do the same. You need to let go of the past. You have a future. Ace doesn't. Live your best life for both of you. You know that's what he would have wanted, and I'm pretty sure it's what Padraig would want for you to."

I frown at him. "Even if my future lies with his own brother?"

Duke shrugs. "Love is love. None of us get to choose. We've just got to grab hold of it where we can."

CHAPTER THIRTY-NINE

JAINE

Jaine's Apartment, Upper East Side, New York

FIN IS WITH SARAH AND CILL TODAY AS THE ACTIVITY THEY'VE gone on is for children that little bit older than my youngest.

I've just fed JJ and now we're watching *Dumbo* for the nth time. I'm not sure which of us love that movie most.

I drop my nose to his black curls, inhaling his perfect baby smell as he lies on me with his thumb in his mouth and his soother clutched tightly in his chubby little hand.

I've lost count of how many times I've silently cried over *Baby Mine* these past few weeks, and here I am crying over it again.

My poor little JJ. My heart aches when I think of how much he's lost out on. I'd give anything for him to grow up with his daddy. I'd give anything for me to grow old with him too. But neither will ever happen.

I turned my grief into anger in order to achieve my plan. Once it was mission accomplished it then returned with a vengeance.

It was crippling. It was debilitating.

But then I lost Ace. It was always going to be.

It's been a month since I walked out of Eoin's apartment. He hasn't tried to contact me once in all that time. I haven't contacted him either. I needed time. Time to heal that I never got after Ace passed. I was still at the peak of grieving when I returned to New York, but I was given no choice in the matter. The Exterminator had a role to perform.

The sniper show had to go on.

I guess, in the end, losing him caused me to lose part of myself. And losing Irish caused me to lose even more. I was fractured. I needed to try to piece what was left of me back together.

I couldn't just do what Delaney did and go off somewhere for months on end. That shit's difficult to do when you're a single parent. So, I created my own little sanctuary at home where I've spent some much-needed time with the kids, because I realize now that despite their young ages, we all miss Ace in our own way. We needed healing time. We also needed time to regroup as the smaller family unit that we are now.

Ace will always be part of us. In spirit if not in person.

I still speak to him every morning or when I'm feeling lost. I probably always will. It helps me feel close to him.

Sometimes I spin around, so sure I can feel him behind me or certain I can smell his familiar aromatic cologne. Then pain sucker punches me once more when I realize he's not there.

For as long as I'm alive, Ace will live on in my memories, and I'll do my best to pass on as many as I can to Fin and JJ so that he's never forgotten.

And when I pass, and we're reunited, we'll just pick back up where we left off. We'll run up that dusty old dirt track and he'll show me how to skim stones, just like we did on that very first day.

Until then, I have to accept that he's gone and he's never coming back.

I've also used this time getting to know myself again. Not Jaine Jones the wife, or Jaine Jones the mother, or Jaine Jones the confidant.

Just Jaine Jones, the plain girl from Rising, California.

I've forgiven myself. Accepted myself. Learned to love myself again. I needed to do all of that before I could let anyone else in. To allow someone to love me, I need to love me first.

Ace has gone. The relationship I once had with Irish has gone.

Do I want a future with Eoin? I think maybe I do.

Do I love him? I'm not sure how I feel about him. It's different.

With Ace, it was love at first sight. I knew straight away that we were end game. With Irish, it's like we shared an intangible connection. And I know even though it hasn't worked out for us this time around, it will in the next life. Irish and I are soul mates. I truly believe that.

With Eoin, it's neither of those things. Maybe the feelings I have for him have evolved due to proximity. Maybe our being forced into this arranged marriage created something that under normal circumstances would never have come to pass.

Sure, there was an attraction between us before, as much as I try to deny it. Let's face it, we've bickered over the years like a pair of pubescent high schoolers who'd developed an embarrassing but not entirely unwelcome crush on each other. But if we hadn't kissed, would it ever have gone anywhere? Probably not.

Our relationship is physical in the main and toxic by its very foundation, so will it really stand the test of time? Will the physical attraction wear off? Will the toxicity burn like acid, destroying everything else in its path?

Who knows?

What I do know is that he's made me feel alive again. I've fucking missed him. I want him, and the thought of him being with anyone else makes my trigger finger itch.

Maybe it's not love. Maybe not yet. Maybe not ever.

But it's something.

Something that could potentially turn into so much more?

Only time holds that answer. Then again, will Eoin want to try again, or has he already moved on with his life?

It's been a month, after all. That's a long time in our world.

And could he ever forgive the way I deliberately led him on, achieved my goal, then subsequently threw his declaration of love back in his face?

I guess I'm about to find out. JJ reaches up for Duke as he enters the room, and I smile as he takes him from my lap before throwing him in the air and catching him.

It's the most beautiful sound. My baby's laughter filling the air.

"You ready to speak to Eoin?"

I smile. "Yes. It's time."

Private Dining Room, Palace Hotel, Manhattan

"How have you been, Jaine?"

Rod and I decided to meet since he's in New York on a fleeting visit once again. Is it a woman, I wonder? Has my handsome Mexican school friend finally found the elusive one? He's never normally in New York this often.

I glance around. I haven't been in this establishment with its vulgar gold, cream, and crystal décor since the worst night of my life.

If I hated this place before, it was nothing compared to how I feel about it now. But it's secure. You pay enough and you have a signed-in-blood guarantee that the walls don't have ears. If they grow any, the head to which they're attached will be blown off well before the associated mouth can even think about spilling its guts.

"Improving, Rod. And I apologize that I went off radar briefly. I needed some me time. I never realized quite how much until I had pretty much reached breaking point."

I can be honest with Rod. I witnessed him go through similar when he lost his younger sibling, Rafael.

"You did the right thing. I know it's cliché, but time really is a great healer."

I smile at him, but it quickly turns into a frown. "About Abel."

He looks at me almost sympathetically. "You did what you had to do. If it helps your peace of mind, I would have made exactly the same call. I know both Lucifer and Ghost held respect for you before, but perhaps that's now sprinkled with a little fear."

"Great." I roll my eyes.

He laughs. "Instilling fear is no bad thing in this life, Jaine. They know you have their town's best interests at heart. They also know how serious you are about unearthing the faction behind all this. That those behind Ace's death are also indirectly responsible for Abel's demise, and my little brother's too."

I place my hand over his and squeeze gently. I know it's still difficult for him to talk about Raf. "Any news?"

He shakes his head. "Nothing. It's all gone quiet. But it's too quiet if you know what I mean."

"The calm before the storm. Which typically means something's about to go down."

He nods. "I think they're strategizing. Things were simple when they could control Reaper. Now he's gone, and with both Ghost and Lucifer refusing to play ball, they'll have to approach things differently. Their bully-boy tactics didn't work. That approach just resulted in three dead Colombians. They won't make the same mistake twice."

"And right now, we have no idea where or when they'll strike."

"Or even if they do. Who knows? Maybe they'll find someone else to help sell their inferior goods and assist with their trafficking. Our weapons order is double this time. We want our men prepared for any eventuality. We've accepted the same percentage reduction as last time. I've already discussed it with Aidan and Jessie. As you and I were meeting up, I told Aid I'd pass you the official paperwork."

He hands it to me, and I place it in my briefcase. I'll personally deliver it to Eoin O'Connell after this meeting.

"Aid?" I raise an eyebrow and smile. "Best friends now, are we?"

He laughs. "Let's just say I'm glad you introduced us. He definitely knows his way around weapons. He's recommended some alternatives based on our requirements. He's also going to throw in a few new models for us to trial."

"Bringing him on board was a good move by the Dusters for once."

He narrows his eyes. I know exactly where this is headed.

"Spit it out, Rod."

I just say it how it is. We've known each other a long time, so there's no need for either of us to be coy with one another.

He leans back in his chair as he surveys me. "Speaking of good moves, rumor has it that Eoin and Molly have parted company." He smirks, raising an eyebrow. "Rumor also has it that you are now Mrs. Eoin O'Connell and that you and he already share a son."

I take a sip from the hundred-dollar glass of sparkling water as he surveys me over the top of his own glass.

"You know I never feed the rumor mills, Rod. I'm surprised you're paying them any mind given how often you've been the subject of gossip and speculation, typically with a pretty female in tow."

"True." He chuckles.

"Brunette, I might add." I smile.

"But of course." He laughs out loud at my reminding him of the fact that he turned down the opportunity to enter into an arranged marriage with Jessie as he doesn't like blonde hair.

How to answer. Truthfully and from where things stand is probably best.

"The rumors are true, Rod, but as you know, I never let my personal life impact on my professional one, so you have my assurance that it will not in any way affect our business relationship."

"Congratulations, Jaine. Tell me, have you been practicing that response?"

He laughs out loud again, and this time, I join him.

The Hudson Dusters' HQ, Manhattan, New York

My stiletto heels click on the marble flooring as I make my way past the reception quartet. The color of the day?

Fuchsia.

They keep their wary eyes trained on me as I walk past. No words are spoken, and they don't try to stop me either.

Number one slowly picks up her phone. She's trying to be discrete, but it's difficult to do wearing inch-long fake pink nails.

Is she letting her boss know that I'm on my way up?

I press the call button for the elevator.

Nothing's visually changed in the building, but the atmosphere feels different somehow. But then I've been gone for some time. A lot could have changed in my absence.

I'm currently playing catch up in all areas of my life. I haven't only stayed out of Eoin's way, but my taking some unplanned time out has meant I haven't really spoken with Dyl or Jessie either.

I've seen Sarah most as she comes to pick up the kids, but all she ever talks about is babies these days, more so now she's finally pregnant with number two. She's not remotely interested in the inner workings of the Duster organization. Not that she ever was. She seldom attends their meetings, hence never has any insider gossip to share.

Rightly or wrongly, I've taken my finger off the Duster pulse. Regardless, it was a necessity. Dealing with grief and mental health issues should always take priority.

When I reach Eoin's office, I'm surprised to find that Candice the rottweiler isn't sitting outside. Her desk phone's ringing out. No doubt it's receptionist number one trying to pre-warn her that Jaine Jones has turned up unannounced.

Where is she? Is Eoin fucking her over the desk? Has he simply slipped back into his old ways?

Figures.

Preparing myself to catch them in the act, I open the door without knocking. The sight I'm met with is worse than I anticipated.

Much worse.

My heart sinks in my chest at the visual.

Eoin's standing at the window. He's up close and personal with a woman, but it's not Candice.

It's Ava Di Matteo.

Both turn to look at me. They're so close their bodies are almost touching. It's an intimate pose. It's not the type of pose you'd find yourself in with a business acquaintance or a friend. At least, not unless you were planning on taking things to the next level.

What have I disturbed? Were they kissing? Were they about to? If I had walked in ten minutes later, would I have caught them fucking? Are they seeing each other? Have they been the whole time I've been gone?

With the alliance between the Sicilian mafia and the Dusters now imminent, it's my guessing her brother introduced them.

Aquamarine eyes connect with mine. His face is impassive.

I turn my attention to Leo's twenty-five-year-old sister.

Tall. Slim. Subtly elegant.

Ava is beautiful inside and out. She's also extremely intelligent. She has it all going for her. She's wearing her dark hair straight down her back. Her heart-shaped face is graced with full lips and large crystal blue eyes. She's the perfect match for Eoin O'Connell. An arranged marriage between them would secure a bond between two of New York's oldest and most influential families.

I want to hate her, but I can't. There isn't anything about Ava that I don't like. Just like her brother, she's an astute and well-respected businessperson. I doubt there are many who would have a bad word to say about her, myself included.

"Jaine." She smiles widely as she continues to stand just in front of him. "It's been years."

She walks over and kisses me warmly on both cheeks.

"Just over two." I smile back at her.

"We must do lunch and catch up." She turns back to Eoin. "That's if I can ever squeeze anyone else in these days as Eoin has already claimed most of my lunch and dinner dates for himself." She chuckles across at him.

He doesn't respond.

She must know he's estranged as he's wearing a ring. Does she know it's me he's currently married to? Going by that comment, likely not.

"Well, I'm sure Mr. O'Connell can spare you for one afternoon." I smile at her once more before turning my attention to him, my poker face firmly in place. "I was just passing. I've had a meeting with one of our mutual business acquaintances this morning and he asked me to drop in some paperwork. I'm told Aidan is expecting it and is already aware of its content."

I open my briefcase, pull out the very lucrative documents from Rod, then toss the manila envelope on top of his desk. The desk that I bought and that he was potentially just about to fuck Ava Di Matteo over the top of.

I snap my briefcase closed. "Sorry, but you'll both have to excuse me. I have another appointment I need to get to."

"I'll give you a call tomorrow, Jaine." I return Ava's genuine smile and accept her kisses a second time.

"I look forward to it."

I close his office door behind me and lean against it briefly.

He told me he loved me. He clearly lied.

Eoin O'Connell isn't my future. It seems he's simply another person who belongs firmly in my past.

CHAPTER FORTY

EOIN

The Hudson Dusters' HQ, Manhattan, New York

As soon as Ava leaves, I call Jaine. One ring, then straight to voicemail. Infuriating, evil woman.

Eoin: *Answer your phone.*
Jaine: *Are you dating Ava?*
Eoin: *We're getting to know each other.*
Jaine: *Isn't that just pretty words to disguise the fact that you're fucking her?*
Eoin: *I'm not fucking her.*
Jaine: *Have you kissed her?*
Eoin: *I might have.*

The phone rings immediately and I answer.

"You might have." She laughs dryly. "I know you're getting on in years, Eoin, but you're not senile quite yet."

I don't reply. She can assume the worst. She will anyway.

"So, I've been gone a month, and in that time, you've started dating Leo's younger sister and you've reached the kissing stage. Who am I kidding? There's no way you'd ever stop at just kissing."

"You're jumping to conclusions, Jaine. Some might say you were jealous."

"I'm not jealous."

"Are you sure? Anyway, I can't understand why you're so bothered? You were quite clear when you left my apartment and before you fell off the face of the earth without explanation for a month that you and I had no future."

There's a pause so lengthy I have to double-check she's not disconnected the call.

"Yes. About that. That's the reason I dropped by." She pauses. "You may or may not know, but I had to return to New York earlier than planned." Her voice is hesitant, almost like she's struggling to find her words. "There was something I couldn't get out of. An event I had no option but to attend where the date couldn't be changed. Having to deal with that. Having to witness it… it was too much on top of everything that had already happened. I just needed to take some time out to…."

She pauses once more.

"With Ace and Irish…you know… I just needed some time out to process things in my own way before I could move on. My head was all over the place. I'm sorry. I should have explained…"

"Yes, you should have, Jaine. I'm not a mind reader."

"I fully appreciate that."

"You fully appreciate that." It's my turn to laugh dryly. "Well, I'm glad one of us has something to be appreciative about. On the contrary, I'm not appreciative of the fact that I was the recipient of your covert revenge attack for the five months preceding. Lies. Deceit. Pretense. Tell me, Jaine, was there any part of our relationship that was real or was it all just a mere fabrication."

"I had my reasons for doing what I did, and you know it."

"Oh, I know it all right, Miss Jones. Misguided vengeance. I think you'll find that was your sole reason."

"I didn't believe it to be misguided at the time."

"You really didn't do your homework where I was concerned, did you? Do those words sound familiar? They were *your* words."

"I'm sorry, Eoin."

"It was my ma's decision. I could have saved you from making assumptions and answered all your questions if only you'd bothered to ask. I didn't go out of my way to ruin my little brother's life, regardless of what you may think."

"Your delivery could have done with a little work," she bites back.

"I'm a mobster, Jaine. I get the job done. I admit that I underestimated you in your tomboy attire, but even knowing what I do now, I wouldn't have changed my delivery. I did what I did for good reason. The Dusters had signed a blood oath with the mafia. I needed to separate you and Padraig and quickly. I also needed you to make him think it was over between you because if Paddy had thought there was any chance, he would have flouted the contract, dishonouring Sophia in the process and earning you both a bullet. A bullet that would also have ended the life of your shared unborn child, I might add. So, tell me, Jaine, what would you have had me do differently?"

"Your homework." Another bark, but this time with a much weaker bite.

"And what would that have unearthed? The fact that Paddy was still in contact with a female he dated for three months when he was nineteen. You told me yourself that you didn't reconnect with him until you were taken by the Bratva, which was exactly when the contract was signed. Doing my *homework* wouldn't have unearthed anything of significance, thus it would have changed nothing!"

Silence.

She must know I'm right.

I'm not saying things couldn't have been handled differently or better. As is always the case in these situations, of course they could have. But Jaine's far from stupid. Deep down, she must know that the person most responsible for this situation is Paddy himself because he kept her a secret.

She's refused to face facts and simply shot the messenger who delivered the unwelcome news. She made me the scapegoat before taking all her anger, turning it into hatred, and directing it at me. It was then much easier to blame the person she hated for everything that had gone wrong as opposed to the one she loved.

"I apologize for the part I *did* play," I say. "I should have come clean when I found out about the messages. At that point, I should either have ended it, or I should have allowed you to communicate with each other. Discreetly, of course. Your love would have seen you never put the other at risk, so I was confident that no truths would ever be revealed. You would simply have assumed Paddy was happy with his lot and vice versa because for either of you to convey otherwise would have put the other's life in jeopardy."

"Then why didn't you?"

She doesn't sound angry, which is what I expected. More curious.

"Because I was selfish, Jaine. By that point, I wanted you for myself. If you were able to speak with him, then you would have had no need to ever speak with me. I didn't want that, so I continued to let him suffer, even though I could have easily ended his torment."

And there it is. The guilt I choke on.

Jaine has no axe to grind with me. She must see that now.

Paddy does, but it's not for her to avenge him. He'll be quite capable of doing that himself when the truth finally comes out.

"Because you love me."

"Yes."

There's no point in denying it. I've already admitted it aloud. I realize now that I always have.

There's a long pause.

"I accept your apology, Eoin. I understand your reasons. Why you did and said what you did. Even though you clearly thought of no-one but yourself at times, you did it for Irish mostly. And I'd be lying if I said that the message exchange didn't help me as much as it did him. If I'd known it was Padraig, I'm confident I would have put an end to it, so maybe it did all work out for the best." She pauses once more. "I hope that you can also accept my apology. I'm sorry. Those two words pale into insignificance when contrasted against the magnitude of what I've done. I'm not proud of my behavior. My plan was pre-meditated. It was a personal and deliberate attack based purely on revenge, which is not like me. I now know that the responsibility wasn't yours exclusively. Subconsciously or otherwise, I chose to make it so as it's often easier to stick the pins of blame into someone you hate."

She pauses. I can tell there's more to come, but I'm not sure I want to hear any more.

Someone you hate.

"There's one thing that we will have to disagree on, however."

"And that is?"

"That you ever loved me. Because you didn't, or at least not in the true sense of the word."

"And you know that how?" I ask quietly.

"Because love is what I felt for Ace and for Irish. And I would have waited a lifetime for either if I thought there was any chance of a future together. Love completes you as a person, and without them, I never felt truly whole. Real love isn't something you get over in a day or a week, or in your case, a month. Real love is something you never get over. You just learn to survive each new day without your person. So, I'm sorry, but I call bullshit on your claim that you ever loved me because it's clear you never did given how quickly you moved on. All I've ever been to you is an infatuation. The biker chick with the mouth of a sailor who dared stand up to the future Irish king."

I exhale slowly before asking my own burning question. "And did you ever love me, Jaine?"

There's a pause.

Even though I suspect I know the answer, I want to hear it. I need to know for sure. Once and for all.

"No. I've never loved you, Eoin."

I don't respond. Not because I don't want to, but because I can't.

I've never loved you.

I think back over our time together. Over the *toxic* two years. Over the past months when she's acted out of character in so many ways. I understand why.

Grief.

Not just for Ace, but also for Padraig. For reasons known only to herself, she watched him take the vows. From a front row seat, she watched as the final curtain of their doomed relationship fell for the last time. I'm certain the loss of him will also feel like a death to her. And I'm sure she'll continue to process each regret and *what-if* moment as they arise. I'm also sure that top of her list of regrets will be the five months of her life she'll feel she wasted with me. Squandered in her eyes, but quite the opposite in mine.

She's wrong. I haven't moved on. I would have waited a lifetime if I thought there was any chance of a future together with her, but there isn't, so there's no point attempting to explain what she thought she saw. It won't change anything. So, I'll just have to accept that I'll never feel truly whole. That I'll need to learn to survive each new day without my person too. That I'll need to settle for someone else simply because, to fulfill the role I was born into, I need a wife.

Silence.

It stretches almost indefinitely until she finally disturbs it with even more unwelcome words.

"I'm aware as the future Da Duster that you have responsibilities and obligations to fulfill, so I'll have the marriage annulled. That way, you can move on."

With Ava. She doesn't say it, but it's silently implied.

"To ensure confidentiality, I'll handle the paperwork personally at my end then push it through as quickly as possible."

As is Jaine's way, she then terminates the call.

"Fuck." I watch my phone shatter as it connects with the wall on the opposite side of the room.

I'm not sure why Dylan finds it so hilarious that I was fucked off enough to smash my phone to smithereens. I don't find it amusing in the slightest. And since yesterday. my foul mood has only worsened.

I pass him the manila envelope.

"This paperwork was delivered this morning. The annulment has been requested on the grounds that she was forced into the marriage. She's already explained verbally that she'll push it through as quickly as possible and handle it all personally."

He frowns as he flicks through the content. "You'll still have to agree."

He looks back and forth between me and the documentation.

"Yes, but my dragging my heels will simply delay the inevitable. She's a lawyer. And an extremely good one. Even if I employ the best attorney money can buy, she'll still use one of her own to run rings around them in court."

"Has she asked for anything?"

I snort. "You've seen her bank statements. She also has an extensive property portfolio on top these days. Jaine Jones has more money than she knows what to do with. She doesn't require any handouts either from her estranged husband or from the Dusters."

"Have you mentioned any of this to Da? He's going to go nuts, Eoin. If she insists on going through with this, he'll likely try to force her to marry the only other option. Our Aidan."

The contents of the surface of my desk follow the same destructive path as my phone, this time colliding with the adjoining wall.

"He will never fucking marry her! He will never lay a fucking finger on her!"

Dylan visibly pales.

It's understandable. It's not often I show this side of me in the office, but the thought of Aidan touching her in any way… I'd drag him to the docks and tear him apart, family or not.

"Calm down, Eoin."

"I am calm!"

He side-glances at my smashed laptop. "Clearly."

Running a frustrated hand through my hair, I lean back on my chair and place my feet on the desk.

Her fucking desk.

"Jaine thinks she's doing me a favor by pushing the annulment through," I admit reluctantly.

He frowns at me once more. "And why would she think that given the reason you agreed to marry in the first place was for the protection of Fin. Even if you've both decided to do your own thing, surely that should still be the priority."

I exhale. "Because I did something extremely foolish."

He smirks. It's wiped off his face when I glare at him.

"Jaine walked into my office yesterday and saw me with Leo's sister. Ava was just passing and thought she'd drop in. Jaine stopped by at precisely the same time to hand in the official paperwork from Rod…"

Dylan's frown deepens as he interjects. "But I thought there was nothing going on between you and Ava."

"Nothing *is* going on. Since we were introduced by Leo, we've met up for lunch and dinner once or twice, and it has always been strictly business-related. There's been nothing untoward. There will be nothing untoward with any female while I'm still married to Jaine. I would never disrespect her in that way. She's my fucking wife."

"And?"

"Ava implied that she and I were meeting up for breakfast, lunch, and dinner most days, and that I was monopolizing her time."

"In front of Jaine?"

"In front of Jaine. And to make matters worse, when Jaine entered my office, without knocking I might add, Ava was standing extremely close."

"So, Ava was staking her claim, not knowing that Jaine's your wife."

"That's what I took from it, yes. Ava knows I'm estranged. She's keen. She doesn't even try to be coy about it."

"And I'm guessing Jaine then made her own assumptions based on what she saw and heard."

"Yes. And I didn't correct her. In fact, I made the situation far worse by neither confirming nor denying when asked directly if I'd kissed the girl."

It's his turn to run his hand through his hair. "Jesus Christ, Eoin. Were you trying to make Jaine jealous?"

"Perhaps."

"But Jaine doesn't do jealousy. I'm not saying she doesn't feel it, but she'd never act on it. She'd rather walk away and chalk it all up to experience. She'd never lower herself by getting into a catfight over any man. It's not her style. Look at what happened with her and Ace."

"I know that now."

"So, what happened next?"

"Jaine suggested that I'd mistaken my feelings for her given how quickly I was able to move on. That it wasn't love and never had been."

"Shite."

"I'm sure she wouldn't have been so hellbent on rushing the annulment through had she not misinterpreted what she saw."

"A sight that you encouraged her to misinterpret because you thought it may work in your favor."

"Yes!"

He ignores my sharp tone. "So, she didn't get angry?"

"Quite the opposite. It was a civilized conversation for the most part. I also apologized for my part in all of the deceitful shenanigans, and she apologized for her personal vendetta against me. We both accepted each other's apology, and then she insisted on pushing the annulment through as quickly as possible so I can move on with my life."

His eyebrows almost reach his hairline.

"So, she's forgiven you? For everything? Just like that?"

I nod. "There was never really anything to forgive."

"And you've forgiven her for leading you on all these months."

I nod again.

"Well, I'm only sorry I missed that conversation."

"There was nothing to miss. I don't think you realize how well she and I understand each other now. We were together for five months, after all. It really wasn't difficult to see it from the other person's perspective when everything was calmly explained. Jaine's also quite clearly spent the past weeks analyzing and filing things away in her head. I think that process helped. She's pretty much back to being her old self."

"So, no more flying off the handle."

I shake my head. "I then asked her outright if she had ever loved me."

"And what did she say to that?"

Someone you hate. I've never loved you.

I pause before I respond because I'm not sure I want to hear the words out loud a second time. "That she never has and that, in fact, she still hates me."

"Ouch." He grimaces.

"Indeed." I run my hand over my face.

"But you're in love with her."

"Yes, Dylan, but did you not hear what I just said? Jaine's feelings for me remain unchanged. In fact, they're worse than I feared. She achieved her plan. A plan she regrets, I might add. Now that it's over, her guilty conscience won't allow her to continue to hold me to ransom when she clearly sees no future for her and me, and especially not now she thinks I've found my perfect Ma Duster."

"Do you want me to have a word with Jaine? To explain what actually happened, and that it was all a misunderstanding?"

I shake my head. "There's no point, Dylan. It won't change anything. I'll just have to accept that her feelings for me are what they are and move on with my life the same as she's doing."

CHAPTER FORTY-ONE

JAINE

Jaine's Apartment, Upper East Side, New York

"YOU CAN'T PUT IT OFF FOREVER, PARTNER."

"No? Just watch me."

I'm working from home and so busy that I answered the phone without looking at the caller ID. After twenty minutes of a pretty much one-sided conversation, it's now something my ears are regretting.

"You can't not go. It's for Finian's and JJ's birthday." She's resorted to whining now, and I can't help but smile.

"It's a month too early, so it's not like it's their official party or anything."

"It's the only date the clown was available." She huffs at my excuse-making.

It's been four weeks since I last spoke to Eoin O'Connell. The New York grapevine is buzzing with news of his and Ava's budding relationship. Talk of two of Manhattan's founding influential families potentially merging? I'm sure the wedding invitations when they eventually go out will be like gold dust and sold off to the highest bidder in order to add to their soon-to-be-amassed combined fortune.

Well, good luck to them. I truly mean that. Let's hope the ceremony goes without a hitch because my alter-ego won't be showing up to dispatch any bad guys this time around.

At least not without an invitation. I learned my valuable lesson last time having almost lost my life at the hands of my O'Connell father-in-law. And as I'm the soon-to-be ex-wife, it's highly unlikely an invite with my name on will be forthcoming. The future Da Duster ship has sailed. It sailed when I walked out of his apartment having just spat out the ugly word 'karma'. I'm not proud of my out-of-character behavior. Far from it. All I could think about was my own personal vendetta. I was so blinkered I couldn't see past it.

Everything that subsequently followed on from the utterance of that one spiteful word was just nail after nail in the coffin that contained our toxic relationship.

Do I regret ending things? I'm not sure, but I do know that it *was* the right thing to do. Eoin has signed the paperwork to enable our marriage to be annulled.

Why did I put the offer on the table when the sole reason for getting wed in the first place was for Fin's protection? A protection that's still very much needed given the bad guys are still on the loose.

Our nuptials should have been just one more match in the compendium of games that he and I insisted on playing with each other. But something that should have remained fake very quickly turned into something that felt way too real. The lines became blurred.

Could we have given it a proper go? Yes, but the fact that we didn't is perhaps a blessing in disguise as, in hindsight, would any attempt at trying to become a genuine couple have been doomed to failure given where we started?

Marriage is a sacred union of two people and a merging of souls. Until death do us part and all that. Like it was with me and Ace. It's for life. You vow to love that person forever.

Eoin and I didn't love each other. I was only willing to go ahead because I was game-playing, and Eoin wasn't willing at all as he felt obligated to marry Molly.

We had no solid foundation for any marriage, and when you try to build on a bed of shifting sands, at some point, everything is going to crumble and fall.

The marriage vows were repeated, but it was without the necessary intent or promise. They weren't meant. They weren't heartfelt, and we all too quickly reached the point where we could go neither backward nor forward.

In the end, it wasn't checkmate after all. It was stalemate.

All that aside, there were two other important considerations that had to be taken into account. The fact that I loved his baby brother. The fact that he'd moved on with someone else.

In the end, I think it all worked out for the best because he shouldn't have to settle, and that's exactly what he would have been doing with me. He deserves to experience true love at least once in his life.

And now? Well, given that he's Finian's uncle and Ava may soon be his aunt, it's time to wipe the slate clean and move on. We have no choice.

My life is back on track.

Professionally, I'm in a good place. Mentally, I'm in a good place.

Emotionally? I'm getting there slowly but surely and one day at a time. I'm just not there yet, and that's why tomorrow is just too soon.

The signed annulment paperwork was only received from Eoin yesterday. No explanation as to the delay, not that I'd bothered to chase it up.

Was I having second thoughts? Was he? Who knows?

I guess he's been busy moving on with his life. I'm not sure what my excuse was.

So, no, I'd sooner not have to attend Finian and JJ's joint birthday party at Chez O'Connell. Quite frankly, shooting myself in the head with one of my own engraved bullets is more appealing than the thought of colliding with the happy couple and having to pretend everything is A-okay. Even though I continue to hammer nail after nail after nail, each one a resounding affirmation of all the reasons why things had to end between us, I miss him.

Our intense conversations. Our heated arguments. His pomp. His arrogance. His light. His dark. I miss all three hundred and sixty fucking degrees of Eoin O'Connell.

I may not like the fact that I have feelings for him, but I can't deny them any longer, at least not to myself.

But it's not love.

I also have no interest in meeting Roisin. Despite what Jessie thinks, I *can* put that off forever. I've managed to avoid any interaction with her up until now, and I'd like for it to remain that way.

I'm not blood. I'm not family. I'm merely the biker female who birthed her grandson.

"Do you want them to think you're a scaredy cat?"

I snort. "Excuse me, but are we back in kindergarten?"

She ignores me and continues, which is what Jessie does when she's about to get on her soapbox. She thinks if she's talking loudest then she's winning, and sometimes it's easier not to argue and to just let her get on with it.

"Well, do you? Because the Jaine Jones I knew would never have backed down from anything or anyone. She was strong. She was fearless. She was…"

"And maybe that Jaine Jones left the building when her husband got killed."

"So, in other words, she *is* a scaredy cat."

"Not at all. She just needs a little more time to heal."

It's a flimsy excuse. Jessie doesn't need to know it's because I don't want to collide with the future Ma and Da Duster.

She scoffs. "You can't keep hiding behind that old chestnut, Jaine. It's been eight months."

"There's no time limit on grief."

"Ace wouldn't want…"

"It's not just about Ace."

"Paddy…"

"Might as well be dead too."

"No one can force him to make contact, Jaine. He's doing what he needs to from a business point of view and that's all we can ask of him. I guess he's just living his best life."

"Yup. Maybe he is."

Jessie pauses. She's thinking up her piece de resistance. I smirk at the phone and wait.

"You know, the strongest, wisest, and most successful woman I have ever met said something to me once."

"Did she really? And what did this brilliant woman have to say?" I smile.

She clears her throat exaggeratedly, and I can't help but chuckle. "She said to me 'Jessie. You put your big girl pants on and you show those O'Connells exactly what you're made of'. And do you know what I did?"

"I do, but I'm sure you're going to remind me."

"I am indeedy, partner. Because I, Jessie O'Connell, did exactly what that wise legal eagle told me to do."

She's right of course. I need to move on in all areas of my life and stop being so goddamn selective. I'm thirty-one years old. A single mom with two beautiful little boys.

A successful lawyer. A successful sniper.

I need to stop wallowing in my own private lake of what might have been.

It's time to put your big girl pants on and get over it, Jaine Jones.

I don't have Ace. I don't have Irish. I don't have Eoin. But I still have me and my boys, and I'm sure God has me somewhere on that big old masterplan of his. He's not going to give biker trash like me any clues as to where exactly, but I can live with that.

"I'll be there." I sigh exaggeratedly.

"Is Sarah bringing the kids?"

"She is. She's also bringing Duke."

"So you'll be showing up in traditional biker style?"

"I sure will."

"Well, I guess I'll hear you tomorrow, partner."

We both snicker.

CHAPTER FORTY-TWO

JAINE

The O'Connell Home, Darling, New York

THERE'S NOTHING QUITE LIKE THE FEEL OF A HOG'S ENGINE thrumming between your thighs, the wind whipping through your hair, or the smell of clean outdoor air infused with road dust, fuel, and grease. I'm so glad I had my Softail shipped to New York.

I've had this hog since I was eighteen years old. My birthday gift from my pop. This ride is what carried me all the way from Rising to New York, then all the way back again a decade later. It's part of my soul.

My memories drift to the past. To Ace, and tears prick my eyes. Some days they do, some days they don't. Mostly they do when I'm filled with overwhelming regret at the wasted time we won't get back.

Do-overs seldom happen in our life. Duke's right. You have to grab what you can when you can. If you don't, then chances are, you'll spend the rest of your life living with regret like I do every day.

It's been eight months.

It feels like yesterday. Feels like a lifetime ago.

I've come to realize that grief is the heavy price we have to pay for love. That to experience the good, you have to be prepared to roll with the bad.

Jessie and Sarah think I'm lucky to have experienced real love more than once.

Maybe I am. Maybe I'm not.

What they don't understand is that loving more than one person isn't the blessing they think it is. In fact, it can be quite the opposite. Because one of the guaranteed side-effects of love is that it instantly creates an opportunity for your heart to get broken. More love just equals more opportunities, and given the number of times my heart has been broken, I'm surprised it's still beating in my chest.

I still wouldn't change anything.

Not with Ace. Not with Irish.

Not with Eoin.

I pull up at the gated entrance and press the keypad to be let in. While waiting, I take in the vulgar O'Connell residence once more with its too much of everything going on. It's only the second time I've been here. I never wanted to return after my last visit and came up with every excuse under the sun to avoid having to do so. Who can blame me after what I was backed into the first time around? I've also chosen to stay away because I've had no wish to meet Ma Duster. And Fergal? We tolerate each other from a business perspective. Why would I want to play happy families with him when I still wear the scar of our cozy little heart-to-heart on my cheek? With the right make-up, it can easily be hidden, but it will always remain. Out of sight but never out of mind. An invisible reminder of the time I danced with the Duster Devil and lived to tell the tale.

I watch as the security cameras fix on me. They'll no doubt follow my every move. Is it big brother watching this time, or is it the matriarch herself? She must be rejoicing in the fact that her son and heir is going to be heading down the aisle with someone of a suitable caliber second time around and he'll no longer be tied to biker trash like me.

The gates slowly open. I rev my engine and ride through.

I've been told to head towards the rear of the building this time. The party is outside. It's my guess it will be extravagant, over the top, and everything two little boys don't need. Still, I can accuse the O'Connells of being many things, but I can't accuse them of not being family orientated. I may mean nothing to them, but my two little boys mean everything. They are both embraced and loved by this family. Their acceptance of JJ surprised me. Eoin's acceptance of him even more so given he's always been way too selfish to sacrifice any part of his big, conceited self for anyone else.

He loves JJ, and in turn, JJ loves him.

All eyes turn in my direction as my hog roars into view. I smirk inwardly as Jessie points exaggeratedly. She'll no doubt have been taking credit all morning over the fact that she's the one who managed to prize Jaine Jones out from under her goddamn rock.

All the casually dressed O'Connell men are standing together in an almost identical pose with their hands slung low on their hips, Aidan's messy blonde hair making him contrast against the others.

The only one missing is Eoin.

I'm guessing it won't be long before I see my eldest son in a similar stance given the same blood runs through his young veins.

My eyes then drift to Roisin. She's standing beside Duke and holding Fin in her arms.

I frown. Where's JJ?

It's then I see him. Or should I say them.

Eoin and Ava.

Her arm is linked through his and he's holding a smiling JJ in his arms. They look like the prefect little family enjoying this pleasant summer's day.

I swallow thickly. I can't describe the feelings that run through me.

Guilt that my little boy doesn't have a mommy *and* a daddy. Regret that it could have been me with him. Acceptance that it is what it is and it's time to just suck it the fuck up and move on.

Everyone stands and stares at the female biker as she parks up her gleaming classic hog. The girl who was verbally warned to stay away but who is now being reluctantly welcomed because she's produced something they'd all quite literally kill for.

A male Duster heir.

I take off my half helmet and swing my blonde hair free before removing my black aviators and my patched leather jacket.

I immediately feel Eoin's intangible darkness caress my soul, and I almost groan out loud at the sensation. I don't make eye contact with him. I can't.

It's been four short weeks. Nowhere near long enough. Fake marriage or not, I've missed him. I've missed our conversation. There was no acting involved in our shared intimacy, and I've missed that too. Even now, the raging hot inferno inside of me still burns for him.

"Mommy."

A beaming smile crosses my face as I watch my little boy try to wriggle free from his grandma's arms. She smiles lovingly at him before placing him gently on the ground.

He runs. He falls. He picks himself back up. Then, knowing all eyes are now on him, and just like his daddy would, he exaggeratedly dusts himself down while wearing the cheekiest of grins, then he runs some more. When he finally reaches me, he shrieks his delight as I lift him as high as I can before spinning him around.

"Hey, little big guy."

Tears immediately prick my eyes. Happy-sad ones. Happy that I'm so fucking blessed to have this part of my Irish. Sad because he's never met his son and he's almost two years old.

"Hey, Jaine."

"Sarah." I blink back my tears as I hug Delaney's baby sister, Cillian's wife. We see each other most days as she's always shuttling the kids back and forth.

"Jaine."

"Jessie." I hug her even closer. The bond that's grown between us is beyond any I share with the rest of my friends.

"Now, there's someone I'd really like you to meet, partner."

She's trying her best to sound authoritative but failing miserably. I can't help but chuckle in response.

Jessie has a unique gift that enables her to lighten any mood, and right now, I've never been more appreciative of that.

I turn my attention to Sarah briefly, my expression serious once more. "Take Finian and JJ somewhere else to play. Just for now."

She nods as I pass my wriggly little boy across, fully understanding why I'm asking. If anything's going to go down here today, I will not have either of my children witnessing it.

Jessie's right. I've delayed this meeting for as long as I can. I can't put it off any longer.

I approach Roisin O'Connell confidently, noting that Fergal has now moved to stand by her side. A show of solidarity? Or maybe they're expecting me to bow to the Irish royals.

Hell will freeze the fuck over first. Jaine Jones bows to no-one.

I look at him first. The man who would have slit my throat had

Dylan not intervened. He looks almost normal in his grey slacks and cream button-down shirt.

"Fergal." I nod.

He nods back. I have no need to look beyond the surface. I've already seen what lies underneath on several occasions, and vice versa.

I then turn my attention to Roisin, conscious that all eyes are watching this long-awaited interaction.

I stood her up. In return, she indirectly threatened my life. There's no love lost between us. There never will be. But we will have to learn to tolerate each other for Fin's sake.

She's a petite woman. I'm around five-ten in my fuck-off biker boots while this grey-haired older lady with her stubborn glints of auburn is barely five-feet tall. Her small stature in no way diminishes from the large aura she omits.

Power. Death. Destruction.

All currently hidden behind a pale pink twinset and pearls.

"Roisin."

I stare at her.

She's taken a lot of lives. I can see each and every one of them clawing to escape as I stare into eyes the exact same shade of green as mine. But she hasn't taken as many as I have. Nowhere near, and somehow, she knows it. Somehow, she can feel it like some sort of fucked up sixth sense because, right now, Roisin O'Connell is introducing herself to every single one of the diseased souls that reside within me.

She clearly misses nothing. That makes two of us.

She shares a look with Fergal, and I watch as they silently communicate with each other. I recognize the connection. It's the same intangible one that Irish and I share. She then turns her attention back to me and nods.

"Jaine."

A New York accent with a Dublin undercurrent.

Silence once more as we try to assess one another. An impossible task with neither of us prepared to give anything away.

"Jaine, could we have a private word, please?"

I swing my attention back to Fergal. "No."

A fleeting look crosses his lined face. It's gone as quickly as it arrived. I have no idea what it was. I don't fucking care. I doubt there are many who would dare say no to Da Duster. Not even his own sons. Perhaps not even Roisin.

"Perhaps you and I could have a word alone after the festivities."

I swing my attention back to Roisin.

I stare. She stares.

"Jaine." My name is quietly spoken from behind me.

I immediately spin around with a grin on my face. "Dyl."

"We have a shooting range on the property if you fancy yourself an expert shot. I mean, I'm rubbish, but…." He smiles at me and it's like a welcoming hug.

"I'd like that, Dyl. I'd like that a lot." My own smile silently thanks him for his timely intervention.

"I'm sorry it's not your usual style or quality of weapon, Jaine, but for us mere mortals a gun's a gun."

I can't help but laugh out loud in response.

Dylan and I have walked the one hundred or so meters to the shooting range on the property. I knew it existed. Fergal mentioned it last time I was here. I declined his offer for him and I to pay it a visit then for obvious reasons. I'm quite partial to my head being attached to my body.

I guess, as mobsters, they need all the practice they can get, as when push comes to shove, it's either our skull or someone else's. Speed and accuracy are essential. Trust me, I know that better than most. I also understand their choice of practice weapon as it's what the majority of our kind carry in real life. Two-legged targets are typically short-range unless you're a professional sharpshooter like yours truly. I pick up one of the pistols. Its solid weight feels good in my hand but it's not quite the same.

"I can use a pistol, Dyl, but I do have a preference for rifles, as you know."

"There's a suitable weapon in my office."

We both turn and stare at Fergal. He silently followed us. Did the gentle breeze carry any of our private conversation back to him? Not that we said anything condemning.

Dylan and I know when to talk mundane matters.

I know the gun Fergal's referring to. It spoke to me silently last time I was here.

I look beyond him to see the others filing in our direction. All except for Sarah, Cillian, and Jessie. They'll be looking after the little ones.

"Dylan?"

Dyl glances at his da. They share a look. It's an exchange that says, *go fetch the rifle and be quick about it because I want to see exactly what this biker chick is made of.*

Dylan swings his attention back to me with a knowing smirk. "I'll be back in two ticks, Jaine."

I nod.

"The targets are electronic."

"Good to know, Fergal." I don't even look at him.

"You like guns, if I recall."

"I do."

Business is business. I speak then because I have little choice.

I'm not remotely interested in his goddamn small talk, and he knows it.

"Have you fired a Glock before now, Jaine?"

I smile inwardly. If only he knew what I did in my spare time. "I can shoot short range or long range. Sight, scope, or neither. Pistols or rifles."

"We have an electronic target at five hundred meters, but for that…"

"We'll need the rifle," I interject. "Let's wait for Dylan, then, shall we?"

"Will you shoot against me, Jaine?"

My heart immediately starts pounding in my chest. It's been a month since I've heard his voice. I forgot how fucking perfect it is.

I side-glance at Eoin as he stands with Ava by his side. She's dressed in a flowing cream-colored dress with matching kitten heels, both of which contrast her olive skin and dark hair perfectly. Meanwhile, I'm standing here in my black tank top, black leathers, and my monstrous *don't mess with me, or I'll kick your fucking head in* biker boots. I don't make eye contact with him. I do with her. She smiles warmly, but she's not her usual engaging self.

Maybe she knows who I am now. That *I'm* Eoin's estranged wife. She'll also think we share a son.

She never did call me after she promised she would. I was disappointed by that out-of-character behavior from her.

Does she love him?

I know from personal experience that love can make you do crazy things. It can make you run for a decade before tossing you into a sea of eternal regret where you then struggle to keep your head above the surface every day.

Love can also make you so sick that you see things that aren't even there. Until you find yourself seeking retribution from someone who wasn't guilty just because you needed anyone to pin your blame on.

He deserves her love if she does. I want that for him. I want him to experience the heady highs that being on the receiving end of love can bring. I want only good for him.

"I'll take you on, Jaine." Aidan disturbs my brief moment of reflection with a smile, a wink, and what I suspect is a double-entendre.

"I think us ladies should show the men how it's done, don't you, Jaine?"

I turn my attention back to Ava.

Being Leo's sister, she'll have used countless enemy heads for target practice over the years, so she'll be a very competent shot, I'm sure. She's confident enough in her abilities to challenge me in front of the O'Connell family.

I smile. She smiles. Hers feels just a little forced.

Movement at her side causes me to switch my gaze, and I finally make eye contact with *him.*

Big mistake.

Aquamarine meets green. I struggle to look away. Is it the same for him? Is this physical attraction we share obvious to everyone else around us? It's like a ravenous beast that wants to feed at every turn and a million times a day. That if we don't succumb to its hungry demands, it will devour us both whole.

It's a two-way street with us. Our bodies are so in tune they're silently screaming, each craving fulfillment from the other.

My gaze trails slowly over him as he walks towards me. Dark. Dangerous. Panther-like. He'll feel its heat, I'm sure. My traitorous brain immediately visualizes him naked. A sight I've imprinted to memory more times than I can count.

Taut, toned, hard flesh. Perfectly inked. Imperfectly scarred.

By the time he's reached me, his eyes are already green, no doubt as a result of my blatant ogling.

I smirk at him as I pick up a pistol.

"Ava." I say her name without breaking eye contact with him.

I've slapped him in the face with his challenge, and instead, I've accepted hers. His nostrils flare in annoyance.

Does he not realize that I want to annoy him? That I deliberately want to fuck him off? That I want to push him over the edge until his alter ego comes out to play?

That's exactly who I want to make me pay for being annoying. Inside that rusty old shipping container on the docks. His fucking monster.

I tilt my head. His eyes narrow.

If he didn't know it, he does now.

What the fuck are you doing, Jaine? Touch the naked flame and it's you who gets burned this time around.

Right now, I'm not sure if I care.

And then I finally heed the warning issued by my common sense. I drag my eyes reluctantly away and they instantly connect with Roisin's.

She nods her head slightly. She missed none of that silent interaction between me and her eldest, I'm sure.

I turn my attention to Ava as I pass her the pistol. If she's serious about Eoin, then she'll want to prove her Ma Duster potential here today.

I'll be proving nothing to anyone but myself.

She helps herself to muffs. I help myself to plugs.

"Fifteen rounds. Fifty-yard target. All shots fired. Accuracy wins." Fergal announces the rules.

Ava lifts her chin determinedly. She probably thinks she's got this in the bag. I mean, I'm a suit. A lawyer. What could I possibly know about guns and killing people?

I side glance at Dylan. I can almost feel his excitement. He's known for over two years what my pastime is, and for the first time ever, he's about to witness the skillset of my alter-ego.

I stare at the electronic screen on top of the shooting table beside me.

"It's the best system money can buy. It doesn't make those of us who are…"

Raising the Glock, I wait for the weapon to connect with my soul before firing while Dylan continues to talk. Rude perhaps, but I won't interrupt him for very long.

Ava immediately follows.

Me.

Fifteen rounds. Four seconds.

Ava.

Fifteen rounds. Ten seconds.

The results are instantaneous. Adrenaline flows through me as my efforts are met by a wall of shocked silence.

I can see the ninety-eight percent accuracy result. Not bad for a weapon I seldom use. I can also see Ava's seventy-seven. A good effort, but not good enough.

"Congratulations, Jaine."

She shakes my hand firmly and smiles graciously in her defeat.

Never underestimate the underdog, and always expect the unexpected. You'll live longer that way.

"Do you still want to have a go with Da's rifle, Jaine?"

I smile at Dylan as he passes me the weapon, my sniper soul instantly soothed as I run my finger lovingly along the full length of the cool metal barrel.

Sitting on the bench, I load the weapon before standing in front of the table. There are several elements to respect when working outdoors at long range, the main ones being wind strength and direction.

Always do your homework before pulling the trigger.

Retaking my seat, I check the scope. I can see the target in the distance. It looks much larger than some of the skulls my bullets have connected with over the years, so I'm not foreseeing any issues. Then again, I don't typically have a crowd. The only positive is my captive audience is clearly still in shock over my accuracy with the pistol, so they're currently deathly silent.

"Can you see the target, Jaine?" Fergal finally speaks.

"Yup."

I blank out everyone after that. It's just me, the rifle, and the target I need to hit.

My finger hovers over the trigger. I'm about to squeeze just as Roisin lets out a small, forced cough. She'll no doubt want to see if I can maintain accuracy having had my concentration disturbed.

The only time I almost missed was when I received the message from Dylan. The message that turned out not to be from Dylan. My last ever message from my Irish.

My finger hovers once more before gently squeezing the trigger.

The bullet has already reached the target by the time I've got to my feet. I know in my soul that it's as good as dead center. I always know. I can feel it. It has to be.

"Nice rifle." I break the silence just as the ninety-nine percent accuracy score shows on the screen.

"If you can do that with it, you can keep it, Jaine."

I shake my head and smile at Fergal. "Thanks for the offer, but I already have a few of my own."

I can feel Eoin's dark penetrating gaze as he silently takes me in. Surprised. Impressed.

"Am I still okay to have Dec drop me off?"

Ava interrupts the stretched silence. Even though everyone can hear what's being said, for some reason, it still makes me feel like I'm intruding on an intimate conversation between her and Eoin.

I remember when Dec used to drop me off too.

"Yes, of course. Shall I walk you back to the gates?"

"No, it's okay, Eoin. I don't want to spoil your fun. If you could message Dec and get him to meet me out front. Let's just say our goodbyes here."

Without a word, I turn and walk away.

CHAPTER FORTY-THREE

EOIN

The O'Connell Home, Darling, New York

As soon as Ava left, I went searching for Jaine, finding her eventually in the downstairs cloakroom of my parents' home.

She doesn't seem at all surprised that I've sought her out. It's like she half expected it. Subconsciously, she welcomed it.

I want to know what game she thinks she's fucking playing.

"Where did you learn to shoot like that?"

It's déjà vu from when we were at The Meeting Rooms all those months ago. Her standing in front of the basin conversing with my reflection in the mirror. Only this time, she's not nervous and wearing an exquisite gown. This time, she's confident and dressed head to toe in her biker attire.

I'm not sure which I prefer.

All of it. Everything.

Her. I will always fucking prefer her.

"I told you before that I grew up a tomboy on an MC compound and that I liked to play with guns."

"What you just did goes beyond just playing with guns, Jaine."

I've never known anyone who can rapid-fire a Glock with such pin-point accuracy the way she can.

I lean against the wall of the full-tiled, all white space with my arms folded. Her eyes are immediately drawn to my torso. I welcome back their heated gaze.

She shrugs. "I have a natural talent. What can I say?"

There's a pause. She knows exactly what I'm going to ask next.

"And why did you leave the shooting range without a word?"

I know why. We both do. Will she admit to it?

It's been a month since Jaine and I had any form of contact. She issued the annulment paperwork, I received it, and we left it at that. What else was there to say or do? Everything had been done and more than enough was said during our final telephone conversation.

She doesn't love me. I've moved on.

Have her feelings now changed? If not, then what game is she playing?

I had hoped that the physical attraction we shared would wane over time. It hasn't. It's stronger.

She may not love me. She may not wish to share a future with me. But she wants me.

I'd love nothing more than to lift her on top of the counter, wrap my hands around her pretty little throat, and sink my dick in to the hilt. And that's exactly what she wants too because she just gave everything away by staring at me like I'm her favorite fucking snack.

I'm sure everyone else witnessed it, including Ava.

What now? Does she want to continue to starve herself, or does she want to binge just for old time's sake?

I don't think she can make up her mind, and therein lies both of our problem.

She doesn't want me, but she does.

Does she expect me to just sit around and wait for her to figure it all out?

Sorry. No can do.

"That's none of your goddamn business."

"I already know." My tone is confident.

She stares at my reflection, swallowing thickly as I close the space between us.

"And what is it you think you know, Eoin?"

I smile as I inhale the scent of wildflowers from her hair, a subtle movement that causes her breath to hitch.

"You couldn't bear the thought of me being intimate with Ava, so you ran."

Silence.

I fucking knew it.

Spinning her around, I force her back against the wall, my arms boxing her in. Her heart is pounding. I can almost hear the fucking thing. "Admit it."

She tilts her chin up in one last ditch attempt at defiance. "Admit what, Eoin?"

"That you were jealous."

She frowns. I've asked a direct question. Will she tell a bare-faced lie, or will she be honest with me for once?

"What if I was?"

I stare down at her and she licks her lips. I can't help but admire their glistening fullness.

Pouty. Pink. Perfection. Which she then parts invitingly. She wants me to kiss her whether she realizes it or not.

"I won't do anything unless you beg me, Jaine."

"I won't beg. Don't worry."

"Are you sure about that? Because we both know you're asking me to do all manner of things to you without saying a word."

"I know it will be difficult for your conceited self to believe, but I'm pretty sure I can manage to control myself," she snaps.

Smart-mouth comments. I expected nothing less. I breathe out, running my hand through my hair in frustration.

"What the fuck are you doing, Jaine? What game is this that you insist on playing?"

Guilt crosses her face, then she frowns again. "I'm not trying to play games."

"Well, you could have fooled me." I release her from my caged arms. I can immediately sense her disappointment.

She wanted me to do each and every one of those things she was silently begging for. Something's holding her back.

Is it the lack of love, or is it something else?

She pauses as she considers what to say next. "You and I both know that we share a physical attraction."

"Yes. It's called lust, Jaine, but what you were displaying outside was envy so is it lust or is it something more."

I stare at her and watch as a flicker of something crosses her face. Realization?

"I don't love you."

Is she trying to convince me or herself?

"So you've said on numerous occasions, Jaine. Quite frankly, whether you do or whether you don't now is moot. You need to decide once and for all what you want."

"I'm sorry, Eoin. I think it's best for everyone that we just stay out of each other's way."

I stare at her. She's a fool if she thinks separation is the answer. Removing the temptation doesn't mean it doesn't exist. As we've just witnessed, all it does is exacerbate the situation and intensify the craving. Next time, we may not have the willpower to walk away.

What then? We fuck on a whim? Again and again and again?

Despite the temptation, it's not enough for me anymore. From anyone else, I can accept half-measures, but from her, I want all or I want nothing.

I rub my hand over my frustrated eyes.

What Jaine doesn't realize is that she had no need to run for the hills. I merely gave Ava a polite kiss on the cheek as a farewell. I've never kissed her. I've never fucked her. I will touch no other female while Jaine is still legally my wife.

I don't want the annulment. I reluctantly returned the paperwork because I need to move on with my life. It's time to throw in the towel now as my wife is clearly adamant that she and I will never share a future. We need to draw a line under these mind games once and for all.

We stare at each other, but neither of us walks away because neither of us is prepared to accept that this is it.

"Eoin, are you in there?"

A voice from the other side of the door. I close my eyes, cursing silently before slowly reopening them. How much has she fucking heard?

"Ma," I reply.

"Do you know where Jaine is? She and I were going to have a girly chat."

Jaine rolls her eyes. She hates my ma, and who can blame her after what she did? But she's still my ma. The woman who birthed me and gave me life. The woman who birthed Paddy, without whom, Finian would not exist. Ma's trying to offer an olive branch. Jaine needs to rise above the past and accept it for all of our sakes, but more so for Fin's and Paddy's.

"I know where she is, yes."

"Where?"

Jaine moves across to open the door. A door that she left unlocked as a silent invitation to me, even though she won't ever admit it to herself.

The door swings open and Ma takes us both in.

"Interrupting something, am I?"

CHAPTER FORTY-FOUR

ROISIN

The O'Connell Home, Darling, New York

SOMETIMES EAVESDROPPING IS THE ONLY WAY TO FIND OUT WHAT'S going on.

Molly had the right idea, even if at times it was a little misguided. The main problem that silly girl had was that she insisted on mixing it with lies.

A Molotov cocktail unless you know how to handle it.

As a parent, it's difficult to listen to your children in pain. And that's what Eoin currently is, try as he might to hide it.

From the family.

From her.

He's not been himself this past month. He portrays himself to be all right on the outside. He may be able to fool everyone else, but he can't pull the wool over his mother's eyes.

I've watched him grow from boy to man. I've watched him

practice and master his mobster craft, including all of his facial expressions. I know what's going on behind each and every one of them. I know he's been covertly pining for the biker. The biker who turned out to be the mother of my grandson. The biker who kept Finian from us for almost a year and a half.

Do I understand her reasonings? Of course I do. She was protecting her son. And she was also protecting my Padraig.

Now I'm going to do the same, only this time, I'm going to protect Eoin.

I was dead against their union. Even when Fergal insisted that she was the perfect match for our eldest, I still wasn't accepting of it.

Until he relayed in detail the way she stood up to him. That she quite happily stepped up to the plate and danced an Irish jig with Da Duster himself before telling him to fuck off.

Twice.

And that when he cut her, she didn't flinch an inch.

Molly McGrath would have emptied both her bladder and her bowels before spilling her guts as she begged for her life.

Jaine Jones would sooner die than beg. And she almost did.

There was also Finian to consider. Protection of that child must come before anything else, so in the end, I had no choice but to relent.

And now I've met her.

A successful lawyer and also a serial killer. And she knows I know. She did nothing to mask their countless souls from me.

My eldest boy loves her.

It's not an infatuation or a case of wanting what his baby brother had, which is what I suspected it might be. He worships the ground she walks on.

She insists she doesn't love him. Who is she trying to kid? She stormed off the shooting range because she couldn't bear to watch him with Ava. A girl who, on the surface, is a perfect match for him having been born and raised in the mafia life. Also, a girl that Jaine wiped the floor with on the shooting range.

Accuracy like that takes years of practice.

I'm going to make it my business to find out all there is to know about Jaine Jones. The girl who will step into my very own shoes in due course. The girl who's loved by two of my sons and who loves both in return, even though she can't or won't admit to the second.

Paddy's lost to her now, and Eoin will be too if she's not careful.

For an intelligent woman she's not seeing what everyone else can. Or at least what I can.

I'm standing outside the downstairs cloakroom having just listened to their exchange.

The door swings open and I take them both in.

"Interrupting something, am I?" I smile politely.

"Nothing at all," Jaine replies, her expression deadpan.

I'll have my work cut out for me with this girl, even if all I'm doing is forcing her to look past the end of her nose.

The physical attraction is there between her and Eoin. Her jealousy. Their push and pull. Everyone witnessed it outside. It's more than just sex. She's lying to herself, and there's a reason for that, but I'm not sure what it is.

I'm not sure she knows herself, and that's the problem.

"Is now a good time, Jaine?"

She nods reluctantly. I'm sure she'd much rather repeat her experience with Fergal than have anything to do with me, but I'm her mother-in-law whether she likes it or not. Whereas that may or may not change in the future, I'm also her son's grandma. That will never change. She has no choice but to let me into her life whether I'm welcome or not.

Liam's having a day off, and Dec's currently driving Ava, so I've asked Jaine to take me to Hell's Kitchen. There's a deli there that my Fergal likes to use. We try to purchase what we can from our little community. These people pay us for protection, so the very least we can do is give a little back where we can.

I didn't bother to tell the others where we'd gone, I just left a note on the kitchen table. If I had, they would only have insisted that one of them come along for the ride, and I need Jaine to open up to me.

We're ten minutes into the journey and still not a word has been said. It's time to break the ongoing silence.

"Did you enjoy the party, Jaine? The boys seemed to enjoy themselves."

She'd rather pull her nails out one by one that partake in idle chit chat with me, I'm sure, so it's best to keep it to safe topics.

For now.

"It was quite the unforgettable experience."

The corners of my mouth twitch up. She's trying to be polite by not speaking her mind and saying it was over the top. Which it was.

"And what did you think of the live entertainment?"

She half-smiles. "The clown was more frightening than all of the O'Connell men put together. I'm sure Finian and JJ will have plenty of sleepless nights and will most likely need therapy."

I chuckle. She's right. Clowns aren't for everyone. Little JJ looked terrified and hid his face in the crook of Eoin's neck for the entire show.

"I thought it best we…"

"We're being followed."

She just announces it matter-of-factly.

"And why would you think that?"

"There's a black Mercedes behind us. I've deliberately driven down a few side streets, and it's done the same. It may just be a coincidence, but my gut's telling me not."

We don't get to discuss it further. Perhaps the driver had a sixth sense and realized that we were on to him as the vehicle overtakes us then cuts us off, causing Jaine to have to slam on the breaks.

"I'm no one of interest. I'm just Nicole, your driver."

I nod at her as the occupants of the other vehicle step out. I recognize who it is immediately. We did suspect there may be some form of revenge attack, and here it is now, several months later.

"Roisin."

I smile politely at the man who's opened my car door. "It's nice to see you, Malky."

I respond as though everything is normal as I take in the morbidly obese individual with his comb-over black hair, watery blue eyes, and rosacea-infused cheeks. Clearly, Molly takes her looks from her ma.

I watch as his goon pulls Jaine from the driver seat. She doesn't put up a struggle and neither does she speak. Wise on both counts.

"Who's the blonde?"

"She's my new driver. My old one retired."

"Her name?"

"Nicole."

I watch as his eyes drift over her while his heavy pushes her into the back of the Mercedes.

"She's a bonnie lass."

"She's also married with two children." I know exactly where his mind's going. I also know that if he harms one single hair on her head that my eldest will move Heaven and Earth to find him then tear him apart with his bare hands.

"A pity. Anyway, shall we, Roisin" He smiles at me with nicotine-stained teeth before offering me his hand and helping me down from the vehicle.

I'm not pushed inside the car like Jaine was. As Ma Duster, I'm treated with a little more respect, even if the ending he has in store for us both is the same.

I make eye contact with Jaine briefly, but nothing is said as we sit side by side in the back of the vehicle. She's had her phone confiscated and I've had my handbag taken.

I'm only sorry now that I didn't alert the others to the fact that we were popping out. Still, there's nothing we can do to change that now.

Our future is in God's hands, and Malky's too, of course.

Regardless of whether Jaine and I survive this ordeal, Malky's life is now in the hands of all the male O'Connells, but he'll already be aware of that.

By the looks of him, his health is already in steady decline, probably down to poor lifestyle choices. He doesn't look like he's long for this world, so he'll no doubt be more than happy to meet his maker sooner rather than later if it means he can avenge his only daughter on his way out.

In his defense, she was humiliated by Eoin. In Malky's position, and had we been blessed with a daughter, my Fergal may well have done the same.

The vehicle comes to a standstill, and I look up at the large spires of the gothic-looking cathedral.

St. Patrick's.

Mine and Jaine's final destination if Malky has his way.

It's closed to the public this week while several of the handmade pews that were destroyed in the shooting incident are replaced. The O'Connell's have, of course, paid for all of the remedial works to be undertaken, including the costs of any fixtures and fittings. Many were irreplaceable, so we've also made a considerable donation by way of an apology and for all the inconvenience caused. We needed to atone for the atrocities that took place in The Almighty's own house. It's a small price to pay given what we could have lost that day.

Malky and his goon alight the vehicle.

"Ladies."

We're both helped from the car before being led up the church steps. Nothing is said. Malky will likely wait until we're inside before he communicates further.

We all know the reason behind all of this. We're just waiting for him to furnish us with the plan of what he has in store for us both. Me in particular, because right now, Jaine doesn't factor in his plans. As far as he's concerned, she was simply in the wrong place at the wrong time.

He obviously doesn't realize that she's Eoin's wife and the woman he jilted Molly for. If he did, he would quickly become her captive audience and I would be the one then surplus to requirements.

Let's hope he doesn't find out.

CHAPTER FORTY-FIVE

JAINE

Saint Patrick's Cathedral, Manhattan, New York

I MUST HAVE THE WORDS 'PLEASE ABDUCT ME' INVISIBLY INKED ON my forehead. First time with Ace and Irish. Second time with Sarah, and now here I am, third time unlucky with Roisin O'Connell.

Malky. That's what Roisin called him. I have no idea who Malky is, but he's Irish, as his accent is strong. It's also clear that he feels the Dusters have wronged him in some way and now he wants his pound of flesh.

We pull up in front of St. Patrick's Cathedral. All the memories of that day immediately come flooding back.

Irish's wedding.

Like with Ace, I can think about it without tears most days now. Or at least visible ones.

Malky and his goon open the car doors. I get yanked out while

Roisin gets the VIP treatment. I'm just glad to escape the confines of the vehicle as it stinks of bad breath. Going by the state of Malky's teeth, I think he's the guilty party with the extreme case of halitosis.

It's still warm and sunny out. It's as good a day as any to die, I guess. They haven't brought us here to admire the kaleidoscopic effect of the stained-glass windows.

"This way, ladies."

Malky makes eye contact with me, and I turn away. There's no point in antagonizing whoever he is.

We enter the building. It looks the same as before aside from remedial works that appear to be ongoing. The most notable thing missing is the overwhelming stench of lilies.

Malky chats animatedly to Roisin as we walk upstairs, his fat thighs chaffing together the only other sound. We're led to a small room. I know it well. It's right beside the one I used when I took out the sniper bad guys. The only reason I didn't use this one is because it has no view over the proceedings. It's fully enclosed.

I glance around at the natural stone walls and the bare floor. A chair has been prepared in advance, which has already been set in concrete. It's obviously a mobster thing. It reminds me of Mr. Unfortunate at the docks. The sounds, sights, smells, and tastes all come flooding back.

I watch as Roisin is bound to the chair.

"Sit." Malky finally addresses me, pointing toward a small wooden pew that's around twelve feet in front of where Roisin's sitting. She's done as I asked as Malky here obviously sees me as nothing more than a Duster toy soldier.

"You'll never get away with this, Malky. You know that, don't you?" Roisin breaks the ongoing silence.

"I know that, Roisin, but I want justice to be served."

"We promised nothing."

"You promised to make my daughter Ma Duster and then you reneged on the deal." He hisses his fury, spraying saliva over the floor.

I frown inwardly. Is this Molly McGrath's father?

"No promises were ever made, and you know it. And your girl wasn't harmed in any way."

"On the outside, perhaps not, but on the inside, it's a different matter. She's still struggling to come to terms with the fact that your eldest jilted her."

"That was always his prerogative. The role she applied for could not be compromised and you know it."

"And how would Molly have done that?"

"She was found out to be deceitful, Malky. And not just once, but on several separate occasions. We can't have a bare-faced liar at the head of our organization."

"But you can have a biker."

"The biker in question birthed an O'Connell. Eoin's son."

He laughs smugly. "Come now, Roisin. You and I both know that Padraig is the boy's father. There was no need for Eoin to ever be dragged into the mess when clearly any O'Connell would have done."

There's a pause. No one was meant to know that intel outside of the immediate family.

"What makes you say that?" Roisin quizzes.

"Eoin told Molly himself. She asked why they couldn't just adopt his son and Eoin explained that the lad isn't his."

I suddenly feel sick. Why would Eoin tell her that? She was never to be trusted. It was the reason I didn't want her knowing in the first place.

Who else has she told?

Hell hath no fury like a woman scorned. The old saying immediately springs to mind.

The only thing that has more fury than a scorned fucking woman is Jaine Jones if anyone threatens her babies.

I can't die here today because now my boys are at risk.

I glance at Roisin. If she wanted to, she could give me up, save herself, and walk away. I'm pretty sure old Malky would much rather end my life than hers since I'm the female responsible for ruining his daughter's happily ever after.

"That aside, she's a liar." Roisin ignores his revelation.

"My daughter is no liar."

"She told the family she saved Eoin's life, but she didn't. She blatantly lied to secure the Ma Duster position, Malky. Eoin had discounted her, and she knew it. He only reconsidered her as he thought himself obligated."

"She did save his life. She told me so herself."

"Then she's a liar, but you're also a fool."

He storms towards Roisin. She'll never withstand a beating from him.

"Leave her alone!"

He turns and glares at me before grinning, the saliva he was spitting earlier having now formed a hard white crust in the corners of his mouth.

"Ah, the pretty little blonde driver." He walks across and backhands me across the face with his gloved hand. My teeth rattle. It's a similar hit to the one Fergal inflicted.

Another mobster thing.

"Every time she lies, shall I give you her punishment, blondie? Is that what you want?"

Another backhander and I'm immediately seeing stars.

I wait until the darkness passes before spitting out the blood that's accumulated inside my mouth.

"Yes. That's what I want."

"Set it up." Malky addresses his side kick.

We all turn our attention to the heavy. He's dressed head to toe in black and is reminiscent of a fatter, older version of Dec. He puts on a pair of leather gloves before removing a replica of the Sword of the Spirit from the wall. What are they going to do? Run us through. Decapitate us?

The heavy takes some rope and ties it firmly around the hilt, then throwing the rope over the exposed beam in the room, he positions the sword so it's directly above Roisin's head.

"We thought the driver would be a man, so perhaps this will be over quicker than we thought." Malky smirks at his comrade.

The goon's expression remains impassive as he walks over to me. Using tape, he binds my left arm to my body before taping up the fingers of my right hand, leaving only my thumb exposed. He smirks, his first facial expression of the day as he places the other end of the rope between by taped fingers and my thumb.

I look at it, then stare at Roisin.

I let the rope go and the sword drops on her head.

"So, your plan is to kill Roisin?" I ask the obvious question.

Malky looks at me but doesn't make any attempt to move towards me this time, which I'm grateful for. I still feel partially dazed from the backhanders I've already received.

"Molly has shut herself away. She feels sullied. She told her friends that she was going to be the next Ma Duster. Now she feels like a laughingstock. She's as good as dead inside. Given that the Dusters have destroyed the most important woman in my life, I think it only right that I destroy the most important woman in theirs. Wouldn't you agree, Nicole?"

I don't respond. There's no point. It won't change anything.

In the distance, I hear a phone ring. It's my business phone.

The others will have noticed our absence not long after we'd gone, I'm sure, but given we've been AWOL for the best part of an hour, I guess they'll now be realizing that something is wrong.

I then pray to God that no one tries to ring my burner.

It's on silent, but it will still vibrate.

CHAPTER FORTY-SIX

EOIN

The O'Connell Home, Darling, New York

"I'VE TRIED BOTH NUMBERS. NEITHER JAINE NOR MA IS answering."

We're gathered in the kitchen, each of us pacing the floor while running our hands through our hair, which seems to be the O'Connell men's way. Sarah and Jessie are putting the little ones down for a nap. I halt my pacing to stare at Dylan as he speaks. This is not what any of us wanted to hear.

We've just found Ma's note. We all stupidly assumed that she and Jaine were sitting down and sorting out their boatload of differences.

Obviously not.

Obviously, they've gone out without telling a fucking soul when we all currently have targets on our backs.

"Try the deli. Ma's note says they were on the way to the deli.

Call them. See if they've arrived, and if they did, how long ago it's been since they left."

We all watch as Dylan dials the number then laughs and jokes with Aoife, the lady who runs the place. She and Ma are friends. They have been most of their lives. Even with that in mind, he'll want answers, but he won't want to give anything away. It's at times like this when all you can trust is blood.

If they never turned up, then this is not good. Not good at all.

Dylan's face pales. He disconnects the call. We don't even need to ask, but he says it out loud anyway, just to reaffirm what we all already know.

"They haven't been into the shop today. Aoife says the order Ma placed is still under the counter. I've told her I'll get one of the drivers to drop by and pick it up. That Ma must have gotten waylaid as she had a few errands to run today."

I nod. "I'll ask Dec to go."

"Shall I try Jaine's other phone?"

He's referring to her burner. My reply is instant. "You will do no such thing. What if it rings or vibrates? If it's still in her possession, it may be the only lifeline they have."

He shrugs. "So what should we do, then?"

"Use the tracking system to locate the vehicle. If they have been abducted, then it's unlikely those involved would have taken them anywhere in a Duster SUV. It will at least give us a place to start. We have nothing else to go on. Once we've located the car, we can check the surrounding CCTV in the area. Try to track their path or at least find out who took them and to where."

"I'll set off for my apartment now. It'll be easier to access the systems from there."

"Quickly, Dylan. We've not a moment to lose."

He knows exactly what I'm saying. That every second they're gone they become more at risk and less likely to be alive.

I look at my da. He's aged in the space of an hour. The love of his life taken by God knows who and to God knows where.

I'm grateful that he's letting me handle things. He knows I'm more than capable. That the only thing missing from my life is a wife.

But then, I have a wife. A wife I promised to protect.

I can feel my monster surfacing, but I need to remain calm and focused. There are little ones in the house. Women. I'm not in a shipping container on the docks and there's no one to kill.

Yet.

But there will be. Because if anyone has harmed her then there will be hell to pay, and I will personally extract that payment limb by limb and with my bare fucking hands.

Nothing must happen to her.

Nothing.

CHAPTER FORTY-SEVEN

ROISIN

Saint Patrick's Cathedral, Manhattan, New York

MALKY AND HIS HEAVY HAVE GONE, LEAVING JAINE HOLDING ON TO the end of a piece of rope, the other end of which is tied, one can only hope quite firmly, to the hilt of a sword that's currently hanging over my head.

I can't topple my chair. For one, it may just see me splayed out on the floor with another part of me then directly exposed to the McGrath's Sword of Damocles, and I'm not sure my old bones could sustain the cold of the hard ground for very long. For another, my chair has been set in a concrete slab. Weighted so it drops like a stone. I know the method well. The Dusters use the same one to sink bodies to a watery grave.

I take in Jaine Jones. While she's beautiful in her own unique way, both my boys have wined and dined females with far greater claims to beauty. I know that's not what's attracted each of them to her. It's because she has a certain *je ne sais quoi*. It's difficult to put your finger on exactly what it is about her. It's a combination of many things. She has an air of something.

Strength. Determination. Fearlessness. Loyalty. The ability to commit cold-blooded murder with ease.

Fergal knew he was looking at the future Ma Duster. That by hook or by crook we had to make it so. Don't get me wrong, knowing what we do now and factoring in young Finian, we would never get in the way of her taking the vows with our Paddy if he were available. But he's not. He's already taken them with Sophia, and nothing can free him now apart from Sophia's death. And I've seen where they live. It's the Sicilian equivalent of Fort Knox. No one is getting anywhere near her or Paddy.

Like Eoin, I underestimated Jaine Jones. Or should I say Jaine O'Connell.

My daughter-in-law. Married to the brother she insists she doesn't love. My eldest. While pining over the one she does. My youngest.

A woman I had Molly verbally threaten the life of. A woman who has my very own life in her hands.

Having been on the receiving end of two brutal backhanders from Malky, her face is so badly bruised her eye has almost swollen shut. She didn't make a sound.

She took what he gave, and she did so for me. She knows as well as I do that as much as I'm young and strong mentally, at almost seventy years old, my body is becoming older and weaker.

"Thank you."

She looks across at me as she's sat there dressed head to toe in black and wearing biker boots.

"For?"

"Taking the hits."

She snorts. "I need you alive, Roisin. Without you, I'm as good as dead."

I nod. She's right, of course.

There's a pause.

"Thank you."

"What for?" It's my turn to ask.

"For not telling them who I am. You could easily have traded your life for mine. I'm the reason Molly was jilted in the first place having issued Eoin with the ultimatum."

I smile politely at her. "You're the mother of my grandson. What sort of a grandma would I be if I willingly allowed him to grow up without his ma in his life? He needs you. Both of your boys do."

I pause before I say the next part.

"You're also my daughter-in-law. What sort of a mother would I be if I took from my own boy the person he loves most?"

Silence.

I can tell she's digesting what I've just said. She's probably wondering which of my sons I'm referring to, and she's probably hoping that it's Padraig.

She stares at the rope that she's been made to hold on to. We both know that, for now, it's a simple enough task. Simple until it feels like she's holding up a slab of concrete. Simple until her fingers get pins and needles, or worse still, they go numb and she can no longer feel it slip between her fingers.

"Eoin."

I put her out of her misery as I know she won't lower herself to ask.

She lifts her gaze to look at me, disappointed. I can feel the emotion radiate from her. She wants the love of my youngest, not my eldest. Even though he's lost to her, she craves it more than anything.

But I need to move her mind away from him. It won't help anyone.

"Eoin doesn't love me. Love doesn't allow you to move on as quickly as he did."

I snort. "You played him for five months, Jaine. You told him that you didn't love him, that you never would, that you hated him. What did you expect him to do? He needs to step up and we all know that every Da Duster needs his Ma Duster by his side in order to be able to do so."

She knows what I'm saying is true. Did she just expect to walk off time after time and for him to be sitting around waiting for her to change her mind?

Her forehead creases.

"I never said I hated him. At least, not recently. I don't hate him."

"Then perhaps he misinterpreted your words. but that's what he believes to be the case."

"He told you that?" Her frown deepens.

I know what's going through her head. The fact that if neither of us get out of here alive that Eoin will continue to think that she hated him.

What does it matter what he thinks if she's so insistent she doesn't care about him?

"Eoin would never tell me anything of such a personal nature. He's an extremely private person as you know. He told Dylan. Dylan told me."

She nods. Like me, she'll be only too aware that since the Jessie fiasco, Eoin and Dylan have become close, the same as she and Jessie have.

"Why did he tell Molly the truth about Fin?"

It's my turn to frown because even I'm confused by those actions. "I'm not sure. From what Malky said it seems Molly had suggested that she and Eoin adopt him. Perhaps he chose to tell her the real reason why they couldn't. That he trusted her enough because if she loved him, she would never betray him."

"She never loved him." It's said matter-of-factly.

"How do you know?"

"No woman has ever told Eoin they love him. He told me so himself."

I feel pain in my heart over such a frank confession. That my eldest boy has never felt love aside from that of his immediate family. I thought I knew him better than he did himself, but I wasn't aware of that.

He told Jaine he loved her. He wanted desperately to hear the words back, but he never did, and she's determined that he never will.

"How did it make you feel when he confessed such a thing to you?"

She releases her breath slowly as she considers my question. "Guilty. Sad. He deserves to be loved. Everyone does."

"This coming from the woman who tried to ruin his life." I snort.

"This coming from the woman who blatantly threatened to end mine," she snaps.

"Touché."

"I held him responsible when I shouldn't have. I'm well aware of my own goddamn mistakes and that he didn't really do anything wrong."

"The only thing Eoin did wrong was fall in love with the same woman as his brother, but he wasn't in control of that. We don't get to choose who we love."

Surely, she must know that he still loves her. She's far from being stupid or naïve. Or is she deliberately not wanting to see what's in front of her because her feelings mirror his and she doesn't wish to accept them?

To embrace the future, Jaine needs to let go of the past, and right now, she's not willing to do that.

"I saw him with Ava."

"Doing what? Nothing is my guess. Come now, Jaine. I believe you know deep down that Ava means nothing to him. He's taken the vows with you. He won't have kissed the girl, let alone done anything else with her, no matter how much she may try to tempt him. She wants him for herself, but the same could be said for most of the females in the city. He has no interest in them. Ava's merely in reserve because he has no option but to find himself a suitable, willing wife."

"And I'm not willing." She speaks quietly before her mouth slowly curves upwards. "But I'm not suitable either, am I, Roisin? As a biker, I'm lower than pond life in your eyes. Why is it that you hate bikers so much?"

She's right. I do hate bikers and I've never denied it. I reluctantly let my mind drift back to when I was twenty-one. I seldom let it go back there for reasons I've told no one apart from my Fergal.

"There are several motorcycle clubs dotted around New York, as you know. As young girls, all our heads were turned by the handsome young men wearing their leathers and driving around on gleaming motorbikes." There's a lengthy pause. "I very stupidly got involved with one. A handsome lad with a mop of blonde hair and the most sparkling blue eyes you've ever seen." I can't help but smile at the bittersweet memory. "Coming from a strict Irish Catholic family, my parents instilled in me that I had to remain pure for my future husband. That it was a sin to do anything out of wedlock and that I would be cast aside by The Almighty if I even had such wicked thoughts, let alone acted on them. My biker boy filled my head with nonsense about the rosy future he and I would share. He was full of sweet talk and charm. In the end, I gave in, and I ended up pregnant. When I told him, he explained that he couldn't be with me because he'd also gotten the president of the club's daughter pregnant. He claimed he had been put under pressure to make her his old lady and that they were going to have to jump over the broom together or whatever it is that you lot do instead of taking proper vows."

We both chuckle, but it's tinged with sadness.

"In the end, I had to confess everything to my parents. In their defense, they were more understanding than I thought they'd be. They simply sent me away to live in a house with girls in a similar situation. Once I'd had the baby, he was immediately taken from me. My parents reassured me that he was found the very best of adoptive homes.

"I was broken for a long time after until my Fergal found me. He had his choice of every Irish girl in Hell's Kitchen, but he chose the tarnished one who was classed as used goods."

We stare at each other for a time. There's no rush to speak. We won't be going anywhere soon, if at all.

"Did you not ever try to find him?"

"Who?" I stare at her as I drag my mind back from the past to the present.

"Your son."

I shake my head. "My life had moved on. His would have moved on too. It would have been unfair of me to try to shoehorn my way in."

"And only Fergal knows?"

I nod. "My parents have long since passed."

"If you change your mind about finding him, I can gain access to records, and for any I can't, I'm sure Jessie can…"

"Thank you for your kind offer, Jaine, but I won't be changing my mind on the matter."

A pause.

"I'm sorry for what happened to you, Roisin, and I truly mean that. But you can't simply condemn all bikers because of one bad experience."

"I just didn't want my sons to go through what I did. In my experience, bikers live by their own rules. They live hedonistic, almost nomadic lifestyles. Maybe that's why they stick to their own kind. There's no expectation for them to behave like normal people that way."

"Is that why you wanted me to be kept away from Padraig? Because I'm a biker?"

I look at her. "Partially, but that wasn't the main reason."

"Do you mind telling me what was?"

"Aside from the fact that he was part of an arranged marriage before your existence became known to us, if I recall, you were in love with two men at the time. The biker you went on to marry and Padraig."

She nods.

"My youngest was hurting, and as a mother now yourself, you know it's the hardest thing to see. Your child suffering. I didn't want Padraig's pain to drag on or for him to get his hopes up when, from experience, the likelihood was you were going to choose one of your own. Tell me, Jaine, who would you have picked if you could have chosen only one?"

She stares at me, her reality now sinking in. That maybe with hindsight, the decision we made for Paddy was actually a blessing in disguise for all of them.

She doesn't answer because she can't.

Not then. And not now.

"I admit that I didn't want any of my boys becoming involved with bikers based on my own experience, and I apologize for that. It was wrong of me to pre-judge the rest of you."

She still doesn't reply.

"Going by your silence, perhaps we did you a favor when it came to Padraig by taking that impossible decision out of your hands. Maybe, in the end, our doing so was the kindest thing for everyone concerned. It's time to move on now. You need to let go of the past and accept the fact that you love him too."

I stare at her, and she frowns.

"Who do I love?"

"Eoin."

She shakes her head. "I don't."

I tsk. "You're lying to yourself. Everyone can see it, even if you can't. The boy can sense that you do, and that's why he's refusing to walk away. Subconsciously or otherwise, you're giving him hope then refusing to commit."

CHAPTER FORTY-EIGHT

JAINE

Saint Patrick's Cathedral, Manhattan, New York

I don't answer. Not only do I not know what to say, but I can't even think about that right now.

For now, I just need to sit here and hold on to a piece of rope that feels like it's getting heavier with each passing hour.

We sit in silence. It's not awkward, and even if it were, it's not like we can go anywhere. We're both pondering what's been said, I'm sure.

Roisin's reveal about the son she gave up. Her next reveal that Eoin's still in love with me.

Then the $64,000 question.

If I had to choose between Ace and Irish, which way would I have gone?

It's a question I refuse to ask myself because even if I knew the answer, which I don't, it wouldn't make a damn bit of difference.

Ace is dead. Irish is as good as dead. What our conversation did do is explain her reasonings. It's clear she wants me to move forward with Eoin.

I won't. Even if I wanted to try, I know the relationship would be short-lived if the key feeling isn't reciprocated, and regardless of what she thinks, I don't love him.

I tried to force things with Delaney. I didn't want to hurt him or let him down, but in the end, I succeeded in doing both. My taking four years to reach the conclusion that I no longer wanted to be with him almost destroyed him mentally. I'm not going through that with anyone else. I'm not saying it would bring Eoin O'Connell to his knees if we tried and subsequently failed, but I know he wants it all. The wife. The marriage. The children.

Do I even want more kids?

It would need to be all or nothing, and I can't commit to all as easily as I can to nothing. I care, but it isn't enough. I'd rather him face rejection now as opposed to in years to come. Surely Roisin must see the sense in that. It's what she's just admitted to doing for Irish. He deserves better than me. I want more for him.

Then why is it that I hate the thought of him being with anyone else? She's right. I'm confused, and in turn, I'm confusing him. I'm not playing fair.

But now is not the time. At the moment, the chances of either of us getting out of here alive are slim to none.

I exhale. It's dark. I have no idea what time it is, but I reckon we've been in here for around six hours, give or take.

"You should try to get some sleep." I speak quietly. At least if she's asleep and I accidentally drop a sword on her head, she won't know anything about it.

She doesn't answer, but I hear her breathing even out not much later.

Seconds. Minutes. Hours.

I've no idea how long passes. There's no clock in here counting down the time to Roisin's expected doom by my hand.

My arm aches. My fingers are numb.

But worst of all, I'm struggling not to fall asleep in the pitch dark. I keep jerking awake in a panic thinking I've let the rope go. My fingers are so cold that I can barely feel it, and I don't want to adjust them in case I accidentally let it slip and kill my little boy's grandma. I want to shout across to make sure she's still okay, but there's no point in both of us being awake.

So, I sit in the dark, surrounded by the non-existent stench of lilies and death and the unwelcome memories of Irish's wedding.

Malky's expecting to walk in tomorrow and find the deed done. As soon as Roisin's dead, the blonde driver will be next as she'll be surplus to requirements.

There really is only one option. I'll have to let the rope go because there is no Plan B.

I spend the rest of the night jerking myself awake until I'm not sure whether I'm asleep or not, or whether it really is just one big nightmare.

Dawn's breaking.

At least now I can see the rope, even though I still can't feel it. My arm's now threatening to snap. I can't hold on much longer.

Roisin's staring at me.

She knows it too.

Even though she's slept, it's clearly done her no great favors. She looks old and haggard. I can't imagine I look much better. I can barely see out of my left eye, so the bruising to my cheek must be pretty extensive. What's one more bruise if not just another visible reminder that you've survived one more day with what this life has to goddamn throw at you?

"I'm going to have to let go of the rope." My voice sounds stark against the silence, and I can see my breath in the frigid air.

It feels like a morgue in here. Seems fitting somehow.

The church is closed for repairs because of the extensive damage suffered when The Exterminator took out the bad guys.

When The Exterminator took out the bad guys. My rifle is still behind The Virgin Mary in the room next door.

"I know."

"I have access to a gun."

"How did you manage that?"

"I can't say."

"You having access to a gun doesn't change the fact that I have a sword hanging over my head."

"I realize that."

"And how do you suggest we get around that small problem?"

"I'm going to let go of the rope then run and push the sword out of the way before it connects with your skull."

"What if you trip?"

"Then it's game over for you."

"What if it cuts you in half?"

"Then it's game over for me."

"It's not much of a plan."

"Well, it's all we've got, unless you've got any better ideas?"

"You know fine well that I haven't."

"Then we are where we are. Any last words in case at least one of us makes it out of here alive?"

"Tell my boys that I love them. You?"

"Same."

We both take in what could well be our final surroundings. The old stone-walled room with its ancient artefacts.

I don't say another word. I don't let my nerves get the better of me. I don't let the now-familiar taste of vomit deter me either.

I simply count down in my head.

Three.

Two.

One.

I let the rope go and I run, grimacing in pain when the blade cuts into my shoulder as I struggle to push it backward. It moves freely, which means it hasn't connected with anything or anyone else.

Yet.

I can't see the blood, but I can feel it instantly turning cool in the freezer-like conditions. Not that my bleeding matters. The only thing that matters is hearing the sound of metal as it collides with the stone flooring.

I'm breathing heavily.

It has nothing to do with running or the exertion of pushing the heavy blade away. My heart is pounding over the permanent image now engraved in my brain of what I could have been facing had I been too slow.

Roisin is pale. I didn't announce that I was going to act. I just did it.

It was intentional. That way, if I had been unsuccessful, her death would have been pretty much instantaneous, which is all any of us can ever hope for.

I glance at the wound on my shoulder which is currently dripping blood all over her pink cardigan. It's deep and will need sutures, I'm sure, but I'll live.

We make eye contact. We both know that we've stared Death in the face today and survived. But we also both know that he never leaves empty-handed.

It's then we hear the entrance doors as they open then close.

Roisin is still bound. There's no time to deal with that when whoever's come to join the party is mere minutes away.

I can't switch on the location finder on my phone as it will be dead. I never charged it as I wasn't expecting to have to use it during a kids' birthday party.

Cursing, I use the now horizontal sword to cut through the tape on my right hand until my fingers are free and the blood is circulating once more. Then I use it to cut off the tape binding my left arm to my body.

Fuck.

Did they lock us in?

Roisin watches as I quickly make my way to the door. I nod at her. It's a silent promise, letting her know I'll be back. I breathe out in relief when I turn the handle and the door clicks open. Closing it behind me, I make my way to the room next door.

There's been no mention of any weapon having been found, but that doesn't mean that it hasn't. I reach behind the statue of Mary, then pull out my rifle. It's covered in a fine film of dust, but it's exactly as I left it.

"Thank you, God." I close my eyes as I whisper to the ceiling, grateful that for once The Almighty has answered my silent prayers.

CHAPTER FORTY-NINE

ROISIN

Saint Patrick's Cathedral, Manhattan, New York

I WATCH AS THE GIRL WHO WOULD HAVE BEEN MY DAUGHTER-IN-LAW enters the small room. She looks surprised initially, then it changes to one of distaste. I'm not at my finest having spent the time I have tied to a plastic chair. I'm covered in filth and blood. Meanwhile, Molly is professionally dressed in a grey pin-striped suit. Has she already found herself a new job and a new fancy man? She definitely doesn't look as devastated as Daddy Dearest was making her out to be. One of them is lying. Then again, it's a trait that typically runs in families, so it's probably both. One thing's for sure. Molly McGrath wasn't expecting to walk in here to find me alive and well. She was expecting me to have a sword sticking from my skull.

I tsk as I shake my head in disappointment. "Molly, surely there could have been another way."

"He betrayed me, Roisin. You both did." She pouts like a child.

"So you thought taking my life was the answer?"

"I wanted to take away the thing that meant most to him."

"Then surely you should have set your sights on Jaine."

"Daddy says we can go after her next time. He said she would have been far more difficult to take as she seldom leaves her building."

"Not really. We were traveling in the same car."

She frowns. "What do you mean?"

"Just as I said, we were in the same vehicle. Are you not wondering where my female driver is?"

I nod at the empty pew facing me. She glances at it and her frown deepens.

How could I have ever thought this girl suitable for the Ma Duster role when she's walked in here and has neither assessed her surroundings nor identified where both hostages are?

I glance behind her exaggeratedly. Her eyes widen as her life no doubt flashes in front of them. She now knows exactly where my driver is.

I smile as she spins, knowing her last sight in this world will be Jaine Jones pointing a rifle at her head. I know what Jaine can do from five hundred meters away. She doesn't need to bother checking the wind direction today. And I know she won't hesitate. Not with a person who's just admitted to wanting her dead.

"Hi, Molly. Bye, Molly."

I smirk at Jaine's words then close my eyes before she pulls the trigger. Not because I don't want to witness the execution of this deceitful girl. It's because I don't want any of her brains getting in my eyes.

We both stare down at Molly as she lays on the floor, her eyes wide open, a perfect round hole in her forehead and surrounded by an expanding pool of her blood. Placing the weapon on the pew, Jaine unbinds me.

I stand, stagger, and she holds me upright until I find my balance.

"What now?" I ask.

"Before we contact your family, I need to make a quick call."

She rummages through Molly's jacket and pulls out her phone. She then uses Molly's thumb to unlock the screen before going through the phone. A few minutes later, she makes a call.

"It's me."

I can hear a mumble, but I've no idea who it is.

She faces away from me as she talks in hushed whispers, and while she's speaking, I use the opportunity to stretch my legs. It's then I see it on the floor behind me. I know what it is even before I pick it up.

"Fifteen minutes and no longer."

Putting the phone in her pocket, she turns around to take me in, and I hold up my finding with a smile on my face.

"I shared my secret with you, daughter. Is there anything you'd care to share with me?" Silence as she takes in the engraved bullet that I'm holding between my finger and thumb. "Are you not going to try to deny it?"

It all adds up now. Her coming back to New York ahead of time. Her being at our Paddy's wedding. Her abilities on the shooting range.

"It goes no further."

"So, you're admitting it. That you're The Exterminator."

"You're holding the goddamn proof in your hand, Roisin. What do you expect me to say?"

She saved Eoin's life in Nevada. Our whole family in this very building.

The infamous sniper is a female.

The infamous sniper is Jaine Jones.

In fact, not Jaine Jones. Jaine O'Connell. The infamous sniper is an O'Connell.

"Your word, Roisin."

I stare at her.

"Give me your fucking word that this goes no further. Not even Fergal. My secret. My reveal. It's the only goddamn way."

"I give you my word." I pause. "Who were you speaking to?"

"Delaney."

"Why?"

"To come pick up my rifle."

"Jaine, what the fuck?"

Paul Delaney stares at her. I can see the biker's rage trying to take over as he witnesses the mess she's in.

He stops in his tracks when he notices me. Obviously, Jaine has told him as little as possible. Just the location it would seem.

"Roisin." He stares at me, the mother-in-law of his sister, Sarah.

"Paul."

He turns back to her.

"Yes, she knows, Delaney. Never mind that for now. Molly's daddy could turn up any goddamn minute. Your Glock." She holds out her hand and he pulls it from the back of his jeans and passes it to her. She removes a bullet and tosses it in the puddle of brains before sticking the weapon in the back of her leather pants.

"Take this and go." She hands him the sniper rifle. "On your way, call Dylan. Let him know what's happened. We need picking up. Tell him we also need the cleaners here urgently, along with a Molly-sized body bag. Tell him that Eoin is to stay away. He can't come here. He'll react, and it's neither the time nor the place."

"On it, Jaine. I've got Blaze and Jamie keeping the place under observation until the others get here."

"Thanks, Delaney."

He places her rifle in a holdall, they hug tightly, and then with a nod in my direction, he leaves.

We sit side by side on the pew.

"Dylan knows?" I ask.

There's a pause before she replies. "And Padraig."

I'm proud of my boys for keeping her secret. That they've both shown such loyalty they've not even revealed it to the immediate family.

"You said Eoin would react."

She laughs dryly. "He would. You know he would."

"At what?"

"At the state I'm in."

"You're right. He would. Have you seen what he's capable of?"

"I had a front-row seat in an old shipping container at the docks. He ripped out a pedo's heart and made him eat it right in front of me."

I don't show my surprise, but even I've not witnessed Eoin kill. He typically does so in private. He really has shown all three hundred and sixty degrees of himself to this girl.

If that's not a declaration of love, then I don't know what is.

"And did you find his sentence harsh?"

She chuckles. "Not in the slightest. I passed judgment personally. Eoin merely delivered it on my behalf."

I smile.

My Fergal was right. Jaine is indeed Ma Duster material. Even more so given she's the surreptitious sniper.

CHAPTER FIFTY

EOIN

The O'Connell Home, Darling, New York

WE'RE IN THE FAMILY ROOM AT HOME. MA AND DYLAN ARE SITTING whereas I'm doing my usual pacing of the floor.

"I need to see her. It's been two days."

"Give her some time."

I stop my pacing and stare at ma. "Time to do what exactly?"

"You know what she had to do, Eoin. I'd suggest rather than worry about what Jaine's doing, we focus our energies on finding Malky. He'll have returned to the church to find it wiped clean and his daughter missing. He'll now be on the warpath a second time."

"Eoin's just worried about Jaine, Ma. He just wants to see with his own eyes that she's intact. She's still his wife."

"I can speak for myself, Dylan," I hiss at him.

"Sorry."

"You should be." My tone is accusing.

"You can't blame me for the secret getting out." He shakes his head in denial.

"No?"

"You told Molly about Finian. That was your choice, Eoin."

"Only because I thought she cared about me since she saved my life. That she would never betray me. But it turns out she didn't, did she, Dylan? It was The Exterminator all along."

"Enough!" Ma barks as she looks between us. "We can't change what's happened. All we can do is deal with the consequences. We have no idea who else Molly has told, if anyone. Jaine has agreed that for the time being both children are to stay here with me and your da. Duke has agreed to move into the summer house, so he's close at hand and also out of harm's way. We'll get through this together. As a family. As we always do."

"And meanwhile Jaine's living on her own. What if they target her? If anything happens to her. Jesus Christ." I'm pacing again.

"She has a company to run. A business that's located in the same building where she lives. She doesn't need to leave the property. I've also witnessed firsthand what Jaine's capable of. Trust me, Eoin, she'll be just fine."

Eoin's Apartment, Hudson Yards, New York

Swirling the whiskey around the glass, I throw it back in one. At this rate, I'll be pickling my liver faster than our Paddy.

Two days.

I haven't asked to see her, so she hasn't directly said that she won't. It's ma who's been insistent that I give her space and time. It's obviously something they mutually agreed on before they were picked up by Dylan.

Jaine specifically asked that I not attend.

Reading between the lines, there's only one reason. They don't want me to react to what I'll see, which means the fuckers have hurt her, and badly.

She saved ma's life. She ended Molly's.

My moment of reflection is disturbed by a knock on my door.

My phone immediately rings. Dylan. He'll be even more observant now that we're not just at risk from this unknown faction but also from Malky and his mob.

I answer.

"It's Jaine."

I disconnect the call. I don't need to know anything else. Why has she turned up here?

I've showered but not shaved. I run my hand across my stubble, then through my still-wet hair. Grey sweatpants finish off my not finest look, but I haven't time to change when she's waiting at the door.

I open it. Indescribable rage spirals through me as I take her in. Her face is a mass of purple down one side, her eye swollen tightly shut. She's wearing a grey tank top which does nothing to disguise the bandage wrapped under her arm and across her shoulder.

Did the fuckers cut her?

"What did they do to you, Jaine?" I whisper.

"It's nothing. It looks worse than it is."

I pull her inside my apartment, and she grimaces. I've hurt her. Guilt spirals through me, followed by even more rage.

With a roar, I turn and punch the wall. If she's in pain, I want to feel it. I want to share it with her. I want to share every-fucking-thing with her.

But she won't let me.

I punch the wall again and again, and every time she tries to grab my arm.

Anger. Frustration.

Love.

Malky McGrath will suffer like no others have before him for what he's done to my fucking person.

"Eoin."

I let her soft murmurs soothe me as I stand there panting, my skin now sheened with sweat. Then I watch as she gently captures my clenched fist, kissing my knuckles until my blood glosses her lips.

I swallow thickly. Does she have any idea how much I fucking love her?

Leaning over, I capture her lips with mine. I need to taste my blood from her mouth. I kiss her gently. I don't want to hurt her again. She doesn't pull away or try to stop me. She's letting me take what I need as she does the same. Her hand reaches up to grab the back of my hair, and I can immediately sense her disappointment that I've had it cut. She never said anything, but I know she liked that it was too long. She liked me being imperfect.

Because she's imperfect too.

I part our lips, my mouth now filled with the metallic taste of my own blood, and then I stare at her.

Bruised. Battered. Bloodied.

Beautiful.

"Why are you here, Jaine?"

She frowns. Does she regret coming now I've asked a question I wished I hadn't? I don't want her to ever regret coming here. I don't want her to ever regret anything with me.

But she does. She has five months' worth of fucking regret.

"I can't sleep properly. I haven't since it happened. Every time I do, all I visualize is the sword and what would have happened had I let go."

I pull her tight against my chest, inhaling the scent of wildflowers from her hair. "But you didn't let go."

She snorts. "Try telling that to my brain every time I drift off."

I exhale slowly. I don't want to move. I'm enjoying the feel of her being back in my arms too much, her chest pressed against mine. Our hearts beating together and her soft breath on my neck.

Lifting my head, I take her by the hand. "Come."

I walk towards my bedroom. We enter the same room as before. The lights are off. There's just the warm, welcoming glow coming from a bedside lamp.

She turns to look at me. "This isn't a guest room, is it?"

I shake my head. "There's never been another woman in my apartment, let alone in my bed."

She nods slowly in acknowledgment.

I watch as she removes her clothes, then she watches as I do the same.

We're both naked, but this isn't about sex or giving into lust. This is about me being here for her because she needs me to be. Tonight, it's all about me offering her a safe refuge. We both get under the covers, and I switch off the lamp. Wrapping my arms around her from behind so her small body is safely cocooned by mine, I wait until her breathing evens out before placing a soft kiss on her hair, then let myself sleep.

I'm not sure how long passes when I feel her straddling my hips. She presses her slick pussy against my cock and I'm instantly hard. There's been no one since her.

She rubs herself against my full length, and I raise my hands to her hips to let her know she can use my body as a means of escape if that's what she needs to do to get out of her own head space.

She rocks back and forth until the blunt head of my cock slips inside her, and she raises herself up and down over and over again until I'm fully sheathed.

I say and do nothing. I just keep my hands on her hips to let her know that I'm here with her. This isn't about me, it's about her.

I can only see her outline in the dark as she rocks back and forth, but for some reason, that seems to make it feel even more intimate.

Her movements quicken, her walls clenching tightly around me every time until I'm struggling to hold back.

She must feel my cock swell as she increases her pace, desperate to find her own release before I give in to mine.

"Eoin."

I grip her hips and I thrust upward, slow and deep. She grinds against me, desperate to take everything I have and silently begging for more.

I increase my pace as she rides my dick. I wish I could turn on the light. I wish I could see the expression on her face that's causing her nails to dig unapologetically into my abdomen.

Her movements are erratic, then she finally shatters on my cock, her soft mewls of pleasure the only sound against the blinding silence, sounds that encourage me to spill deep inside her, and with one final thrust, I do just that.

She doesn't move away.

Instead, she leans forward, then stretches her legs across mine, so her body is laid atop. Placing a soft kiss on my chest, she tucks her head under my chin. Within seconds, she's asleep once more with my dick still nestled inside her.

Wrapping my arms tightly around her, I soon find my own contented rest.

When I awake in the morning, she's gone.

CHAPTER FIFTY-ONE

JAINE

Jaine's Apartment, Upper East Side, New York

IT'S BEEN FIVE DAYS SINCE IT HAPPENED.

I've been working from home as the kids and Duke are still on lockdown at Roisin and Fergal's place. Given the state I'm in, I'm sure my co-workers are pleased they don't have to look at my beat-up face on a daily basis.

The bruising is starting to turn yellow, and the swelling has all but gone, so I could hide most of it with make-up if I tried. I can't say the same for the ugly red scar on my shoulder. The cut made by the sword needed six sutures in the end.

Still, I'm alive.

Meanwhile, Malky is still at large and no doubt searching for his beloved and very dead daughter.

I'm not sure what the O'Connells did with the body, but it's my thinking that acid was involved. They wouldn't have risked chucking her in The Hudson as there's every likelihood her daddy would have employed a set of divers to search the riverbank and scroll through the sea of water-bloated faces.

I haven't asked Eoin how he felt about the fact that I ended the life of the woman he was set to marry. We've exchanged messages, but all of them have been polite and about nothing much in particular.

We also fucked. There was nothing polite about that.

I shouldn't have gone to his apartment. I know I've caused even more confusion by doing so, but I needed someone.

I needed him.

I was selfish, thinking of my own goddamn needs and not his. Taking and never giving anything back in return.

My thoughts are interrupted by my vibrating phone.

"Jaine."

"Dyl." I smirk.

"We've got Malky." My smirk turns into a frown at the abruptness in his tone. "He's at the docks. I'll pick you up. Eoin will want you to be there."

I CAN TELL DYLAN'S IN SOME SORT OF MOOD THE MOMENT I GET IN the SUV because there are no niceties and no eye contact, both of which aren't like him.

Given recent events, the surveillance will be heavily monitored. There's no way he won't have seen me showing up at Eoin's apartment. Arriving late at night and leaving before daybreak. I suspect he's pissed at what he sees as me leading his brother on yet again. He's right. Unintentionally I am because I can't seem to stay away.

"What are you doing, Jaine?"

I knew it.

"I don't know." It's the honest answer.

He laughs dryly. "You don't know. Well, let me tell you exactly what you're doing. You're messing with my big brother's head. Again." There's a pause. "I understand your reasons for doing what you did, Jaine, but you've paid him back now. Isn't that enough?"

I stare out the window. I deserve his frustrations. What he doesn't realize is that his mirror my own.

"You've always insisted that you hated Eoin, but you never actually did. That's just what you wanted us to believe because it's what you wanted to believe. You then used that hate as something to focus on throughout this whole Paddy thing. I understand. It's what you needed to do to get through it. But it's done now, Jaine. It's time to move on."

I side glance at him as he runs a hand through his hair before turning my attention back out the window.

"You know as well as I do that there's always been something between you and him. You loved Ace. You love Paddy. You're obviously capable of loving more than one person, so why can't there be room in your heart for Eoin too because he loves you, Jaine. He really fucking does."

He exhales loudly, no doubt at my lack of response.

I want to speak, but I can't.

In order to meaningfully respond, I have to say what's on my mind, and I don't know what's going on in my fucking mind, so how can he expect me to find the right goddamn words?

Time passes. I'm well aware that with every second it appears more and more like I don't give a fuck, but I do.

"I don't have the answers to give right now, Dylan. I'm sorry if that's not what you want to hear, but it's all I have."

He lets out a long sigh. "No, I'm sorry Jaine. I appreciate it may not have been the ideal timing for this conversation to have taken place given everything you've just been through." Another sigh.

"When you and Eoin wed, it was meant to be for the protection of Fin, but it's gone way beyond that now. You've both stepped so far over the line there's no coming back. It has to be all or nothing. There can't be any more of this back and forth because that's not fair on him, and you know it. Eoin needs to move on with his life. You both need to. And Ava… well, she's not like Molly. She's a nice girl from a good family. So, if you don't want Eoin, for Christ's sake just let him go and let him be with someone who does."

Having been delivered a heaped plate of food for thought, we travel the rest of the way in frigid silence.

The Docks, Hudson Yards

There's no chair.

This Mr. Unfortunate has been suspended by chains until only his bare feet reach the floor. He's wearing pants and nothing else, just like his unlucky predecessor, the folds of his obese body hanging in multiple layers over the top of the stained black material.

This time I'm guessing the thick metal bound around his wrists will be used to sink him to the deep like some sort of fucked up human anchor.

"Leave."

Dyl knows it's directed at him. He's probably heard the same single word order on numerous occasions. Big brother is as private about his killings as he is everything else in his life.

Despite our awkward journey, Dyl reaches out to squeeze my arm. Is it in comfort? Maybe he doesn't realize I've been here before.

Maybe it's because he's stuck between a rock and a hard place.

I get it. He cares for me a great deal, but I'm not foolish enough to think it isn't surpassed by the love he feels for his own flesh and blood.

I take in Malky McGrath as I wait for Dylan to leave. The man who bitch-slapped me until I was almost blinded in one eye and the one who tried to end the life of the reigning Ma Duster.

He looks confused.

Wondering why I'm here. Wondering who I am. Wondering why 'blondie' has a front row seat at his very own private execution.

"What's Roisin's driver doing here?" he hisses, spitting blood and saliva all over the floor as he does. The left-hand side of his face is swollen. Eoin has obviously been playing with his prey by inflicting on him exactly what he did to me.

I turn my attention to my husband as he stands wearing a pair of coveralls over the top of his all-black clothes. He really must mean business if he's wearing that level of protection. It's my guessing not much of Malky's blood will be left inside his body by the time Eoin has finished with him today.

A shiver runs through me. I know why.

It's because Death is standing beside me. I can feel his ice-cold fingers whispering across my skin once more.

Eoin looks at me, his eyes blazing green.

Anger. Arousal. Adrenaline.

I feel his darkness as it descends across the room, its seductive arms wrapping around me. This time, I welcome them.

The sounds. The sights. The smells. The tastes. They now come flooding back. There's only one thing currently missing.

Good old-fashioned fear.

He'll be here soon enough. He won't want to miss this farewell party.

Eoin turns his attention from me back to Malky.

"This is Jaine. She's not my ma's driver, she's my wife. She's also responsible for blowing your two-faced lying scheming bitch of a daughter's brains out for attempting to bring harm to our fucking family."

He sounds Irish once more, his monster now front and center.

Wrong time, wrong place, but arousal flows through me all the same.

He looks back at me, his nostrils flaring. He can sense it.

I don't want to hear Malky begging for his life or cursing me for taking his daughter's. It's done. It's over.

I walk across the room, and I pick up the murder weapon. There's no sword, but it will do just as well.

I pass Eoin the axe. "End him."

He takes the weapon, then stares down at it before slowly lifting his gaze to meet mine. His head is now cocked, making him look deranged, just like before. It's a sign that he's relinquished control to his monster. Well, as much as he ever dares.

He grins. He's obviously pleased with my choice of weapon.

With a roar, he turns and swings the axe against Malky's leg. I know he'll strike him numerous times before landing the final blow.

He'll make him suffer. He'll make him bleed.

And I know he's doing it for me.

Because *I* was made to suffer. I was made to bleed.

And because he loves me.

I'm standing in a sea of blood when he levels the final blow against Malky's skull. He leaves the weapon in-situ, jutting out from between Malky's bulging, lifeless eyes.

And then he turns to face me.

He storms forward and pushes me back against the cold wall of the container. I grimace when my shoulder makes contact, but unlike at his apartment, this time he shows no guilt or remorse for causing me pain. Fisting my hair and pulling my head back, his lips capture mine and his tongue sweeps deep, drowning all my senses.

I taste blood. Malky's blood. Its rancid flavor will forever seal Eoin and I in this fucked up moment. A taste and a memory that neither of us will ever forget.

With one hand, he rips off his coveralls, then yanks his black t-shirt over his head.

I groan as my hands connect with smooth, inked flesh that's damp with sweat. I can't get enough of the feel of his skin under my fingertips or the taste of its saltiness under my tongue.

His skin is hot, like the raging inferno that burns inside us both can no longer be contained and has finally reached the surface.

I now know that I'm ready to burn in hell with him.

There's no waiting as he rips open the crotch of my pants before lifting me with ease so my legs are secured over his arms. I'm fully exposed to him, and I can't move.

With one hand, he unzips himself, then we both watch as he strokes his huge cock once, twice, before lining up and thrusting deep.

I can't breathe. I can't speak. I can't do anything as he fucks me.

Fast. Furious. Frenzied.

His mouth connects with my neck, and he bites down. I hiss my appreciation, and in return, he fucks me harder.

This isn't about me. This is about the monster within finding his release. Whether I find mine or not is irrelevant. It's his turn to be selfish.

My back scrapes against the container as he pounds into me harder, deeper, each thrust alternating pain and pleasure.

One final thrust. Too deep. Too hard. I grimace in pain as he reaches his crescendo with a roar. His liquid darkness fills me, the sensation pulling me over the edge with him.

Hot. Sweaty. Slippery flesh.

Panting, I rest my forehead against his as I look deep into eyes of aquamarine.

Realization.

Finally.

WEARING EOIN'S JACKET TIED AROUND MY HIPS TO HIDE MY TORN pants, I'm chauffeur driven home by Dec while Eoin coordinates the clean-up.

I know what's been holding me back all this time. Subconsciously or otherwise, I think I've always known.

I need his blessing.

My love. My loyalty. It doesn't matter which. Neither would have allowed me to move forward without him being accepting of the situation.

I pull my phone from my pocket.

Jaine: *I need Padraig's blessing. I need him to tell me he's okay with me being with his brother. That he's accepting of that relationship.*

Roisin: *Leave it with me.*

My future now lies in Irish's hands. If he refuses to accept Eoin and I, then I will respect his decision and end things with his big brother once and for all.

CHAPTER FIFTY-TWO

EOIN

The Hudson Dusters' HQ, Manhattan, New York

IT'S BEEN TWO DAYS SINCE I HACKED MALKY MCGRATH INTO pieces before submerging his remains in acid and turning him into human soup.

Two days since I fucked Jaine hard against the wall of the container while standing in a sea of blood. I hurt her, bruised her, used her for my own self-gratifying purposes.

Is that what she wanted? I can't be sure.

The red mist had yet to lift when I carried out the selfish act.

And now, as seems to be our frustrating way, we've simply reverted back to the mundane like it never happened.

We've been on this merry-go-round for months. I'm getting too old for these playground tactics.

I'm sitting at my desk with my feet on top and our Dylan facing me.

"Spit it out. Say whatever is on your mind. You're going to anyway."

I know exactly what he's going to say.

"I've been doing some thinking."

I don't reply. It's more of a general observation than a question.

"All this time, Jaine's been forcing herself to hate you when anyone with a pair of eyes can see that she cares. How much is anyone's guess as she's refusing to admit that even to herself."

"Go on."

"Jaine's never indecisive about anything, but this situation is causing her to question everything and anything, and she's admitted that she doesn't have the answers."

"When did she?"

"I've already had this conversation with her on the way to the docks. Did she not mention it?"

"Not a word."

He pauses before he continues because he's now going to tell me what I don't want to hear.

"I wish I could encourage you to persevere, but I'm not sure it would make any difference. I think Jaine's reluctance stemmed from Ace initially. Guilt. Betrayal. You and she was all too much too soon, which is perfectly understandable. They shared a life together."

"She was also game playing the whole time." I throw in.

"There's that too. But I think there's a second reason. Paddy."

"In what way?" I frown at him.

He shrugs. "She loves him. She birthed him a son. In her mind, it should be her and him living the happily ever after, not you and her. At the back of her mind, she must surely be worried about how he'd react if you became a genuine couple. She'd be part of the family for real and not just tied to us because of Fin. She'd be your wife. The mother of your future children. Whether he's married or not, if Paddy's not accepting of that relationship, then birthdays and Christmases wouldn't be very pleasant for the rest of us, would they?"

He smiles as he tries to lighten the mood, but it quickly vanishes when he takes in my less-than-receptive expression.

"Think about it, Eoin. Everything Jaine's done these past two plus years has been for him. To protect him. To keep him safe. Because she loves him. She's now being asked to consider doing something that could hurt him more than anything ever has. Something that could potentially destroy him. I honestly think, subconsciously or otherwise, that's what's also been holding her back. You and I both know that Jaine's not the type to sit on the fence. She never has been. She always just says it how it is. In my opinion, it's because she doesn't know which side of the fence she's meant to be on."

I take on board all that he's said, and it makes complete sense. It's true. Everything she's ever done has been in Padraig's best interests, and yet here I am expecting her to choose me over him. The one person she's gone out of her way to protect all this time. The one person I insisted she protect.

It was clear-cut, really. I'm not sure why I didn't see it. Maybe subconsciously I didn't want to face my own reality either.

Jaine was never going to choose me. When it was game-playing, it was fine, but now things have gotten serious it's a different matter.

She may not love me, but she cares enough that she doesn't want to hurt me, and she doesn't want to hurt him either.

In the end, she's the one who's hurting.

I complain that I can't move forward with my life, but she's living in limbo too. She can't move forward with hers either.

If she can't make the choice on our behalf, then I'll have to make that decision for us. I won't see her pulled apart by all this push and pull any longer. In truth, her choice has already been silently made. Actions speak louder than words. If she wanted to move forward with me, she would have done so by now.

"Ava's a nice girl, Eoin. She's a strong businesswoman. She's from a good, solid mobster family. You could do a lot worse than Leo's little sister."

He's right about that too, of course.

I've been keeping the girl hanging on and that's been unfair of me. She deserves better. She'll have an army of suitors, I'm sure, but it's me she's chosen to spend time with and get to know. A far cry from Jaine, who never wants to discuss anything personal, goes AWOL every five minutes, then when you do manage to locate her, she gets all hissy because she's been backed into a corner.

And all because she doesn't know how to let me down gently or otherwise.

"I love Jaine. You know that, Eoin. She's the sister I never had. But it's time to draw a line under this for both your sakes."

I nod silently and he takes that as his cue to leave.

"I meant to say." He stops at the door and turns around. "Ma's asked if you can pick Finian up from Cillian's and drop him off at Jaine's. Apparently, Cill's going on a job with Aidan and Sarah has an appointment with the ob-gyn."

"And JJ?"

"Watching movies with Duke."

I'd forgotten the children had moved back home now that the Malky threat has been permanently handled.

"Let Dec know the timings and tell him to set it up in my calendar."

"Will do."

I CLOSE THE DOOR TO CILL'S APARTMENT, CARRYING A WRIGGLY FIN in my arms and with his bag over my shoulder. Who knew a small child needed so much stuff?

He's chattering away. To me. To himself. To anyone who'll listen.

He's such a beautiful lad. Our Paddy's mini-me in every way.

I miss my brother. We all do.

I glance down at the little boy in my arms with his pale skin, black hair, and sparkling blue eyes. He could easily pass as my son. No one would ever think otherwise. I'm annoyed with myself for telling Molly. I thought I could trust her. That she would never betray me or my family. My misjudgment means we now have no idea who else may be aware of Fin's true parentage. Hopefully no-one.

I step outside the building. It's a sunny day. I pass a giggling Fin to Dec, who's come up the stairs to meet me before handing across his bag.

There's no time like the present. I turn my face up at the sky and take a deep breath in before taking out my phone.

Eoin: *Can you deal with the annulment paperwork swiftly please, Jaine? I'd like to draw a line under this matter once and for all and move on.*

My finger hesitates. I inhale and exhale. I don't want to send it, but I must. For both our sakes.

I press send.

Looking up, I see the black SUV as it crawls along the sidewalk. My gut's already telling me that something's not right and it's seldom fucking wrong. My phone flashes in my hand.

Is it a warning?

I click on the message, but I've no time to read it as the window on the vehicle lowers and the gun barrel glints in the sunshine. I immediately push myself in front of Fin who's in Dec's arms.

I feel the bullet hit. I feel myself fall. I feel blinding pain in my head.

Then nothing.

CHAPTER FIFTY-THREE

JAINE

Jaine's Apartment, Upper East Side, New York

Padraig: *You and Eoin have my blessing to move on with your lives together, darlin'. I wish you all the best.*

I'VE BEEN PACING THE FLOOR AND STARING AT THE MESSAGE FOR hours. I'm not sure why. It's not like it's going to miraculously change with the passage of time.

Twenty words.

I'm not sure how I feel about that number. Is twenty words adequate given what he and I went through together? If the twenty words were heartfelt and meaningful, then maybe so.

I wish you all the best.

Those are words you'd write in a greeting card to a nameless, faceless person who's no one in particular. Those words aren't meant for someone who was your confidant for nine years of your goddamn life. Those words aren't sufficient for someone you blatantly lied to for the two years following because you couldn't bear the thought of letting them go.

Surely *that* fucking person is worthy of something more. Surely *that* person who sacrificed so much of their life for yours deserves something more than 'I wish you all the best."

Unfeeling. Unemotional. Unloved.

There's no love in those few generic words. Not even a love that should stem from the rarest of friendships that we shared over so many years.

I sigh as I read them one final time. In his defense, he doesn't know what I had to do or who I've had to keep hidden.

And who's to say his messages aren't being monitored by Sophia? If they are, then maybe he has no option but to keep things unfriendly and impersonal.

Rightly or wrongly, I still feel fucking cheated. I expected more. Needed more. Not *War and Peace* or a declaration of undying love or anything like that. I expected a goodbye that allowed the past to be buried with the love and respect that it truly deserved so we could both move on to the future with a clean slate and a guilt-free conscience.

Because it's kind of a big deal for me. Saying goodbye to even more of my past. Letting go of *him*.

I stare at the message. I'm tempted to delete it, but I don't.

Like the others, I'll keep hold of it for old time's sake and to remind myself of a relationship that spanned over a decade of my life. A relationship that ended, even though I never wanted it to.

A relationship that meant something to me, even if it meant nothing to him.

I love you, Irish.

Always have. Always will.

I have no regrets.

Never have. Never will.

All I'm left with is more memories that I no longer have anyone to reminisce with over. I mentally box them away, tears pricking my eyes when I realize that I've filed away way more than I'll ever have left.

That between losing Ace and Irish, I've had to box away most of my life.

What now?

Life moves on, I guess. It's time to start afresh and build new memories.

I smile. It's a bittersweet one, but it's a smile, nonetheless. Saying hello to my future.

Letting *him* in.

Do I message Eoin? Do I wait for him to arrive with Fin? Things have been more awkward than usual these past few days. He expected a suitable reaction after what happened at the docks, which is understandable, but I wanted to wait until I had clear direction from Irish first. So I knew what reaction I was going to be able to deliver.

A message I wasn't sure was going to ever come.

But it did.

I pick up my burner and stare at the screen before typing the message. He may as well use this number now as I'll have no option but to introduce him to my alter-ego.

Jaine: *I love you.*

My finger hovers.

Send. Not send.

I smile at the screen. I want him to know. He needs to know. He's waited long enough for me to say those words back.

He's waited a whole lifetime to hear them.

I press send.

My phone rings moments later.

"Dylan."

"Jaine, I don't know how to tell you this." His voice is panicked. It immediately brings memories flooding back. Memories from the worst day of my fucking life.

Please, God. Not again.

"Is it Fin?"

"Fin's fine. It's Eoin. He's been shot."

"Where?"

"Outside Cillian's apartment."

"Where on his body has he been fucking hit, Dylan!" He knows exactly what I'm asking and why, and his silence speaks volumes.

"Dylan!"

"In the gut, Jaine." I can tell by his tone that he didn't want to go into that level of detail over the phone because he now knows exactly what I'm thinking.

That's he going to die.

"Where is he?"

"New York Presbyterian."

New York Presbyterian Hospital

Deja-vu? History repeating?

Given I can recall every single shitty detail of the previous two occasions, I guess it's the latter.

Raf. Gut shot. Dead.

Ace. Gut shot. Dead.

Eoin. Gut shot.

I arrived at the hospital on my hog with no recollection of how I got here. I don't even remember entering the building. All I recall is an endless maze of identical white walled corridors, each ending with a set of revolving doors offering three choices.

Turn left. Turn right. Straight ahead. Turning back was never an option.

And people. So many people milling around getting in my way while getting on with their lives.

Then there's me. No longer able to get on with mine.

I don't stop to ask where he is because I know I'll find him. He's just down one more corridor, through one more set of revolving doors.

Walk don't run. How can I walk when I need to get to him?

I need to tell him.

Jesus Christ, what if he can't hear? What if he never fucking hears again?

Regret and guilt. Words spoken but never heard, same as with Ace.

Please, God, no. They can't remain unspoken because they're too important.

"Dylan."

It doesn't even sound like me. It's not my voice. I look around but there's no one else here but me and him.

It *was* me.

With the voice of someone who's slowly falling apart.

With the voice of someone who's just buried one husband and is about to bury another.

With the voice of someone who's desperately trying to hold it all together as their world comes crashing down around them once more.

I take back what I said. Every goddamn word of it.

I'm a fucking liar.

Love's not fucking worth it. Love's not good. Love is evil. Love destroys you.

It rips you into so many pieces that it's impossible to put yourself back together again. You can try, but you'll never be the same. The invisible wounds never heal. In the end, you just learn how to plaster over the cracks to keep them hidden below the surface, but you will always be fucking broken.

Ace.

Irish.

Eoin.

I haven't been lucky in love. I've been un-fucking-lucky.

Dylan looks up at me from where he's sitting.

"What have they said?" I blink because I can't see.

"Jaine." His voice is soft and caring, unlike the last time we spoke. When he gave me a talking to for leading his big brother on.

His hand reaches up to my cheek and he wipes away tears that I didn't even know were falling. I step back, using the back of my hand to hastily wipe them off.

"What have they said, Dylan?"

Fuck emotions. Fuck tears. They won't bring him back if he's already dead. If I'm already too fucking late.

It's then Dr. Kelly turns the corner.

Jesus Christ, anyone but him.

"Miss Jones." I clearly made so much of an impression on him the first time around that he still remembers my name.

He stops in his tracks, and his eyes flit between me and Dylan. "I need to speak to Mr. O'Connell's next of kin."

"That's me," I reply, and he switches his full attention back to me, coughing nervously as he stands there all blonde-haired and boyishly handsome.

"And your relation?"

"I'm his wife."

He stares at me, likely wondering why Eoin, who could take his pick, would willingly choose to marry a woman as clearly unaccommodating as I am.

"We're waiting, Doc." I want to give him a goddamn shake and tell him to get on with it, but I don't want to scare him.

"Mr. O'Connell's been shot, as you know. In the abdomen. Fortunately, it went clean through and miraculously missed any vitals. If it hadn't, well…." His voice fades.

Relief floods through me, but it doesn't last long as he's still looking worried, and it must be over what he's about to say next.

"Is there a *but*, Doc, or does that mean he's going to be okay?" I know there's a but. I'm just trying to encourage him along in as non-threatening a way as I can.

His face pales. "Unfortunately, when the bullet impacted, he fell backward down some steps. He banged his head. There's significant brain swelling. Thankfully, he was brought in just in time. I was on standby, and we drilled into the base of his skull to release the buildup of fluid as soon as he arrived. Unfortunately, we had to do that without permission. If we hadn't acted with haste, he could have… We've also had to place him in a temporary coma…."

"The prognosis, Doc." I interject his ramblings, my words still quietly spoken. I'm grateful that he's alive, but I now want to know how much of the old Eoin is going to come back.

"We don't know for sure. At the moment, he has machines doing everything for him to allow his brain the chance to heal. There's activity, so he could make a complete recovery, but it's just too early to say. We'll know more once we have the swelling under control and once he wakes up."

If he wakes up.

He doesn't say the words aloud, but we all know they're silently implied.

"We did everything as quickly as we could, so the prognosis is as good as can be expected. I'm sorry I can't give you any more than that."

I glance around the clinical corridor that stinks of Lysol and coffee and is decorated with white boards and fancy charts.

"So, what do we do now?"

"All we can do is wait."

"Can we see him?"

He nods slowly. I'm guessing he's not a pretty sight. Given that I saw Malky McGrath with an axe lodged in his skull not so very long ago, I'll take my chances that I'm able to cope with the visual.

We follow Dr. Kelly. Dylan walks beside me and takes my hand, giving it a gentle squeeze. Is it to give me strength?

I want to pull it away because it's not making me feel stronger. It's making me feel weaker.

He's offering me reliance, but I don't want reliance because when you rely on someone else, it just opens up the doorway to being let down. In the end, I don't pull my hand away.

Maybe it's him who needs my strength.

We enter the white hospital room.

They've tried to disguise the smell of death behind some fancy vanilla-based air-freshener. It hasn't worked. It just makes the stench even more noticeable.

You can't hide the smell of death from a serial killer.

I look around. I wanted to see him, but my reluctant eyes now want to look anywhere but at him.

State of the art machines beep and flash, all competing with each other to keep the man on the bed alive.

I finally look at him.

And I take it back.

I try to swallow the painful lump that's just appeared in my throat.

I was wrong. I'd rather stare in Malky McGrath's glazed

bulging eyes for the rest of my days than look at Eoin O'Connell right now. At the sight of him lying there with wires going in and tubes coming out like some sort of fucked-up spaghetti junction.

Aside from the machine making his lungs work, he's motionless.

He's bandaged from the chest down, and his head is also swathed. It's not the ocean of white gauze that's the emotional deal-breaker. It's the sea of purple bruises covering that perfect GQ model-like face of his and making him unrecognizable.

It's not him.

It doesn't look like him, so it can't be him.

My brain is clutching at flimsy straws. Eoin O'Connell can't fucking be here. This is a sick joke. He's in a container on the docks, killing deserved people. Or in his office with his perfect Italian leather-clad feet on his desk, looking all pomp and pristine as he dishes out orders to his yes-people.

I hear the sob. It's loud. It's ugly. It's painful.

And I know it came from me.

I don't want him to be in here. I don't want him dependent on machines to keep him alive.

I want him to be awake. I need to tell him.

I turn and walk. It's too much. It's too private. I don't want to share my pain. My grief for a man who's not even dead.

When I get outside, I gulp in air, but I still can't breathe. Resting my hands on my thighs, I bend over, and when it finally fills my lungs, I use it to cry my frustrations to the world.

Because he can't.

He can't die without hearing me tell him that he's loved.

CHAPTER FIFTY-FOUR

JAINE

New York Presbyterian Hospital

"Excuse me, Miss."

I turn to stare at the man behind the desk. He's around mid-twenties with an unruly mop of the reddest hair I've ever seen. Hair that he's tried but failed miserably to tame with some hair product or another. My gaze then drops to a face that's covered in a plethora of complementary freckles, a beaming smile, all topped off with round black glasses framing happy blue eyes, and a pair of regimented scrubs.

My gaze drifts back to his hair. I imagine people stare at its brightness a lot as he immediately points to his head.

"It's ginger. I inherited it from my Scottish mom, along with these." He points at his freckles.

I nod silently.

"Mind if I ask where you were going?"

I've already had to provide ID to two armed guards to check off against the O'Connell's strict list of approved visitors to get on this private wing. It's understandable. The future Irish king was shot by an as yet unknown entity and is currently in a medically induced coma. He must be protected at all costs. I naively thought that once I had gotten past those goons, and as it was out of hours, I'd be able to access Eoin's room pretty much unnoticed.

I was wrong.

I walk back to the desk. I suddenly wish I'd taken more care over my appearance as I realize I must look like a tramp, wearing the most worn tank top and combats combo I own.

He's never going to believe who I am. What if he calls the family to seek clarification. Then everyone will know where I am.

"I'm here to see Eoin."

He grins. "I'm sure Mr. O'Connell will appreciate the visit, Miss…."

"Mrs. I'm Jaine O'Connell. I'm his wife."

He nods. He doesn't look me up and down or act surprised in any way. Instead, his smile widens. If I was feeling defensive, I don't anymore. His expression is so warm and welcoming. I can't help but return his smile with a small one of my own.

"So, you've decided to come out of hours. Are you and Mr. O'Connell planning on having a party and trashing the place?"

I laugh out loud. "I think my partying days are long gone." My smile widens. "Sorry, I know it's after ten. I just figured that now's when he's most likely to be on his own." I glance at his name badge. "And I don't want him to ever be on his own, Tim."

A flicker of sympathy crosses his face, which causes me to swallow yet another lump. I don't want pity. I want Eoin to be awake and back to how he was before he risked his own life to save my son.

"And you know where he is, right?"

I nod before turning and walking away. I pause before walking back.

"What should I do? I mean, in these situations. What's best to do or say or…" My words fade out.

I don't know what I'm going to do or say when I get in there. Tears prick my eyes, and I blink them back, but I'm sure they won't have gone unnoticed.

"I've seen lots of weird and wonderful things relatives do to help their loved ones back on the road of recovery, but let me tell you what I would do."

He rests his elbows on the top of the desk. The tears from earlier fill my eyes before he even gets a chance to speak.

"Mr. O'Connell is in a coma. He can't respond to you, but that doesn't mean he can't hear you. He can't squeeze your hand, but that doesn't mean he can't feel you squeezing his. There's no guarantee he can hear or feel, but I think if there's even a slim chance that he can, then it's worth doing, right?"

I nod with an ugly sob.

"Because right now he's all alone. And as his wife, I'm sure he loves you more than anything else in the world. So, I think it will mean the absolute world to him that you don't treat him any differently. That you interact with him like you would normally."

"Anything else?" My voice is a shaky whisper.

"Tell him that you love him as often as you can."

He's saved the latter for last because it's the most important. It's in case he doesn't wake up. In case he doesn't make it out of here alive. So I have no regrets.

But I do.

I have five months' worth of fucking regrets.

Tears and snot. It's all going on, but it's my guess Tim's seen it all before more times than he can count.

He passes me a Kleenex.

"Sometimes music helps too. Songs you've shared or listened to together in the past."

I nod again.

Guilt flows through me that we never did much of anything together in the past. He wanted to more than anything, but I refused to because it was all about me and my stupid fucking grudge.

"Tim?" He smiles at me once more. "My being here? Let's just keep that between ourselves."

He nods. "Your secret is safe with me, Mrs. O'Connell."

"Jaine. You can call me Jaine."

I STRUGGLE WITH THE WIRES AND TUBES THE MOST. I WANT TO RIP them out, then shake him and tell him to wake up. But he won't wake up, and those wires and tubes are the only things keeping him alive.

I look down at the man who's turned my whole world upside down. The man who until recently I regretted having any feelings for. The man who, despite everything I've thrown at him, has refused to give up on me.

And now it's my turn to never give up on him.

"Thank you."

I feel stupid saying the words aloud knowing he might not even be able to hear me.

I sit on the edge of his bed and take his hand in mine. It feels warm. Not like Ace's did when I last held his. It's comforting. The warmth of his skin is giving me hope because it means he's still alive.

"For what you did. For saving Fin. If you hadn't stepped in front of him…" My voice breaks.

Dec's already confirmed the gun was pointed in Fin's direction. That my little boy may well be dead if not for Eoin.

This man would do anything for his family, including die for them.

"And I'm sorry for everything. I should never have done what I did. I wanted to hurt you so badly I couldn't see straight, but in the end, all I succeeded in doing was hurting myself. I threw your love back in your face when deep down it was the thing I wanted most."

I pause. My emotions threaten to drown me, but I can't let them. If I break now, I know I'll never be unbroken. If he dies, there won't be anyone left who can piece me back together.

I exhale shakily.

"I love you, Eoin O'Connell. I sent you a message…it was from my burner, so you probably didn't…." I suddenly can't breathe at the thought of a life without him in it. It doesn't matter in what capacity just so long as he's still alive and not dead.

Not like Ace.

I take a few slow, deep breaths.

"I'm so sorry. I'm trying so hard to be the brave Jaine Jones that everyone expects me to be at all times, but I guess I'm only human. And sometimes even the brave ones fall apart."

And then the tears fall hard, steady, and ugly.

For him.

For me.

For an us that might never be.

Wiping my face with my hands, I reach into my pocket and pull out my ear pods.

"I told you a while back that I'd pick us a song. Well, I have. I chose it the very next day, but there just never seemed to be a right time…" My voice fades once more at the realization that there never was a right time because I never allowed there to be one.

He didn't ask for much from me.

For my love. For me to spend time with him. For me to let him in.

He wanted to be part of my life. He wanted to be part of my family. I dangled it all in front of him then deliberately pulled it away.

"Anyway, I hope you like it."

Standing, I place one of the pods in his ear before placing the other in my own. Then I curl up on the chair beside his bed, take his strong hand in mine, and let our song play on repeat.

"The Lady with the Lamp returns."

"Very funny, Tim. You definitely missed your calling. You should have been a comedian."

He chuckles heartily. "I'm sure your husband will be very appreciative of the overall effects of your dedication. I'm not too sure he'll have enjoyed you talking his ears off every night while he's trying to sleep, even if the equipment is showing that his brain activity goes through the roof any time you're nagging him."

I laugh out loud. "Once again, it's conversing, not nagging!"

I've fallen into a routine where I'm having a one-sided conversation with Eoin from the minute I get here until the moment I leave. Telling him about my day and my life, both past and present.

I'd give anything to hear one of his pompous responses. Sometimes I think I do, but then I look at him, and he's still sleeping.

No one knows I've been coming here at night. Maybe they think I haven't bothered to come at all. Perhaps that's for the best. I'd rather no one pretend to just be *passing by* because they feel the need to drop in to keep me company, thinking they were doing me a favor.

They wouldn't be. This is my time. Our time.

He wanted me to let him in and I have. There's not much I haven't told him over the past four nights. He may not remember any of it, but I've spilled my guts all the same. Tim said I should be prepared for the fact that something may trigger these memories for Eoin one day. Maybe by then I'll have had the chance to say it all face to face, so it won't matter.

I spoke with Dr. Kelly at length earlier today. The family has agreed that the drugs that have being keeping him in the coma all this time can be stopped. The brain swelling has reduced significantly. Early indications are that he should make a complete recovery with no lasting ill effects, although that still can't be guaranteed. We won't know anything for sure until he wakes up, and even though the drugs have been withdrawn, we still have no idea how long that will take.

All we can do now is wait.

"Jaine."

I jerk awake and stare up at Tim from the chair.

"Is he…." I sit bolt upright and look at Eoin. While he's still a swathe of white bandages, his bruising has significantly reduced, and he has way less wires and tubes. He's looking far more like his normal self.

"He's fine, Jaine. There's been no change. Sorry, I was called away on an emergency and I've only just returned to the desk. I thought it best I wake you as the others will be arriving soon."

"Shit."

He frowns. "You don't need to run. It's to be expected that his wife would want to be at his bedside, surely?"

"They don't know that I've been here, Tim."

His frown deepens. "Still? Why the big secret?"

I run my hand down my face.

"You just wanted it to be you and him."

I nod. "We're sort of estranged you see. I'm his wife, but then I'm not. It's complicated. We're complicated. His whole family is complicated."

"That all sounds very…. complicated."

I smile and roll my eyes exaggeratedly. "I'm going to get out of here. I'll just grab a coffee from the machine first."

I stand and stretch before bending to place a gentle kiss on Eoin's lips.

"I'm going off duty shortly, Jaine. I've asked the nurse taking over to let me know if there's any change. I'll let you know if I hear anything."

I place my hand on his upper arm in thanks. "I'm sorry for all the cloak and dagger, Tim, but it really is for the best."

With a smile, he squeezes my hand with his own in silent acceptance.

I make my way along the corridor and into the restroom. It's white and clinical, the same as everywhere else in this place. I wash my face and hands before staring at my reflection in the mirror. I look exhausted. My skin is pale, and my hair is lank. I'm surviving each day on whatever sleep I can get on the chair beside his bed, but it's not a lot because I spend all my time watching over him.

Duke and the children have moved back in with Roisin and Fergal. At the moment, I'm spending my nights here, and my days there. In a few days, the kids and I will be moving into the safe space underneath the property and will remain there for the foreseeable future.

I have no choice.

Like the Malky situation, this new threat wasn't veiled. It was blatant and a deliberate attack, made in the cold light of day and right outside a Duster property. My own son the target.

I make my way back into the corridor.

It's a proper coffee machine with regular cups and not paper ones. Given what the O'Connells are no doubt being charged for Eoin to have hands-on specialist treatment and care, it's the least they can throw in.

Drink in hand, I glance into Eoin's room on my way past.

It's then I see her.

Ava.

Has she been visiting him too?

My thoughts are interrupted when she stands abruptly and starts getting animated. "He's waking up. Quickly. Someone. Anyone."

Am I disappointed that I won't be the first person he sees when he wakes?

Yes. No.

CHAPTER FIFTY-FIVE

EOIN

The O'Connell Home, Darling, New York

I GRIMACE AT THE PAIN IN MY STOMACH.

I was discharged one week after I woke up from the coma, and that was two weeks ago now.

Opening the manila envelope that's been left on my home desk, I stare at the Decree Absolute. The confirmation in black and white that the annulment has been processed and that our marriage is now deemed to have never taken place.

I've never been Jaine's husband. She's never been my wife. At least not in the eyes of the law. The document can't eradicate that, in every other sense of the word, we were exactly that, even if only for a short while.

Nothing contested. Nothing requested. It was always going to be clear cut. She wanted nothing from me. And the one thing I wished from her was, in the end, the only thing she couldn't give me.

Love.

I take my seat before flicking through the paperwork. She obviously has friends in high places given that she's been able to turn it around within a matter of weeks and without me having to be in attendance. But then, I'm well aware of who she rubs shoulders with. I also know she excels at her job.

I should be pleased. I've got what I wanted. What I requested in the message I sent to her before I was gunned down, she's delivered precisely.

I can now move on with my life without her in it. With someone else in her place.

Ava.

According to Dylan, I had a regular female visitor when I was in the medically induced coma. It can't have been anyone else as the only female visitors that were allowed entry were family members and Ava.

It can't have been Jaine. By all accounts, she attended on the day I was shot then stormed out and never looked back. It's nice to know that my own wife didn't give a fuck whether I lived or died.

Ex-wife, I should say.

I run my hand through my hair in frustration. Why couldn't she have loved me instead of fucking hating me?

Maddening, evil woman.

Eoin: *Can I see you?*

Jaine: *We're currently living in the same house, so I'd say that you bumping into me is pretty much inevitable.*

Eoin: *I'd like to discuss this recent paperwork.*

Jaine: *It's a Decree Absolute. It signifies the end of the annulment process and the legal termination of our marriage. There really isn't anything to discuss.*

She's right of course. It's over.

I stare at the slim silver band on my finger. What it signified. What it meant.

Everything. *Nothing*

Hope. *Disappointment.*

I never paid much attention to it after she placed it on there. It just became part of me. A sign to those who saw it that I belonged to someone.

It's only now as I slip it off my finger that I realize just how much a part of me it had become. Just how much a part of me *she* had become.

I immediately miss it, but it's not like I can continue to wear it. I stare at my bare finger, a sign that I no longer belong to anyone.

I place the ring in the desk drawer before glancing around my temporary office.

We've all been living under my parents' roof. Until the threats have been permanently eradicated, it's been agreed that Jaine and the children will live in the safe space underneath the property, while Duke will stay in the summer house. Until I'm fully convalesced, my ma has insisted that I also reside here. I have my own suite which caters to my every possible need, but it still doesn't stop her from barging in every five minutes to fuss over me.

This place affords me no privacy whatsoever. Not that I need any. I'm under strict doctor's orders that sex is banned until my body has fully healed. And not that it matters. I no longer have a wife with whom to undertake the act with anyway, and the thought of fucking anyone apart from Jaine holds no appeal whatsoever.

There's a soft knock on the door. I know immediately who it is.

"Come in."

I look up at my nurse as he enters the room.

"Tim." I smile. He's a nice lad. Very Celtic looking with his bright red hair and matching freckles. His ma's Scottish. He definitely found his calling as he has the right personality for this role. He's friendly and chatty with a joke thrown in here and there to distract you from what he's doing.

"It's good to see you, Mr. O'Connell."

"I've asked that you call me Eoin."

He smiles warmly as he pushes his glasses further up his nose. I'm not sure why I waste my breath repeatedly asking him. I know he'll never call me Eoin. I'm his employer. He's my employee. He's respectful of that.

"How's the head? Still getting headaches?"

"Yes, but they're slowly reducing in number and intensity."

The hole in my head has all but healed, although I still get occasional pain. I'm also currently not allowed to drive, so I have Dec on constant standby.

The stomach wound is taking a little longer to resolve, as most of the time I forget all about it then aggravate the wound by moving or bending too quickly. That's why Tim's been tasked with calling in several times a day to keep an eye on things while he changes the dressing.

I exhale as I stand and pull my black t-shirt over my head.

"Melancholy moment?"

He keeps his gaze on what he's doing, his fingers working deftly.

"My Decree Absolute came today."

He glances up at me before continuing with what he's doing. "Not welcomed?"

My silence is all the answer he needs.

"I suppose you can now move on with your life."

I laugh dryly. "With my Florence Nightingale."

He looks up at me in confusion.

"Dylan said you mentioned that I'd had a regular female visitor keeping me company. He also overheard you mentioning to one of your colleagues that she was my very own Florence Nightingale and that her one-sided conversation had aided me on my road to recovery."

His hands stop.

"It must have been Ava. I'm told my wife attended on the first day then never returned. Or should I say ex-wife."

There's a quiet knock at the door. Tim and I both look toward it at the same time.

Jaine.

How much of that did she overhear?

If she heard anything, she gives nothing away. Her eyes drift slowly over my exposed torso and my dick twitches. We can end our relationship. We can end our marriage. But how the fuck do we put out a fire that refuses to stop burning?

"Tim. How are you?" She smiles widely at him.

"I'm good, Jaine. You look… different."

He looks her up and down and laughs. It's not in a leering way. If it had been I'd have ripped his throat out by now.

She's wearing a navy suit. A skirt this time, instead of pants. My eyes drift unwittingly up her long legs and beyond until they reach her face, and our eyes connect.

Her face is flushed as a result of my blatant admiration. Her bruising has gone. No visible reminders of what she went through with Malky remain.

On the outside at least.

Neither Ma nor Jaine have divulged in any great detail what they went through at his hands and during their time in captivity, but given the state Jaine was still in days later, I figure it wasn't a pleasant experience for either of them.

Neither do we know what they discussed during the time they spent alone together, but whatever it was has enabled them to reach an amicable truce and move on. They'll never be close. They'll never be friends. But it's clear they do now share a mutual admiration for each other that wasn't present before.

The only positive from the negative.

She drags her gaze away and turns her attention back to Tim.

"What can I say? Your job calls for scrubs and mine calls for ridiculously priced tailor-made suits," she jokes.

"You two know each other?"

There's a pause as she glances at him. It's a look that says *let me handle this*. Her gaze connects with mine once more, her expression now impassive.

"We met once and spoke once on the phone."

I don't miss the look of relief that crosses his face. What are they hiding? Because I don't believe a word of that. And he's calling her Jaine, yet he refuses to call me Eoin.

She interrupts my thoughts.

"My last message didn't require a response, but as I was just leaving and you hadn't replied, I thought I'd make sure that everything was okay before I left. Roisin has gone out and Fergal's with her."

"Thank you for your concern, Miss Jones. It's better late than never, I suppose. I'm fine. As you can see, I have Tim."

I regret both the abrupt tone and my condemning words as soon as they leave my mouth. They sound bitter.

They taste bitter.

Maybe that's because I *am* bitter at her lack of care and compassion. That she shed no tears and showed no concern over the sorry state I was in. While there's every likelihood that Finian was targeted because of my dropping the ball over his parentage, I still stepped in front of a bullet with his name on.

Her expression remains impassive.

"I'll go, then. It was good to see you again, Tim." She smiles.

"You too, Jaine."

We both watch as my ex-wife closes the door.

"You were too hasty, Eoin."

We're in the family room. I'm resting on one sectional, Dylan is on the other playing *Call of Duty,* and Ma's standing by the window.

Unbeknown to her, I've started making plans to return to my own apartment, and it's not a moment too soon. I love my family.

In small doses.

"Jaine was the one who asked for the annulment in the first place, Ma."

"And is that what she still wanted? When was the last time that she mentioned it before you sent her a message chasing her up?"

It's then I realize it had been months. She issued the paperwork, then never mentioned it again. It was the main reason it took me so long to complete and return it in the first place.

Had she been having second thoughts? Not that she'd ever admit as much.

I don't even get the chance to respond.

"I love Jaine, but she's been messing with Eoin's head with her constant back and forth, and there was no sign of her ever committing. In turn, he was leaving Ava dangling. Leo's sister's a nice girl. He could do a lot worse," Dylan answers, his face never leaving the screen.

"Can you even hear your hypocritical self, Dylan O'Connell?" Ma hisses at him.

She's clearly not happy that I've asked Jaine to push through the annulment. Which means Da won't be either.

Dylan pauses his game as he looks at her while wearing a confused frown.

Happy that she's now got his undivided attention, she continues. "Grace was a nice girl. So was girl number two and girl number three on the list of names that me and your da compiled for you, but you insisted on marrying Jessie because you were in love with her. Are you suggesting your brother accept a fate that you weren't prepared to settle for?"

Dylan frowns, and I do too. Ma's right, well partially at least. Dylan would have walked over hot coals to be with Jessie because he loved her. After Grace bowed out, he wasn't prepared to accept anyone else. But Dylan's situation differs from mine. His love was reciprocated. Mine isn't.

"Jaine asked me to obtain something for her recently. Something that she wouldn't have been able to get access to. She explained that she needed it before she could move on," Ma continues.

"And what was that?" I mutter.

"Our Padraig's blessing."

Dylan immediately stands and punches the air. "I knew that's what was holding her back all this time."

"Sit down and stop crowing. You're also the person who encouraged me to push the annulment through." It's my turn to hiss.

He sits back down. He knows I'm right. He admitted to having had a similar conversation with Jaine which no doubt spurred her on to also do what she thought was right for all parties concerned.

I know I can't blame Dylan entirely. I typed the message. I sent the message. It's what I wanted. What I asked for.

I run my hand through my hair, annoyed that I can't pace the floor, but it's just too much effort to stand and Tim's already told me off once today for doing too much.

"That revelation changes nothing. The fact of the matter is that Jaine doesn't love me, and she never will. Sadly, Paddy's approval or otherwise won't alter that."

We sit there in silence. We all know that part is true at least.

Jaine's always been brutally honest about how she felt about me. That the arrow points firmly to hate. So, even with Paddy's blessing, even if she did want to try again, it would still come with no guarantees of permanency or longevity. I have no more time for game-playing. I can't simply settle for half-measures when I know with certainty that in the end she won't. For her, it's all or nothing.

She's already confirmed on numerous occasions that she can't give me her all. Our trying again would simply delay the inevitable.

"And did Paddy give his blessing?" Not that it makes any difference.

"Yes. He did," Ma replies.

CHAPTER FIFTY-SIX

JAINE

The O'Connell Home, Darling, New York

TIME TICKS. TIME TOCKS.

Things stay the same. Things change.

From one day to the next, people come, people go.

You never know which thing. You never know which person.

Nothing surprises me anymore. Nothing prepares me either. So, I've learned to welcome each new sunrise and appreciate each new day for what it is.

It's been two weeks since I hand-delivered Eoin a copy of the Decree Absolute. His message was received very loud and clear having been stuck in some sort of telephonic abyss which no doubt resolved itself as soon as he switched on his phone. I'm guessing he discussed the situation with Dylan beforehand. That the verbal ear-bashing I received from his younger sibling in advance was the tag-team back-up that Eoin asked him to perform to let me know that he wanted to move on with his life once and for all.

And so, I let him.

He and Ava haven't gone official yet, but rumor has it that it's only a matter of time as they've been seen together in all of the usual hot spots our kind frequent, no doubt in advance of any formal announcement being made by both families. I'm also aware that Ava's introduced him to Leo as someone who may transpire to be more than just a casual business acquaintance.

I know because Leo told me.

Once he was aware that Eoin may have other intentions about his baby sister, he immediately did his digging. He's now fully aware that he and I share a past, and also that we share a son.

He doesn't know that Finian is Irish's boy.

But someone does as that's still believed to be the reason he was targeted and why my kids and I are still having to reside in the safe space below the O'Connell residence.

Now that I'm no longer married and wearing the Duster brand like some sort of invisible protective shield, it's my guessing I'll be expected to stay put for the foreseeable future. At least until the faceless faction becomes known and we figure out who's been gunning for my eldest.

Hopefully, they're one in the same.

I can live with this situation. Then again, I have no choice. I have to do everything in my power to protect Fin and JJ.

I refuse to marry Aidan as a Plan B. Not that there's anything wrong with him, it's just that I'm not going to be railroaded into marrying anyone else again. From here on in I'll just be plain Jaine Jones.

Eoin and I are still on speaking terms. We even text on occasion like we did before, but it's not the same. It never will be. There's been way too much water under the bridge because I've seen both sides of him.

Ditto. Aside from my secret, that is.

We must remain civil as we're family whether we like it or not. There isn't anything that's going to change that.

Did he receive the message I sent from my burner?

Maybe he did. Maybe he didn't. I'll never know because I'll never ask him.

Maybe one day he'll see it. If he doesn't, then that's God's will. I truly believe that things happen for a reason. So, I've decided to adopt Ace's way of living. You've just got to go with the flow and be grateful that you get to wake up to enjoy just one more sunrise.

Do I still love Eoin? Of course I do. You can't switch feelings like that off once they're on. I still love Ace. I still love Irish. Forever. For always.

I let them get on with their lives without me in it. Ace from when I was eighteen to twenty-eight. Irish for almost three years now. The same applies to Eoin.

Like I said before, loving more than one person just creates more opportunities for your heart to be broken. It's not all roses, chocolates, and happily ever afters. From my experience, it's regrets, what-if moments, never-ending loneliness, and living on memories that fade with each passing day until you feel like the moment never happened because the person you shared it with is no longer there to remind you that it did.

That's what I miss most. Reminiscing. Having someone to remind me that I did have a past and that it wasn't all just a dream.

Still. I'll survive.

The important thing is that Eoin is alive, as is Irish. That's what matters. Nothing else.

I smile as I answer my flashing phone.

"You dressed to impress, partner?"

I roll my eyes exaggeratedly even though she can't see me as I glance down at my cream wrap dress. "How many times? It's a business dinner, Jessie."

"With Nathan Hawke, District Attorney. Aged forty-five. Divorced with two young daughters and dare I add extremely fucking hot."

I laugh. "Quit running internet searches and drooling over images of other men or I'll tell Dyl. I've already said it's purely business. It could never be anything else considering he wants to send most of my goddamn client list to Rikers Island, your husband included."

"But you could still have a little taste. He looks mighty delicious."

"I never mix business with pleasure, and you know it, or at least not since Delaney."

"You never mix pleasure with pleasure these days. Not since you and…"

"Jessie, we agreed not to get into the whys and wherefores of me and Eoin. It's done. It's over. We've moved on."

"But have you moved on?"

"Jessie." I say it warningly. "Anyway, I need to go. I'll talk to you tomorrow and let you know how it went."

"I want all the juicy details."

"If I fuck the District Attorney, you'll be the first to know."

"I'm so jealous."

"You're so married."

"Thanks for reminding me, spoilsport."

"That's me, Jessie. Goodbye." I disconnect the call with a smile on my face.

Public Dining Room, Palace Hotel, Manhattan

I've agreed to meet Nathan outside. As District Attorney, I know he likes to be seen to be watching over his citizens at every opportunity he can get. Like some sort of fucked up caped crusader, protecting their city streets from crime, but without the cloak and wearing a ten-thousand-dollar business suit instead.

I know the tailor. I use the same one myself.

His ex-wife, Emily, is my age. A supermodel in her heyday, she's also an extremely savvy businesswoman. Emily's an Ivy League graduate and runs her own marketing and PR firm. They have two young daughters aged eight and six.

Rumor has it Nathan's biggest regret over the failure of his marriage is losing the ability to have his handsome face plastered across the press at every available opportunity courtesy of his ex-wife.

Who knows, maybe he and Emily still work in tandem for the greater good of their now-dispersed family. It's unlikely. Rumor also has it their split was down to the fact that he cheated on her with a teenage cheerleader, but who knows?

Maybe she's the forgiving type.

"Nate, it's good to see you."

I lean forward, but he takes a further step in so he's deliberately in my personal space before kissing me on both cheeks.

"You don't mean that, Jaine."

He's right. I don't.

He smiles wickedly. His auburn hair is perfectly groomed and his blue eyes sparkle on a face that gets better looking with age. He's around six-three. Like me, he's also a fan of the martial arts, hence his impressive athletic build.

He smiles at me with perfect white teeth. It's not veneers. There's nothing fake about Nathan.

"How's Murdoch?"

I smile through gritted teeth as he refers to one of my clients he's managed to successfully send down on a first-degree murder charge.

"Already receiving death threats. He'll be lucky to survive the week."

He smiles politely as he offers me his arm, which I take. "An eye for an eye."

I'm only glad he doesn't know about my own killing spree.

We make our way into the public dining room. It's still private, but it means we're seated among other guests. It restricts the conversation somewhat, but Nathan always likes to be upfront about who he's meeting with, especially if it's his legal nemesis.

He orders for both of us before smiling politely at the waiter. It's a painted-on smile that says *we've ordered, now fuck off.*

"Now, Jaine. As much as I'd like for it to be the case, I'm sure this isn't a date since I want nothing more than to see most of your clients sent down for one felony or another."

I chuckle as I take a sip of water. "Well, thank you for being so honest with me, Nate."

"You know me well enough to expect nothing less."

I pause. "As you know, there was a recent incident that involved my son."

"And your ex-husband." He smug smiles to let me know that he's fully aware of the mobster I was married to, albeit briefly.

"And my ex-husband."

"The drive-by shooting."

"That's the one."

"What about it?"

"Some of my west coast clients have been experiencing a little unrest. An unknown faction has been flexing its muscles, and it's resulted in the demise of a few of their high rankers."

He takes a sip of his own water. "Your first husband being one of them."

There's a pause. Nate was always going to have done his homework given who he was meeting with, so there's no point in me trying to deny any truths.

"Yes. I'm concerned that they may be behind this recent shooting although at the moment it's mere speculation."

"And if it turns out that they are, what do you expect me to do about it."

"I want your help in bringing them down."

He smiles wickedly once more. "You now have my undivided attention, Miss Jones."

I smile politely back. "While my clients are more than capable of taking care of their own business, my concern is that the potential numbers involved may make this too large an undertaking even for them."

He knows what I'm saying. That my clients will shoot as many as they can in the head, then dispense with the bodies, but they can't do that for an unlimited quantity. If we've bitten off more than we can chew, then we need to have a Plan B in place or, once found, the assholes that we can't contain will just scatter to the wind and spread like a cancer. Where or when they'll next appear would be anyone's guess.

"Do your clients know you're discussing this with me?"

"No, but that's not my concern right now. My main concern is if this faction's reach extends all the way to New York, then it may be a much larger entity than we first thought, so I'd sooner get all my ducks in a row to be on the safe side."

"So, you want convictions and jail time."

"As they're now encroaching on your territory, then for any that fall within your jurisdiction, yes."

We eat as he considers what is effectively my offering to form an unofficial alliance.

Good guy lawyer. Bad guy lawyer.

This could earn him a lot of brownie points in his career, and he knows it. He places his cutlery on the plate, wipes his mouth, and then takes a sip of water.

"And what's in this for me, Jaine?"

"Exposure. We know this faction is involved in human trafficking among other things. Being seen to serve them justice would earn you quite the feather in your cap and would look extremely impressive on your legal resume."

He nods. "I'm interested, but only if I get to convict someone of a suitable caliber. If all I'm doing is dealing with the lower hierarchy, it won't earn me a great deal of exposure. Not for the work it may entail handling the throughput."

"And what if I offer you their leader?"

"Then I may be interested." He pauses before continuing. "Is that all you could offer me, Miss Jones?" His tone has turned suggestive.

I stare at him. Is he for real?

"Well, I'm not fucking you, Nate, if that's what you're asking."

"No, she's right. She's not fucking you, Hawke." A veiled threat comes from directly behind me.

Nathan grins past me. I did wonder why he'd lowered the tone. He must have seen my ex-husband come in and then walk over. He'd love for Eoin to react further so he can haul him into court. Eoin is probably top of his list of people he'd like to bring to justice.

"As if I would ever suggest such a thing to your very beautiful *ex-wife*, Mr. O'Connell." He smiles charmingly at him before standing and turning his attention back to me.

"I'll be more than happy to work with you, Jaine. Call me anytime. Day or night. Both my personal number and address are on the back of the card. I can send a driver to pick you up at a moment's notice."

I stand and he kisses me on both cheeks, again closer than would be deemed polite and most likely for Eoin's benefit this time. He then passes me the hand-written business card.

"Miss Jones. Mr. O'Connell."

He smiles at us both before walking away.

I then turn my attention to my ex-husband as he stands there in a dark business suit, the whiteness of his open-neck shirt contrasting against the material.

Darkness. Power. Strength.

He radiates all three, the combination intoxicatingly magnetic.

Roisin mentioned Eoin had a business meeting. I really should have asked where.

I allow Nate time to leave before making my own way to the exit. I'm aware I'm being followed.

"Dec will drive us."

I nod as I walk out of the building.

"Are you not going to respond?"

"When I'm able to do so." I smile politely at the other guests as we pass them.

"And what does that mean?"

I wait until I get into the SUV and he's pulled the privacy screen across before I reply.

"What it means is that I wanted to wait until I got inside the vehicle so no one would hear me calling you a goddamn asshole."

"The District Attorney was suggesting that you sleep with him."

"And? Do you honestly think it's the first time in my life that I've ever had a man come on to me? I'm a big girl, and I can handle myself. Nate's single. I'm single. Maybe I've got an itch that needs scratching and I wanted to take him up on his offer. Who the hell are you to intervene?"

I can already feel the shift in atmosphere. Eoin needs to get over himself. I'm not going to stay celibate for the rest of my life because he doesn't like the thought of me being intimate with another man.

"What were you discussing with him?"

"That's none of your business."

"Tell. Me." He grabs my arm and I wrestle it from his grasp.

"Fuck you, Eoin. I don't need to tell you anything. What I do in both my professional and private life has nothing to do with you anymore. I'm no longer your wife, remember?"

He spins, grabbing me by the throat and pinning me against the leather seat. "Tell. Me."

"I said, fuck you."

"That. Fucking. Mouth." His breath is hot against my lips, his mouth so close I can almost taste his addictive arrogance. Tendrils of darkness infused with spicy cologne wrap around me.

I can't move. I don't want to move. I'm exactly where I want to be.

"Don't." I shake my head weakly. We both know I've already surrendered. A groan escapes me as his lips capture mine.

Hot. Wet. Firm. And so fucking demanding.

His tongue pushes past, and arousal flows through me.

I can't stop it. I don't want to stop it.

My common sense is screaming at me to push him away, but I make no attempt to stop him when he drags me across to straddle his lap, causing my dress to hitch up around my thighs.

My hands fist his hair, and he hisses in pain. My fingertips then soothe the scarring at the back of his head. He growls in appreciation as his hands grip my hips, pulling them down to meet his so he can grind that huge dick of his against me.

His fingers skim my pussy. No panties. My empty core clenches at the thought of them being thrust inside me as an appetizer.

His chuckle is low. He knows exactly what I'm thinking.

"Greedy, evil woman."

"Fuck. You."

"Anytime, Miss Jones."

"Then how about right now?"

I know I won't be able to turn back, so I may as well embrace the carnal sin that is lust one last time. I pull on the tie of my dress and let it fall to the floor. His eyes drink in my naked flesh. Reaching down, I unfasten him to freedom, my hand gripping tightly around his thick, throbbing shaft. He hisses his appreciation as my fingers lubricate the tip with his pre-cum.

We pant against each other's mouths as I lower myself onto his thick, waiting cock, hissing at the burn as he fills me inch by perfect inch.

Our groins connect, and I stay there, relishing in the feel of him being so deep inside me I don't know where he ends and I begin. My hands grip the seat at either side of his head, and I ride him.

Hard. Fast. Selfishly.

Because this time, it's all about me. This last fucking time, it's me who's in control.

His fingers dig into my flesh as he tries to slow me, but all I want is to reach my goal. What he wants doesn't matter.

We're not together. We're not married. This is nothing more than the most perfect exchange of bodily fluids.

"Jaine."

His dick swells.

Impossibly hard. Impossibly long. Impossibly thick.

With a low growl, he thrusts upward, spilling deep inside me. I shatter around him, my tightening walls taking him for everything he's got.

Panting, I lay my head against his shoulder as he wraps strong arms around my waist to pull me close.

Neither of us speaks. What's there to say? Clearly, when it comes to each other, we have zero control.

Eventually, I lean back. It's then I see the blood.

The dark patch against white, expanding with every beat of his heart.

I scramble off his lap and open the privacy screen.

"Dec. New York Presbyterian. Now!"

New York Presbyterian Hospital

Same room. Same chair.

Wires going in. Wires coming out.

He was unconscious by the time we got here while I was cradling his head in my lap and sitting in a pool of his blood.

According to Dec, he'd been warned several times by the doctor that he was doing too much. While his stomach wound looked like it was healing just fine on the outside, it was simply masking the damage that was still struggling to repair underneath.

He's been in surgery for the past two hours. He's fine. He's not in a coma, and he'll make a complete recovery.

But it could have been quite the opposite. He could have bled out.

Like Ace. Like Raf.

"Jaine."

I look up and exhale loudly as I take in the familiar smiling face and happy blue eyes. "Tim." My voice breaks and tears prick my eyes.

"He'll be just fine, Jaine."

"I know, but…"

"No buts. He'll be fine. There's no point in dwelling on something that's not going to happen."

I'm sitting, wearing a dress that's damp and sticky with Eoin's blood.

"I've called Dylan. He's on his way with a change of clothes," he adds chirpily.

"That's good of him."

"His wife wanted to come along too, but I explained that we could only allow two visitors per bedside."

"Thank you for that." The relief is evident in my voice.

Jessie would have been one hundred miles an hour. As much as I love her, I'm in no fit state to handle her gregariousness right now.

I link my fingers with Eoin's. It's then I notice that he's removed his wedding ring. I'm not sure how I feel about that. Disappointed, I guess. That he discarded it so quickly. But we're no longer married, so why would he continue to wear it?

I glance down at my own hand, both of mine still firmly in place.

Two little bands signifying a promise of the vows I'd taken. I upheld them with Ace. With Eoin?

I let him down in every way because I didn't even try.

CHAPTER FIFTY-SEVEN

DYLAN

New York Presbyterian Hospital

"How is he?"

Tim smiles warmly at me from behind his desk. He's already been signed up as part of the Duster emergency medical team to work alongside Dr. Kelly in the future.

"He'll be just fine. Jaine was with him when it happened. She had him here in record time."

I frown. "What were he and Jaine doing together?"

Tim's wearing a look I know well. It's a sheepish one that says he's riddled with guilt because he kept a secret that maybe he shouldn't have. It's difficult not to recognize it when you've been seeing it reflected in the mirror for years.

"Spill, Tim."

I watch Jaine as she comes back from the restroom. Eoin's still out for the count having slept all night because of the anesthetic, while she's not slept a wink.

She looks royally fucked.

I can't help but smile at the sight of her in my wife's clothes. Jessie is at least three inches taller than Jaine, and even though she's slim, Jaine is borderline skinny.

I frown inwardly. Seeing her as often as I do, I've stopped looking so closely at her these days. She's lost a lot of weight.

What she's gone through in the past year would have destroyed most people, but here she is, still trucking on and putting others first as she's always done, even to the detriment of her own health and well-being.

Who I now know to be my big brother's very own Florence Nightingale then retakes her seat at his bed. A bedside that she didn't let on to the rest of us that she spent five full nights at while he lay in a coma. A bedside she's just added a sixth night to.

All so he was never alone.

"I'm sure Tim can find you somewhere to have a lie-down, Jaine," I urge gently.

"I'm not leaving him."

She sounds exhausted. I watch as she links her hand through his once more. I'll bet as soon as he gives any indication that he's waking up, she'll remove it and leave. She'll pretend that she's never been here. That she didn't care enough to even visit.

And he'll be none the wiser, just like he wasn't last time.

She loves him and he doesn't even know. And she doesn't know that I know.

When she figures it out, she'll expect me to keep quiet like I've done with everything else.

I'll bide my time, but I won't. Not this time.

I'm partially to blame for this mess. In part because I encouraged Eoin to push the annulment through, but also because I knew the reason Jaine wouldn't or couldn't commit to him.

Our Padraig.

She loves my baby brother too much to ever cause him pain. She'd rather self-flagellate from now until eternity than ever allow him to suffer. Everything she's done these past years she's done for him. Her love for him will see her loyal and protective always. Same as it did with Ace. Same as it does with her two boys.

Same as it's doing now for Eoin.

She will simply absorb, and she will carry on. She may stumble and fall at times, but she gets back up, dusts herself down, and keeps right on.

She has to. She's never had any choice.

Ma's already confirmed that Paddy has given his blessing to their union, so why can't Jaine and Eoin be together if that's what they really want?

"Can you manage?"

"I'm not an invalid, Dylan."

It's been three days. I'm driving Eoin back from the hospital. Ignoring his protestations, I help him maneuver his way inside the back of the SUV. He rests his head against the seat. Even with my help, he's exhausted and got a sweat on. It's an alien feeling seeing my big brother weak. I'm pretty sure it's an alien feeling for him too. He's always been the strong one, but right now, he looks tired. It's like he's worn out with it all.

And I'm sure it's not just his health that he's exhausted with.

I switch the engine into life.

"If you want to regain full strength, you need to not be hate-fucking your ex-wife in the back of an SUV." He needs to start listening to what the doctors are telling him, or he'll never be back to where he was physically.

He glares at me.

"Your sex ban has been extended until you're given the all-clear. I was there when Dr. Kelly passed judgement. I know it will be hard for you given abstinence isn't really your thing..."

"Where's Dec?" he interjects, obviously not best pleased at being reminded that he's on a sex hiatus for the foreseeable future and that the only thing he can fuck is his hand. I had a self-inflicted one for thirty years. I'm sure he can manage without for six weeks or so.

"He's sparring with Jaine."

I look in the rear-view mirror and watch as he frowns. He's in pain, but it's not that that's affecting his face. He's frowning because he's not liking the thought of Dec putting his hands on Jaine, even though it was he who suggested she use him.

Just Eoin being madly possessive over the woman he's madly in love with.

I wait until we're on the road, then I switch on the music.

It's a CD.

Tim said that sometimes certain songs can trigger the memories of people who have been in a coma.

This is Plan A. I also have a Plan B which I've listened to in its entirety and which even I didn't survive with dry eyes, so Eoin's got no chance.

I've never seen my big brother cry. I think he will when he hears that content, not that he'll ever admit as much to anyone.

I press play and the song fills the space. Their song, chosen by Jaine.

Seemingly, my big brother wanted them to share a song. Tears prick my eyes when I realize that, despite having everything, all he ever wanted was normalcy, and with her.

The intro plays. I glance at him in the rear-view mirror.

Nothing.

I'm disappointed. I wanted it to trigger something. When she wasn't talking at him all night, she'd share her ear pods with him and play their song on repeat.

According to Tim, Eoin's brain activity went through the roof whenever Jaine was around, so he knew she was right there with him, even if he can't remember a thing.

"That song." He frowns.

"Do you like it?"

"I've heard it before. What's it called."

His forehead's marred, and I immediately feel bad. I forget about his head sometimes. That he still gets headaches too.

"It's called *Chasing Cars* and it's by Snow Patrol. Do you want me to switch it off? Is your head hurting?"

"No, leave it on."

We drive in silence with the song on repeat. We're on our way to my parents' house. Ma says Eoin can't be trusted to live on his own as he's clearly not been looking after himself. He's there for the next six weeks minimum, which means he'll be living under the same roof as Jaine for all that time.

After today, maybe that's something they'll both be happy about.

Fingers crossed.

The O'Connell Home, Darling, New York

Ma's standing outside, waiting. She's got little JJ in her arms and he's opening and closing his fist, his tiny fingers making a little pudgy starfish shape each time as he tries his best to wave. He's Ace all over, from his quiet demeanor right through to the fact that he's the caring sort. If JJ thinks you're sad or unwell, he'll automatically come over to comfort you by giving you a sticky hug and offering you his own precious saliva-soaked soother.

Finian, on the other hand, is more likely to escort you personally to the reaper's door by talking you to death.

He's our Paddy all over.

We're just parking as Jaine comes to the door. She's in her trademark tank and cargoes, her hair wet and hanging down her back no doubt after her recent shower following her workout with Dec.

The inside of the SUV instantly feels cooler. I know it's caused by Eoin's now foul mood that she doesn't care about him. That she doesn't love him.

What he doesn't realize is that he travelled to the hospital with his head cradled in her lap as she sat there in a pool of his blood. What he also doesn't realize is that she rarely left his side, and when she did, I was under strict orders to replace her and not move an inch.

Or else.

I've seen Jaine's 'or else' and I'd quite like to keep my head attached to the rest of my body.

He'll know it all soon enough.

I've not seen the message that she sent to him, but I know it's there on his phone. Missed somehow. Likely because it came from her burner and the fact that she sent it at the precise moment he was shot.

Was she planning on telling him about her alter-ego? I think she must have been. She was clearly giving her permission for him to use that number, and everyone else who has access already knows her heavily guarded secret.

I open the car door and the music filters out. Jaine stares at me, a small frown on her forehead.

She's not daft. She now knows that I know.

I'm sure she won't appreciate my meddling, so I reckon if I value my life, it's best I just keep out of her way and let them get on with it.

I step out, then help Eoin down from the back.

"Dr. Kelly said you'd been doing too much, Eoin." Ma immediately starts nagging him, and he rolls his eyes at her. "You were told to take it easy and to rest. What on earth possessed you to do something that would hinder your healing? What were you doing, for goodness' sake?"

"You don't want to know, Ma," I mutter with a small smile, which earns me a glare from my big brother. "Although I'm sure Jaine can fill you in on all the details woman to woman if you really insist."

Cue awkward silence.

Ma now knows exactly what he was up to and with whom. She looks between them both.

"Surely, there's a time and a place for that sort of thing, and it's not in the back of a moving vehicle with Declan driving," she mutters, her lips twitching upward.

Who would have thought we'd ever see the day that Ma would appear happy about Eoin and Jaine spending time together.

So, Plan A. had some success, but it wasn't the momentous occasion it could have been, but I guess this isn't a movie. This is real life.

So, it's on to Plan B.

I follow Eoin into his bedroom suite then quickly set up the laptop I've brought with me. A laptop that contains all the footage from when Jaine was at the hospital.

We had armed security outside the ward. Surely, she must have known that we'd also have surveillance installed throughout. He's the future Da Duster. He'd just been shot.

He was never going to be left unattended without top-of-the-range security.

I guess what none of us realized was that he had the most lethal of guardians holding his hand and sitting by his bed the entire time.

I watch as he lies back on his bed. He looks fucked. This whole thing has knocked him for six.

"What are you doing, Dylan?" He huffs as he covers his tired eyes with the back of his hand.

"I need you to watch something. Or at least listen to it."

"I'm exhausted."

"It's important, Eoin. Really important. I know you're not feeling great. I know you're tired. I'm not saying that you need to listen to all of it in one sitting, but you need to hear it. It's about your Florence Nightingale."

He removes his hand and frowns at me as I start playing the audio.

There's a pause before it starts.

"I love you, Eoin. I sent you a message…it was from my burner, so you probably didn't…."

I watch as he starts looking around. He's searching for his phone because he can scarcely believe his own ears. He wants to see the physical proof. I can't say I blame him.

I pass him his phone with a grin on my face.

Jaine: *I love you.*

"She'd obviously sent it just as you got shot, then when she got yours, she's assumed that you'd never seen it or that you no longer cared, so she let you move on. Your happiness took precedence over her own. It always will. That's just how Jaine works."

"Shite." He runs his hand through his hair. It's difficult to describe how he looks.

Happy. Sad. Annoyed. Frustrated.

Hopeful.

"I should go to her."

I sit on the edge of the bed. "This footage contains her whole life story. She knew that you wanted her to let you in and that she deliberately never did. So, now that's exactly what she has done. She's let you in. This is warts and all. She went to the effort of saying these things, so you need to take the time to listen. Watch it. Absorb it. Digest it. Find out who Jaine Jones really is and then go find her. Because she knows now that you know."

"How?"

And then it dawns on him. "The song that was playing."

"It was your song."

CHAPTER FIFTY-EIGHT

JAINE

The O'Connell Home, Darling, New York

I PACE THE FLOOR AS I GLANCE AROUND THE SAFE SPACE IN ITS tones of whites and creams.

Calling it that makes it sound like we're living in a prison. We're not. Or at least it doesn't feel like one.

It's luxurious, the floor space even larger than that of my penthouse apartment. It's spatially furnished, which works well when you have two kids who are still finding their feet and forever bumping into things.

Eoin's been back forty-eight hours now, and he's remained holed up in his suite pretty much the entire time.

This morning I received a single-word message.

Eoin: *Noon.*

I've had to ask Roisin and Duke to take the boys to visit with Auntie Sarah and cousin Caoimhe for the day.

I couldn't miss their grinning faces as they left. I'm only grateful that Fergal is out with Cillian and Aidan. I'm not sure I could have coped with Da Duster's smirk on top of theirs.

I'm sure the entire family already know that Eoin and I fucking in the back of an SUV is what landed him in the hospital.

I message Dylan.

Jaine: *You left without saying goodbye the other day.*
Dylan: *I was just safeguarding my head.*
Jaine: *What did you tell him?*

There's a pause.

Jaine: *Dylan!*
Dylan: *He has the recordings from the hospital, Jaine. All of them.*
Jaine: *Shit.*
Dylan: *You told him all of it already. There was always the chance that he would remember everything. That he still could even without the aid of the recordings.*

He's right. Maybe it's best that it's all out in the open as opposed to it potentially coming out at a later date.

Dylan: *He's also seen the message on his phone. The one you sent him at the precise moment he got shot.*

So it's *all* out there. He knows *everything.*

I rub my sweaty palms down my pants, suddenly nervous. What to say? How to act? He'll be here any minute.

There's a knock on the door. My heart immediately thuds in response.

Jaine: *He's here.*
Dylan: *Then answer the door to him. He was always going to come and find you. Nothing was going to keep him away. Don't keep him waiting. I wouldn't want to be the door standing between my big brother and the woman he now views as his.*

I place the phone on the side table before running sweaty hands down my cargo pants once more and opening the door.

I take him in as he stands there in snug black jeans and a black fitted sweater. His clothes do nothing to disguise the perfection hidden underneath. He leans against the door frame with his arms folded and wearing a confident smile as I blatantly admire him.

His hair is messy, he looks exhausted, and the eyes on his GQ model-like face have dark rings around them, but nothing can detract from this man's presence.

Dangerous. Powerful. Addictive.

All topped off with spicy cologne that together create the most intoxicating of aphrodisiacs.

His eyes are already green and my core throbs in response, but I know we can't go there. Not for six weeks at least.

Doctor's orders.

His eyes trail slowly up my body. He's taking in what's now his.

I'm no man's possession.

Never have been. Never will be.

But there's something about Eoin O'Connell that makes me almost want to be possessed. To be owned.

And he knows it.

"You should be resting." I'm not sure what else to say.

I walk backward as he starts to walk forward for no reason other than to give him space to enter the room. Or at least that's what I'm telling myself.

He stops right in front of me. We're mere inches apart.

Too close. Not close enough.

He lifts his hand and strong fingers grace my throat. Closing my eyes, I swallow thickly before reopening them. His thumb then tilts my chin up so I can't look anywhere but at him. He smiles darkly. He can feel my heart pounding, I know he can.

"Concern for my well-being coming from the mouth of who I now know to be my very own Florence Nightingale. Well, I suppose it makes a pleasant change from being cussed at." His tone is low and mocking.

"Once an asshole, always an asshole," I bite back,

"That fucking mouth just can't help itself, can it?" He drags his thumb across my bottom lip and my tongue flicks out to lick the now-dry skin, tasting his unique saltiness on the surface.

We stare.

"Say it."

He's heard it on recordings. He's seen it on a message. He now wants to watch the words fall from my lips.

"I love you."

His face gives nothing away, but his nostrils flare.

Possessiveness.

I've just sacrificed my soul at the altar of the Duster devil himself.

"Again."

"I love…"

He backs me against the wall as his tongue sweeps deep inside my mouth like he wants to somehow taste the words he's been waiting so long to hear.

Because Eoin O'Connell is loved.

I love him today. I love him tomorrow.

Forever.

For always.

I snake my arms around his neck as strong hands explore my body.

Memorizing. Remembering.

There's no urgency. He's taking his time because he knows that's what he now has. All the time in the world.

I groan as his hand cups my pussy before twisting out of reach.

"Six weeks for you means six weeks for both of us."

"I want to give you pleasure, Jaine. It's my right as your…"

He stops.

Reality check.

We both know what he was going to say next. Something that's no longer the case. I can immediately sense his frustration. He'll think he's acted with haste.

He didn't. He was more patient than I ever deserved.

Taking his hand in mine, I lead him to the cream leather sofa. It's reminiscent of the one back home in Rising, but it holds no old memories. Only new ones.

He takes a seat then pulls me down beside him, and I turn so I'm facing him.

"Can we reverse the Decree Absolute?"

I shake my head. "No. We can't. It's a legal document."

I link my fingers through his, his skin hard and calloused. How little did I know about him? Back when I assumed his hands would be soft and unblemished because he instructed his toy soldiers to do all the dirty work on his behalf.

I was so wrong about him.

"I knew we should never have had the marriage annulled." He rests his head back on the sofa and closes his eyes.

He looks tired, his complexion paler than usual and his cheekbones more pronounced. I realize it's partially my fault.

What I've done. How I've behaved.

Unreciprocated love can do a lot of damage even when it turns out not to be the case. I should know.

"I'm glad we did."

He opens his eyes and frowns at me. "Why?"

I shrug. "Because we got married for all the wrong reasons using a platform that was both toxic and unstable."

"Then we have to marry again. A fresh start. Now that you're in love with me." He says that with a confidence that only he can.

"That sounds almost conceited."

He smirks. "Isn't that one of the things you love about me?"

Mr. Smug. Selfish. Pompous is completely right.

It is.

I roll my eyes with a smile before my expression turns serious. "We don't have to get married, Eoin. Or at least not straight away."

"Why not?"

"Because protection is no longer such an issue now. I've agreed to live here with the kids. There's no immediate rush."

"I appreciate your kind are somewhat unconventional but, in my faith, people court and then they marry."

"My kind?"

"You know what I mean."

There's a pause.

"When did you first realize, Jaine?"

"When did I first realize what?"

"That you loved me. When did you know?"

"At the container. After you killed Malky. You did what you did to avenge me that day. As much as it was brutal, I realize it was done out of love."

"Not before?"

"I can't be sure, Eoin. Even if I did, I'd have told myself I didn't."

"Because of Paddy."

"Yes." I sigh.

"Do you love him more?"

My heart fills with emotion at the uncertainty in his voice, and I instinctively lean against his side and let his arm wrap around me.

"Not more. Differently."

"In what way?"

I lift my head to look at him. "I love you, Eoin. Isn't that enough?"

"In what way?" He repeats the question which is what he does when he won't take no for an answer.

"Irish and I share a connection."

"You didn't have that with Ace?"

"No."

"And not with me either?"

"No."

"So, you love him more."

"Don't twist my goddamn words."

He ignores my hissy tone.

"Describe it. This love."

How do I describe something indescribable?

"If I reach my mind out far enough, I'm sure I can feel him. It's like he's ever-present."

"Fate."

"Perhaps."

"Describe ours. Our love."

I pause before I speak. I want to be completely honest with him.

"I was never destined to love you, Eoin. You made me love you by showing me all of you. Every layer. No matter how evil or twisted, you never kept anything hidden from me. I didn't fall in love with your light or your dark. I fell in love with the fusion of both. With the man as well as the monster. I would kill for you. I would die for you. When I realized I would do anything for you, that's when I knew."

I sit up and I look at him.

"I love you, Eoin O'Connell. But I also love your brother. My love for you won't ever change my feelings for him and vice versa. You have to be prepared to accept that. And that's why I think we should wait. There's no other reason. Let's get our heads around all of this first because the fact remains. I will always love him. And he will always be your brother."

CHAPTER FIFTY-NINE

EOIN

The O'Connell Home, Darling, New York

How frustrating.

That the woman I love has finally confirmed that she loves me back and I can't even fuck her as a proper thank you.

I sit on the sofa in the safe space with my legs stretched out in front of me and Jaine Jones, my now ex-wife, curled up against my side.

My mouth curves upwards. I can't stop it.

I feel euphoric.

Is this how my brothers felt when the women they had feelings for reciprocated? How our Paddy felt when Jaine confirmed the same to him?

Guilt will always be there.

That she's only mine because she can't be his.

But as it was with him and Ace, I think she'd now be unable to choose between us. Her loyalty to both would see her unable to decide.

I understand her reasons for not wanting to rush back into marriage, but I don't think she sees herself as being unwed. She's still wearing both of her wedding rings.

She still sees herself as being tied to both Ace and me.

There's also probably an invisible one on her finger tying her to our Paddy too.

If she won't agree to retaking the vows immediately, then I'll ask that she remove the ring that I placed on her finger. Then I shall have the most extravagant and largest of diamond engagement rings commissioned, get down on one knee, and force her to wear it until she relents.

She'll hate that. Having to wear something vulgar and ostentatious.

I chuckle at the thought.

"Something funny going on inside that big head of yours?"

"You could say that."

Her phone vibrates.

She looks at the screen. She's not hiding anything. We can both see that it's a message from my ma.

Roisin: *We're going to stay at Sarah and Cill's tonight, Jaine, so you have the place to yourselves.*

She leans her head back on the sofa and rolls her eyes exaggeratedly. "Great. Everyone will know by now."

"Know what?"

"What landed you back in the hospital."

"You mean when you took advantage of me in the back of the SUV."

She laughs out loud. "I so did not."

"You so did, Jaine."

She frowns. "I'm sorry. I never even thought about your injuries."

"If you'd had chance to think about those then I would have to deem myself as not being very good at foreplay. I'm only sorry it was so rushed now we have to abstain for six weeks."

"You're allowed to masturbate. Dr. Kelly told me so. After he told me there was to be no more enthusiastic sex and after his cheeks turned bright red."

I laugh out loud. "You scare him, Jaine."

"You scare me."

There's a pause. I capture her chin with my fingers and tilt her head up to look at me. My eyes graze her face.

She's so fucking beautiful.

"Do I frighten you?"

She nods slowly. "I'd never experienced fear before. Not until that first time at the container."

I'm not sure how I feel about that.

"I would never hurt you or cause you pain, Jaine. Unless I knew that you wanted me to or unless you gave me reason to."

"I know."

"And how did that fear make you feel?" My voice is coaxing. I already know the answer. I can almost hear her heart pounding in her chest at the thought of admitting it.

She licks her lips, and my eyes drop to their now glistening fullness. "Aroused."

"And how does the memory of it make you feel, Jaine?"

"Aroused." It's whisper-like.

So, seeing me at my worst turns her on. Could she be any more fucking perfect?

My lips claim hers, and I swallow the soft groan she makes as I taste her addictive sweetness once more.

She climbs onto my lap and straddles me, and my dick's instantly rock-hard. I feast on her mouth, searching and demanding, questioning and answering. I can taste it now.

Love.

"I want to fuck you, Jaine," I whisper against her lips as my hand fists her hair so there's no escape.

"You can't."

I release my grip on her, leaning my head back against the sofa while exhaling in frustration. "I can't say the thought of fucking my hand fills me with any great sense of excitement."

"I can't say the same."

A heated pause.

"What are you saying, Jaine?"

I know exactly what she's saying, and my dick gets even harder at the thought.

"That I'm happy to be your captive audience."

Naughty, evil woman.

I grind against her once more before lifting her off my lap and standing in the middle of the floor. Pulling down my zip, I free my cock.

She licks her lips. She clearly wants it in her mouth, but I know she won't give me access to that hot little vacuum either as I fuck that as hard as I fuck her pussy. That's how we both like it.

Hard. Fast. Deep. With plenty of saliva.

She yanks off her tank top to display her tits. They may be small, but they're perfectly formed. My eyes graze over a slim torso that's covered in an array of scars, each one looking like it's been intricately carved onto her skin. She's a work of fucking art.

She's my work of art.

My gaze drifts to the recent scar on her shoulder. A permanent reminder of when she saved my ma's life. It's still red and angry-looking. As red and angry as my own recent scars.

I am her. She is me.

We're the same.

Imperfectly perfect.

She stares at me, and my eyes bore into hers as I rub my pre-cum around the tip of my dick before stroking its full length. I haven't removed my clothing intentionally, so her focus remains on my cock. I already know that she likes what lies underneath my clothes.

Her gaze drops.

"Is this what you wanted to see, Jaine?"

"Yes."

I smirk as she replies without taking her eyes off my now slick length, her skin flushing and her nipples pebbling with arousal at the sight of me jerking off.

Her little pink tongue flicks out to lick her fingertips before she traces them around her already peaked tips.

I grunt my approval as my hand works faster. Knowing I'm getting close, she gets on the floor and crawls towards me before kneeling in front of me so close I can feel her breath tickle my balls.

"I want to fist your hair and fuck you hard in the mouth. Make you choke. Make you gag. Make you gasp for fucking air."

"But you can't." She gives a smug smirk.

She's right. I can't, but the thought of it has my balls tightening, and with a low growl of pleasure, I release ropes of hot cum all over her perfect face and tits.

Panting, I stare down at her.

"You will receive my cum in any way I see fit to give it to you. In return, it is yours and yours alone. I give you my word, Jaine."

I watch as she dips her finger into my release before sucking it into her mouth. My dick twitches at the sight.

If my lifestyle choices aren't going to be the death of me, Jaine Jones fucking will.

I tuck my cock back inside my jeans as I watch her rub my cum into her skin, then I offer my hand, she takes it in hers, and I pull her off the floor.

She smells of me. I smell good on her. Maybe masturbation won't be quite so bad after all.

Tucking her hair behind her ear, I smile down at her.

"I love you, Mr. O'Connell."

Eyes of green.

Open. Honest. Sincere.

"I love you too, Miss Jones, soon to be Mrs. O'Connell once more."

We both chuckle. I'll wear her down quickly and she knows it. She knows how persistent I can be. That when I want something, I won't stop until I get it.

I want her to be my wife. I want her to be the mother of my children.

I place her hand over my heart. "As long as it beats, it's yours."

She looks emotional. She knows I'm not very tactile, that I never wear my heart on my sleeve, but with her, I will try to do both.

"Well, given that there's no one here to call me a promiscuous biker, you might as well spend the night."

I raise an eyebrow at her.

"Now, that really would be making things official."

CHAPTER SIXTY

DYLAN

The O'Connell Home, Darling, New York

Once Dr. Kelly gave Eoin a clean bill of health, we didn't see much of either him or Jaine for the best part of a week.

It didn't take a rocket scientist to figure out what they were up to.

I've just dropped in at my parents' house to check on an issue with the CCTV, and even now the pair of them can barely keep their hands off each other. They managed to stop their canoodling to acknowledge my presence by saying hello, but that was about it.

My brother's never been tactile. He's never been emotional either. Jaine brings out both in him. She's softened him. Humanized him. He no longer thinks about himself. He only ever thinks of her and the kids.

In the end, Ava was accepting of the fact that Eoin and Jaine wanted to try again. We'd already created the illusion that they shared young Finian together.

By all accounts, her and Eoin's relationship had never gone beyond wining and dining anyway. I think in his heart of hearts, he never lost hope that he would end up back with Jaine.

They had chosen to focus on a toxicity that, in my opinion, wasn't really there to begin with. It was just something they invented as they both needed someone to hate on for the guilt they were feeling over Paddy.

Were they destined like Jaine and my little brother?

Probably not.

I don't think Jaine was ever fated to love our Eoin, but it doesn't mean that he wasn't fated to love her, and they do say love conquers all.

That and perseverance. For Eoin, the latter paid off.

My brother had everything. The only thing he'd ever been missing in his life was that one special person, and now he's found her.

And Jaine?

I don't claim to understand it. How one person can love so many.

When she lost Ace, she lost part of herself. When she lost Paddy, she lost even more. Eoin has helped her find herself again. Not the parts she lost, as they're gone for good, but new parts. They may not be the perfect fit, but they've made Jaine Jones whole once more.

Their constant bickering stopped her from drowning in a sea of grief. He's been the buoy that's kept her afloat. A distraction that's captured her attention and held it even though she refused to admit it to herself and to him.

The way I see it, our Paddy is her sun and her guiding light. Ace is the stars that illuminate her path and surround and protect her everywhere she goes. And Eoin? He's her moon. A strong light that's there for her in our world of darkness.

Jaine Jones needs all three.

Who knew?

Now Eoin has her, his life is complete. Well, almost.

He wants to marry her a second time, and it's my thinking she'll give in sooner rather than later given she's currently sporting an engagement ring that's as big as the Rock of Gibraltar.

We all know Jaine doesn't do showy, but he's insistent that she can't have her simple wedding band back until they've retaken the vows.

We also know Eoin wants children. That's an even bigger commitment, so maybe that's for another day. They're just enjoying getting to know each other in every way and lining themselves up to grow old together.

Old age isn't something we're blessed with in this life, but one can live in hope.

And my folks? They're delighted. A complete one-eighty from Ma, but then Jaine did save her life. And Da? Well, he let slip that he knew he was looking at the future Ma Duster as soon as Jaine uttered the words *fuck you*.

He manipulated the situation by coercing them into marriage. Turns out, there was no need to marry. In hindsight, Jaine could just have moved into the safe space like she's done now.

Protection problem solved.

It was a manipulation that went on to spectacularly backfire, but by then it was too late for Eoin and Jaine as they'd already stepped over the line from hate to love.

There's a niggle at the back of my mind, though.

Well, two, actually.

The first niggle is that Jaine has yet to mention her alter-ego to Eoin. I get that it's early days, but Eoin is an extremely private person, yet he's still told her everything there is to know about him. She's even witnessed him kill.

Twice.

Why hasn't she told him?

The second niggle and perhaps the most concerning of the two. Jaine told me that Paddy had messaged her to give his blessing, and she's just now shown me the message on her phone.

What she doesn't know is that Paddy changed his number before he left for Sicily.

The message came from Paddy's old number.

Who could have sent it?

Well, given that the handset is still here in New York…

Who do you think?

Author's Note

I hope you enjoyed Eoin's story.

DIRTY EOIN is NOT standalone.
DIRTY EOIN is BOOK 5 of a SERIES, which contains an ONGOING STORYLINE that CONCLUDES in BOOK 6, DIRTY PADRAIG.

These books contain MULTIPLE POVs from characters across the entire series.

Due to the nature of the CONTINUING STORYLINE, these books MUST be
READ IN ORDER.

The Outlaw Chess Reading Order

ACE

DIRTY CILLIAN

RAZR

DIRTY DYLAN

DIRTY EOIN

DIRTY PADRAIG

These books are NOT standalone.

Due to the nature of the CONTINUING STORYLINE

PLEASE READ IN ORDER.

Acknowledgements

For Nikki.

About the Author

Harley Diamond is a writer of romance novels with plot twists that will leave you begging for more. In every dirty story, an angsty bad boy and a badass queen lead the cast.

When Harley's not reading, she's writing. When not doing either, she's plotting to unleash her next novel on you from her non-working farm in West Yorkshire, England, surrounded by her faithful but very needy companions. Her seven rescue dogs.

Facebook Group: Harley's Hangout
Facebook Group: Harley's Spoilers